Mark of the Magpie

K. Bannerman

ISBN 978-0-9864701-5-8

This book was created in Canada.

For more information, contact kim@kbannerman.com.

To my mom, Cindy Bannerman,

whose Victoria roots run deep.

"From too much love of living,
From hope and fear set free,
We thank with brief thanksgiving
Whatever gods may be
That no man lives for ever;
That dead men rise up never;
That even the weariest river
Winds somewhere safe to sea."

—From *The Garden of Proserpine*,
by Algernon Charles Swinburne

The Magpie Song

One for sorrow,
Two for joy,
Three for a girl,
Four for a boy,
Five for silver,
Six for gold,
Seven for a secret
Never to be told.

—Traditional

Prologue

He started awake in the night, cold with sweat. A body moved next to him, rolling as languid as a drop of mercury into the curve of his back, and one thin arm snaked over his torso to caress the expanse of his chest.

"You awake, luv?" she mumbled in his ear.

He grunted in reply.

"Sweet mercy, you've been having dreadful dreams again!" she said, pressing a kiss to the nape of his neck, to the top of the scar that ran down his spine. "I weren't sure if you were still sleeping, after all that ruckus you made."

Shifting onto his elbows, he looked down at her face: a gaunt triangle of white against the gloom of the bedchamber, framed with sparse hanks of tangled black hair. Her eyelids were still closed. The black lashes made little crescents against her cheek bones. She was young, but the wrinkles that gathered around her eyes added years to her appearance, and by the faint light cast by the lamp down the hall, she seemed papery and frail. Well-used, he thought, and weary as a tired horse.

But out loud, he asked, "What'd I say?"

"The same as every night, luv," she yawned. She still had most of her teeth, a feature of which she was very proud. Her dark eyes opened. "Ain't nothing I haven't heard before."

He scowled to hide his embarrassment.

"Aw, don't look so fussed!" she said, "You yelled a bit, then swore as if you were chasing the devil back to Hell. These walls are thin, luv, and I'm sure you've given the other girls a scare." She cast him her brightest smile, the only part of her that he found pretty. "They're gonna think, either you've tried to kill me, or you just had yourself the best damned fuck in the history of the world."

She chuckled sleepily at her own comment, but he didn't like that he'd spoken aloud without knowing what he'd said. It didn't matter that he was already naked; knowing he'd spoken—and revealed a piece of himself—made him feel vulnerable and exposed. He raised himself up to his elbows. His voice became grave.

"Nell," he pressed, "What'd I say?"

She groaned. "Oh, I don't know, luv. Something about your mother. Something about a man swinging high up in a tree." Maybe she saw how deeply this affected him; she ran her hand down his shoulder in a gesture of comfort and pressed a sweet kiss to his cheek. Then, with a saucy grin, she added, "And I don't know who she is, but the way you moan her name that Lizzie musta been a lucky gal."

ONE

October 15, 1898

Another murder of the foulest kind was committed in the neighbourhood of Whitechapel in the early hours of yesterday morning, but by whom and with what motive is at present a complete mystery.

At a quarter to 4 o'clock Police Constable Neill, 97J, when in Buck's Row, Whitechapel, came upon the body of a woman lying on a part of the footway, and on stooping to raise her up in the belief that she was drunk he discovered that her throat was cut almost from ear to ear. She was dead but still warm. He procured assistance and at once sent to the station and for a doctor.

London Times, September 1, 1888

The tattered copy of the London Times had arrived by post from San Francisco only a few days ago. I'd scarcely put it down since its arrival. I'd read it so many times that the paper had gone soft, like old cotton, and the words had emblazoned themselves upon my mind. Most arresting of all was the single phrase ending the first paragraph, "… by whom and with what motive is at present a complete mystery."

For everyone else, that might be true, but not for me.

My hands trembled a little as I laid the clipping gently in the enameled tin jewelry box, where I had carefully organized a sheaf of articles by date. They were of varying lengths, and the paper quality ranged wildly, from thick expensive rag to paper so thin the light leaked through it. Some articles had cramped text, and others had wide set type spattered with spelling errors and lurid illustrations. They'd come from the street corners of London, New York, Montreal and Toronto, but all had arrived in my possession by way of Miss Rose Fish, a woman obsessed with collecting newsprint, who (according to her brother) was drowning in a sea of broadsheets. The generous and accommodating Rose had sent me twenty-three newspapers in total, and I had carefully snipped the articles that had caught my fancy to assemble my own, more precise collection. All manner of stories filled her tabloids and broadsheets, but I only cared for the ones detailing the rise and disappearance of Jack the Ripper. I especially cherished the ones describing the heinous crimes he'd inflicted upon the wayward women of Whitechapel, ten years ago. Anyone who opened this jewelry box would doubtlessly think me to be a girl obsessed, seized with a gloomy fascination for gore and terror, titillated by murders unsolved.

But they would be wrong. I took no pleasure in reading these words. They were shards of glass. As I read about the women who had been left to die in bloodied pieces in dark London alleys, each detail wormed its way deep into my brain. The lurid stories reduced them to featureless shapes with blunt words like 'whore' and 'prostitute' and 'unfortunate victim', and I could not bear that they been stripped of their humanity, so I committed their names to memory: Martha Tabram, Mary Ann Nichols, Annie Chapman, Elizabeth Stride, Catherine Eddowes, Mary Jane Kelly, Rose Mylett, Elizabeth Jackson.

More and more, on and on, woman after woman. I filled my mind with them, tried to rebuild them from newspaper rumors and gossip. Maybe only five, maybe thirteen, maybe any number in between.

Or, I suspected with dread, maybe even more, and their names lost forever.

I kept a careful tally of each incident, each missing organ, each slice, gash, and stab, because Jack the Ripper was not a mystery to me. He was a monster, an obsession curdled by self-importance. He was a warning of the path where my own impulses might lead me.

He was my father.

A knock at the door broke my focus. I closed the lid and set the box on the bedside table, and through the wood slats came the puzzled voice of Mr. Fish.

"Lizzie?" he said, "I don't wish to intrude. Are you awake?"

"Yes, sir," I replied, "Please, do come in."

The door opened. He smiled to see me.

Mr. Harris Fish was not the sort of fellow to show happiness openly. The expression sat ghoulishly on his narrow features. He was a hawkish, peevish sort of man, possessing few friends and having no hobbies beyond his beloved island railway line. For the last week, he'd been discussing its future construction with agents of the provincial government, which meant that most afternoons, he disappeared in meetings, debates, and arguments. To the best of my knowledge, his ideas had met with fierce opposition from both sides of the legislative house, and the war had given him a spring in his step and a blazing fire in his bright brown eyes. He came from a long line of railway industrialists, and his brother had amassed a fortune in Australia constructing transportation networks, so I suppose the love of trains resided in his blood, spurred to a froth by fraternal competition. No one would dare call Mr. Fish 'friendly' or 'warm', but neither would they call him 'weak' nor 'easily discouraged'. He was churlish, contrite, and unforgiving of those he deemed as fools, and most of his neighbours knew to avoid him. As thin and unyielding as an iron rail spike, Mr. Fish used his sour demeanor and vast investments to fight battles with the tenacity of a pit dog.

But I was neither an adversary nor an ally in his railway battle, so he didn't know what to do with me. He lingered in the doorway, unused to having a guest in his house. He'd never married and most people thought that was a blessing—he'd make a most cantankerous husband. But, while he had only a few close friends, he possessed a very loyal staff, and during the last four weeks that I'd been living under his roof, it became clear that he preferred the company of his housekeeper to any wife or paramour. An unmarried elderly bachelor was often the topic of much speculation, but Mr. Fish didn't seem to give a fig what others thought, and I rather like that quality in a person.

I'd taken residence in one of the attic rooms of his grand James Bay mansion. The series of sparsely-decorated chambers had once been furnished for staff, and now served me quite comfortably. I had a private space with a wrought-iron bed, a full-length mirror, and a chest of four drawers that provided me with far more storage than I needed. A small window looked east over the garden and alley, and another offered a southward glimpse of the sea. At night the room could be quite cold and silent, but with a thick wool blanket and a clay pig warmed by the kitchen stove, I was very comfortable.

He spied the clipped newspapers on the bed and floor. "I've interrupted. You're pouring over the package from Rose. You carry the expression of a pensive scholar, Amaryllis, and your hands are black with printing ink."

I glanced at the remains of the paper, strips and squares scattered like streamers and confetti. "Your sister was very kind to send me these back issues, especially of the London Times. I must write a letter to thank her."

"Don't bother. It will only be lost in the piles of papers towering around her apartment," he huffed, "Really, I ought to thank you, Liz! Rose's hoarding has grown worse with age, but you've been kind enough to put her stacks of rubbish to good use. If my sister's trash aids your research on The London Match Girls' Strike, then so much the better!"

Ah, the match girls. I smiled and mustered my story before I spoke.

"I've learned a great deal, sir," I said. "The prohibition of white phosphorous has not yet come to pass, and those poor girls still work in atrocious conditions. Our work is not yet done!" I brandished my small fist. "I shall not be content until they've won their fight."

Lifting the plight of the lower classes was a noble cause, taken up by many girls my age. It provided a perfect excuse.

"I dare say, the suffragettes are lucky to have you on their side, Lizzie," he said as his face squished into an ungainly smirk. Then he waved one long hand in dismissal and said, "But, I didn't come to debate the atrocious living conditions of the poor. I came to tell you, you have a visitor."

"I do?"

"Indeed. And you will be very pleased to see who it is." Without waiting for my reply, he turned and descended the stairs, trusting that I would follow.

Because the attic was designed for the accommodation of servants, the rear stairway was steep and dark, and led directly to the kitchen on the first floor. With his long legs, Mr. Fish was able to descend them two at a time, and he reached the bottom long before I did.

I was still only half way down the case when I heard him say, "Here is your guest, Liz, right where I left him."

I thumped into the kitchen as Chen Shaozhu rose from the table.

To see him, my heart lifted from the shadows like a sparrow taking wing. His smile was a ray of sunlight slicing through my gloomy thoughts.

I hadn't seen Shao in five days. I tried not to count the passage of time; I knew he was busy working, building a place for himself in this city, establishing a business network that would provide him with much-needed security, but some things are difficult to ignore. His absence was like a sliver of wood in my thumb: persistent, uncomfortable, and relentless. Now that he stood before me in the sunny kitchen, my eyes ranged over every feature, every nuance, every movement, ravenous for the sight of him.

His plain grey suit had no adornment except for carved bone buttons, but the simplicity of his clothes only accentuated the handsome features of his face. His blue-black hair had been cut short, except for one wayward lock that persisted in falling over his brow. Mischief sparkled in his eyes. When he smiled, I felt my pulse race.

"*Ni hao, Lei Zi*," he said.

"*Ni hao ma*," I replied, stumbling over the inflection. Up, or down? God's teeth, it was hard to remember!

To Mr. Fish, he said, "Good afternoon, sir. You're well?"

The man scoffed. "Why waste time asking after my health, boy? We all know, you're here for her." He lowered his voice theatrically. "And who can blame you? Liz is a far more attractive host than me."

"I certainly agree," said Shao.

Mr. Fish raised his head and yelled through the kitchen doors, into the parlor. "Jess, my girl? Be a dear and make enough tea for all. But I'll take mine in the study." To me, he cast a wink. "The sun is shining full and bright upon the back porch, Liz. Best to enjoy it before the winter arrives." He strode out of the kitchen, leaving us together, rasping a chuckle under his breath.

Shao and I moved out to the porch. The rich October sunlight cast a honey-thick glow over the dry leaves of the oak trees, and a fresh sea breeze ruffled the last roses in the bowers. There wasn't much of summer left. The season wished to expel one last burst of sunshine before the cold rain arrived. I sat next to him on the top step, not so close to be improper, but I set my hand down next to his, close enough to feel the warmth from his skin. Oh, how I missed him! The mere presence of him made me giddy, and the rational part of my brain scolded my heart for being so ridiculous, romantic, simpering. I tried to stamp down the gallop of my pulse, but then I felt the touch of Shao's smallest finger against my own, and my blood was set racing again.

"How have you been?" he asked. He kept his voice low, but I heard a tension there, as if he was having trouble keeping his own happiness restrained.

"Well enough," I replied.

"You've been practising your vocabulary?"

"A little," I replied. "But Xi laughs at my accent. I spend most of my time talking to myself in the mirror. Mr. Fish seems very amused by my efforts."

"He's a strange old fellow, isn't he."

"He's been very accommodating," I replied. "And Eddy's a wonderful cook. I think I'm gaining weight."

I saw clearly in his face that he didn't believe me. Mr. Fish's housekeeper, Edwina, was very skilled in the kitchen, that part was true, but I never had much of an appetite these days. Before Shao could press the issue, I said, "What about you? How've you been?"

"The rib still hurts."

"Let's see," I urged.

He faltered. "But the neighbours ..."

We might not be able to show affection, but there were loopholes. I mustered up any sense of authority a 15-year-girl can hold, and scowled fiercely.

"I'm your physician, Mr. Chen," I reminded him, then added, "Sod the neighbours."

He chuckled as he removed his grey coat, turned his back to me, and lifted his white cotton shirt.

I ran my palms down the left side of his lean bare torso, where the fierce bruise in the shape of a boot had almost completely vanished. Shao flinched but said nothing. I felt the strong, well-defined muscles covering a brace of bones, each one straight and well-healed.

"Breath in," I instructed.

His rib cage rose evenly. He released his breath, wincing a little.

I let my touch linger, then helped him replace his shirt, but I was reluctant to hide away his handsome form. I ached to wrap my arms around him. I felt so few strong emotions that it was an agony to stifle these delicious desires. However, I leeched any passion from my voice and said, in a most scientific and scholarly way, "I think your pain may simply be the last of the healing process."

He settled back on the step before shaking his head in wonder and frustration. "Three months!" he snapped. "It's been almost three months since …" The furious words snagged in his throat.

Since he'd been beaten at the hands of vengeful, hateful, spiteful men. I brought my head close to his.

"You're getting better," I reminded him. I ran my fingers over his hand, caressed the small bones of his wrist, let myself take delight in the touch of his skin. "Rib injuries take a long time to heal properly."

"*Pok gai*," he muttered through clenched teeth.

For the last two weeks, I'd barely seen him; his work at Mr. Lim's apothecary shop kept him too busy for social calls, if such a thing would even be allowed between him and me. Shao's infrequent visits to James Bay came in the form of deliveries to wealthy patrons, and when he could spare a moment, he'd drop by the house to see me. He seemed content, very happy with the job he'd secured. I suppose Mr. Lim recognized a valuable employee when he saw one, and considered Shao to be an investment worth nurturing, rather than a slave to drive hard. The two of them ran a neat little shop on Herald Street, and Shao spent almost every day in the bustling alleys and dens of Chinatown, where he could practise the arts of pharmacy in the company of men who respected him. He'd left English society behind, and after the beating he'd received at the hands of white miners, I couldn't blame him.

But he'd left me behind, too. The thought stung. I missed him terribly.

He straightened his white shirt, turning his gaze to me. "Liz, how are you, really?" he asked, and before I could craft a lie, he said, "You look terrible. You've got shadows under your eyes."

"Newspaper ink, I bet."

"You look like you haven't slept in days. You're as pale as custard."

I shrugged.

How could I tell him he was right—I hadn't slept, I didn't eat—without explaining to him why? Maybe it was better that our lives were drawing apart. With Shao engrossed in his own life, it meant I never had to tell him about mine.

"Have you heard from your father?"

I winced. "No."

"He left for Europe last August!" he exclaimed, his eyebrows arching in surprise. "And not a single word to you?"

"I don't wish to talk about it."

"He's abandoned you, Liz. *Zao gao*! Does he even know where you are?"

"Stop it," I hissed.

Shao recoiled, only a fraction, but it was enough: I saw from the look on his face that my own expression had changed. The mask had fractured, the dark beast peeked out. I closed my eyes, willed the warmth of human emotion back into my features.

Since the events of last summer, I'd begun to suffer lapses in my composure, and I hated the flash of rage and sense of detachment that now rose quickly in moments of anger. I feared that those last minutes in my father's company had dredged something sinister from the depths of my soul. I was hardly eager to recognize it. I dared not name it. I felt as if confronting it was tantamount to giving it power, and I didn't want to lose control. With my eyes firmly shut, I struggled to suppress the rising dark—I struggled to forget how good it had felt to plunge that knife into firm, living flesh.

I am not like him, I thought, banishing the memories to the basement of my soul. *I will never be like him.*

When I opened my eyes, Shao was watching me, concerned and perhaps a little afraid.

I took his hand in mine. "Please," I said quietly, "I don't want to talk about it."

We sat for a moment in awkward silence.

Then, Shao stood. He fidgeted, he faltered. "I should leave," he said, "Mr. Lim is expecting me back. I … I only wanted to know how you were doing."

He didn't look back as he walked down the stairs and across the lawn, towards the back gate leading to the alley. He'd crossed the garden path and was reaching out for the latch when I called out, "Shao, I'm sorry."

He paused, turned.

"I'm sorry," I repeated.

"For what?"

For not being honest with you. For not telling you everything. For not admitting I killed my own father and dumped his body in the ocean. For lying again and again to you, never admitting you into my confidence, for not trusting you. For ripping your life apart and putting you in harm's way. For loving you.

For everything, really.

My throat hitched.

"I … I don't know."

He frowned, puzzled by my answer, then disappeared out the gate. I heard his footfalls on the hard clay of the alleyway, disappearing towards the harbor.

A light step in the kitchen door caught my ear. I looked up to see Jess, standing in the doorway, holding a silver tray.

She looked much younger than her twenty years, with soft, rounded features and wide-set eyes. There were very few negro people in Victoria, and the complexion of her skin set her apart from other women her age, but I think Jess' childlike face was more arresting than any other difference that divided us. Her body showed every clue that she was older than me, taller and shapely and womanly, but her face seemed so much younger and girlish than mine.

"Um, miss?" said Jess in her soft, timid voice, "Would you still like your tea?"

"No thanks."

She hesitated. Jess only spoke after great thought, and she rarely did anything impulsive. Rarer still was speaking her mind, or telling someone what to do.

"I think you ought to have something to eat, miss," she insisted. "I've made you an egg salad sandwich."

"I'm really not hungry—"

"You're heartsick, miss, nothing more. He's a lovely boy, but he ain't your type, and this heartsickness, it'll pass." She laid the blue-and-white china plate next to me on the step. "Trust me, I been through it myself." She smiled warmly, and her voice adopted a motherly tone. "Now, I shall not interrupt you as you eat, but I'll be watching you from the kitchen window, miss, and I'll know if you throw it to the birds."

I scrubbed one hand over my face, feeling hollow inside. "Thank you, Jess."

"There's a sing-along at the theatre tonight. You're coming with me."

"I'm not really the musical type—"

"Of course you ain't, miss," she agreed, "You're the type to lock yourself in an attic and turn your back on the people who wish to drag you into the light." She set a cup of tea alongside the sandwich. "I've told Mrs. Thornton to expect us. We'll leave by 6:30, the show begins at seven. We'll be taking the trolley, and Mr. Fish said he'll pay our fare." She gave me a pert smile to show that she would accept no refusal, and before I could protest further, she left.

Her soft, steely resolve brought a small smile to my own lips, and I begrudgingly took a bite of the sandwich. A quick glance at the window showed that yes, she was watching, so I nodded in thanks and continued to eat. I did like Jess, very much; I wonder if she would've allowed me to not like her? She was headstrong in a quiet way, so that she could steer a person's opinion without them even noticing, and she kindly guided Mr. Fish to compromises when her fusty employer and her mother would have otherwise argued. Jess was a soothing spring breeze, and I had liked her since the first moment I met her, on a sunny afternoon in mid-September, only four weeks ago.

TWO

September 14, 1898

I ought not to have been surprised. I don't know why I expected anything modest or small. I immediately recognized my folly as we reached the address on the card, and lifted our eyes to view an imposing mansion on the corner of Turner Street and Dallas Drive.

The main section of the house was three stories, with a steep roof of dark wood and a round tower in the north-east corner, topped with a conical roof. At its peak, a brass wind cock cast in the shape of a train whirled in the breeze. The house was covered with scalloped shingles, painted a crisp white, and every window box had a trim of deep red. Bay windows ran along the front of the house, and a series of gables along the upper floors created an irregular, picturesque roof line. The yard was small, but immaculate. A line of plush pink roses along the fence released a sweet perfume, and covered the arbor over the front gate so that visitors were forced to bow their heads as they passed under the thorns. The drone of industrious bees filled a garden containing a riotous collection of flowers, so that the mansion seemed to float on a sea of blossoms.

"*This* is the house?" Shao whispered in awe.

"Stay here," I said, leaning him against a bare section of the arbor. He released his breath in a groan and hugged his injured side with both arms.

I walked up the slate path and climbed three stairs onto the verandah, which followed the south side of the building. Squaring my shoulders and mustering my courage, I seized the brass knocker and gave a confident knock upon the door.

The woman who opened it was slight and spare, with skin that was the warm, comfortable color of melted chocolate. Her eyes, large and spaced far apart, formed a sharp contrast of black iris and white sclera, like marbles of jet in pools of milk. She wore a plain brown dress, polished leather shoes, and a necklace of gold at her throat, with a modest cross laying in the hollow at the base of her thin neck. Cautious, careful, and quiet, she looked a little afraid of what she might find on the porch.

And this is what she found: a small girl standing at the door step, wearing a dark wool coat and a pair of grey trousers that were dirty at the knees. The girl's hair, more red than brown, had been pulled into a ponytail at the base of her neck, and a number of strands had broken free to frame a face that was sun-tanned and smooth. She possessed a short stature, but she was still young and hadn't yet stopped growing. I can vouch for this, for this girl was me, and sometimes my knees ached with the pains of stretching.

"Yes?" said the maid.

I folded my hands before me, trying to look proper. "Is Mr. Fish available?"

"No, miss," the woman said, "But I'll be happy to take your card, and tell him you've called." She looked over my scrawny shoulder to the man behind me, hunched against the gate with a walrus-hide bag at his feet. He was Chinese, but he'd abandoned the queue, as a few in the city had done. His arms were wrapped around his chest, and he breathed with difficulty. "Are you alright, there?" She looked back me. "Your boy, he isn't looking so good."

"We've come a very long way to see Mr. Fish," I said again, "And I don't have a calling card to give you, but if you could—"

Shao groaned, an unintentional sound full of pain. "Uh, Liz ..."

"Oh, stuff and nonsense!" I said, leaving the woman at the door. I wrapped my arms around him and helped him to sit on the lowest step.

"You should've told me it was this bad, Shao!"

He glared at me with a mixture of frustration and affection. "I didn't want you to worry."

"So you'd rather drown in your own blood, is that it?"

"It's not so bad, Liz—"

"But it's not so good, either," I replied. I ran my hands over the side of his torso, and felt the swelling underneath the tightly-bound bandage. "You need to rest, Shao. We shouldn't have left ... a week or two more, and you would've been strong enough to travel."

"I made it this far, didn't I? It's just a broken rib." His ragged hair fell across his face. He grinned weakly at me, but he didn't release his hold on his chest to push the hair from his eyes.

I growled at him, at his stubbornness, at his bravado. I wrapped my hands around his face and said, "If you push yourself so hard that you die, I'll ... I'll ... I'll bloody well murder you!"

A deep female voice interrupted. "Hey, what's all this going on, now?"

We looked up from the bottom stair to see a second woman stepping onto the porch, cleaning her large hands with a rag. She was as dark-skinned as the girl who had fetched her, and she wore a crisp white apron speckled with blood, protecting a fine and serviceable grey dress. Her black hair carried a sprinkling of matching grey at the temples.

"We don't want any beggars around here, and we've got no openings for employment, so you both best be on your way," she began, then stopped at the sight of Shao, "But, man alive, Jessie said you looked like death warmed over! Boy, you don't look good at all!"

"He has a cracked rib," I said, "And we've come from Cumberland to see Mr. Fish."

The woman pointedly ignored me. "Sweet mercy, boy! You came all the way from the coalfields with cracked ribs?" She turned to the house, to the girl lingering in the doorway. "Go get him some hot milk, Jess, with a dash of the brandy from the kitchen cupboard. Go on, girl! Scoot!" Then she hurried down the steps and helped Shao to his feet, and ushered him up to the porch, and brought him inside. I followed, slinging my leather satchel over one shoulder and carrying the walrus-hide Gladstone bag in both hands.

We went straight through the main hall, passed fine oil paintings of red Australian landscapes and an imposing grandfather clock, to a narrow corridor leading into a warm kitchen, immaculately clean with white tile walls and a black polished stove. The air smelt of basil and rosemary, along with the heavenly perfume of baking bread. My stomach roared. We hadn't eaten since our boat had docked that morning, and the grandfather clock said the hour was now almost five.

"You sit here, boy," said the woman, helping Shao down on a wooden chair, then rounding on me with flashing teeth and angry eyes. "What possessed you to drag this poor man all the way from the coalfields, miss? Glory, that's just cruel!" She jabbed one finger in my direction. "Couldn't you spend the bucks to hire a fella that's got his health?"

I set the suitcase down by the door. "He assured me, he was well-enough to travel," I said, "And I, being a fool and in a hurry, believed him."

"Well, you ask for double wages, friend," she said to Shao, "You make her pay for her hurry, understand?"

As Shao took the cup of milk which Jess offered, the agony in his face was momentarily replaced by a crafty grin. "Oh, she'll pay," he replied.

The woman turned her attention to me and crossed her meaty arms. "Now, you say you've come all this way to speak with Mr. Fish?"

"I made his acquaintance this summer," I began, "He gave me an invitation to visit, should I find myself in Victoria. We've only just arrived off the SS Joan, and I'd hoped he'd be available to see me."

The housekeeper looked me up and down, appraised my coat, rumpled clothes and scuffed boots. From the look on her face, I fell short of quality. "Mr. Fish is currently out, and is not expected to be home until supper," she said, "But you can stay in the kitchen until he returns, if it pleases you."

"Yes, thank you, that would please me very much." I gave her a tired grin. "My name is Lizzie Saunders, and this is Chen Shaozhu."

"I'm Edwina Garry, but everyone around here calls me Eddy, so you can, too," she said, holding out one flour-speckled hand to shake mine. "This is my daughter Jessica. I cook for Mr. Fish, Jess helps with the house."

Jess lowered her face shyly. Her fingers toyed with the gold cross at her throat.

"Be accommodating, girl," her mother snapped, then to me added, "Don't you mind her. She's too timid for her own good."

"I'm very pleased to meet you both," I said, and glanced to the cup of brandied milk in Shao's hands before saying. "Are you feeling any better?"

"A little," he said, "It's good to get off my feet."

Eddy plucked up her knife from the counter and returned to her work: sawing a hunk of bacon into long thin slices. "You're in a curious get-up, Miss Saunders, what with a pair of men's trousers and all. Are you one of those wags who rides a velocipede?"

"Me? No," I replied, "I've never even sat on a bicycle!"

"Well, Mr. Fish is a grand proponent of those infernal contraptions, so I thought you might have such in common with him." Eddy gave a throaty laugh, showing lots of square teeth. Then she paused as a thought occurred. "But cor! You must be half-starved hungry, if you've been traveling! Jess, get them a bit of soup and a slice of bread. We've got ourselves a nice cabbage stew, and a bit of pork, and I just pulled the bread out of the oven not an hour ago."

"That's very kind of you," I said, "We haven't eaten since the morning."

"Well, that's no way to treat your help, healthy or not!" Eddy admonished, and shook her finger towards Shao. "You serve him first, Jess. Poor man, dragged all over God's green earth and for what! Not even a decent meal! How'd you get yourself in such a mess, man?"

"He consorts with the most wicked type of person," I replied. "Stubborn, headstrong, and without a lick of good sense."

Eddy pursed her lips. "You'll be referring to yourself then? Well, he best do what's best for him, don't you think? Let him get a bit of rest and hire yourself a healthy fella to cart your luggage for you!"

"You're mistaken, Eddy," said Shao as he took a bowl of soup from Jess, giving her an appreciative nod, "Lizzie is stubborn, that's true enough, but she hasn't let me lift a thing," Shao turned his eyes to me, "And we've hardly made good time because of it. As you saw, her luggage weighs more than she does."

I heard the front door open and close. All faces turned to the arch leading from the kitchen to the main hall. A familiar voice called out, droll and dry.

"Jess, my girl! Where are you at?"

"We're all here, Harris, in the kitchen," shouted Eddy.

Footsteps sounded in the corridor. "Jess, too? I've got a few parcels I need delivered by the close of the afternoon, and I wondered—"

When Mr. Fish appeared in the doorway, his sentence abruptly ceased.

He looked just as I remembered: tall, miserly, with a sharp brown suit and bowler hat. He normally appeared unshakable, but at the sight of guests in his kitchen, his jaw dropped open and his arms fell to his sides.

"Well!" he said, "Amaryllis Saunders! What a shock!"

I stood and held my hand out to him. "Mr. Fish. I hope this isn't an intrusion."

"Not at all!" He took my hand and pressed a dry kiss to the back of it, "When I gave you my invitation, I fully expected a girl of your nature would seize upon it, but I hadn't expected to see you so quickly. I only left Cumberland a few short weeks ago, and yet here you are, standing in my home!"

"I wanted to take you up on your offer," I said carefully, "To stay with you for a while, in Victoria. You had said I would be welcome to come, and to bring," I glanced towards Shao, "To bring my Adonis."

Mr. Fish regarded me for a moment, his eyes flitting thoughtfully between my face and Shao's.

"Perhaps we should discuss this in the parlor," he said. Did I catch a flicker of amusement crossing his lips? "Will you join me, Lizzie? Alone?"

If the house had seemed large from the outside, it seemed positively palatial within: a maze of rooms, anti-chambers, closets, stairways, bolt holes and corridors, all paneled in dark wood with parquet floors. Mr. Fish led me through the corridor, making comments about the Australian landscapes, then into a library, where my amazed reflection peeked at me from the high polish on the walnut furniture. Three narrow windows gave a pleasing view of the street, but I barely glanced at them; instead, I salivated at the sight of long book shelves carrying luxurious leather-bound volumes. Mr. Fish saw me pause, gave me a heartbeat to read a few titles from the spines, then led me through a pair of French doors to enter his parlor, and he held out his hand to welcome me.

The walls of the parlor were bare of paintings, but quite purposefully.

While the library windows had looked upon a pleasing street scene, the parlor took up the south-west corner of the house, and two large windows gave a scenic view of the sea. Three barques had caught the wind, and their full white sails urged them through Juan de Fuca Strait as their bows cut ivory curls from the blue water. The Dallas roadway ran between the house and the cliffs, so that as I admired the passing ships in the straight, I saw, too, a surrey with a trotter and fine ladies in their dresses admiring an afternoon ride.

The parlor enhanced the magnificent view, for it was modestly decorated, yet luxurious in its quality. There were few adornments. The only furniture was a couple of chairs and a couch, but the smallest details had been finely wrought, and added together, resulted in a most delightful sitting room. Persian rugs, patterned in crimson and cream, felt thick under my boots, and the tea caddy in the corner—a locked mahogany box on a carved stand, protecting a cargo of the finest exotic blends, most certainly—was the finest I'd ever seen. Even the potted fern looked lush and rich. I had grown so accustomed to the houses in the coalfields that I assumed everyone lived that way, with floors scarred by hobnail boots, old iron stoves in the room for warmth, and all of one's belongings covered in an oily coating of coal dust. As I stood in Mr. Fish's parlor, I was swiftly cured of my misconceptions.

He held out his hand. "Have a seat, Liz," he said. I sat on the horsehair sofa, sinking into its soft cushions. Mr. Fish closed the French doors. Then, from a sideboard, he took a crystal decanter and portioned out two glasses of raspberry cordial. He handed one to me, then he sat across from me, unfolding his long legs.

"How is your father?"

I took a sip of the sweet drink before answering. "Not well, I'm afraid."

"Mason Briggs told me that Dr. Saunders left quite suddenly for England; here one day, and gone the next."

"You must understand, sir, that with Mother's death, then Violet's ..." I fumbled for an explanation. "Frankly, I think the impact was more than he could bear."

"But you did not go with him to Europe," he probed.

"Where he has gone, I don't wish to follow," I replied, "I want to stay in Canada. This is where I am meant to be."

"And your father had no disagreement with this course of action?"

"He's left me well-established, if that's what you mean," I replied, "And I am happy to pay for my room and board—"

"Good Lord, girl! You'll stay as my guest, and as long as you like!" He scoffed, but in a way that was more affectionate than gruff. "What I'm trying to ask, as delicately as possible, is this: does your father know you've fled Cumberland in the company of a Chinaman?"

"My father told me, once, that he was unconcerned by my friendship with Shaozhu."

Mr. Fish narrowed one eye. "That doesn't quite answer my question, Lizzie."

I pondered how to best reply. I didn't like to lie, especially to someone I respected like Harris Fish, but I could see no way around it. "My father knows that I've left Cumberland and come to Victoria," I claimed, "But he decided to withdraw from practising medicine and spend time touring the continent, and I do not begrudge him his decision. Father recognized that it's best for us to part ways. I've spent the last few weeks, closing our house and liquidating our possessions, and during that time, I have ministered to Shao's injuries and kept him safe from harm. But once the company took back possession of the house, I simply couldn't abandon Shao. He's fallen out of favor with certain affluent members of Cumberland's Chinese community and no one there will take him in. To leave him there would've been a death sentence."

Mr. Fish cocked one thin, grey brow to me. "Did you have anything to do with that?"

"I'm afraid I had everything to do with that." I squirmed in my seat. "Discretion is not my strongest suit."

"No, quite," he agreed, "Which is rather what I like about you."

I felt a blush rise to my cheeks to hear such kind praise.

"But the problem, Liz, is this: I can not have you and your friend living under my roof. As much as I appreciate your lack of discretion, I must be careful to keep the illusion of discretion in my own house." He held up one hand to shush me. "Not because I think there is anything inherently immoral about such a tryst—goodness, such delights make life worth living! The Good Lord in His wisdom knows, the romantic dalliances that I've enjoyed would make gentle society quiver … but I can't have you and … Shaozhu? This is his name?"

"Yes."

"I can't have you and Shaozhu living as man and wife under my roof. It would cause great upset to the neighbours. You do understand, yes?"

I nodded. Appearances were difficult to reclaim, once lost.

He grinned. "This does not mean I will cast you out, dear girl. I have a spare room on the top floor of my dwelling, most suited to a young lady's accommodation, and the carriage house has been converted into a dwelling where my gardener resides. It isn't much—two bedrooms and a sitting area—but Shaozhu will be more than comfortable there, and Lou Kwan Xi will be a gracious host." He took a sip and shook his head in disapproval. "And from one look at that poor boy, he needs a place to lie down! When last we spoke, you were training to be a doctor. Didn't your father teach you about the importance of rest?"

I felt the weariness settle upon me, and only then did I realize how worried I'd been that Mr. Fish would throw us to the street. "Thank you, sir," I said, "A place for Shao to recover—Mr. Fish, this is very generous of you!"

He reclined in the chair to take a sip of his cordial, and a ghoulish grin spread across his thin lips.

"Yes, I'm a bloody saint," he replied. "Now if only I could convince my neighbours of that fact. Go on," he tipped his chin to the kitchen, "Fetch your things, Lizzie Saunders, and Eddy will show you to your room."

THREE

The carriage house had two bedrooms, joined in the middle by a common area where Lou Kwan Xi had arranged a sitting area, a pile of dog-eared books, and a corner table where he might eat. There was no kitchen; meals were provided by the main house. The furnishings were as clean and modest as those in the parlor, but these were well-used. In Shao's room, we found the chair and bed to be serviceable, although when I'd helped him lay down, the springs in the mattress howled and the legs wobbled. A small dresser by the window was made of solid bird's eye maple, and looked like it might have come from a wealthy house, but a closer inspection showed that one of the legs was riddled with wormholes and it would soon lose all strength.

"Who is—" Shao's question was interrupted by his own groan of pain, but once he'd reclined on the bed, he took a shuddering breath and began again. "Who is this man?"

"Harris Fish," I replied. I grabbed a blanket from the drawer and whisked it over Shao's legs. "He's a friend of Mason Briggs."

"Your sister's friend?"

"Poor Violet. She'd hoped Mason could give her a life beyond the coal fields," I said; then shaking off the memories of my sister, I gave him a stern look. "Now, lift your shirt and I'll tighten the bandages."

"No, I'm alright, it doesn't hurt if I lie still," he replied. The muscles of his face relaxed and I believed him. "Can we trust this man?"

"I think so," I replied, sitting on the edge of the bed. I took Shao's hand in mine. "He works with the government, lobbying for a train system on the island. He doesn't disagree with you and I together but I think he's mindful of his public face, and I don't begrudge him that."

"No, I suppose not," Shao said, "I wouldn't want to risk such a comfortable house and property, either." He looked around at the small carriage house, its walls freshly papered with a gold-and-red floral design, its small square windows looking out onto a beautifully-tended garden. "Tell me about him."

I sat at his side and waiting for the springs to stop howling before I spoke. "He's from a prosperous family, but he never married."

"And he doesn't mind that your father has left for Europe?"

I paused for only a moment. "I don't think so," I replied. The words stuck in my throat. "I don't want to talk about it."

"Of course not. Forget I mentioned it."

When I glanced sideways at him, he had that peculiar expression on his face; not quite pity, but close.

"I won't mention your father again," he assured.

"Good."

"But I don't know how Dr. Saunders could just abandon you, Liz. It's cruel."

"Yes," I agreed, dropping my gaze to the wooden floor.

"And leaving you to close up the house? And sell your family's belongings? And without a word in person to another living soul? Only a letter of resignation, left on the dining room table?"

"Shao," I growled as a warning.

"It beggars belief that a good man like John Saunders would neglect his duties, even with the stress of his daughter's murder, and the suicide of Kelly, and—" He paused. "Sorry. I promised, didn't I."

"You did, yes."

I stood and gazed out the window. My breathing was slow and steady, but I knew from my own observations, the pace was unnatural. Ought I not be upset?

"You're too calm, Liz."

"I'm always too calm."

He stared at me, hard, as if he was trying to see through me. "Are you angry?"

"No." My face softened.

"What do you feel, Lei Zi?"

This was a question Shao asked often these days. I recognized it as an effort to understand me, and while the question coming from anyone else would've been pesky and annoying, I found myself enamored by Shao's inquiries. Lord knows, I didn't always have a good answer. Violet had never tried to understand me. As much as my sister had loved me, my personality had always proven a trial for Violet to bear. For Shao, though, I was a puzzle to solve.

"What do I feel?" I repeated, "Not much of anything, these days." I dropped my shoulders and sat on the edge of the bed again, careful not to jostle the thin mattress and cause him pain. "I've been so occupied with thoughts of getting here, to the sanctuary of Mr. Fish's home, that I haven't been feeling fear, or sorrow, or anything more."

His mouth kinked into a grin and he closed his eyes. "I've been so afraid that my uncle would seek some sort of revenge ... honestly, Liz, this is the first time in a month that I've felt the smallest bit safe."

I leaned towards him and pressed a kiss to his forehead. "Then rest. Recover. Mr. Fish assured me, we can stay here as long as we need."

I helped him wash the grime from his face, unpacked our few belongings, fetched him a bite to eat from the kitchen and mended his shoes; they were frightfully worn in places, and it took a bit of ingenuity and a scrap of leather from the garden shed to patch the soles. By the time I was finished, he was sleeping soundly, and the sun had set.

I, too, was tired from our travel, but I was too fretful to sleep, so I left our sanctuary, crossing the small garden and taking a deep breath of the cool evening air. The hour was close to nine. The night closed in like the drawing of velvet curtains, and while the day had retained its summery warmth, the evening brought the first clue of an advancing winter. A bracing chill in the air sunk its teeth into bare flesh, and brilliant stars pierced the clear night sky like diamonds.

I sat on the back porch. A sense of calm washed over me.

Shao's question turned over in my mind. What did I feel?

Safe, I suppose, but it was a tenuous safety, tinged with the need to keep myself in check when others were watching. Sometimes, I wished I lived on a boat—only me, alone—with no other people around. I liked being alone. If I was alone on the sea, I would never need to hide myself; I could speak whatever I wished, do whatever I liked, dress however I felt most comfortable. Best of all, I wouldn't need to lie. I hated lying, hated that it was necessary. It baffled me that I had to lie because no one would understand my actions; why should I suffer because they couldn't understand my reasons? Their basic emotions would drive them to shun me, imprison me, question me, distrust me.

I had driven a knife into the back of my father's neck, severing his spinal cord and killing him instantly. From everything I read, I was supposed to feel guilty about such a drastic action, but I didn't feel a speck of regret. It needed to be done. Like a rabid dog, he would've killed again. I could not let him live.

I thought about my family as I looked at the distant stars. My father, Dr. John Saunders, had been put together wrong, like a doll with mismatched parts. I didn't know why. I wasn't yet sure if I was as poorly constructed as he, but I had my suspicions. For all my life, I had admired his cool intelligence, his collected demeanor in the face of adversity, and his ability to care for my mother's needs. Now, all these traits seemed dark and cruel. What I saw as calm intelligence, could easily have been calculating. His care for Mother was not love as others might feel love; their relationship had been a cocoon, where they kept each other safe from a world that did not understand their perverted desires. Molly's madness was not insanity as others might define it, but the repressed torture of a woman terrified by her own sexual impulses. The medical books said madness ran through the female line, and mad mothers gave birth to mad daughters. Of that fact, they were quite clear.

So as I grew to adulthood, who would I resemble more? My mother, with her unnatural lusts? Or my father, who delighted in tearing women apart?

I dropped my forehead into my hands.

"God's teeth," I muttered to myself and the flowers.

If I ever wanted to be fixed, I needed to know how he'd become a broken monster. A hunger woke in my belly. Not the hunger for sex, to which I had recently been introduced, or the hunger for blood, which hummed like a distant engine in the back of my brain. This was a hunger for knowledge, and it grew like a fire in my mind. It was a cleaner, sweeter, lighter hunger that the other two, and I seized onto it with desperation. The world might not understand an unmarried woman's lust for sex, and they certainly wouldn't condone a young girl finding comfort in killing, but they'd be perfectly fine with a student pursuing research.

I would dive into the stories of my father's fiendish exploits. Surely, somewhere amongst the newspaper columns and tabloid cartoons, I would find a hint of how the man had become a devil? Somewhere, someone must know.

The click of metal on metal came from behind me, at the corner of the yard.

There at the gate stood Jess, her hand lightly opening the latch from the alley.

"Good evening, miss," she said.

"Were you making deliveries?"

Jess paused, then said shyly, "Only a few packages." She hesitated, shifted from foot to foot.

I saw plainly enough in her face that she hadn't intended to be seen, so I smiled. "I won't say a word."

"Thank you, miss."

"Out meeting a paramour?"

When Jess smiled, her face blossomed into beauty. "Something like that.

Please don't tell my mother I was out so late; I don't know what she'd do, she'd be so angry." Jess looked passed me to the carriage house. "Is your boy—is he going to be alright? He looked sore awful."

"He looks awful, yes," I agreed, "But I wager he'll be fine, now that he can rest. Traveling took a terrible toll on his injuries."

Jess hesitated. Her large eyes gave away the questions that lingered, unspoken, behind them.

"He was beaten," I answered.

"Well," Jess said softly, "I guess some things just ain't allowed." She took two steps, then said, "Do you know who did it?"

"Yes," I replied, and my throat hitched at the rage I felt. "I was made to watch."

Her face twisted in pity and sorrow. "And did you have justice?"

"No."

Jess lowered her large eyes. "I guess that's too much to ask. You're lucky you've still got him with you, here on God's earth." A moment's pause passed, and Jess gave a strained, shallow smile. "Good night, miss. Sleep well."

FOUR

September 15, 1898

In the morning, I fetched a pan of water from the house while I left Shao to attend to his more private needs. When I returned, I carefully unraveled his bandages and washed the sweat from his chest and back. By the light of the bedroom window, the bruises appeared faded: what had once been the clear outline of men's boots had now become murky patches of grey-purple against his tanned, bronzed skin. He gasped when I removed the bandages, but he breathed easier without them, and when I placed the cold disc of the stethoscope against his sternum, his lungs and heart replied with a strong, steady rhythm.

"Much improved," I pronounced.

"Leave the bandage off, just for a bit," he asked, "I don't feel like I need it to breathe today."

"We can keep it off for a little while—good Lord, it's filthy!—but it'll have to go back on." After days of use, the reams of cotton cried out desperately for washing, and I gathered them up with arms outstretched, as far away from my nose as I could reach. "Don't push yourself, understand? You aren't so healed yet that you can't do yourself more damage!"

"Yes, doctor," Shao replied as he stood gingerly, the bed springs squealing. He gave a few grunts of discomfort as he took a step to the birds-eye dresser but, as he reached his arms upwards, he smiled triumphantly. "I think I'm more stiff than sore, Liz and—ow!"

His face greyed from the pain. I dropped the bandages and helped him sit down again.

"Easy, Shao! You're still not healed! You won't be for at least a month."

"Alright, fine," he relented, "But at least let me sit outside!"

I helped him stand, together we shuffled into the garden. Lou Kwan Xi raked leaves in the far corner, and he watched as I fetched a blanket and pillows from the bed, then openly laughed as I constructed a comfortable nest for Shao in the shade of a gnarled oak. Xi possessed a broad, square face with an easy smile, and a smudge of dirt garnished his cheek. He was short, stocky, and strong, built like a bull, but he was friendly, too, and a little silly. In the past few hours, he'd demonstrated an easy personality, and he had a way of making Shao grin that I appreciated. Xi shouted something in Chinese, and Shao laughed in reply.

"What did he say?"

"That if you want to make him a spot to rest, he'd be happy for it," Shao replied.

"You laughed a little harder at his joke than at your interpretation," I smirked.

"I'm paraphrasing," he said, arranging a pillow under his back. "Let's just say, Xi's comment was a little more rude, Lei Zi."

"I need to learn more Cantonese."

"I'll teach you a phrase right now," Shao said, then to Xi, he replied with particular fire, "*Gau si gwai!*"

Xi looked shocked, then laughed at the insult and went back to work.

I looked at Shao for a translation, but he smirked.

"Trust me, it's not very nice."

With a chuckle, I gathered a tin pail of water and a handful of soap flakes from Eddy. When I returned, I sat next to Shao and began the laborious task of washing the stinking bandage.

Shao folded his hands over his knees. "So tell me, Liz: how long until I'm healed? And what do you propose we do, when I'm better?"

"That magical point is probably a month away, Shao, and frankly, I'm not planning that far in advance." I lifted the dripping fabric and cringed when I saw that the water was already grey. "We're lucky to be where we are, right now. For that, I'm grateful."

He closed his eyes and tilted his head back, resting comfortably in the shade. "We could open an apothecary shop in Victoria," he said, and his voice had adopted a dreamy quality, lost in thoughts. "A fusion of Eastern and Western medicine. You'll diagnose them, and I'll sell them the tinctures and salves they need to be well."

"I don't know if I'm quite the caliber of doctor that you assume, Mr. Chen," I began, "My education has come to an abrupt standstill. You're the sum of my patients, and your maladies are few, and I rather want to keep it that way." I plunged the bandage into the tin bucket again, scrubbed and rubbed until the water roiled with suds. "And I don't know who would take me on as an apprentice, to continue my education, now that my father is—"

I almost said, 'dead'. My teeth clamped on my tongue.

"Now that my father is gone."

He mistook my pause for a rare show of emotion. His hand caressed my forearm. "Lizzie, I'm sure he'll come back."

"No, Shao. I'm quite sure he won't."

"How can he have been so cruel?" Shao said, bewildered, "He loves you, Liz. He's always been so supportive of you, that to abandon you so fully—I can't understand it! Why wouldn't he take you?"

"I wouldn't want to go. He knows me well enough, Shao, to realize that I have no interest in leaving this place."

"Because of me?"

"Oh, don't you think highly of yourself!" I said with a laugh, but he didn't respond to my levity, so I smiled and said, "Do you want me to leave? Do you want to wash your stinky old bandages yourself, while I spirit around Europe with a gaggle of fluff-headed young ladies, wearing white skirts and painting watercolors of Grecian ruins?"

He looked at me in my grey trousers, my shirt sleeves rolled up past my elbows. "It doesn't seem your style."

"Precisely."

The backdoor to the main house opened. Mr. Fish emerged, wearing a pressed grey suit and a silk top hat with a purple band. When he descended the stairs to the yard, his footsteps were as quick and merry as a man of his sour disposition can muster. "Good morning to you both," he greeted, "How is the patient today?"

"Much better, Mr. Fish," I said, sitting back on my heels. "Less than a day, and I can already see improvement."

"My strength is returning, sir," Shao said, "I'm very grateful to you for giving us such comfortable lodgings."

"Good to hear," he said. "Eddy's made a fine breakfast of fried kippers and some kidney chop, and if you ask nicely, she may even toast you a bit of bread to go with them. I have a meeting to attend this morning, Lizzie, but I've received an invitation that you might find interesting."

"You did?" I was puzzled; who could possibly know I was here?

"Dr. Briggs is hosting a gentleman's gathering this afternoon. When I sent word that you had arrived—like a bedraggled stray cat on my doorstep, mind you—his wife Emma nearly fell over herself in her haste to invite you. Are you free this afternoon to join her for tea?"

"I'm afraid I can't, Mr. Fish. Shao is still unwell, and—"

"I'm perfectly fine," Shao replied.

"Yes, but—"

"Go, enjoy yourself," he insisted. "You've ordered me to rest and relax, Lizzie, and now I'm doing the same for you." Shao struggled to his elbows, wincing. "Thank you, sir, for your hospitality. I hope to repay you however I can, once I am healthy again."

Mr. Fish bowed his head crisply. "Lizzie speaks nothing but praise for you. It's my pleasure to have made your acquaintance, Mr. Chen. Your grasp of English is quite phenomenal."

"I was raised in San Francisco, sir."

"And Lizzie tells me you worked in an apothecary."

"Yes, sir."

"A useful skill to have. And your head tax—is it paid?"

"In full." Shao reached for his pocket, where he kept the document detailing his status. "My papers are here, in order—"

"Put your papers away, young man; I've no interest in seeing them. I fully believe you when you say you're a free man." Mr. Fish nodded his approval. "May you recover quickly, Mr. Chen, for a fellow with your talents is always in high demand. Now then, Lizzie," he began, turning to me, "I've hired a carriage. It will arrive at one. Do you have suitable attire for a tea?"

I wrinkled my nose. I was still wearing grey trousers, old leather boots, and a stained linen shirt, and now my sleeves were wet to the elbows. I'd brought almost nothing with me. In addition to the ones on my back, my only clothes were a black cotton pinafore, and a black smock with no slip or petticoat. Certainly I had no hat or gloves in my possession. There was nothing in my portmanteau suitable for an afternoon party, and while I normally wouldn't care for social niceties, I didn't wish to embarrass a man who'd been so kind to us. If I was going as Mr. Fish's guest, I'd rather look presentable, if not simply clean.

"I brought only one other outfit, sir, but it's a simple frock, and quite plain. I currently own nothing suitable for a formal call."

"I thought not," he smirked. "I've asked Jess to fetch you anything you need, and," He looked to the timepiece in his pocket, a heavy gold watch on a thick fob, "She knows a spot downtown to buy a pre-made dress, clever thing that she is." He snapped the watch shut and tucked it in his pocket again. "If you're going to assemble some manner of presentable attire, you'll have only a few hours to do so; might I suggest you hurry?" His eyes glanced at the sopping fabric in my hand. "In a pinch, Lou Kwan Xi has been known to do my washing. I suggest he take over for you here, and entertain your friend with tales of their shared homeland."

I glanced at Shao who, having come to North American at the age of four, had very few memories of China upon which to draw. To call it 'home' was as absurd as me returning to England.

"Will you be alright if I go?" I pressed.

He grinned. "*Mei wen ti.*"

I frowned, squinted one eye, thought hard. "Not a problem—yes?"

"Well done."

Mr. Fish gave a gruff cough, perhaps to hide his amusement. "I knew you were learning medicine from your father, but I had no idea you were also learning Chinese from Mr. Chen." He turned to leave, and over his shoulder, he added, "What other talents do you have trapped in that brain of yours, I wonder?"

Cumberland had been a city, but a small city, a modest industrial burg constantly perfumed with the acrid smoke of coal mines and trains. The streets were dirt, the buildings constructed of rough-hewn timber. Almost everyone worked for the same colliery company, so everyone knew each other—people's private affairs provided the juicy topics of daily conversations.

In contrast, Victoria was a city in the truest sense of the word. Its buildings were constructed of brick and stone and steel. The bustle of life infused these cobbled streets with a different flavor: varied, exciting, vibrant. Here, people made their living in a vast array of different ways, and not everyone within view was employed by the same company. The boardwalks teemed with government officials, traders, furriers, fruit vendors, ship merchants, insurance brokers, carters and fishermen. Victoria, as the new capital of British Columbia and a port city, possessed a sense of grandeur, international purpose, and civility that Cumberland had sorely lacked.

I followed Jess through the corridors of people as we hurried along Belleville Street.

I tried very hard to keep from staring at the bustling shipyards, the stone turrets on the partially-constructed parliament buildings, and the wooden Indian canoes that floated on the muddy slough of Victoria's Inner Harbor. At the edge of the beach, a group of Indian women—the Songhees, Jess called them—had pulled their narrow boat ashore and they rested on mats of woven cedar bark, selling freshly caught fish to pedestrians. They wore hand-me-down flannel shirts and multiple layers of hand-stitched skirts, the colored fabrics faded by sun and time into a dull brown. On their heads were conical hats woven from cedar bark, dyed black and scarlet, with wide brims designed to protect their faces from all sorts of weather. Long silvery salmon lay in cedar bark baskets at their sides, ready for purchase, and while the younger women smiled and bartered for coins, the older women watched us with eyes that were hooded, unfriendly, distrustful.

"Hurry up, miss!" Jess demanded.

A skinny pedestrian bridge crossed the wide mudflats between James Bay and the downtown district. Jess turned onto it and strode across. I tried to follow close after. While I didn't want to look like a bumpkin who'd just stumbled out of the woods, the newness of these surroundings threatened to overwhelm all my senses, and as I crossed the bridge, I abandoned my efforts to ignore my surroundings. How could I? There were so many things I'd never seen before! At the midpoint of the bridge, I stopped to catch my breath and my wits, and I stared unabashedly at the skyline of the glorious city and the fine sailing ships moored in the bay.

I couldn't quite believe I was here. Only a month ago, I had been living in a company house with my father and sister, my clothes mended by our Scottish housemaid, my future as a doctor's apprentice at the Cumberland Hospital firmly set. And now? I stood alone on a bridge in a strange city. I'd been cast adrift. I was an orphan.

I held the handrail and took a deep breath of sea air. It smelt salty and fishy and fresh all at once.

Shouldn't I feel something more than this, I thought. Shouldn't I be sad, or afraid, or confused? Where would I be, a year from now? Or, for that matter, in a month? I leaned my elbows on the railing and marveled that my future had become a wholly uncharted ocean, with no clear landfall in sight.

Jess had returned to tug at my elbow. "Quit with your daydreaming, Liz!" she said, "If we're going to fetch you a dress, we haven't time to admire the view!"

I quickened my pace to catch up with her. "Where are we heading?"

Her soft voice barely carried over the rattling of carriages on the wooden cobbles of Wharf Street. "A little dress shop on the corner of Yates and Broad," she said over her shoulder.

"We don't have time for a dress to be made!"

"No, no, Mrs. Thornton sells 'em already put together, miss," said Jess, "She caters to all sorts of ladies who need clothing, all quick like!"

"What an odd clientele," I replied, but Jess didn't hear me, and scurried on at her rapid clip.

When I finally caught up again, I asked, "How long have you lived here?"

"Quite a few years, miss," Jess said with surprising ease; we'd covered many blocks at a fast clip, and while I was winded, she seemed unaffected. "Me and Mama, we came up from San Francisco in the spring of '89."

"Do you like it here?"

"It's nice enough," she replied. She led me around a corner, onto a quieter side street, and we fell into step alongside each other. Perhaps she took pity on me, for she slowed her pace. "Better than California, I s'pose. Mama hoped to have a business of her own in California, but it weren't the right place for people like us. They said the negro would have his freedom once the North won the war, but it ain't happened yet, and I doubt it ever will."

"Have you found freedom here?"

Jess gave a hard laugh. "It's better, but it sure ain't grand!" She warmed a little. "You heard about Belle Adams, last June?"

I shook my head.

"I figured you might've—it was in all the papers."

"We didn't always get the most recent news in the coalfields."

"Well, it was about two blocks from here, over on Johnson Street, that Belle Adams damn near took the head off Charles Kincaid with a straight razor. He was a friend of my mother. Mama said Belle done it cause he was negro, and an unnatural affection across the races causes white women to go mad as hops."

"Really, now," I said.

"Poor old Charlie, he died in the road," Jess added as we crossed a street, narrowly avoiding a cab and horse. She continued after we hopped up onto the safety of the opposite boardwalk. "She stabbed him in the front room of the Empire Hotel, and he staggered out onto the street, and she chased after him screaming her apologies for taking his life, but her cries came too late. He gave up the ghost and died in her arms." She clucked in her throat sadly. "All because he fell out of love. I figure, if you can't tell someone you don't love 'em anymore and get away with your life intact, then you aren't really free."

"I think love makes everyone go mad. It doesn't matter, their skin color."

Jess smiled shyly. "Well, maybe that's true." Then the smile melted and she said, "Here we are. This is the spot."

On the corner of Yates and Broad sat a squat warehouse, built of soot-stained yellow bricks, with a line of small dark windows across the upper level. The main doors, which fronted onto Yates, were closed up tight and shuttered, but over them hung a wooden, hand-painted sign that read 'Temple of Thespis'. I peered through the crack but saw nothing, for it was pitch black inside.

Jess laughed at my efforts. "Not here," she said, and led me around the corner from Yates onto Broad. I saw at once that this side of the building had been split into a handful of small businesses, both on the street level and a few on a basement level. We passed a butcher, a tin smith, and a piano tuner's frontage before Jess descended a short stairwell and knocked on the narrow blue door leading to a basement suite.

When the door creaked open, we were greeted with a matronly shriek of delight.

Mrs. Thornton had ample curves to fill her fine, embroidered corset. Her thick honey-brown hair was swept up into a roll, perfumed with lavender to hide the musty smell of a dirty scalp, and her make-up was not quite thick enough to hide the pits and hollows that smallpox had left on her complexion. She had a squat nose and tiny sharp brown eyes set deep in her face, like two currants pushed into a lump of bread dough.

"Well, goodness, my Jessie, my little songbird!" she squealed, throwing her pudgy hands wide and enfolding Jess in a pair of meaty arms. "I thought you were working for Mr. Fish today. Have you come by to help me with the sewing?"

"No, ma'am," Jess said with her chin down, "I'm afraid I'm too busy with work to spend time at the theatre."

Another shriek. "Pish posh! Too busy? The theatre is LIFE, girl!" She emitted a wet belch of a laugh. "And who's the scamp at your side, hey?" Mrs. Thornton leaned forward and squinted. "Larks, it's a wee girl! I thought for sure you were the Nelson boy from three blocks over!"

"No, ma'am," I said, and extended my hand. "Lizzie Saunders."

Jess introduced us properly. "Miss Saunders, this is Alma Thornton, the matron of the Yates Street Amateur Theatrical Company."

Mrs. Thornton took my hand in a fierce grip and nearly broke my fingers with her enthusiasm. "Lovely to make your acquaintance, sweet Lizzie! Have you ever considered the life of a thespian?" Without releasing my hand, she pulled me close. "I always have use of a creature that looks like a boy, but is able to retain her lines with the precision of a girl. Are you familiar with Wilde?"

"Uh, no …"

"Come in, come in, both of you," she said, and she pulled me down the basement steps into a cramped, sweaty, smelly little hole, the walls hung with reams of fabric. Two treadle sewing machines sat in one corner, and a long table with shears took up the center of the room. Three gas lamps hung from hooks on the ceiling, providing the only illumination, and in the close air, the fumes of burning coal from the iron stove in the corner reminded me of home. A small doorway at the back of the room led into a dark chamber beyond.

"We're putting on a production of Wilde's 'Duchess of Padua' in October," she continued, "I could use an urchin like you to play the role of Taddeo Barti." She turned and looked over my head to Jess. "Have you brought her to me for the role? I shall be pleased as Punch if you did!"

"Miss Saunders has come from the coalfields up north, arriving yesterday and with no decent dress to call her own," Jess said, "She's a friend of Mr. Fish."

"Oh!" said Mrs. Thornton. I detected a hint of levity in her admiration.

As she studied my legs, she said, "So this is how they dress the womenfolk in the wilderness! Jess told me Mr. Fish didn't have a friend in the world!"

Jess looked uncomfortable. "I didn't mean no harm by the comment, Liz."

Mrs. Thornton laughed. "I've met the man a few times, and I bet he'd see that as a compliment, not an insult! Quite the hermit, so I've heard." She rolled her eyes. "It's a rare occasion to see Mr. Fish in the theatre, and so I'm left a-wondering why a friend of his would be here, in my shop?"

"Miss Saunders is in dire need of a dress for an occasion later this afternoon."

"Ah, the city has wrung the desire for a nice frock out of you!" Mrs. Thornton peered closely at me, studying my form. "Now … let me see … What sort of occasion are we talking about, luv?"

"An afternoon tea," I said.

Jess added, with much gravity, "At the house of Dr. Mason Briggs."

Mrs. Thornton tipped her head back and snorted. "Good Lord! Not yet in town a day and already cavorting with the upper crust! By the look of you, I would've thought you to be a pickpocket or a guttersnipe. Certainly not a lady of any quality!"

"I have been kindly invited," I said, suddenly bashful. "It would be rude of me to refuse, but equally rude to arrive in the clothes on my back."

"Well, the Yates Street theatre has a wide range of costumes and disguises for any occasion," the seamstress boasted, "I bet we can get you into a fine dress in only the time it takes for me to hem it." She strolled around me, appraising my form, clucking low in her throat with some disapproval. "A bit chicken breasted, you are, but that's not a problem. I have a few smocks that are skinny on top, and we can pad any bodice to fill out your bubbies …" She stopped in front of me again and gave a clipped nod. "I will lend you a dress, but only on three conditions."

"Name them," I said.

"One: you will tell Mrs. Briggs that there is to be a production of 'Duchess of Padua' running from October 28th to November 5th, and two: that you recommend she comes to see it, as you've heard it will be quite entertaining."

"I can do that," I agreed.

"And three," Mrs. Thornton said, taking my hand and leading me through the small door at the rear of the shop, into the dark chamber, "You will audition for Taddeo's role."

"You won't give it to me," I warned, "I'm a frightful actress."

"At least give me a chance to make that decision myself," said Mrs. Thornton.

And so I agreed, although the thought of performing on stage made my stomach queasy.

Jess brought a lamp from the front room. She followed us, and the light spread out across the floor, and suddenly the walls were bathed in a dim glow. I let out a small gasp, for all around us were hung hundreds of costumes: dresses, jackets, military uniforms, a vast array of clothing encompassing all shapes and sizes. On the floor sat wooden boxes of hats, gloves, scarves, masks, ties and shoes. My surprise filled Mrs. Thornton with pride.

"I don't think I've ever seen so many clothes all in one spot!"

"Welcome to my costume shop, dear. See that door there?" She gestured to a wide oak door of formidable strength on the opposite side of the closet, snuggled between the racks of dresses. "It leads directly to the back stage of the Yates Street Theatre, or as we've come to call it, our own little Temple of Thespis. Perfect, isn't it! During the day, I keep my dress shop, and in the evening, I clothe the characters. It's proven to be a most lucrative arrangement for all involved." From over my shoulder, she added in a matronly voice, "Jess, dear, keep that lamp away from the skirts. We can't have it all go up in a blaze."

Then she stepped back to appraise the color of my complexion by lamp light. "What color for you, then …" she mused, "Ginger hair, sun-brown skin, plenty of freckles, hazel eyes." She grinned. "Eyes which, I might add, unintentionally reveal a clever, observant mind behind them. Ah, and look at that! A puckish smile to go with them."

"You flatter me so I'll accept the role."

"No, luv," she replied, reaching up into the thick folds of clothes and pulling out a dress made of sumptuous purple velvet. "I'm not full of empty praise. Let's try this one, shall we?" She handed the dress to me, and continued. "The Yates Street players are a family, my dear, and we do not plump each other up with false hopes and empty flatteries. We are dedicated to our craft, isn't that right, Jess!"

"Yes, ma'am."

"We meet twice a week for rehearsals, and provide only the highest quality of theatrical productions for our audience. Why, last autumn we performed William Brough's 'The Caliph of Bagdad' to good reviews …"

"… And in the summer, we did Phillip Watt's play, 'Maud's Peril'. It was quite well received," said Jess. "We played it on the green at Beacon Hill Park!"

Mrs. Thornton held up another dress to my chin, this one a pink-and-tan monstrosity of embroidered beads and ruffles, and shook her head as she reached for third. "In the winter months, we perform in the theatre, right through that door, and it's been a good arrangement between the landlord and myself." She gave me a saucy wink. "He's a lovely chap, a nice fellow, but unable to pursue a thespian's life."

"Why not?" I asked as she held the third garment to my chin.

"He's upper class, poor boy," she crooned. The way she said it, this state was a tragedy suitable for Shakespeare. "His father bought him the building to manage, but has expressed disapproval at the son crossing the stage himself. Quite heartbreaking."

"But he's happy for the dress shop's ridiculous rent," Jess said. "Far too much."

"Now, Jess, don't be bitter. We are provided with a good space, and we are fortunate for our connections!" Mrs. Thornton may have wished to say more, but the click of the latch on the door leading to the theatre drew her attention. It swung open on creaking hinges.

A young man stood in the doorway, his boyish face made more masculine by a sparse moustache and thick eyebrows. He was very handsome, with beautifully chiseled features and an athletic form, and eyes that were as dark and as deeply-set as Mrs. Thornton's. His short honey-colored hair was the same hue as hers, too, but it had not been combed, and like waves on a storm-tossed sea, the messy scrub crested in all directions. He wore brown denims and a stiff white shirt with patched elbows; the sleeves had been rolled up, and in his belt loop, he'd slung a mallet. His outfit gave every indication of being handy and clever with tools, but he gaped and blinked rapidly at the sight of three women by lamplight, fussing over frocks. By his startled reaction, I wondered if he was not so quick witted.

"Andy, dear," said Mrs. Thornton. "Aren't you supposed to be hanging the new lanterns?"

At her questions, he found this tongue. "I didn't think anyone was here," he stammered, then added, "Hullo, Jess. How's by you today?"

"Fine, Andy," she replied with a warm smile.

"Well, don't just stand there with your bare face all hanging out," said Mrs. Thornton, "Come in, close the door, you'll let the heat of the shop into the theatre." She turned an exasperated expression to me. "Miss Saunders, this is my son, Andrew."

I nodded at him, but he didn't glance at me.

"I went and cut my thumb," he complained to his mother. "God damn that nail!"

"Language, boy!" she admonished, then softened to him, and said, "Let Jess help you tend it. Go on, into the front room. Jess, you'll find a bottle of liniment in the kitchen, and some clean cotton by the sink." As he passed, she said, "Oh, silly chick!"

Mrs. Thornton took the lamp from Jess as she left and set it down on the floor. "My Andy, his head is soft as a lump of tallow," she said quietly to me, "But his heart is soft, too, so Lord love him and keep him, I say!"

There was genuine affection in her words; she did not seem to hold his clumsiness against him.

"Andy works for the landlord?" I asked.

"When he isn't attempting to learn his lines or building the sets. I'm afraid an enduring passion for the theatre runs in our family." She tittered as she held a bodice to my chest. "He's been blessed with a sweet nature and a kind temperament, even if he's a bit short on brains."

Through the door, I saw Jess applying the liniment to his hand, pressing the cloth to his injury. Her eyes remained riveted on his wound as she spoke to him, but he watched the top of her head.

"He seems quite fond of Jess. They're good friends?"

She scoffed at that. "Andy is driven keenly by the capricious whims of a young man's biology," she said, rolling her eyes. "He fawns over anyone in a skirt. If you loiter long enough, Miss Saunders, he'll doubtlessly turn his puppy dog gaze to you, too. Such a silly boy!" She held up a dress and gave a nod. "Now, I believe I've found the one!" she laughed. "Try on the skirts and I'll hem the ruffles to your length of leg. We'll have you dressed like a proper lady in no time!"

FIVE

Jess and I brought the outfit home and she took me to a small wing off the main floor of Mr. Fish's house, where Eddy had arranged a comfortable apartment of three adjoining rooms. It was a fine space, decorated tastefully and cheerfully, with a private bedsit for each woman and a shared sitting area. A floral couch and a table made it very homey. A vase of flowers on the table brightened the room. Jess welcomed me in, brought a hairbrush and pins from her bedroom, and bid me to open the packages from Mrs. Thornton's shop, for she would help me to dress.

First, a slip of white silk that reached to my knees, and over that, a whalebone corset that had seen better days. Jess tied the laces tightly at the small of my back, then helped me adjust a petticoat of stiff white linen. Over this, the camisole, then the bustle tied around my waist; Jess giggled to herself as she arranged the plump pillow, padded with hay, squarely over my hips. "Finally, a bit of shape to you," she said.

Next came the underskirt, and I fumbled with the buttons at the waist, but Jess had deft fingers. She grunted slightly at the weight of the skirt, helping me dive head first through it and settling it on my hips before lacing it up in the back, then arranging the shirt and jacket over my bony shoulders. The outfit was made of wool and matching silk dyed deep blue, the same shimmering color as the feathers of a mountain jay, and more lovely than any outfit I'd ever owned.

Jess disappeared in her room, and returned with a black hat and gloves in her hands. "You can borrow these," she said, "But don't you lose 'em!"

As the clock on the wall stuck one, I heard a carriage rattle to a stop at the front of the Fish residence. I stomped down the corridor, out of the apartment and into the entrance hall. I held my skirts above my ankles with both gloved hands.

We found Mr. Fish standing by the front door. He passed the time by doing frivolous things like wiping a smudge from the head of his walking stick and adjusting his hat in the mirror by the coat rack.

When he looked up from his primping, he promptly coughed into his hand to hide his shock.

"I never would've thought it possible," he muttered, more to himself than to me.

"What?" I challenged.

"Your hair is … the dress … gloves and polished shoes …" He laughed. "Well, you still trudge about like a coal miner, Lizzie, but if you stay perfectly still, you look like you belong to a grand European family." He peered closer at my throat. "Where did you find that cameo?"

"It belonged to my mother," I said.

"That glorious piece of jewelry was hidden in your luggage? Mercy, I wonder what other treasures you've squirrelled away there!"

I smiled but said nothing. The walrus-hide portmanteau had been my father's, and it held a great deal. If Mr. Fish opened my bag, he'd find inside an extra change of pants and shirt, a pair of stockings, and the leather tool case that had been my father's, containing the medical implements of his trade. He would have found a well-worn letter from my grandfather, a photograph of my parents and Violet, a scrap of purple fabric from a woman's dress, and a dog-eared book on human anatomy filled with handwritten notes. In the side pocket, he'd find two glass vials of opium, to use in case Shao's pain was too great to travel, and a roll of bills that totaled almost $800, the sum of all my family's hastily sold possessions. Lastly, he would've found a wickedly-curved apothecary knife, given to me as a gift to keep me safe.

But these were my secrets, not suitable for sharing in present company.

"Very little, I'm afraid," I replied as he held the front door open for me. I hooked my hand over the crook of his elbow to steady myself as we descended the steps. "I left in a great hurry, with the intention of purchasing what I need when I reach my destination."

"And where is that, exactly?" he asked.

I thought carefully about my answer. "I don't truly know," I said as we boarded the carriage. "But I'm sure I'll recognize it when I get there."

When Mr. Fish smiled, his face creased into a map of wrinkles and his mouth became ghoulish. "Spoken like a true wanderer, my girl."

The carriage took us along the waterfront then veered inland, past grand houses of stone and timber that were flanked by wide green lawns. Long dusty memories of Wiltshire bubbled to the surface of my mind, but the salt air and the cry of gulls reminded us that we were close to the sea. It all seemed so pristine, so exact, so clean. I felt a little pang of stage-fright—

would Emma Briggs see instantly that my dress was part of a theatre wardrobe, hastily hemmed and tucked to fit my body?

But as the carriage pulled to a halt outside the Brigg's residence, I forgot my nervousness.

Here stood a house plucked directly from the green fields of Surrey. The country mansion was comprised of wings and additions, sprawling outwards and upwards with enthusiasm, but all clad with neat green boards trimmed with crisp white edging and decorations. I counted three stories, and on every floor, stained glass windows with thick lead and bright colors displayed a range of flowers: daffodils, azaleas, roses, foxgloves. On the building's south-east corner, a glass conservatory provided a civilized place to take breakfast or tend orchids, and along the south-west side of the home, a broad verandah looked out over prim, precise gardens. Box hedges marked the paths and lined the banks of flowers still abloom.

The carriage stood abreast of the main entrance, which protected guests from the elements with an imposing stone porte-cochère. Wide stone steps led from the portico to a set of double doors, carved with ivy and flowers from a rosy, polished hardwood.

Mr. Fish held my hand as I disembarked.

"You look astonished," he said.

"God's teeth! I thought your house was huge! The Briggs live in a bloody castle!"

Mr. Fish laughed openly at my comment. "I suppose it must look like that, to someone accustomed to a company town. Mason comes from an established family, but he's done very well for himself in Victoria, too."

"I had no idea!"

As we paused at the base of the stairs, Mr. Fish said, "You know, Lizzie, your father could have done equally well, if not better. Why did he choose a position in Cumberland, where he could never advance past the position of a mine doctor? I wager he'd have done very well in private practice here."

"Mr. Dunsmuir hired my father for the Cumberland practice, and Father wished to do well by his employer's faith in his ability," I replied, knowing that this was not exactly true. "Father was a man of duty before ambition."

The carriage rolled away, and Mr. Fish said, "I assumed it had to do more with your mother's condition."

I bristled.

"He cared greatly for her, didn't he," Mr. Fish continued. "I never met her, but Mason tells me your mother was a lovely woman."

"You tease me, sir."

He heard the cold edge in my voice. "I do no such thing! Why would you think that?"

"My mother was quite insane, Mr. Fish," I admitted baldly, and he startled a little at the bluntness of the comment. "She was given to bouts of depression, manic energy, and delusions. All Cumberland knew it. The gossip that followed her exploits was vicious and far-flung, but I didn't realize it stretched all the way to Victoria."

Mr. Fish, this man who had taken me in and provided me with friendship, looked aghast. "Liz, I meant no harm at all in mentioning her! Mason doesn't gossip about her; he tells me she was a sweet soul, full of good humor, but that she had a delicate condition for which your father tended her! I assumed she was weak of constitution, as your sister was."

My heart softened to him. "No, sir, Mother was weak of mind. She could be quite difficult to bear, at times."

"Though I can see, when you think of her, how much you loved her," he replied.

"I did."

"And the madness? This was the cause of her death?"

I shook my head. "Consumption."

"Mercy—to lose your mother and sister within the space of months. And your father now gone from you, too, for all intents and purposes."

"This has been a most unfortunate year."

He took my hand. "Liz, I never meant to upset you." He paused. "Have I? You are as composed as a flower."

"My heart aches for them, I assure you," I said, "But I'm not given to flights of emotion, Mr. Fish. It's a trait of which Father was most proud."

"He's a man of science," Mr. Fish said with approval. "I know it can be difficult when one you love is weak of mind; my own younger sister, Rose, struggles with compulsions that we can barely comprehend. She lives in San Francisco, all on her own, and fills her days by collecting stacks of newspapers." His eyes rolled, his face grew exasperated. "She fills her apartment with the damnable things, so that she sleeps on a sofa and must go to cafes to eat her meals."

"Really?"

"The paper, the lamps … the sheer flammable danger of her living situation keeps me awake at night. It's distressing, but what can I do? Her madness gives her a headstrong tenacity that none of my brothers can break."

"But you love her."

"Very much." Then he held out his arm to me and guided me up the steps. "Come, come, come. Let's enjoy an afternoon of frivolity and leave all these sad and gloomy discussions on the doorstep. Agreed?"

"Agreed."

After a moment of consideration, I asked, "Do you think she would give up any of her papers? If, for example, I was looking for information on a point in time?"

"I suppose she might. She only loves to collect, she barely reads." Perhaps feeling like he'd slighted me, he hurried to make the offer, for here was an opportunity to make amends. "I'll write her, and ask."

When he took hold of the great brass knocker and rapped quickly on the door, a Chinese butler appeared. He stood only as tall as Mr. Fish's shoulder, but he moved with considered movements that gave him a powerful, quiet presence. His brown-black hair was tied in a queue that reached down his back, and a sprinkle of dark birthmarks covered his wide face. He wore a plain black suit with a crisp white shirt, and he ushered us inside the main foyer with a gesture of one flattened hand. Here we waited as he retreated into another room to announce our arrival. We had arrived on time, but this moment was artfully provided to give us a few minutes to admire our surroundings.

I knew Dr. Mason Briggs to be a sprightly man of good humor, only a few years older than Violet had been, and he'd decorated his home in a manner that was simultaneously austere, conservative, and extremely merry. The stairway was grand, but not overly showy. The paintings on the wall consisted of portraits, but not of dour people; these subjects giggled and grinned, wore gay dresses, and invited the viewer to join them in their canvases with twinkling eyes. Plush carpets in rich colors warmed a wooden parquet floor. In spite of the foyer's spacious size and vaulted ceiling, complete with a glittering crystal chandelier, the entrance to Dr. Brigg's home felt very welcoming.

And then, as my head was craned upwards, admiring a young lady with a lamb in a pastoral scene, Dr. Briggs appeared in a far door. He looked just as I remembered him: animated, youthful, with a head of curly brown hair and a trimmed, waxed moustache. His smile, warm and inviting and playful, gave his face a boyish quality that was both disarming and innocent. He moved like a marionette. He threw his arms up in a gesture that some might see as exaggerated, but I thought enthusiastic. "Harris Fish! Good to see you again!" he greeted, shaking the older man's hand with both of his own. Turning to me, he said nothing. Instead, he paused to behold me, then held out his long arms and embraced me like a long-lost brother.

"Hello, Dr. Briggs!" I laughed.

Mason laughed in my ear. "My dear sweet lovely Lizzie!" he said, "It is so very, very good to see you! I tell you, Feng Soo had to pluck me right up off the floor when he delivered me the message that you were staying in the home of grumpy old Mr. Fish! Well, come in! Come in! We have sandwiches and tea, and Harris, can I interest you in an Irish whiskey?"

I followed the two men as they chatted, down a short hallway and into a sunny parlor where ten or twelve men had gathered on couches. The goods and trinkets that filled the room were glamorous and marvelous: a clock made of copper and glass, an ornate bird cage with a mechanical finch sitting on a perch, a brass barometer. A table with a display of silver teapots glinted in the sunlight, and on the wall behind was a framed map of the world, rendered in bright inks and gilded gold. Lacy curtains, billowing in windows thrown open, separated us from the sumptuous rose garden outside. The men greeted Mr. Fish one at a time with much shaking of hands and guffawing, but one young lady leapt to her feet and walked lightly to me, her face aglow with a sunny smile.

"Emma, my dove," said Briggs, and his words were filled with genuine adoration, "This is Amaryllis Saunders, the youngest daughter of Dr. John Saunders."

What adjectives can I use to describe Emma Briggs that would be adequate? She was more lovely than 'lovely', more graceful than 'graceful'. She was as light on her feet as a tabby, and while she may have once been lean and lithe, she was now round with pregnancy. Her mahogany-colored hair glinted with strands of gold, and her cheeks were as white as alabaster, save for a rosy blush that spoke of robust health. But in spite of all these angelic qualities, her expression was one of utmost humility, showing every hint of true joy at making my acquaintance.

"Oh, Lizzie, I have heard so much about you!" she said with a voice that was musical and light. "Please, first, let me give you condolences on the horrors that you have endured!" At this, she brushed a kiss against my cheek. Its touch was as delicate as a butterfly's wing. Her hair smelled of beeswax and orange blossoms. "Mason told me of your trials. Please, I wish to extend myself to you in any way possible! My home is your home!"

"Thank you," I stammered, taken aback by her concern.

"It is the very least I can do! Mason tells me such wonderful things about you—but he described you as far more adventurous, and I certainly did not expect such a stunning beauty in a breathtaking gown to appear in my door way! I feel so underdressed!"

To have such a vision of femininity refer to me, a scrawny little dormouse, as 'beautiful' and 'breathtaking', might in any other circumstance have led me to think that she was teasing me for the benefit of the men. But her expression and words seemed humble and genuine. She laughed, but not at me.

I stammered again. "Thank you."

"Let me introduce you to our guests," she said. "This is Dr. Collins, of

Oak Bay, and Mr. Franklin-Milne of Vancouver, who is staying for the autumn season." These two men—one portly and young, the other wiry and old—bobbed their heads in greeting. "And here," continued Emma, "This is Judge Carter and his son William. You've no doubt heard of Judge Carter's work? His name has appeared regularly in the Daily Colonist since taking the bench. You keep our fair city safe, sir."

Judge Carter was a barrel-chested man with a sweep of white hair atop a wrinkled, square face. In another place, he might have made an adequate blacksmith or lumberman, but he was dressed in a prim grey suit that spoke of great wealth, and his hands had no callouses or scars. The unadorned fob at his pocket boasted the soft luster of 24 karat gold, and when he smiled, one of his teeth was similarly golden. "You are a kind girl, Emma," he flustered.

"A pleasure to make your acquaintance, Amaryllis," said William, bowing. The son had the same robust physique as the father, but his hair was black, instead of white. He was a little taller than his father, and he gave a low bow when he took my fingers and pressed a kiss to the top of my hand. I found it amusing that his hand was softer than mine.

"And here," said Emma, gesturing to an elderly man standing by the fireplace, as straight and proud as a poker, "This is Mr. McMurdo, from Edinburgh."

"An' a fine welcome tae you, miss," he said in a deep brogue. "Mason tells me you've come from Cumberland, only recently."

"Yes, sir," I replied.

"And your father, he's gone on a Grand Tour?" said William, "Where is he now?"

"I'm not certain," I replied, "I've received no postcard from his current location."

I congratulated myself—this was not, technically, a lie.

"What will you do now, with your father overseas?" said Emma, but Judge Carter interjected before I could reply.

"A young girl left alone? A travesty!" He turned to me. "Surely you have a mother that cares for your whereabouts?"

The room chilled. Mason looked horrified. I, however, felt quite unaffected. "My mother is dead, sir, and so is my only sister. I am quite alone."

"No, you are not," Mr. Fish grumped. "You have a place under my roof for as long as you wish."

"Oh, Harris, you old softie," growled Mr. McMurdo with a wry grin, "You make us all think you're prickly, but here you are, taking in strays."

Mr. Fish took a sharp breath, no doubt to say something in my defence, but I spoke first. "Mr. McMurdo, surely you know: kick a stray dog and it will tear out your throat, but show it kindness and it becomes immeasurably loyal." I bared my teeth, just a little. "Why, some of the fiercest guard dogs were once scrawny strays."

An uncomfortable silence dropped over the men, but when I cast a glance to Emma, she looked satisfied. She hooked her arm over mine. "Come with me, Liz. Let's retire to the garden and leave the boys to their cigars and gossip," she said. The gentlemen, including Harris, chuckled at her dismissal of their conversations; was that a sense of relief in the air? "Lizzie my dearest, you and I have a million things to discuss, and I can't wait to get to know you and call you a friend."

SIX

In the middle of the garden, Feng Soo had set a small wrought iron table with plates full of dainties, and two chairs waited for us to use them. I sat, arranged my layers of skirts, and watched as Emma waved her hand for someone in the kitchen window to bring us a piping hot pot of tea.

"Oh, my goodness!" she tittered, leaning across the table, "McMurdo is a pompous old ass! I half-hoped you'd leap across the room and give him a good old slap!"

"Don't tempt me," I replied. "We've only just met, and I wouldn't want you to think poorly me!"

"I wouldn't think poorly at all," she huffed. "He's staying with us until December, and goodness! I can barely stand it! He's such a fussy old fishwife, bossing me about as if he's been pregnant himself." She took a slice of devilled kidney on toast onto her plate and cleaned her fingertips on a napkin. "Harris has found a friend in you, I think, and none too soon."

"What do you mean by that?"

"Only that he is a prickly hermit, and it's refreshing to see him show kindness to another human being." She took a small bite, then said, "Oh, he's good enough to his servants, but he's less than accommodating to the rest of society. When my husband heard he'd welcomed you into his home, Mason's knees almost buckled. Now, then," she said, "Tell me all about yourself!"

"I don't quite know where to begin," I said.

Ever the helpful host, Emma offered a suggestion. "How old are you?"

"I'll be sixteen in November."

"And what is your favorite subject in school?"

"I'm no longer in school, I'm continuing my studies on my own. My father had taken me as an apprentice, and under his tutelage, I was learning to become a doctor."

"Sweet mercy!" Emma said, "That's truly amazing! Do you think it possible?"

"Absolutely," I replied.

"I was studying to be a teacher when I met Mason, and I dearly loved geography. It was my best subject." She looked towards the house with a satisfied smile. "I had hoped to travel to Africa to see the Great Rift Valley, and Australia to see Ayers Rock, and then to Indochina, to see the remains of Krakatoa. But ..." She tipped her head in acquiescence, "My father thought I ought to accept a match with Mason, instead. Father owns a shipping company, and all of my brothers are underwriters and accountants, so truly, I was pleased to escape the world of business and marry a doctor!" She laughed lightly. "It has been a good match, so far. Krakatoa will have to wait."

"You? Adventuring to Krakatoa?"

"Of course!" she beamed. "Wouldn't it be simply amazing?"

I reclined in my chair. "I would've thought you'd prefer to visit the museums of Europe."

"There are treasures all around us, and only a few of them made by human hands," she laughed. "You think I'd make a poor explorer. I see it on your face!"

"No! No, I only mean—"

"I am not offended, Liz! It's true, I am uninitiated in the mysteries of travel. I was born in Victoria, and I've only left the island once. But I've read all the works of Isabella Bird, and once Mason gives his approval, I shall be off and away to follow in her footsteps!"

Her eyes gleamed like sapphires at the whirl of thoughts in her head. Her skin glowed, not only with pregnancy, but with possibility.

Then she laughed again, at herself this time. "Oh, goodness, I'm being a poor host, taking over the conversation with my daydreams! Will you continue your studies, once your father returns?" she asked.

"I'd like to continue," I said. "But we'll see. The year has been dismal, and I've been left to my own defences. But please, don't feel pity for me—" I added quickly, seeing a look of tragedy cross her features.

"Mason tells me that you're very resourceful and clever."

"Mason speaks too highly of me," I replied. "You know as well as I that he is generous with his praise."

"He has a good heart, it's true," she said, taking a second sandwich for her plate, "He's very fond of your family and, I tell you this in confidence, he was most upset by the events of the last month. From all that Mason tells me, I think I would've liked your sister very much." She grinned. "And I know I'll like you!"

SEVEN

September 29, 1898

They cannot be considered citizens of British Columbia in any sense of the term. If British Columbia had its way, there would be no Chinese in the province.

Victoria Colonist, Nov. 17, 1891

I spent a full two weeks familiarizing myself with Victoria, and I found every facet of the city to be delightful, from the moody fog that materialized each morning to the evening cries of seagulls over the harbor. Both water and land bustled with activity: construction of stone buildings on every corner, gangs of workmen pushing new roadways through farmlands, and great iron ships gliding into the port to bring crowds of new faces. I studied the diversity of people and things with rapturous fascination. My childhood memories of London became faded dreams compared to the vibrancy and urgency with which this growing city blazed. Even the neighbourhood of James Bay, small and sleepy compared to the bustling downtown core, had its moments of vitality. Sitting amongst the manicured houses and gardens were little shops and grocers, and closer to the harbor, a couple of barber shops and industrial brick buildings that housed ship builders and blacksmiths. In the afternoons, the streets flowed with hansoms carrying sight-seers. A jaunt along the Dallas waterfront, around Beacon Hill, and through Oak Bay was much in fashion with the established elite.

Shao's ribs healed quickly. By the end of September, he accepted a position at an apothecary in Chinatown owned by a man named Mr. Lim, the older matrilineal cousin of Mr. Fish's gardener, Lou Kwan Xi—at least,

I think this was the family connection. The Oriental way was much more precise than the English way, and what I might lump under the collective title of 'cousin' could be expressed by over a dozen words in Chinese. Shao tried to explain, but eventually gave up, and said that Xi and Mr. Lim were simply 'related', and left it at that. No matter what the ties between them, Mr. Lim had been in need of an assistant ever since his last employee left for the gold fields of Quesnel Forks, and Xi recommended Shao as a possibility.

Shao told me the news of his employment as we rested on the porch in the afternoon sun. He sat with his legs over the edge of the steps, and I crouched behind him, examining the alignment of his ribs, which (to my satisfaction) were healing straight and strong. Distracted by my work, I was at first quite happy for him.

"That's wonderful!" I said.

"It's not a big apothecary, but Mr. Lim seems to have a very good reputation," he replied, "I've asked around. No one has anything ill to say about him."

"Then his endorsement will be good for you, too," I said.

My finger touched a faded bruise, he winced a bit.

"Ow, that's still sore … and association with Mr. Lim will give me some professional contacts."

I sat next to him on the porch. "One rib is still tender. I'm glad you got the job, but walking to Chinatown every morning? Maybe you should wait until it's fully healed."

He winced again, but this time, his expression didn't come from any physical pain. "Well, that's the other news I have to tell you." He ran his hands through his blue-black hair, buying time to think of the right words. "Mr. Lim has offered me a room above the shop—nothing big, nothing as nice as what Mr. Fish has here, of course—but it's right there, so close, and if I'm working at all hours of the day or night …"

I felt my stomach drop. "You're leaving?"

"It makes sense," he said. "If a shipment comes in at midnight, I can help Mr. Lim. If there's an emergency and he needs assistance, I'll be there. Plus, I won't have to walk back and forth from downtown everyday. You said it yourself, Liz: with my rib still healing, I might do more damage."

"Yes, but—"

"We'll still see each other, every day. You can visit the shop, I'll come back here, you'll hardly notice I'm gone."

I couldn't argue with this logic, but I didn't want him to go. I didn't know what to say to him, or what I would do without him. In the pit of my stomach, I felt a pang of loneliness, the first in such a long time; I loved to be alone, but I had grown accustomed to knowing Shao was near, and taking comfort from his presence. It was clear to me, quite suddenly, that I'd never thought his nearness would end.

"I suppose," I said slowly to hide my disappointment, "I suppose it's such a good opportunity for you. And for you to walk back and forth … well, it's not practical, for us to see each other every day. You'll be busy."

"Well, perhaps we'll see each other every couple of days, then," he said. "Maybe you're right."

He'd misread the quiet timbre of my voice. I was not being practical. I was not being sedate and accepting.

I wanted to grab his shoulders and scream in his face, demand that he stay, and the darkness began to boil inside me, looking for an escape. But no matter how much I wanted to react, I couldn't: I remembered the look on Shao's face when, last summer, he had caught a glimpse of the darkness in my soul, and I thought I would rather die than reveal that side of myself to him again. So I repressed it, pushed it down into the middle of me, until it burned like an ember.

"Then go," I said. I forced a smile to my lips. "You must."

Shao accepted the job and moved into the small room above Mr. Lim's apothecary, and when he left Mr. Fish's residence with only the clothes on his back, I watched him through the library window as he disappeared down the street. I did not cry. Instead, alone in the library, I let the mask slip and I watched with cold, brooding eyes. When I pressed my palm to my chest, I was sure I could feel where a lobe of my heart had been sliced rudely away.

At first, the darkness bubbled and simmered. That first night without him near, I dreamt of blood: the coppery taste of it, the sweet and intoxicating thickness, the liquid warmth and the congealing coolness. For a few days, I was short of temper, peevish. But Jess would not let me be. She brought me buttered toast and talked with me about frivolous, incidental things.

"You don't need to be my friend," I snapped at her one morning.

"I don't need to be anyone's friend," she replied. She fussed over the kettle, scrubbing it clean with baking soda. "But maybe I want to, miss. You've got your heart wrapped up in a man, and I know well enough what that's like." When she grinned at me, it reflected in the polished metal surface, so that I was met with two smiles instead of one. "Life's too short to spend it sulking," she said, and dropping her voice to a whisper, added, "And it's sure the heck too short to tangle ourselves up in the boys we're sweet on."

I lingered, intrigued. "You know that Shao and I—"

"Mmm-hmm," she agreed. "Ain't no stretch of the imagination to see it."

"And your boy—?"

"Ain't none of your darn business, miss," she replied with that playful smile. "Ain't none of anyone's business, 'cept my own."

"What do I do?" I replied in a matching whisper, "I miss him, so much!"

She tipped her face close to mine. "Pour yourself into something you love equally much, I think. That's all I've been able to do." She set the kettle down and threw the rag into the sink. "When I set to singing, I pour all my love into it. My songs give it a nice place to vent."

"Are you suggesting I sing?"

"Heck, no, Liz. I've heard your caterwauling, and I wouldn't wish it on my worst enemy," she replied.

"What do I love as much as Shao?"

"Well, I can't answer that for you, silly girl," she replied. "You gotta figure that out on your own."

The answer soon revealed itself. Really, how could I not have guessed?

Within that first week, I fell to old habits to distance myself from the quietness of the house: I began to read through Mr. Fish's library. Books welcomed me. Most of his collection revolved around mechanics, steam engines, and the technological marvels of our era, but I searched until I found topics more suited to my interests: medicine, anatomy, biology. Even if I wasn't attending any formal school, I was loath to let slip the education my father had given me. I chewed through a particularly gruesome and hilarious book, entitled *Sea and Land* by J.W. Buel, that contained a number of full color plates illustrating the many ways animals and plants attack and devour humans. By the end, I was certain the entirety of God's creation had sworn to slaughter everything on two legs.

And when the first package from Rose arrived, I dove headlong into it: a thick bundle of newspapers tied with string and wrapped in butchers paper that came, addressed to me, upon a steamer from San Francisco. The stories of the Ripper's gruesome murders offered me a welcome diversion from the confusion and sense of betrayal stewing in my heart.

"Great bloody dusty things!" Eddy said over her shoulder as I read one of the papers, using the kitchen table to spread out the sheets and scan the tiny typeface. She stood at the stove, checking on the loaves of bread in the oven, and when she stood up and slapped her hands against her apron, she looked at me with disapproval. "Look at it, all yellow and curling in the edges! That's good for nothing but starting a fire, it is!"

"Ma," said Jess as she passed through the kitchen, "Leave Liz alone."

"Those papers ain't nothing but gateways to Hell!" she called after her daughter. Then to me, Eddy said, "All full of revolting stories and gruesome engravings. Look at that one! That one right there!" She pressed one floury finger to the picture of Jack the Ripper lurking in an alleyway. "All of it, designed to excite the heart and open innocent eyes to lustful sin!"

"I have nothing to fear, then," I assured, "I'm not very innocent."

She scoffed at me.

"Getting my kitchen all dirty with ink and filth, and messin' up the inside of your head with old stories? That ain't gonna help no one," she muttered, going back to her bread. "You be careful now, Miss Saunders. You're a girl alone in a nasty world, and the Devil has plans for you, just as he does for all of us."

"I'm sure the Devil has barely noticed me," I said as I scanned the text.

"Oh, that's what he WANTS you to think," she said, "But he's out there, lurking like that sinner in your picture. And God has got enough to do, without leaping to your aid, so it's best for us to avoid the Devil ourselves."

Jess, returning from the front hall, rolled her eyes. "Ma!"

"Don't you be giving me sass," Eddy snapped back. "Liz hasn't even gone to church once since coming to stay with us. I say she's ripe for the Devil's plans." She returned her fiery gaze to me. "What are you finding so interesting anyway?"

"The London Match Girl Strike," I replied, letting one finger drift over a story in the right-hand columns. "They have to work in deplorable conditions—it isn't right."

There wasn't enough sin in my answer for Eddy's interest, so she simply huffed and shook her head. "Nasty things, those papers," she muttered. "You just make sure you tidy them up and take them to your room when you're done, Miss Saunders. Am I clear? Or they'll be cut up for use in the outhouse, I swear it!"

EIGHT

Another Whitechapel Mystery
Horrible murder in Buck's Row, Whitechapel

Scarcely has the horror and sensation caused by the discovery of the murdered woman in Whitechapel some short time ago had time to abate when another discovery is made which, for the brutality exercised on the victim, is even more shocking and will no doubt create as great a sensation in the vicinity as its predecessor. The affair up to the present is enveloped in complete mystery, and the police have as yet no evidence to trace the perpetrators of the horrible deed. The facts are that Constable John Neil was walking down Buck's Row, Thomas Street, Whitechapel, about a quarter to four on Friday morning, when he discovered a woman between 35 and 40 years of age lying at the side of the street with her throat cut right open from ear to ear, the instrument with which the deed was done traversing the throat from left to right. The wound was about two inches wide, and blood was flowing profusely. She was discovered to be lying in a pool of blood. She was immediately conveyed to the Whitechapel mortuary, when it was found that besides the wound in the throat the lower part of the abdomen was completely ripped open, with the bowels protruding. The wound extends nearly to her breast, and must have been effected with a large knife. As the corpse lies in the mortuary it presents a ghastly sight. The victim seems to be between 35 and 40 years of age, and measures five feet two inches in height. The hands are bruised, and bear evidence of having engaged in a severe struggle … In Buck's Row, naturally, the greatest excitement prevails, and several persons in the neighbourhood state than an affray occurred shortly after midnight, but no screams were heard, nor anything beyond what might have been considered evidence of an ordinary brawl. In any case, the police unfortunately will have great difficulty in bringing to justice the murderer or murderers.

East London Advertiser, Saturday, 1 September 1888.

Shao visited me two or three times, but as his own work consumed him, I saw him less and less. By mid-October, he seemed to have forgotten me completely. I lay awake for nights after his last visit, when I had called out an apology that I refused to explain, and I wondered if I'd ever see him again. He had connections, now. I could offer him nothing.

So in an effort to make my own connections, I began accompanying Jess to Mrs. Thornton's shop to help with the sewing. Let me be honest: I am not the best seamstress. I told Jess, most of my stitches had been practised on living flesh, sewing up wounds from men who'd injured themselves in the mines. Jess laughed at this. I suspect she thought I was joking.

Still, it was good practice. Clearly, I lacked domestic skills. My mother had been in no fit state to teach me, and due to my tomboyish interests, our housekeeper Agnes Gunn had tried but failed to show me the arts of the home. I barely knew a needle from a pin. But the drizzly autumn afternoons provided a cozy time to lock ourselves into the theatre and mend costumes, and it was far more enjoyable that fashioning underwear out of old flannel shirts for the Gunn boys.

Mrs. Thornton was a patient teacher. While I suspect I plucked out more stitches than I kept, she never seemed angry or disappointed. She told me that my pricked thumbs and skewed seams were battle scars, but that we must never give up, for we were slowly winning the war.

The Yates Street group treated Mrs. Thornton's shop like a way station, coming and going to strange schedules that I couldn't quite determine, but I began to recognize a few of the actors and stage men. I don't mean to sound cruel, but they were an amateur group in every sense of the word: people dropped by at their own leisure to perform chores, volunteering an hour here or a half-day there, taking tasks for which they were clearly untrained. Much like my skewed seams, it wasn't unusual to find props built to awkward proportions, or playbills with spelling errors, or other little foibles. The whole organization exuded a good-natured levity, and whenever something was particularly cockeyed, people would shrug and laugh and poke fun at the one responsible, so that over time, their mistakes came to bind them more closely together rather than drive them apart. No one seemed to take anything too seriously. I came to appreciate my afternoons as a wonderful opportunity to watch people enjoy each other's company. The only time I saw any sense of organization was when Mrs. Thornton scheduled a rehearsal. Then, and only then, did the players cohere into a military unit, with all their passion focused on a single goal. The director, Mr. Horatio Stevens, was a bald-pated gentleman who quietly spent his work hours as a minor accountant for the nearby dry goods company, but upon entering the theatre, he became the fiery architect of imaginary lands, red-faced with zeal. He stood upon a chair at the head of the stage and produced great arcs of spittle with every command as he shouted his actors through their paces. He had earned himself a nickname, *The General*, and the title fit as snugly as Napoleon's hand in his waistcoat.

Mr. Stevens had his favorites and I was not one of them. I rarely spoke to the man, but he and Mrs. Thornton shared a particular bond that seemed to run deeper than the theatre. Jess whispered that they had been lovers when they were younger. I rather wish she hadn't told me that, because it painted an awkward picture in my mind whenever I saw the two of them together, heads close, planning the current production.

And, of course, that production would be a rousing rendition of *The Duchess of Padua*. Opening night had been scheduled for the last Saturday in October, only two weeks away. Mr. Stevens claimed the melodrama had proven popular in amateur theatres in Toronto, and felt it might find a similar appreciative audience in Victoria. However, the *dramatis personae* consisted of ten male roles and only two female roles. Because the Yates Street Amateur Theatrical Company split evenly amongst the sexes, many of the women had claimed backstage responsibilities. Some of the girls even helped on the upper scaffolds with the ropes.

One such girl was Greta Braun, a stout actress with a head full of blonde ringlets and a nose that was perhaps a smidgen too generous for beauty, but the smoky shadows under her eyes gave her a sense of mystery. She could run up the ropes like an orangutan, following the boys across the scaffolds, and swing without a care over the (admittedly, shallow and rarely used) orchestra pit. There was something disarming about her blithe nature, but she was not charming in the slightest—the older boys considered her like one of their own, but they teased her, too, like one might treat a rambunctious puppy that gamboled about the ankles. Andy seemed to be the only one to show her any kindness, and I attributed that more to his gentle nature than to any generosity of character. He was incapable of saying a mean word about anyone.

When she wasn't hanging from the scaffolding, she was part of the chorus and sang alongside four other women: sweetly innocent Divinia Grace Goodman, square-jawed Maude Mawson, a sickly sallow waif named Francine, and the matronly baritone Mrs. Carter-Mackie. When they were able to pry Greta from her backstage duties, the five women practised their songs, and their melodic voices filled the theatre with warmth and beauty.

I said this to Mrs. Thornton, and she laughed, "Well, thank goodness for that!" And I knew precisely what she meant, for while their voices infused the theatre with beauty, the building dearly needed all assistance when it came to its physical appearance.

The Temple of Thespis was not a fancy building. While the term 'theatre' might conjure images of velvet seats and curtains, polished brass fixtures, and baroque decoration, I can assure you, none of those would be correct. The three-story brick building had been constructed not long after Victoria's incorporation as a city in 1862, and it had originally been an auction house for livestock in the days when Victoria was the last major supply post for men rushing north to the Fraser Valley gold fields. The miners who visited the Temple in those days didn't care a whit for soft cushions or gilded candelabras. The seats were hard and wooden, the fixtures made of iron. The floor was dark wood and pitted by the passage of animals' hooves. In the far corners, one could still catch a farmyard whiff of hay and urine. The whole space was wide and broad and serviceable enough for an amateur production company, but I wager the owner made more profit off the rental of the storefronts outside than by this ungainly, windowless interior space.

Still, the players loved it. They clearly were grateful for the use of the stage, and they took great care of it. They practised their lines as if they crossed a grand theatre, head held high and shoulders back, confident and proud of their work, and when they weren't running scenes, they each pitched in to make the Temple more presentable: waxing the woodwork, scrubbing the floors, fixing the stairs or painting the seats. The work brought them more closely together, so that they were like a congregation, finding solace and strength in this adopted theatre family.

One afternoon, while hanging curtains with Greta and Andy, I marveled that a contingent of three workmen were refurbishing the wooden seats. There were well over a hundred chairs, and it was no small task. They scrubbed at the old lacquer with sandpaper to roughen it before applying a fresh layer of black paint.

I stood on a ladder. Greta balanced four rungs above me and Andy stood on the ground below us. Both her hands were free to reach up and hook the curtain along its upper edge to fasteners running along the beam. The canvas curtains were beastly heavy and unwieldy, so Andy lifted it up and I held aloft the seams as Greta struggled to hang hooks through the grommets I'd sewn. Beads of sweat formed on my brow.

"They're painting all of the seats?" I panted.

"The landlord says we can," Greta said defensively.

"It won't take so long," said Andy, "They'll be done most of them by opening night."

I doubted him, but didn't argue. Instead, I said, "They're doing an excellent job. It'll make the place look even more grand."

Greta looked down her nose at me and giggled. "Grand? You need spectacles, Miss Saunders. This place is a ruin."

"You seem to like being here," I replied.

"Why would you think that?"

"You're one of the few that come almost every day."

Her voice adopted a spiteful note as she struggled with a particularly obstinate hook. "Well, when you live in a one-bedroom walk-up with five brothers and sisters? You find any excuse to escape." Her hands now free, she stretched her arms. "Lordy, I just love the space of it! And no toddlers hanging on my knee, or my mama nattering in my ear, or diaper cloths to wash!" Her gregarious laugh bounced around the upper rafters.

A conversation gave me an opportunity to rest my tired shoulders, and tipped my head towards the men working on the seats. "I can see well enough that one of them is Joe, the General's son," I said, nodding to the group, "But who are the two other men?"

Greta stretched her arms. "The fat fella is Seamus McGurty, and the skinny fella is Joseph Hala'iwa."

"Hala Eeeva?" I repeated. "That's a curious name."

"He's kanaka," she said, and seeing my confused expression, explained, "He came from Hawaii to work for the Hudson's Bay Company." She lowered her voice and grunted with disdain. "Cor, he's stupid with lines!"

"Greta," Andy admonished softly, "Be nice."

"I think he'd forget his own name if his wife hadn't stitched it on the back of his collar, and he's always moaning about one thing or another," she continued. "I don't think Joseph likes the theatre very much, and the General certainly doesn't like him."

I lurched the curtain up again, waiting until she took the weight before asking, "Why is he still here, then?"

"Well, look at him," she urged. "With his skin tone and features? He plays all the Oriental characters. Other acting groups in town have to paint someone up to look Chinese, but lucky for us, Joseph already tends toward the celestial features." She hung another grommet and added, "Gives Mr. Stevens the chance to do productions that the other troupes can't. Gives us a bit of an advantage, like."

"Why not simply cast someone who's Chinese?" I asked.

Greta looked down at me from her higher perch, and she seemed confused by my question. "Come, now, Liz. You know what they say."

I shook my head. "No, I don't."

"The Chinese carry leprosy." She turned back to hanging the next grommet.

"There's no way the landlord would ever allow one in the building."

I almost dropped the curtain, which would have yanked Greta off the ladder and dragged her into the orchestra pit. "That's preposterous!"

"No it isn't," she said. "They're crawling with disease!"

"What?!"

Andy said, "We ain't allowed to have Chinamen in here. That's what the landlord told Ma."

"That's ridiculous!" I said, and Andy shrank back at the sharpness of my voice, but Greta took my disgust in stride.

"Everyone knows it," she said, "My father says the health authority is moving the sick out to an island, trying to contain the disease. He says we're a cat's whisker from an outbreak, and all that's keeping us safe is our vigilance against the Celestial peril."

An ugly cold knot formed in the pit of my stomach. "Your father is a god damn liar."

"What?" Greta's eyes widened, her mouth pinched in a hard line. "You take that back!"

"I haven't seen anyone sick in Chinatown," I replied, "And even if that's true, the lepers could have just as easily contracted the disease from the English." I heaved the curtain up to her, eager to finish this task as fast as possible. "And who could ever be so barbarous, to leave the sick and dying on an island? That's horrid!"

She seized the fabric and pulled, but the red flush of her face was no longer due to exertion. "I'm not making it up, Liz. Desperate times require desperate measures."

"Desperate men do stupid things when they don't stop to look at the facts, and instead, let their desperation rule them," I spat.

Greta scowled at me and bit her tongue. I bit mine. Andy just looked uncomfortable. We finished our task in angry silence.

NINE

October 27, 1898

If the woman was murdered on the spot where the body was found, it is impossible to believe she would not have aroused the neighbourhood by her screams, Bucks Row being a street tenanted all down one side by a respectable class of people, superior to many of the surrounding streets, the other side having a blank wall bounding a warehouse. Dr. Llewellyn has called the attention of the police to the smallness of the quantity of blood on the spot where he saw the body, and yet the gashes in the abdomen laid the body right open.

The weapon used would scarcely have been a sailor's jack knife, but a pointed weapon with a stout back—such as a cork-cutter's or shoemaker's knife. In his opinion it was not an exceptionally long-bladed weapon. He does not believe that the woman was seized from behind and her throat cut, but thinks that a hand was held across her mouth and the knife then used, possibly by a left-handed man, as the bruising on the face of the deceased is such as would result from the mouth being covered with the right hand. He made a second examination of the body in the mortuary, and on that based his conclusion, but will make no actual post mortem until he receives the Coroner's orders. The inquest is fixed for to-day.

The London Times, September 1, 1888

I thought about what Greta had said, and the idea seemed so outrageous that I scarcely believed it to be possible. The next morning, I met with Mr. Fish over the breakfast table and asked him if what Greta had claimed was true.

"Is there a plague of leprosy in Chinatown?"

To his credit, he did not choke on his toast, as Violet used to do when I asked blunt questions. Instead, he raised one thin eyebrow, dabbed the butter from his lips, and said, "What? No match girl questions? You're plotting your next crusade, aren't you."

"So there is?"

He harrumphed, shook his head. "No, Liz. Not a plague."

I breathed a sigh of relief.

"You are concerned for Shao's safety?"

"Yes, I was, but if there's no leprosy in Chinatown, there's no need to worry—"

"I only said there is no plague," Mr. Fish corrected. "A few men contracted the dreaded scourge, but they were swiftly quarantined."

That cold knot in my stomach returned. "On an island?"

He nodded. "It's no secret." Seeing that I had leaned forward and would not be satisfied with this simple answer, Mr. Fish lowered his knife and fork. "At first, the government tried hard to keep it quiet, but not for shame," he said. "They wanted to ensure no general panic. They purchased D'Arcy Island in '91 and moved five men out there. In official documents, it's called a 'garbage crematory', if you can imagine the gall."

"Who were the men? Have their families been told?"

"Who knows?" said Mr. Fish, "I'm sorry, Liz, but you know how the Chinese are treated. They've been given numbers to tell them apart: Chinaman 1, Chinaman 2 ..."

Even abandoned to die, they were denied the dignity of a name.

"People know this and yet let it happen?"

"Some people were quite determined to *make* it happen," he replied. "You have only to whisper the word 'leper', and chaos ensues. But," and he set down his silverware, "We've been assured by our esteemed government officials that the men are receiving quality medical care in clean, secure facilities." Mr. Fish scowled. "And if that's true, I'll eat my bicycle."

"What's being done?" I said, then before he could answer, I said, "We must inform the press, or write to the federal government—"

"Certain crusades can not be won by shouting," he warned, then in a softer voice added, "But good men work quietly in the background, giving succor where they can, and supporting good notions. And going to the press is not always the wisest notion, Amaryllis. You've been reading too many of Rose's broadsheets; don't give the newspapermen so much credit. They're mostly liars, you know. They'll twist the truth to make a penny."

"But surely if people knew the truth—"

"People know the truth, Liz," he said.

I sat in sour silence, toying with my toast.

Mr. Fish looked at me with pity, and said, "When did you last see Shao?"

When I counted out the days, the answer hit me like a slap. "Almost a week … no, wait. Two!" I startled to realize how busy I'd been. "God's teeth, it's been almost two weeks since I saw him. I've been so busy with my books and helping with the play."

"Mr. Lim keeps him busy, too, I imagine."

I took a bite of toast. "Is Mr. Lim is one of these quiet, background men you mentioned?"

"You may be surprised to hear it, Liz, but with some topics, I keep my ears open and my mouth shut," he said. "However, let me assure you that Mr. Lim is a dedicated man, very aware of his community, and in his own quiet way, not a force to be trifled with. Shao is lucky to have found such a benefactor."

I felt a twinge; I suppose it was shame. "I miss him."

"Then you ought to visit him," Mr. Fish said. When he saw my hesitation, he urged, "Put aside your books and your newspaper clippings, Liz, and get out of the house while the sun is shining. Why would a young fawn as energetic as yourself want to spend the day indoors with a celibate old monk like me, growing dusty on the shelf?"

"If he's been so busy that he can't visit, do you think I ought to interrupt him?"

"Well, I certainly don't know," Mr. Fish harrumphed. "He doesn't confide in *me*."

I faltered. "But what if he doesn't want to see me?"

"Oh, sweet merciful Lord," said Mr. Fish with rolling eyes. "You are young and inexperienced in love, and that is such a dreadfully painful state to be trapped in!" He leaned forward. "Listen to me, Liz. Do what your heart tells you. You miss Shao, you wish to see him? Then go see him. And," he added with a finger pointing in my direction, "Do him the courtesy of letting him think for himself, without injecting your own guesses into his actions."

I poured out the tea and stifled a smile. "Thank you for the advice."

"I'm sure most matrons would feel it's very *bad* advice," he said, "But I have always done what my heart instructed, and it's never led me astray."

"I'll visit this afternoon, on my way to the theatre."

"The theatre, the theatre, what a hive of ridiculous nonsense," he grumbled. "The Victoria Theatre is bringing in a troupe of opera singers from San Francisco tonight, and I'm supposed to go as Mason's guest. Will you attend with me? I'm sure your commentary would lessen the drudgery of it all."

Poor Mr. Fish. Mason Briggs tried so hard to make him sociable. "I'm afraid I can't, sir. I have other plans."

"You? Plans?"

I folded the napkin and set it aside. "Tonight is the dress rehearsal. Mrs. Thornton has invited me to come watch, and I promised Jess I'd go. I've never been to a Wilde play, and I think I might like his work." I toyed with my food. Two theatre invitations in one evening—what had I become? Violet would be proud.

Mr. Fish smirked. "Well, if your calendar has become so full, I ought to inform you immediately." He clapped his hands, looking gleeful. "I'm having a gathering here on the night of All Hallow's Eve, this coming Saturday. Is there time in your crowded schedule to attend?"

"You, having a party?"

"Terrible, I know!" He gave a sinister cackle. "Society only allows me to be curmudgeonly for so long before tongues start to waggle. One night of frivolity will quiet the disgruntled mob that feels, because my house is large, I ought to let them in to drink my liquor and eat my food." He took a sip of tea. "Amaryllis, you should hear the gossip that's begun to circulate about you and I! Eddy tells me, the neighbours have had a jolly time devising how you and I might know each other, measuring the depths of depravity to which I must be stooping: that you are my illegitimate child, or my bride-to-be brought from overseas, or other creative flights of nonsense. It seems the neighbours are unable to fathom that you could simply be my *friend*." He snorted in disdain. "So, you must come and dance with the younger men, if only to show that we aren't romantically entangled."

"I'll do my best."

"Perfect," he said. "It will be a masquerade ball, so that I can avoid looking at their dull, stupid faces. And I had hoped, by sending out invitations with less than a week to prepare, no one will bother to come." He gave a short chuckle. "I may not even come. Perhaps I'll sneak away to the carriage house for a drink with Xi."

"Will there be a séance?"

"After our last brush with the afterlife, I've decided to hire the most frightening medium I could find: a snaggle-tooth gypsy woman with one eye and a great bend for the absurd. Oh, don't give me such a disdainful look, Liz—you know her better as Mrs. Carter-Mackie, one of Jessie's theatre group, and she's agreed to a bit of fun in a ridiculous costume. Our shrieking guests will provide a few moments of amusement, and I'll consider the endeavor a complete success if we can get one of the ladies to wet her petticoats."

I finished my breakfast and bid Mr. Fish a good day, and grabbed my father's portmanteau before leaving. It was a lengthy walk through James Bay to Chinatown, especially with the heavy bag held in both hands, and I had a patient to see.

When I'd first met Shao, he had been working in his uncle's shop, in the back room of a boarding house in the swampy lowlands of Cumberland. Mr. Lim's apothecary was nothing like the rough-hewn, mold-speckled room of jiu fu's establishment. This business was clean, precise, neat. The store was twice as large, with polished cherry-wood floors and matching trim along the shelves. It fronted onto the busy byway of Herald Street, with two big windows to let in the cheerful morning sunshine, and two spotless counters stretched along each side. The shelves that covered the walls carried glass jars full of goods. Stepping inside, the senses were excited by riotous colors, textures, scents: an exotic cornucopia of flavors from far-flung kingdoms. Dried flowers, roots, stems, insects, bits and bobs and all sorts of salmagundi lent a carnival air to the room.

As the brass bell above the door jangled with my arrival, the small figure of Mr. Lim hurried from a room in the back.

"Good morning to you!" he chirped.

Here was a man who had spent forty years building a stable, prosperous business but was not yet eager to leave it for a quiet retirement. With his vigor and good humor, Mr. Lim was a man with goals left to accomplish. Everything about him radiated friendliness, from his outstretched arms to the wide smile that showed one missing incisor. His hair was thin on top, and his ears stuck from the sides of his head a few degrees more than was seemly, but he was energetic and convivial, with a protective streak that seemed almost fatherly. As far as I knew, he had no wife or children—his community was his family, and he loved it dearly.

"*Ni hao ma*," I replied.

"*Hen huo, xi xi ni,*" He grinned. "You are learning well, yes? But such bad accent!"

"Because Shao is teaching me," I replied, and he laughed again.

"That boy—I do not understand a thing he says!" Mr. Lim nodded. "I get him, you wait here." He hurried to the door at the rear of the shop, where one stairway led down into a basement, and another led up to living quarters. He leaned in and craned his head into the stairwell, and yelled something too quickly for me to pick out any words. The meaning, however, was clear.

Shao thundered up the stairs, smiling broadly. "Liz!"

"I figured I ought to check on my one and only patient."

It was so good to see him, even the little things, like the quick movements of his hands or the way his short hair crested above his brow. Especially the little things, I suppose, because they were the qualities of Shao that didn't always stick in my memory, but were the quintessential traits that gave him his Shao-ness. How his smile started on the right and spread across his mouth, or the little scar on his cheek, or the way he held his shoulders. I feasted my eyes on him and felt my heart bursting.

He sat on a stool in the corner where the sunlight slanted in through glass jars, and I set the portmanteau on the ground. I withdrew the stethoscope, polished the brass with the hem of my black skirt, and listened to his chest. I heard the strong, healthy beat of his heart and the steady rhythm of his lungs. When I tapped my fingers over his ribs, he only flinched a little. For the most part, he seemed healed, and I told him so.

"I don't always sleep well," he admitted. "Sometimes, I wake in the night with a pain in my chest."

I nodded thoughtfully at this. "From what I've read, the bone can sometimes ache if you've laid on one side too long."

"You're studying again?"

"I am."

"I'm glad to hear it," he replied.

I wondered if his gladness came from knowing I was busy, too. Did he feel guilt, that we saw so little of each other now? Did he resent taking this position?

Or, I thought with a sharp pang of bitterness, did he resent me, coming to visit without invitation, interrupting a peaceful life, and tying him to a society that detested him? Did I remind him of the moment he'd gained his bruises and broken bones? It was an ugly feeling, and an ugly suspicion, and I tried to stamp it down before it could take root in my heart.

Wholly ignorant of my thoughts, Shao stretched his arms over his head, grinning.

"Have you heard anything from your father yet?"

He tried to keep the question light, but it carried weight and substance. It was only the first of a chain of questions I did not want to answer anymore.

The timing was terrible. The spark of anger became a small flame.

I had bent over the portmanteau to put away the medical tools, and I was thankful he could not see my face; every muscle tensed, my teeth clenched.

"Yes," I said tersely. "I received a letter, two days ago."

"You did?" he replied, and from the brightness of his voice, he clearly hadn't expected this answer. "That's wonderful! Where is he?"

"En route to England," I said, "He wants me to stay in Victoria for the winter. I will not hear from him again until spring."

"That's fantastic news, Liz! I'm so glad to hear he's safe." I plainly heard relief in Shao's voice.

The lie burned, but I felt weightless, too; Shao would not ask any questions again, at least until spring. I kept my eyes down under the pretense of organizing the portmanteau, long enough to compose my face, and when I looked at him again, I asked, "Would you like to go for a walk?"

Mr. Lim gave him leave for an hour, and within a heartbeat, we were wandering the streets of Chinatown, admiring the food in the windows. Shao had made a name for himself, it seemed. Everyone knew him, greeted him in Cantonese or Mandarin, and a vendor even gave us two sweet coconut buns to eat, free of charge. I felt liberated from my past by my falsehood, and Shao seemed genuinely happy to be with me, and when I teased him about his newfound status in this part of town, his laughter was carefree and genuine.

"I like it here."

"I haven't seen you in so long."

He looked down at me, and hidden in the crowd, I felt his warm hand slip into mine. "Mr. Lim has lots of work to do, and now that I'm feeling better, he's had me hauling crates. I'm exhausted by the time the day is done. I've missed you, Liz. I can't tell you how much I've missed you." His eyes blazed with a dark fire; I suddenly sensed he longed for more contact than only our hands. "But I'm so busy, and so are you, I hear." He leaned close, dropping his voice to a whisper, and his breath tickled my ear. "I never guessed you'd have such interest in the theatre."

"How'd you know about that?"

"Xi plays mah jong with Mr. Lim on Sunday nights. I'm kept well-informed." He leaned his head to mine. "You at the theatre, Eddy and her nightly tippling, Jess delivering packages when none are needed …"

I giggled, and under the pretext of the shifting crowd, pressed my body along his. "Mr. Fish knows everything that goes on under his roof, but I don't think he minds as long as we're discreet. There does seem to be a wagonload of frivolous things for people to waste their time doing in this city …" I replied. We paused before a narrow fissure between the buildings, and I realized it was not a door, but an alley. "What's this place?"

"Come with me," said Shao.

The sensation of his warm, smooth skin on my wrist made my heart stutter, and I let him lead me inside. The sunlight vanished. Suddenly, we were plunged into a twilight gloom between towering brick buildings. Five or six stories high, they seemed to arch above us and block out the sky. I could reach out my hands and almost touch each side of the alley. The passage snaked between the buildings to link two busy thoroughfares, and the whole length of it was studded with deep doorways.

"Welcome to Fan Tan Alley," Shao said.

I circled around, admiring the closeness of it. The ground was littered with broken glass and bits of clay pipes, so that it glittered in a multitude of colors like a fine mosaic floor. "What happened here?"

"It might be deserted now," he replied. "But when the sun goes down, it's the busiest spot in the city. Gambling, drinking, opium. You can barely pass from one end to the other, for all the people enjoying themselves."

It was so quiet. Every door was closed, and most windows shuttered.

"But in the day, everyone's asleep?"

"It's just you and me, Lei Zi."

We walked to the midpoint, holding hands. Shao told me that the low doors led to a warren of rooms on either side of the walkway. I couldn't read the wooden placards that hung above each entrance, but from the ribald graffiti scratched into the bricks, I could easily guess what took place in each one. Here, you could find all the pleasures of a mortal coil offered at a reasonable price. The day found the alley at rest, but at night, this place became the beating heart of Chinatown.

"I love Fan Tan Alley," said Shao, looking up at the dark windows above. The alley wrapped around us like a blanket. We stood so closely together that I could feel the warmth of his body.

"It's an oasis," I said, "The calm center in a storm."

I leaned against the building, and together we enjoyed the peace and serenity. I entwined my fingers in his, and then we pressed close in the shadow of a brick doorway, our arms snaking around each other's body. His kiss held all the passion of weeks apart. Both of us were hungry for this connection, desperate to seize the privacy and exploit it for our own animal needs. His fingers plucked at the buttons of my wool coat, his hands slipped under the fabric and brushed the bare flesh of my arms, and I shivered as he caught my lower lip in his teeth. I needed no stethoscope to detect the rapid thunder of his heart; I felt it through his sternum, pressed against my own.

But I was not as distracted as him. A creeping sensation skittered up my back, and the hairs on the nape of my neck bristled. No base instinct was strong enough to drown away the knowledge that this was dangerous. I could not forget how near Shao had come to paying for our indiscretion with his life. Even as he kissed me, ran his hand over the back of my head, pressed me close to his body, I remembered the vision of his assailants pummeling him. I saw the ribbons of saliva and blood running from his mouth. I heard the sharp high scream of agony as they kicked him, again and again.

I pushed him roughly away. "Wait, Shao," I panted, "Wait!" I paused and looked down the alley in each direction. I saw no one, but my ears strained for any hint of a noise.

"What's wrong?"

"What if we aren't alone?"

Shao glanced down the alley. "No one's here." He kissed me again, more gently this time. "There won't be anyone until the doors open in the afternoon."

But the ugly feeling persisted.

"And above? What are those windows?"

Shao looked up. "Boarding houses, brothels. I suppose there could be someone watching ..."

I ran my hands over his face, tracing my fingers over the small scar on his cheek. When I kissed him, it was both an expression of my desire and an apology. "I don't want to get you in trouble again."

He lowered his chin as I ran one hand over his injured side. We both knew this was dangerous. The aching rib was a staunch reminder of the price he'd already paid.

"I should get back to the shop," he said, but his voice was low and full of longing, and his eyes didn't meet mine. "We can go, if you wish."

I did, very much.

TEN

It was with aching disappointment that I left Shao, unsure of when I'd see him again. All indications hinted that it might be a long time: Mr. Lim had work for him to do and, as soon as we appeared at the doorstep, he held up his hand and gave a smile of relief before rattling off a list of demands. A shipment of exotic herbs had arrived off one of the ships from the Philippines, and Mr. Lim needed Shao to run to the customs office, then hire a cart, then hurry to the docks and pick up a crate. Once this chore was done, there were jars to dust, herbs to sort, and accounts to balance.

"I'll see you soon," Shao said to me.

"Until then," I replied. How I ached to kiss him, or even steal a fleeting touch of our hands.

Instead, I heaved my portmanteau against my hip, and left for the Temple of Thespis. All the way to the theatre, I could smell his scent on my skin and taste his lips on mine.

From the outside, the Temple looked drab and rough-hewn, but inside, the space was decorated for the dress rehearsal: the newly-painted wood fixtures, bundles of flowers tied to the ends of each row, and the fresh smell of lavender sweetening the air provided a brave effort to disguise the old livestock auction. It was a bit like putting a fancy hat on a goat. I wandered down the aisle, hauling the heavy portmanteau, and I marveled that the authorities would be so concerned with leprosy carried from Chinese patrons. Surely I was in greater danger of contracting lockjaw from the rusty nails poking up through the floorboards?

Most of the seats were empty. From what Jess had told me, this was to be expected: only a few invited guests were welcome tonight. Five or six people peppered the empty rows of seats. I chose a seat near the front of the auditorium and placed my bag on the ground, and as I sat, I melted into the stiff chair and rethought my opinions: true, it was a rustic building, but it was charming, too. It boasted no luxuries or frills or gilded candelabras, but the acoustics were amazing. When Mrs. Thornton strode to the center of the stage—a massive platform strong enough to hold horses and cattle, with a certain dark patina to the wood that spoke of feces and shellac—I could hear her voice as clear as if she were sitting next to me, even though she stood a hundred feet away.

"Welcome, friends, to our performance of *The Duchess of Padua,* a most thrilling play sprung forth from the pen of Mr. Oscar Wilde," she said to the sparse crowd. "We hope you enjoy tonight's dress rehearsal. If you notice any slips or errors, please temper your criticisms with kindness."

A polite fringe of applause fluttered over the audience.

The long black curtains parted with the squeak of old pulleys, revealing a scene of rural Italy painted on canvas and hung from lines. A few props decorated the stage: market carts, laden with clay apples and pears, and a spire cut from wood, designed to sit at the back of the stage and appear as if it were the roofline of a distant cathedral.

Market patrons appeared from the wings, one by one. A woman strolled across the stage with a basket of flowers in her hand. From the opposite side came a baker carrying bread and a young girl with a live chicken under one arm.

A young man stepped to the front of the stage. Even from my seat in the tenth row, I saw clearly his trembling hands, the beads of sweat on his forehead, and the wide eyes like a spooked horse. His Christian name was Alfred and in his real life, he worked as a bricklayer, but today, he had dressed in a ragged peasant's suit, jerkin and hose, and his round face stood out like the full moon against the dull browns and greys. Poor fellow—he looked mortified.

His voice cracked twice before he found his tongue and proclaimed weakly, "Now by my life, Guido, I will go no … no … no farther; for if I walk another step I will … I will … I will have no life to swear by; this wild goose errand of yours."

He looked wildly around, and only after a moment's hesitation, the character of Guido joined him on stage, played by Andy Thornton. He'd dressed in a similar peasant's garb, his face a ruddy hue from embarrassment at missing his cue to enter, stage left. But as he reached center stage, he drew himself up to a noble height, and adopted a confidence that the real Andy rarely showed.

"I think it must be here." He strode to the flower-seller. "Pray, is this the market place, and that the church … the church of … of Santa Croce?"

Well. Who would've thought? Andy was a marvel! As the play continued,

Andy's prowess increased in bounds! His first stumble on stage had invigorated him, and after that unfortunate slip, he missed neither line nor cue. Mrs. Thornton claimed he was a bit soft, but given lines to learn and knowing exactly what to say, Andy had transformed himself into another person, and one of such wit and bearing that I'd never have guessed his true self. He made a very handsome leading man, and time passed quickly because watching him cross the stage was such a treat. Between the third and fourth acts, we enjoyed a brief intermission, and Mrs. Thornton appeared on stage to invite us to honey cakes, tea, and watered wine in the main foyer.

I left my seat to stretch my legs. A few patrons milled in the aisles, chatting. When I paused in the foyer to massage a cramp in my calf from the hard wooden seat, I heard a polite cough behind me. A man's voice said, "Miss Saunders?"

I turned to see a dark-haired, barrel-chested man in a dark grey suit jacket and a pair of forest green trousers. I recognized him immediately and could not contain my surprise. "William Carter, isn't it? The judge's son?"

He looked pleased. "I didn't know if you'd recall me from Emma's garden party."

"Of course! But what are you doing here?"

"I've always wanted to be an actor, and the Temple of Thespis gives me leave to pretend, if only for a little while, that my father's disapproval is not keeping me from pursuing my dreams." He said this with a broad, unabashed smile; it was the expression of a man who has put aside his childhood wishes for more professional pursuits, but not without a few regrets.

"Really?"

His smile turned into a great laugh. "Also, I own the building," he added.

"You!" I exclaimed.

"I own most of the block. Let me be perfectly honest with you, Miss Saunders," he dropped his voice to a hush, "The Temple of Thespis brings in very little revenue, but gives me more pleasure than any of the other shops." We fell into step together as we crossed the austere lobby. He held open the door as we exited onto the boardwalk. A stiff, cold wind gusted up the street from the ocean, very refreshing and invigorating after the stuffy theatre. "And you?" he said, "Why are you here?"

"Mrs. Thornton is pursuing me, badgering me to join her troupe," I replied. We walked a little ways along Yates Street to the corner of the building, where a small alley separated the Temple from the boarding house next door. "But I, unlike you, have no great thirst for drama."

"Still, it is a fine production, isn't it!"

"I'm afraid I'm not familiar with Wilde's work," I replied.

"This one has an interesting history," William said. A carriage rattled by, and he waited for it to pass before continuing. "It's fairly new. Wilde wrote it back in '82 or '83, but I believe it wasn't played until '91."

"Why so long between writing and the stage?"

"He'd written it for Mary Anderson—you know, the actress? But she turned it down. Then, after five or six years of collecting dust on a shelf, it was picked up by an anonymous producer in New York. Wilde claims this play is his masterpiece."

"Really?"

"You sound unconvinced."

I mused on this. "I am enjoying it, especially watching Andy. Perhaps I'm simply not fond of melodramas? I find the characters to be insincere."

William looked intrigued. "How so?"

"The story is much about revenge, but the characters are too poetic. Revenge is brutal business and they're too clean for my liking. Look at the character of Guido, for example: he doesn't smolder with rage as one would, if they were driven by vengeance."

"You wish for sincerity, yet you fraternize with actors?" He chuckled, but not in a way that was friendly. It was a cold, patronizing snicker. Clearly, I was a silly girl. "If *The Duchess of Padua* is too frigid for you, then I recommend 'The Importance of Being Ernest'. Perhaps that play will inspire your passions." He gestured. "We ought to return. Intermission will be over soon."

"I have a question for you," I said.

"Yes?"

"I was told you do not allow Chinese patrons to enter your theatre? Is this true?"

"Absolutely," he replied.

"You do not, honestly, believe them all to carry leprosy?" I asked, straining to keep a polite tone.

He gave that smile again—oh, silly girl. "My duty is to my patrons, Miss Saunders. The Chinaman is a vehicle for all manner of exotic disease, and I will not expose paying customers to the Yellow Scourge."

My hands clenched at the small of my back. Doubtlessly, my knuckles were white. "Yet you're more than happy to let that same Yellow Scourge cook your food, do your laundry, tend your gardens, and clean your outhouse?" It was becoming increasingly difficult to keep my voice sweet.

He regarded me coolly, looking at me down the length of his nose. "What sort of girl are you, Miss Saunders, who cares about those that plot to overrun our city?" A flare of anger blossomed in my chest, but I stifled it down as he said, "You don't think they're blameless, do you? They've brought the plague upon themselves with their heathen ways. The Celestials live in cramped squalor and filth, you know."

"Because city officials give the Chinese the worst of places to live."

"Because that is all the Chinese know," he corrected. "If you had any experience in these matters, you'd see they are a shiftless, lazy blight upon the coast, Miss Saunders. And if it takes responsible citizens like myself to keep them under control, then so be it. I'm proud to do my duty to Queen and country."

"If you are so concerned with the plague, Mr. Carter, shouldn't you make your own sandwiches and scour your own chamber pots? Or are you just a hypocrite?"

His smile vanished. His face became stone.

"How old are you, Miss Saunders?"

"Almost sixteen."

"Your father taught you to speak your mind openly."

"My father taught me many skills," I replied.

William's eyes darkened slightly; there was no good humor there now.

"Then he must have taught you, to hold your tongue in the company of your betters."

Anger bubbled behind his terse words, but I wasn't intimidated by him. Instead, the rage in my own chest rose like the tide, filling quietly up inside me, and the whole street around us grew vibrant, shivering. The stoic expression on his face changed as I felt my mask slip—he faltered, stepped back, looked at once puzzled and afraid. I'd seen the same expression on Shao's face, and on Jack's, too. I'd become a pale, dead-eyed monster.

"No," I replied, "But he taught me to be unafraid." Then as an afterthought, I added, "Sir."

A bell tolled from inside the building. The play was about to resume. William hesitated; I honestly think he didn't wish to turn his back on me.

"Thank you for the ... illuminating talk, Miss Saunders," he said, giving a quick bow. And with that, he left.

If I could've fled to Mr. Fish's house, right then, I would've. I leaned against the corner of the building as the simmering rage inside me began to subside. I felt it trickling out through my limbs like cold seawater, leaving me an empty husk again. I wanted to go home.

I only wish I knew where that was.

In frustration, I pressed the heels of my hands against my forehead. The portmanteau was inside; I couldn't leave it. And once inside, I'd have to stay. I didn't want to insult Mrs. Thornton. I'd promised Jess to take the trolley home with her once rehearsal was done. I only wanted to leave, but for so many reasons, I could not.

Through my own thoughts, I became aware of a faint conversation happening down the shadowed alleyway, close to the far end of the building. Perhaps there was a stage door there or a loading dock. Two women were talking to each other. The words echoed along the bricks, and it was hard to hear them clearly with the wind howling about the buildings, but when I pressed my head close to the wall, I caught snippets of words bouncing along the flat surface.

I recognized one of the voices as Jess.

"—won't be auditioning in December," she said.

The hiss of whispered words followed immediately. I didn't recognize the other woman's voice, it was too faint. However, I easily caught the shrill edge of frustration, but dampened to keep it from carrying.

"I know it's his dream! I don't *want* to keep him from acting!" Jess insisted, then lowered her voice again. I heard only a snippet. "—not meant to—like this."

I peered down the alley, and saw their two figures lingering in the entrance to backstage. Jess stood fully outside, in my view. The other remained hidden behind the open door, and all I saw was her shoulder, pressed against the frame, and at points, a gesturing hand.

Another bell rang from inside, signaling the end of intermission.

The other woman seethed, reeled away, and vanished fully inside the theatre.

"I want no argument with you," Jess insisted. The whole sentence was clear; she spoke loudly, no longer whispering. Then she followed, but she walked with her head bowed, looking crushed.

The slam of the door echoed down the alley.

I heard the rumble of applause coming from deep within the building. The curtain was lifting, intermission was over. I hurried back and, as I settled into my chair alongside my portmanteau, I saw William Carter glance quickly at me from his own seat, scowling.

The last two acts were wholly unsatisfying. Yes, there was the requisite death and retribution, but whether it was the wooden writing style or the director's interpretation of the script to blame, no one seemed very passionate about the vengeance they sought. Everyone appeared sadly disinterested in the whole tragedy. The characters used the death of Taddeo's father for a good excuse to wax philosophical about the inconvenience of living, and didn't seem to give a care that the man was dead.

William, however, felt it was a ripping production, and this he told Mrs. Thornton at the end of the evening. She was much pleased by his review.

After final curtain, she twittered around the lobby like a bird, although her hefty girth and high wig gave an appearance more like a dancing ostrich than a graceful sparrow.

"You are a kind fellow, Mr. Carter, and always so supportive of our little troupe!" she giggled. "Will you attend Friday's opening?"

"I'll be here," he assured as he set his top hat upon his head, "Of all the theatres in Victoria, Mrs. Thornton, I love yours the best!"

"You flatter me!" she tittered. "We are but your humble players, sir!"

He saw me, and a little flash of ice glinted in his eye, but then it was gone, whisked away with his smooth smile. "No, I do not tell a lie. I find nothing so invigorating as an opening night, filled with fellow theatre-lovers from all castes and occupations!"

It was easy to see what he meant: the common folk, the workers and laborers, gathering together in this old building to enjoy a bit of a farce or tragedy, away from the stuffy upper crust of Victoria's society. He'd put on his roughest suit and walk here from James Bay. William wasn't an actor, but he liked to put on a costume and perform.

"My congratulations, Mrs. Thornton," I said, "Andy made a wonderful leading man."

She pressed a kiss to each cheek in the style of the French. "Thank you for all your help, Lizzie. And you'll be here for the opening, as well?"

"I wouldn't dare take a seat from a paying customer! Thank you again, Mrs. Thornton, and good night." I heaved the portmanteau onto my thigh.

William stepped forward. "Miss Saunders, if I remember correctly, you are currently a guest at Mr. Fish's residence? Can I offer you a ride home? It is only a few blocks from my own house, and I have a coach waiting."

"Thank you for your generous offer," I began, shifting the heavy bag, "But I promised to take a trolley home with Jess."

"Posh, it's a blustery evening, and unsafe for two young women to travel unaccompanied, and you are already struggling with some form of luggage—I shall offer a ride to you both. Yes?"

I balked, but Mrs. Thornton stepped in. "Most generous! Of course they accept. Wharf Street crawls with unsavory characters at this time of night, and I'll not have any of my girls put in peril." She called back into the dressing rooms. "Jess? Are you quite finished putting the costumes aside for tomorrow? Let's not keep Mr. Carter waiting, shall we?"

I wound my scarf around my neck as we headed outside. The night was dark and moonless, but the streets of Victoria's downtown bustled with life: men gathered in doorways to smoke their pipes, sheltered from the wind, and the pubs trembled with music, fights, and drunken revelry. William held up his hand to a growler coach, a covered buggy with four wheels and small doors on each side, which sat under the streetlamps. As it rolled towards us, the flickering gaslight flashed off its pristine, lacquered surface. A driver in a crisp beige suit jacket sat at the front, and he tipped his hat in greeting as William opened the door to let us in. The two horses were strong, straight-legged trotters. Their fine leather bridles must've cost a good deal more than Jess earned in a year.

The rental on such a fine contraption was no small penny, to be sure. Jess looked stunned at the glamour of it. As I sat next to her, she ran her hand over the soft, buttery leather. She sat on the edge of her seat, her mouth tense.

"I was looking forward to a walk," she said.

I grinned. "You'd prefer a walk in the wind to a ride in a cab?"

"Yes, I suppose," she said, and her eyes focused on something behind me. When I turned in the seat, Mr. Carter was leaving the theatre, bidding Mrs. Thornton goodbye.

"I'm very glad you're here, Liz," she said.

I didn't like the enclosed space, and from the way she squirmed, neither did Jess. When William mounted and closed the door after him, a latch clicked and my heart jumped.

"Head along, driver!" said William. He rapped his knuckles against the roof.

I heard the snap of a whip and the whinny of the horse. The cab jumped forward at a brisk trot. Jess gave a whoop of surprise, and both she and William laughed at her shout.

"Hold tight, ladies!" he commanded, "My driver's been known to enjoy a spot of whiskey to shorten the wait while I'm away!"

"Cor, Liz," she said, grabbing my hand and holding it tightly, "I suppose this does beat fighting for a seat on the trolley!"

Any previous hesitation she'd shown had evaporated. The fun of a carriage ride was too great, and while a walk in the wind can be lovely, it couldn't compare to the jostling, merry spring of the growler. The wheels chattered against the cobbles. The seats bounced. Faster than any street car, we rattled along Yates Street, crossing the broad busy thoroughfare of Douglas Street.

Jess stared out the window in delight, but when she noticed Mr. Carter was watching her, she said, "Did you like the performance, sir?"

"Cracking, my dear!" He turned his attention to me. "Now, Miss Saunders," he said as the world whisked by, "I hope our earlier disagreement will not sully our future friendship?"

His expression seemed attentive but flat, like a reptile's.

I did not like being in such a closed space with him. I glanced at Jess, but she was staring out the window again, enraptured by the scenery.

Mr. Carter's eyes remained fixed on me. When he curled his fingers over the knees of his green trousers, the motion was like a feral cat, scratching the earth.

"Will you be attending Mr. Fish's party, on Saturday next?" I asked.

He shook his head. "No, I have another engagement. But Mason Briggs and Emma will be attending, so I'll send my apologies with them." He grinned and that reptilian expression melted into one of conviviality. The coolness still lurked underneath, I'd bet money on it, but if I hadn't seen it before, I'd never have known him capable of such iciness. He reclined and tipped his head back as he relaxed. "I swear, when Mason told me he'd received an invitation to a party at Fish's, I thought he was spinning some ridiculous yarn. Harris the Hermit, opening his home to guests? I'd never have believed it, if I hadn't then received one myself!" He looked to Jess. "Of course, I didn't believe it when I was told Mr. Fish had a houseguest either. I suppose Hell must be frozen solid by now."

Jess smiled shyly. "I think Mr. Fish and Lizzie are similar kinds of creatures. They complement each other nicely, 'cause both of them rarely enjoy the company of others."

"Then aren't we fortunate!" he said. "To know both of them, and be welcomed into their very small circle of friends!"

Jess returned her attention to the world flashing by. "It's a very exclusive club."

I smiled politely because the two of them thought it such a lovely joke. But to myself, I thought very pointedly that someone of Mr. Carter's caliber would never, ever be invited in.

ELEVEN

October 29, 1898

The East End of London was yesterday again much excited by the discovery of two more revolting murders. About one o'clock in the morning, the body of a woman, with her throat cut, was found in a yard belonging to a workmen's club, in Berner Street, and an hour later another woman was found murdered in a corner of Mitre Square, Aldgate. In the latter case the body was also mutilated, and as this was not the case with the woman found in Berner Street, it is supposed that the murderer was disturbed before completing his dreadful work, and he then proceeded towards the City and committed the second crime … The last two murders in Whitechapel are in every respect similar to the four which have already been committed. There has been the same secrecy, the same impunity as yet, the same mystery as to motive and method, and in one case the same disgusting mutilations. The nature of the last is now well known and need not be dwelt upon. The practical things to consider are the attitude which ought to be taken by the public in the presence of this outbreak of crime, and the steps which are most likely to lead to the discovery of the criminal, if there is but one, or the gang, if any gang is at work.

St. James Gazette, October 1, 1888

The night of the masquerade ball was a foul one. Steel grey clouds roiled through an iron-colored sky, bringing a merciless damp cold that gnawed my bones. The oak trees whipped back and forth, their orange leaves ripped from their branches and sent reeling through the air, only to be beaten to the ground by fierce lashings of rain.

From the small window of the attic room, I looked down to the carriage house and saw lamps lit in the windows. Xi and Mr. Lim played a quiet game of mah jong. I'd bet any money that they were telling rude, ribald tales over cups of strong rice wine.

How I wished I was there, instead of here, trying to arrange this ridiculous black, feather-trimmed dress over my bony frame. I hated corsets, I hated skirts. Why hadn't I chosen to dress as something more sensible, like a cattle wrangler or a miner? Someone with pants, and a soft flannel shirt, and maybe a cap to hide my hair.

By eight, the bell rang as the first guests arrived, and yet I still struggled with my costume. "God's teeth! All these bloody buttons!" I swore to myself, once again finding that I'd missed a few and fastened it crooked. I poked my head out the door and shouted down the stairwell, "Jess, are you in the kitchen? Can you help me, please?"

No reply. She was probably helping her mother to prepare the dishes and the decorations. All day, Mrs. Garry had been in a sour mood, and I'd even seen her slap the back of Mr. Fish's hand when he tried to sample the canapés; I didn't dare call Jess again, and risk the full assault of her mother's wrath.

Another gust of wind moaned under the eaves. What a storm! What a miserable night! I'd half-hoped no one would dare go out in such inclement weather, but from the sound of voices assembling in the parlor, the full list of guests were here. No one wanted to miss the opportunity to enter Mr. Fish's fine house. They'd probably brave the fires of Hell and an infernal host of demons if it afforded the chance to breach his defenses and gawk at his decor.

Mrs. Carter-Mackie had arrived in full costume, her teeth blackened and her hair streaked with ash, wrapped in garish shawls and sprinkled with bells, coins, and amulets. She'd even adopted a limp, which required her to drag one leg across the floor in a manner that was particularly unsettling. Her hands clawed at the air, her eyes bulged. She had a mean, cold cackle that caused the hairs to stand on end; the guests loved it. Even now, she was downstairs telling fortunes, and I heard screeches of laughter coming up through the floor boards, then a gasp of collective awe as she performed a magic trick.

I'd avoided the inevitable as long as possible, I couldn't hide any longer. If my buttons were askew, I'd just have to claim it as part of my costume. I put the black feathered mask over my head and left the sanctuary of the attic, and at the head of the stairs, a welcome sound rose above all others: the voice of Emma Briggs.

"One of these people is Lizzie, I'm sure of it," I heard her say, "I have only to sit here in the corner quietly, and I trust she'll find me and save me!"

"You ought not to have come," said Mason's voice.

I descended to the main floor, and made my way towards the sound of their conversation. By this time, a quartet had set up their instruments in the parlor and begun to play, but their voices had come from the direction of the library, which had been set aside for quiet conversations. Here, plates of savory treats lined the sideboards, and extra chairs had been arranged. I saw a man in an owl's mask fussing over a very large swan, which appeared to have nested in the velvet chair in the corner, close to the hearth. "I'm pregnant, not dying," the swan replied with reproach as it selected a bit of smoked salmon from the nearest plate.

"It's not advisable for a woman in your advanced condition to leave the comforts of home, especially on a night like this!" Mason insisted. "We will stay for no more than an hour! I'll tell Brixton to remain with the coach, and we'll leave as soon as I've spoken with Harris—"

Emma waved her hand dismissively at him. "Go and chat with the boys! I'm fine right here. See? Warm and snug!"

I laid a hand on Mason's arm. "And not alone," I added.

Through the eye-holes of his mask, I saw his great relief. "Thank goodness for that, Liz!"

"He says, I am so stubborn, I ought to have come as a mule," Emma laughed, "Do sit with me, Liz. I feel like a whale more than a swan, and I'd be grateful for your company!"

I pulled up an ottoman and sat at her side. I could scarcely believe how many people had gathered in the parlor, and I recognized none of them. Even the ones who came without masks were strangers to me. I'd never have guessed Mr. Fish knew so many people, and said so to Emma.

"Surprising, isn't it!" she replied. "He's a businessman, and it's to his advantage to know many people in all levels of authority. I've heard he even knows the Premier. Do you think such a man would come to this sort of event?"

"Charles Augustus Semlin is far too stuffy to attend a fancy dress ball."

"But you never know," she said, looking at the faces of the guests. There were paper masks of giraffes and naval officers and pirates, four or five gilded Venetian masks decorated with pearls, and a few made of starched lace for the older ladies. Some had even covered their hair with bonnets and scarves, while others wore powdered wigs. Emma peered closely at one gentleman by the bookshelf, smoking a pipe through the mouth of his badger mask. "Any of the men here could be the Premier!"

"But what would someone like Semlin choose?"

"The hind part of a horse, I wager," she whispered. "But it would make a poor disguise; we'd recognize him immediately!" This sent her in a fit of giggles so fierce that she snorted. At that unladylike sound, we both laughed.

"You honked."

"I am a swan," she laughed, wiping away a tear.

"You make a lovely one," I complimented.

"A costume from Mrs. Thornton's shop—yes, you know of her. She told me she'd met you, and wants you to play an imp in Midsummer Night's Dream. How fitting, I thought!"

"I'm not good at acting."

"You'd be a natural!" Emma replied, "And Alma Thornton is a fine teacher, very dedicated to the arts. I've attended the Yates Street Theatre's performances on a few occasions." She pouted. "But Mason frowns on my attendance, and says I ought to save my theatre-going for more established places, like the Victoria Theatre or the Opera." She gave a sudden gasp and raised her hand to her belly. "Oh, mercy!"

"Are you alright?"

"Fine, yes," she dismissed, though her voice was strained. "The baby moves. It's no bother, Liz, just one of the joys of pregnancy." She leaned close, "It is the strangest thing! Your body is no longer your own, and performs a new, more curious trick each day!"

"Like what?"

"Well …" she said, thinking, then casting a sour glance at the man by the hearth. "I can't abide the smell of pipe smoke, and it nearly drives me mad when the men smoke in the house! And I've had great yearnings to nibble the oddest things—strawberry tops, lemon rind, even a piece of chalk!"

"Really!"

"And though I never suffered them before, my feet cramp at the smallest twinge, even when I'm in bed. And, this is the strangest, Liz," she whispered, leaning forward so that the beaks of our masks almost touched, "A line of dark hair has appeared that runs from my navel to … to my … well, downwards. Isn't that ridiculous?"

I'd read a wagon full of medical text books, and I'd never heard of such a symptom. I lowered my voice. "Why?"

"Why, indeed! Who knows!" she laughed, "Why should I suddenly wish for a dinner of chalk and lemon rinds?" Emma shrugged her feathered shoulders and said, "Truly, Liz, pregnancy makes a woman crazy!"

"Well, I think you look very regal."

She tipped the mask back from her face and smiled. "You are too kind."

"And if you need to tell anyone about your strange symptoms, go no further than me," I assured. "I find it all fascinating."

"I will, Liz. This has been—"

She flinched and took a deep breath.

"Are you alright?"

But before I barely finished my question, Emma lowered her chin and closed her eyes as her breath caught in her throat. Her skin paled. She turned limp in the chair. "Emma!" I said, grabbing her hand. It was clammy, so I stood and shouted, "Mason! Mason! Damn it, someone fetch Dr. Briggs!"

The revelry came to crashing halt. The band in the far room stopped playing with a squeal of instruments, the conversations dropped into dreadful silence, and the movement stilled as every mask turned to the chair in the corner. Dr. Briggs pushed his way through the crowd, removing his mask to reveal a look of terror on his face. When he saw Emma, he cried out for cool water, a cloth, and a stool to raise his wife's feet.

Agnes had told me a little about pregnancy, for she'd helped with birth when the miner's wives came to their time, and in her Scottish brogue, I recalled her saying that the blood must flow for a woman to feel hale. I struggled to loosen Emma's dress: I unlaced her corset, and as soon as it was slack, her lungs heaved and filled with air. I removed the mask and the jewelry, took off her tight shoes and set her feet upon the ottoman.

Emma moaned as she revived. Mason held her hand as her eyes fluttered open and a healthy pink color coursed into her cheeks.

Mr. Fish had appeared at my right. "I'll send Jess to fetch a midwife."

"There's no need," Emma assured weakly, "I feel much better—" But Mr. Fish heard none of her words, and hurried to the kitchen to seek out his housemaid.

"I told you, we ought to have stayed home," Mason admonished. "Now you've gone and harmed yourself!"

"There is no harm done, you old fuss bucket!" Emma replied, but her voice was thin. "Help me up, Liz. It's so warm here, and I've overheated under all these infernal feathers!"

Someone bid the music to start again. The conversations swelled as Mason and I helped Emma to her feet. "We should move you to the couch," I offered, "You'll be more comfortable if you can lie down."

We arranged Emma on the couch, removed her mask and her jacket, and lay an afghan over her shoulders. I left them bickering amiably. I didn't want to intrude. People seemed concerned, but gave them space to breathe, and the musicians had started a quick, lively tune to lighten the mood—I recognized it as one of Sousa's marches, very jovial and sprightly. I moved to the arch that led from library to main hall, and for a while I watched a few couples two-step around the dance floor, their grand costumes glittering in the low lamp light.

'Corsets on pregnant women,' I thought, 'What a ridiculous notion!'

I resolved to suggest Emma put away her bindings until after the baby was born. She ought to replace her tight boots with slippers. Perhaps I'd find a book in Mason's collection with more information on a woman's physiology that I could read to define the best—

I felt a hand on my elbow.

"Is the woman alright?" said the man.

"She'll be fine," I said over my shoulder to him, "She just had a fainting spell, nothing severe."

"Would you care to dance, then?"

I turned to face him, to refuse his request. He wore a grey tailcoat and burgundy vest. His hands were gloved, his face obscured with a black satin mask, his head covered with a silk hood and black top hat. I'd never have known who he was, if I was not intimately familiar with his height, his voice, and the brightness of his dark eyes.

My mouth gaped.

"We'll get in trouble!"

Shao took my hand in his and led me to the floor. "Has that ever stopped you before?"

"If Mr. Fish finds out—"

"Who do you think lent me his suit?" he whispered in my ear, and the silk mask slid smoothly against my skin. "No one is paying us any attention, Liz. Just smile, and we'll take one spin around the dance floor."

"I don't know how to dance."

He held my hands in his, our arms outstretched. The band had chosen to play Strauss next, which was more welcoming and suitable for waltzing. "A simple box step, nothing tricky," said Shao, "Just make sure to start by stepping your right foot back, or I'll end up kicking you in the shin when I step forward with my left."

He slipped his hand along the small of my back, caressed the curve of my spine. A frisson of delight skittered over my skin. I felt a blush cross my cheeks and I was happy for the mask that hid it.

And then we were off, joining three other couples on the floor, with me muttering 1-2-3 under my breath the whole time.

When his right arm encircled my waist, I laid my cheek against his chest and let him lead. Whoever had taught him to dance had done an admirable job. He cut a graceful form as we wove our steps around the edge of the room, and soon I forgot the counting. I closed my eyes, lost myself in his embrace. We soared through space held aloft by the music.

Then the band reached the end of the song, and the music came to a close. Couples split apart to give a satisfied round of applause. Shao held me a heartbeat longer, touched the curls of hair that had escaped my mask and framed my face. Before the next song began, we moved to the side of the room. People were watching us, noting that Mr. Fish's young guest had found a man who brought a smile to her lips. "You're full of secrets," I whispered in his ear.

"Now you've been seen by everyone, dancing with a stranger," he replied. "Mr. Fish's reputation as a cranky bachelor has been re-confirmed."

I laughed. "Let's dance again."

But he shook his head. "I shouldn't be here," he admitted. "I'll be out in the carriage house, losing a game of mah jong to Xi. Come visit, after this is all done."

We strolled down the long hall towards the kitchen, and lingered together on the back porch. With the doors between the front of house and the kitchen, it was quite private here, and Shao removed his mask and hood. I pulled off my own mask and laid it on the table.

"When did you learn to waltz?"

"It's always handy to have a few tricks up your sleeve," he replied. "Plus, how often do I have the opportunity to eat a few canapés in the company of doctors, lawyers and accountants? I'm willing to dance with a lovely lady for a plate of savories."

"You're a troublemaker."

"That must be why we get along so well," he replied.

Mr. Fish appeared in the kitchen, coming down from the rear stairs. He looked concerned, his long face set tight in a scowl. When he saw Shao and I by the door, he drew close. "I can't find Jess," he said quietly, "She's not in the house."

"Where would she be?" I asked.

"I don't know," he replied, "Just before the first guests arrived, she told me that she was feeling unwell. She assured Eddy that she was heading to bed early. But her room is empty. Her coat and boots are gone." He looked puzzled, but not angry. "I'll send Xi to look for her."

"An awful night for a walk!" I said. "Has anyone told Eddy that she's missing?"

"I dare not; she'll be furious." Mr. Fish admitted.

"But she might have an idea where Jess would go," I replied. "She could be anywhere, and a night like this is a poor time to search blindly."

"Lizzie, dear," said Mr. Fish, "You don't look well."

I felt my heart hitch in my chest. When I laid my hand to my forehead, my fingers brushed a light sheen of sweat.

"I'm fine—"

But Shao took me by the arm and led me to the kitchen chair, encouraging me to sit. "Bringing back memories?"

I looked up at him, questioning silently, but suddenly understanding his concern.

"It was a night like this that Violet disappeared," he said. "The rain storm—"

"I'm fine," I insisted. But he was right; the whole thing felt remarkably familiar. "I don't know why or where Jess has gone, but I won't jump to conclusions. It's only a coincidence, nothing more."

"I hope you're right," said Shao, then to Mr. Fish, he said, "I'll help Xi, and we'll return once we've found her. Go back to the party." He laid a kiss on my cheek—a most brazen thing to do, considering the proximity of Mr. Fish's guests. "Take ease, Liz, and don't think too much on Violet's death. I'm sure Jess is fine."

Shao disappeared up the stairs to the attic, and when he returned to the kitchen, he'd changed into his own clothes. Mr. Fish gathered a pair of oilskin coats from the hall wardrobe, and handed them to Shao with wishes for a speedy return. Mr. Fish and I sat at the kitchen table while the house filled with the sounds of happy guests, and we watched Shao and Xi leave through the back gate, bundled in their coats against the inclement weather. "The wayward lamb only needs rounding up," said Mr. Fish, "Perhaps the rain will ease for a little while. See, there's the moon, already peeking through the clouds."

"You don't seem overly concerned."

"Jess enjoys a walk along the ocean when the wind is high. I suppose she might have wanted a bit of fresh air." He glanced out the window. "But the night is quite fierce out there … are you well, Liz? You still look a bit peaked."

A smattering of rain hit the glass as the wind changed direction, momentarily drowning out the sounds of the party percolating through the front rooms. I had no interest in returning to the crowd. I ran my fingers over the window, felt the cold glass under my touch. "I do feel …" I struggled for the words, never sure of my own emotions. "I do feel out of sorts."

Mr. Fish stood and disappeared into the front rooms, only to return a moment later with a plate of finger sandwiches and a cup of tea. He'd added a slice of lemon.

I glanced at the contents of the cup. "Is there anything else in here I should know about?"

He grinned his wide, narrow, devil's grin. "Would you like me to stiffen it for you?"

"Yes, please."

And so he did, producing a flask of brandy from the back of the pantry cupboard and pouring a generous dollop in the cup. "Eddy hides this from me, you know. But it's my house, and I make it my job to know all of its secrets. Not to judge, of course—" he added quickly, "But to better understand my staff … and my guests."

He squinted one eye at me, in the manner of a scientist examining a curious new beetle.

"You mean me?"

"The match girl strike is the least of your interests, my dear."

I took a sip of the tea and the brandy burned its way down my throat. "What do you mean, sir?"

As he returned the bottle to its hiding place, he looked at me with crafty glee. "The newspapers you collect come from a very specific period, my girl. There were more pressing concerns in London during the fall of '88."

Fiddling with a sandwich, I said, "I didn't think it was a seemly interest for a young lady."

"But quite seemly for someone of keen intellect, rapier wit, and a thirst for adventure." Mr. Fish reclined in his chair. "You're too young to remember it, I wager, but I can tell you, Liz: the whole world clamored to hear about Jack the Ripper's exploits. The newspapers couldn't get enough!"

"Exploits?" I snarled. "Women died, Mr. Fish. Those are not 'exploits', but brutalities."

A rising chorus of laughter came from the next room; Mrs. Carter-Mackie had told a naughty joke, it seemed. He smiled kindly and waited for the laughter to fade. "I choose my words poorly, Liz, but still I stand by what I say. The tabloid stories were entertainment for the masses. Every time Jack the Ripper killed, the papers ran a lurid story and they'd sell out by noon. His name was on the lips of gossips from New York to Calcutta. He struck fear into the hearts of those in London, but for the rest of the world he made for grand entertainment."

My blood was ice in my veins. "A most vile form of entertainment, sir."

"Your humanity does you credit, Liz," he said. "You are too kind."

No, my reasons had nothing to do with charity. I'd lost my sister to the Ripper's knife. A powerful burning rage roiled in my gut, but I said nothing.

"And of course, he was never caught, and so he became a myth, a bogeyman to scare naughty children," Mr. Fish continued, "There are those—especially the newspapermen—that wait for him to resurface. Good Lord, can you imagine the circus if the police were ever to catch him? The tabloids would make a fortune. They'd parade him up and down before hanging him, or they'd charge admission to see him, or they'd chop him to bits and study his brain …" He gave a laugh, more thoughtful than mirthful.

"You find that funny?"

Mr. Fish shook his head, grinning. "No, not funny, exactly. Outrageous. We live in desperate times, Liz, when men care little for each other and the curiosity of the mob outweighs our morality. But, you know, Liz," and here he leaned forward, tenting his fingers, "There were some folks who claimed Jack the Ripper was an instrument of God, sent to punish sinners and loose women. If he's ever caught, there's some who would hail him a hero." He pushed himself away from the table. "Now THAT'S a gruesome thought."

"Quite."

He stood and tipped his head politely to me. "I ought to see to my guests, but Liz, I'll remind you: you have no need to hide your studies from me."

After he left, I toyed with the sandwiches and sipped at the tea. A most peculiar thought had appeared: I knew the Ripper's identity, and the notion that I could start a whirlwind if I so chose, and vault myself into fame and infamy, made my stomach clench. How could I ever admit I was the Ripper's daughter, a girl born to a legacy of blood and butchered women? How could I ever hope to live a normal life with that dark, dismal shadow cast over me? To make matters worse, the mere idea that some might hail John Saunders as a paragon of virtue, cleansing the streets of filth … well, the notion made me want to vomit.

Jack Hunter had once told me, 'Your father is a very famous man.'

I suddenly realized how terribly right he was.

I still wanted to understand my father, but I realized I could never, ever tell anyone the nature of my interest. Not even the smallest whisper. My research must remain purely academic in appearances, and—

A scream tore through the din of the party, a horrible silence fell over the house, replaced almost instantly by gasps of alarm. I bolted to my feet, burst into the front room, and found the party in the throes of chaos. I pushed through the guests. Emma had fully reclined along the couch, and women hurried to provide pillows and comfort as she gasped in pain. Her hands clutched at her stomach as she let out a second, blood-curdling yell.

I knelt at her side. "What's happening?"

"A sharp stab!" she cried.

Mason took her hand; his face was ghastly pale, even more so than Emma's. "Someone fetch a midwife!"

"Out of my way, Dr. Briggs," I said, and he glared at me as I laid my hands upon Emma's belly. "Forgive me for my presumption, Emma."

She nodded madly as I stuck my arms up under her skirts and felt the swell of her belly. I cast my mind back to Dr. Gould's books, to my father's lectures, to Agnes' stories of women giving birth, to the contents of the glass jars in my father's collection and how they'd looked to my untrained eyes. The glistening scarlet pears, wide at the top, narrow at the cervix, garlanded with golden ribbons of fat. I imagined them tied into the body with ligaments, stretched with childbearing. My fingers gently probed around the shape of the fetus. It jerked sharply at my rude, unfamiliar, uncaring touch.

"The baby is still high. It hasn't turned," I said to Mason.

"Is that bad?"

"No," I replied carefully, remembering that he was only a doctor. It wasn't a man's place to know these things, but a midwife's. "It isn't bad, unless her water breaks; then it's a problem. But her water is still intact—there's no puddle on the floor, and her skirts are dry. Here, I can feel the crown," I closed my eyes and ran my fingers over the top of her belly, concentrating on the shapes below her skin, "And the buttocks are here. See? Already, it stretches its legs."

A tittering of embarrassed laughter reminded me that guests watched from the edges of the room. Mason Briggs glared at them and a few decent souls moved into the parlor. The band struck up a gentle tune in the main hall, and a few women clucked in sympathy and concern. Emma looked like she didn't care at all. Instead, she rested her head against the back of the couch, a faint smile on her lips.

"The pain is leaving," she said with relief. "How do you know where the baby sits?"

I shrugged. "My father showed me these sorts of things."

"Well, good fortune for me, then!"

Another healthy kick hit the palm of my hand. "The baby is lively, but it's not ready to be born. Given where its feet are, I think it might've aimed a kick at your cervix, Emma."

Flutters of affront rippled through the gentle society. Half of them probably didn't even know the word, but it *sounded* naughty, and women weren't to refer to that part of their anatomy at all. Goodness! Such language!

"Nothing to be concerned," I assured Mason.

He was not soothed. "We shouldn't have come!" he said to his wife.

"You'll stay the night," said Mr. Fish, "I'll have Eddy prepare a room for you upstairs."

When it was ready, Mason and Emma retired to their quarters. I saw the beginnings of an argument between them, so I assured Mason that the best thing for Emma was rest and calm. Surely that would keep him from badgering her further.

The last guest to leave was Mr. James Buxton, a politician from Oak Bay, and his wife Charlotta, who had consumed so much of the good gin that Mr. Fish was afraid that, if she stood too close to the candle flames, she'd set her breath alight. The woman had a very difficult time stumbling on her own, but Mr. Buxton was walking at such a severe angle that he was able to prop her up quite well. Together, they managed to trip along like the runners in a wobbly, slow, and crooked three-legged race.

The rain stopped around three in the morning. By the time Mr. Fish bid the Buxtons farewell, he'd long abandoned his costume. We stood on the front verandah and breathed in gasps of fresh morning air, so delightful after a stuffy house full of revelers.

"Thank God that's over," he said, pressing the heels of his hands into the small of his back. "I won't need to host another for at least a decade."

Eddy joined us, quiet and tense. Her expression was full of rigid disapproval. Mr. Fish had told her of Jess' disappearance just before the Buxton's had gathered their scarves and umbrella, and she'd taken the news poorly. Now that all guests were gone, she spoke openly and plainly. "Lord help her, Jessie's gone off with that boy again," she muttered through clenched teeth.

"Now, Eddy, let's not jump to conclusions," he said. "You know Jess is fond of a walk by the sea, especially when it's windy."

"Damnable trouble," she growled.

I saw two figures hurrying down the street, and recognized them at once.

"Here come Mr. Chen and Xi," noted Mr. Fish.

"But no Jess," I said.

"Because that girl knows I'll give her a damn fine thrashing," said Eddy. "And that boy better run too. If I lay eyes on him, there ain't no telling what I'll do!"

"Surely you don't mean that," said Mr. Fish delicately.

"No?" said Eddy as she retired into the house. "I know exactly what I mean, Harris. The two of 'em together means trouble."

"What boy?" I said, but Mr. Fish looked at me sharply, and the warning in his eyes was clear. *Don't ask in Eddy's presence!*

For the whole day, there was no hint of Jess, and Edwina Garry performed her tasks with the sharp, decisive gestures of an enraged bison. She fumed, she muttered, and all of us stayed out of her way, even Mr. Fish. Mason and Emma left after lunch in a hired carriage, and still, Jess had not returned.

After being up most of the night, I retired to my room in the early evening, and laid down to sleep.

Twelve

October 31, 1898

I woke the next morning to the sound of a heavy knock at the door. When no one answered, I realized we were all waiting for Jess to open it.

In slippers and housecoat, I went myself, and as I reached the entrance, I saw Mr. Fish appearing on the upper landing in his own beige robe, his long face drawn with concern.

When I opened the door, the constable had already removed his helmet and held it in a pair of delicate, freckled hands. He had shallow eyes, blotchy skin, and thin blonde hair cut very close to his scalp, along with a pale, neatly-trimmed moustache that hid his upper lip. The pallor of his skin contrasted sharply against the dark wool of his uniform and the two rows of silver buttons that ran down his jacket. I guessed that he must be new to the force, in his early 20s. He held his tall, lanky body as erect as a military statue, fulfilling his duty with an iron-clad adherence to the rules, but the beads of sweat on his brow stood out like little barnacles. He was nervous, and trying every trick to hide it.

"Good morning, miss," he said, overly crisp. "Is this the home of Jessica Garry?"

Mr. Fish now stood at my side. Eddy had appeared from the kitchen, her apron covered with flour. At this simple question, I heard her sharply inhale. Before we had time to soften the blow, she'd stumbled to the sofa, her hands clutching at the collar of her shirt.

"Lord, what's happened?" she gasped, "What's happened to my girl?"

Faced with a mother's raw questions, the constable faltered. He was young and awkward, unschooled in delivering grim news. "I'm sorry, ma'am," he stammered. He recovered his official tone as he turned to Mr. Fish, and said, "I'm sorry, but she's dead."

Mr. Fish sank to the nearest chair as Eddy buried her head in her large hands, great gasping sobs racking her throat. I was stunned—I'd assured myself that nothing was wrong, yet I'd been terribly mistaken. I stepped onto the porch with the police officer to give them privacy in the face of their grief, and closed the door after me. Outside, a soft, misty rain gave the impression that the city was gently weeping. The constable and I stood under the eaves of the balcony, and he shifted his weight from foot to foot, unsure of what to say. A very uncomfortable silence passed between us.

I decided to take the lead. "Where was she found?" I asked.

"Some of the Indians set up nets on McLoughlin Point to catch salmon before winter. She was snarled there."

"Drowned?"

"No, miss."

Here, he paused. Clearly, he didn't wish to say any more, but he didn't know how to conclude our conversation. Maybe he'd stood on the doorstep and rehearsed the delivery of the news, but hadn't foreseen that there'd be questions to answer.

"Well?" I pushed. "How, then?"

He squirmed, then remembered his uniform and stood a little straighter. "She was stabbed." His skin looked a bit green, and the rest of the words came out in a quick gush. "To the gut. Her purse was missing, so it must've been a robbery. But her name was stitched in her dress. The Chief Constable said Mr. Fish had lost one of his staff a few nights back, so we figured" He wrung his hands, thought of his position of authority, and dropped them to his sides. "Her mother will have to come and identify the body."

"She is wholly unfit for such a job," I replied, "I'll dress immediately and join you."

"No, miss, I can't ask that of you."

"I appreciate your concern, Constable ..."

"Grange, miss. Howard Grange."

"... Constable Grange, but this would not be the first young woman I've seen dragged from the water. I am fully prepared for this task. And without the hysteria of grief, you'll find I'll be much faster."

"This is most unorthodox," he pressed.

"Stay here, Constable, and give me ten minutes to prepare."

I returned inside, and I was back to the porch in less than eight minutes, wearing my simple black smock, my boots, and a sweater. I pulled on my wool coat, and not knowing when I'd be back, I stashed a few items in my pocket: from the larder, I took an apple and a tin of lucifer matches, and from my own satchel, a bit of money and a pocketknife. In that time, Eddy's mourning had become a consuming weeping, her back straight and her face pointed to the door, her eyes glazed. Her broad jaw was set tightly, her hands balled into fists.

Mr. Fish stood when he saw me at the base of the stairs. "It ought to be me who goes. This is an employer's duty—"

"Don't be foolish," I replied. "Jess admired you and she wouldn't want you to see her in such a state."

"This is unprecedented, Liz," he said, "I could not ask a guest to perform such a horrific task."

"Eddy needs you here," I said, "Notify the undertaker, Mr. Fish. I'll be back promptly."

He looked unconvinced, but stepped back to show that he would let me go. Still, he warned, "Proper girls do not run after corpses, Liz."

"So I've been told," I replied, "But if my impropriety can serve your household and spare Eddy further suffering, then I'm happy for it."

Constable Grange had taken a buggy, so together we rode back to the morgue, located in the basement of St. Joseph's Hospital. The building occupied the corner of Humbolt Street and Quadra Street, only a few blocks away, so we had little time to exchange pleasantries or endure an awkward silence; before I knew it, the driver had pulled alongside the rear entrance of the brick building. Four stories high, with a noble bell tower sprouting from the center of its long grey roof, St. Joseph's Hospital seemed both official and foreboding. Its long lines of skinny windows gave one the impression of a posh English boarding school, but the lines of wicker wheeled chairs on the front veranda gave a clearer indication of the people convalescing within. A hospital was the last line of defense against Death, and St. Joseph's purpose was only thinly disguised by a veneer of elegant stonework and gardens. The manicured cherry trees in the yard did little to soften the hospital's hard, flinty, battle-weary appearance.

It must have smelt as frightful as it looked, for as I dismounted from the buggy, the horse pranced lightly on its hooves and flicked its ears, eager to leave.

We descended a flight of stone steps to a basement door. Grange ushered me inside, then briskly led me down a white-tiled corridor to a small room. Five gurneys lined the wall, each bearing a familiar shape under a sheet: a nose, toes, the swell of a belly. A wiry middle-aged man with a pair of glasses perched on the end of his nose met us at the door. His dirty white shirt was sprinkled with black dots, and I recognized them as the old stains of blood mist, collected over many months of sawing bodies open.

He looked me over dully. "What's this?"

"She's come to identify the body." said Grange. There was no fondness between them, and as the coroner looked me over—a small girl in a black frock with her hands clasped at her waist—he raised one questioning eyebrow to the constable.

"You're having me on."

"Can we proceed?" I snapped.

He gave a grunt of surprise. "You may wish to brace yourself," he said in a disinterested monotone, "It's not pretty."

"I shall be fine," I assured tartly.

The constable did not come in the room, but waited outside while the man led me into the morgue, to the nearest gurney, to the still form under a grey sheet.

He peeled back the sheet. The pungent smell that followed hinted at old turnips, fish oil, the curds that collected in the folds of unwashed skin. There lay Jessie's head, her cheeks slack and her eyes closed, her dark skin a ghostly grey. Seaweed tangled her matted hair, sand crusted along her hairline. The thin gold necklace with its cross glittered brightly at her throat, untarnished by salt. Yes, she was certainly deceased and disheveled, but she hadn't been in the water long enough to grow plump with moisture, as Violet had. My sister's corpse had been in a much worse state of decay. While I wouldn't be so naive to say that Jess looked as if she were sleeping, she certainly didn't look gruesome, either. Dead, yes, but not disgustingly so.

"That's Jess," I replied.

The attendant began to draw the sheet up.

"Wait," I said. "Might I see more?"

He screwed up his nose at my request. "I beg your pardon?"

"The constable said she was stabbed in the stomach."

"Well yes, but—hey, you mustn't pull back the sheet! That's hardly very Christian of you!" He looked to the door, "Constable, can you please—" He hurried out to the corridor to fetch help.

I laid the sheet along the top of her thighs. They had undressed her to examine her, and she lay naked and exposed on the cold gurney, her hands at her sides with her palms up. I scanned the body, noting the deep gashes in her abdomen: five in total, much deeper at the top than the bottom. The edges of the wounds were ragged and ripped. The tool had not been a sharp one, and the killer had used brute force to tear the life out of her.

But would these wounds have killed? I thought of a miner who had been brought into Father's hospital; the man had sustained a series of gut wounds from an explosion at the coal face. The blast had driven splinters and rock grit deep into his belly. While he had succumbed to his injuries, it took an agonizing length of time—days of excruciating pain, only eased by increasing doses of morphine. These wounds looked similar, and they would've killed Jess, but not in one night.

I peered closer at her body, and soon found what I was looking for:

a depression in the lower back quadrant of her head, where a heavy implement had cracked her skull.

The sharp tap of the constable's shoes on the tile floor drew near. "The killer stabbed her, but she was killed by a blow to the head," I said, pointing to the depression at the point where her hair met her neck.

Grange drew close to my elbow. "Why stab her first, then? Why bother?"

I glanced up at the men, and while the coroner looked at me with horror, Grange looked intently at Jess' soft, relaxed face. "Perhaps they thought the stabbing would do the trick, and had to improvise when it didn't work."

He glanced at me. "Then it was not a robbery gone awry, but an assailant with intent to kill?"

"Not just kill," I said. "Stabbing is vicious, personal. There is great hatred in these wounds."

"You can't look at a wound and know what the murderer felt," said the coroner. "That's preposterous."

But I didn't reply to him; I would've thought a man, accustomed to seeing the bodies of murder victims, would know the difference between an efficient, cold, clean kill and a passionate, messy, brutal attack.

I returned my focus to Jess. The callouses on her right were more pronounced than her left—Jess had been right handed, so I quickly took her right fingers and examined the fingernails, remembering that here I'd found evidence of Violet's attacker. Sure enough, Jess had fought and scratched her assailant, breaking half her nails but taking no skin. This didn't surprise me. After all, on a rainy autumn night, it would be the rare person who wasn't wearing warm sleeves.

But, peering close, I found wisps of green thread snagged under the cracked thumbnail.

"Her attacker was wearing a green coat," I said. "He used a very dull knife to stab her."

"Miss, you cannot possibly know—"

I ignored the coroner and spoke to Grange. "See how the wounds are deeper at the top than the bottom? I wager she was attacked by someone smaller in stature." I thought about this a moment, weighing the idea. "They could've stabbed overhand and used their weight to pull downwards."

"Now see here—" the coroner continued.

"Look, at the firmness of her skin—when did you say she was found?"

"Yesterday, just after dawn," said Grange.

"She was not long in the water," I mused. "Have you yet found the spot where she was killed?"

He shook his head.

"It won't be far from where she was caught in the nets," I replied, once more pressing my finger into Jess' shoulder. "When a body is in the water for more than a few hours, it grows soft and squishy, but Jess is still quite firm. She was killed close to McLoughlin Point."

"Miss, you really must let me cover—"

"Stand back, Albert," said Grange to the coroner. Then, to me, he said, "What else do you see?"

I studied the grey skin, the blue-tinged lips, the sand that had collected in the channels of her ears. I saw the way her long neck became the smooth curve of shoulders. I examined each component as a single item, not as part of a whole body. A hand, a thumb, a hip. As I circled the gurney, I was only vaguely aware of the two men behind me; Jess and I were holding a conversation in which they could take no part. The cross at the hollow of her throat glinted in the low light. I touched it with one finger, felt the cool metal. Her breasts did not fall to the sides, as most women's do when they lay upon their backs, but remained full and round. Grit encrusted the brown flesh of her nipples. The tide had washed the gashes clean of any blood. There was no crust of red that had dried on her stomach or matted her pubic mound. Even the line of dark hairs running from her belly to her thighs was clean, although pronounced and darker than I'd have expected.

I paused.

"Oh." I said, very quietly.

"What is it?" said Grange.

Then he gave a sharp cry as I launched over Jess' stomach and stuck my bare fingers deep into the wounds.

"Dear God!" shouted the coroner, "Stop her!"

Grange shouted in reply, "Go! Fetch the matron! A woman to restrain her!"

But I prodded and dug my fingers into her gut, felt her cold body swallow up my knuckles. Through the rents made by the weapon, her flesh gave only a small amount of resistance. Her intestines squished aside. Then my index finger brushed against something soft and round, knobby and small.

I'd found what I was looking for.

It came away easily; I fished it from her body with a soft, suckling sound and held it in my palm for a heartbeat. So small, so tranquil, so calm. Grange looked at me, repulsed but curious.

"Constable, there is one more thing," I replied.

I held out my hand, unfurled my fingers. There, nestled like a sleeping mouse in my palm, black-eyed and stick-limbed and nub-eared, lay curled a perfect, purple-blue fetus.

Thirteen

When the coroner returned with the matron and two nuns, I very quickly found myself shunted out of the morgue with instructions to return home at once, deliver the terrible news, and—in the matron's most condescending tone possible—be a *good* girl. Frankly, I had no plans to fulfill any of these requests.

Instead, I hurried through the wet, windy streets to the corner of Yates and Broad Street and rapped upon the door of the dress shop. The hour was very early and none of the businesses were open, but I was confident that Mrs. Thornton would be inside; she had too much to do when there was a play to perform, and until *The Duchess of Padua* closed on November 5th, she planned to spend almost every waking hour in the costume shop.

I heard her quick steps on the hard wooden floor. She opened the door to greet me, holding her morning cup of tea in her hand.

"Why, Liz, you look positively frightful!" she laughed, "Such a serious face, so early in the morning? What's happened?"

"I have terrible news, Mrs. Thornton. Jess is dead."

"Oh, dear God!" she whispered. Her knees turned watery. I caught the heavy woman under the arm as she sagged against the doorframe. The tea cup shattered on the floor.

"Oh, how can this be?" she whimpered, "What happened? An accident—?"

"Murder, I'm afraid."

"Oh sweet merciful Lord! Our poor Jess, murdered!" Her chin wobbled, her breath caught in her throat. "How was it done?"

A small crowd of passersby had slowed at the sounds of distress. I guided Mrs. Thornton into her shop and locked the door behind us, taking care not to tread on the shards of broken cup. I sat her down at the table. "I'm afraid it was done in a frightful way," I began, searching the cupboard for another mug and replacing her tea from the brownstone pot on the table.

"I'd rather not say, but I've been to the morgue to identify the body, and I thought you would want to know immediately."

"Oh, poor dear," she crooned, "Oh, poor Jess!" Tears welled in her eyes and tumbled down the wrinkles in her cheeks.

I left her to cry as I cleaned up the broken cup. I was reluctant to leave her alone in her distress. "Where's Andy gone?" I asked as I tipped the shards into a trash bin by the desk in the corner.

"To the wharves, to fix a window at one of the pubs there. He'll be back soon enough—stay with me, Liz! I don't know if I can tell him myself!"

"I can't," I said, "I'm afraid I have too much to do."

"I'll have to tell the other girls …" she said to herself, "And there was the performance tomorrow night, I'll need to cancel …"

She was not speaking to me. "Cancel *The Duchess of Padua*?" I asked, "But Jess wasn't a stage actor. Surely someone else can manage the costumes."

She blinked, her eyes focused on me. "Oh, not those performances," she said. She let her breath release in a great rush of air, collapsing against the back of her chair like a sack of potatoes. "Liz, can I tell you a secret?"

I took the seat across from her.

She dropped her voice to a whisper. "Did you ever hear Jess sing on stage?"

"Jess didn't perform—"

"Oh, she did! She had the voice of an angel! Clear as a bell, sweet as honey, as warm as a summer's afternoon!" Mrs. Thornton looked at me with a sad smile. Her chin trembled. "She was shy, I agree, but when she was on stage with the other girls? Oh, she perked right up and knew a million songs, and all the men loved her." Mrs. Thornton leaned forward. "She never told you about the Sing Song Girls?"

"No," I rose one eyebrow. "I caught her slipping back to the house one night, and she begged me not to tell her mother, and I figured—"

"—She was meeting a boy on some lover's tryst?" Mrs. Thornton gave a winsome sigh in my direction. "Oh, there is a romantic heart in that chicken breast of yours, I knew it! No, she was meeting the Sing Song Girls for a late-night performance." She gave a little chuckle. "They sang a lot of bawdy songs, you know, 'cause that's what the audience demanded, but they were mostly good, decent girls and they didn't do anything to soil their virtue. But Jess thought her mother might get the wrong idea—Mrs. Garry didn't even like her sewing costumes for me, never mind getting up on the stage. So Jess kept her singing engagements a secret. But sneaking out to meet a boy?" Mrs. Thornton laughed again. "Jess was too timid for that sort of thing!"

I looked to the ground, thinking. They can't all have been performances.

Eddy claimed there was a boy, and obviously, Mrs. Thornton knew nothing about the pregnancy.

"She's been a fine help with the theatre, but there aren't many parts for a dark lass, and so I have to put her to work in the back, more oft than not," she continued. "A fine girl, really she is. A shining talent, even, though you wouldn't guess it to look at her, all quiet as a mouse if she isn't on stage." She nodded sagely. "I would've loved to have used her in public performances, and not just on the sly."

"The Sing Song Girls didn't advertise their performances?"

"Never. Only private engagements."

"So they sang at … less respectable establishments?"

The older woman's eyes widened. "Oh, larks, don't be starting rumors like that!" She took my wrist in her hands. "No, nothing sordid! But sometimes the Sing Song Girls were hired privately to sing at a gentleman's club, all up-and-up but private. You understand what I'm saying?"

"Private."

"Exactly."

"And you brokered their talents?"

She let go of my arm just long enough to wring her hands. "I always made sure the references were good! I didn't want any harm coming to those girls!"

"Harm did find its way to Jess—"

"But not through my contacts! I played no part in that poor girl's death!" Mrs. Thornton trembled, her voice pleading, her eyes earnest. "You've got to believe me, Liz! I loved Jess like a daughter. I wouldn't put any of my girls in the smallest bit of danger, even for a pretty sum. I'd do anything to keep them safe!"

She took a long, recuperative drink of tea, draining the mug. I waited until she'd finished it before asking, "When was her last performance?"

"The Girls met on Saturday night."

"The same night Jess went missing."

Mrs. Thornton's face fell. "You mustn't think that had anything to do with—"

"Where was the performance, Mrs. Thornton? Was it out by McLoughlin Point?"

"Larks, no!" she replied. "The Sing Song Girls only performed for the highest caliber of clientele! There'd be no reason for her to go across the harbor! They were performing in James Bay, just 'round the corner from Mr. Fish's house, and Jess figured she be there and back before anyone would miss her. Why, I saw Greta yesterday, and she said Jess sang her very best that night, and earned a good amount of tips."

"Greta was another one of the Sing Song Girls?"

"Greta Braun, Eleanor McCloud, and Maude Mawson. The four of 'em made such a lovely chorus."

"And the other girls are accounted for?"

Mrs. Thornton gave a small shrug. "I spoke with Greta yesterday, and Maude dropped by last night, but I haven't seen Eleanor since Saturday afternoon." She grew alarmed. "You don't think Eleanor might be harmed, too?"

I knew Greta and Maude from the theatre, but I didn't know Eleanor. "Where would I find this Eleanor? I'll talk to her, make sure she's not missing."

Mrs. Thornton shifted in her seat. "She comes and goes, that one. Wild as a feral cat."

"But you must know where to contact her. You'll need to tell her that future performances are cancelled."

She paused and considered, then grabbed a scrap of paper and a pencil. She scribbled an address and handed it to me.

"Eleanor lives here, but don't you tell anyone I gave you this address, understood? And you make sure you leave as quick as you can! It's no fit place for a girl, and I won't be having Mr. Fish scold me for getting you caught up in something unsavory."

I studied the address. "What is it?"

"Not a place for upstanding ladies, my love." She frowned. "I ought not have told you at all!"

I thanked her. Before she could reconsider, I left her shop, holding fast to the address. I turned my coat collar against the wind, and hurried down Yates, to the seedier strip of Wharf Street.

At this early hour, Wharf Street was quiet but not empty. I passed a filthy man sleeping soundly with an empty bottle in his hand, his face pressed against the brick foundation of a supply store. The wind had blown bits of trash around him, and it had collected in the crook of his bent legs. A wolf pack of three skinny boys hunted through the gutters for pennies, and when they saw the sleeper, they scrounged through his unguarded pockets. They were so focused on their task, they hardly noticed me. An aura of desperation and depravity hung in the air like a sour smell.

The address led me to a humble, unpainted wooden door, boasting a tarnished brass knob and a good view of the docks. There were no windows, placards, or hint of a business name. Those facts advertised, more clearly than any sign, what transactions took place behind this door. The knocker was shaped like a mermaid, her tail curved and her hair unbound, with pert breasts and a saucy smile on her brass lips. I took hold of her fins and gave a strong, confident bang on the door.

After a few moments, the lock clicked. The door opened, only a crack, on squeaky hinges.

A face like an eel peeked out. The woman had a knife-sharp nose and fleshy jaws, with a weak chin and bulging, watery eyes. The few teeth she possessed were crooked and yellow. She did not look happy to see me, and began to shut the door at the sight of me, but I laid a firm hand upon it. It took only a little effort to stop her.

"Is Eleanor McCloud here?"

"What choo wan with Nelly?"

"I'm a friend of Jessica Garry. I need to speak with her."

"Oi don't know no Jess'ca Garry," she spat, "And Nelly's busy, so screw off."

"Listen," I said, "Jessica Garry is dead, and if you don't let me in, I'll tell the police to have a word with you." At this threat, the watery eyes bulged a little more.

"Oi don't wan no bloody coppers here!"

"I thought not. I shall happily hold my tongue if you'll give me an opportunity to chat with Eleanor McCloud myself."

With pursed lips and flared nostrils, her fishy face twisted into an expression of disgust. "Get in, then," she spat. "But choo don't go no farther than the door, got it?"

I was quite happy with the arrangement, and I'd have rather she kept the door open while I waited in the hall, but no luck. She slammed it shut behind us and threw the latch, trapping me inside a dingy, windowless entrance with nothing to keep me company but a sad potted fern and a staircase leading up to gloomy rooms. The air smelt of sweat and vomit, softened by the fug of cheap, cloying perfume. I heard voices on the upper landing, but they were too low to discern any words.

When the eel woman appeared on the top step, she said, "There's the bint, Nelly," and pointed down at me. A woman in her mid-twenties appeared on the top step. Her straight black hair hung loose about her bony shoulders, and her high, sharp cheekbones cast deep shadows over her sallow skin. She wore very little: a thin floral shift, grey with too many washings, and pale wool stockings that sagged around her knees. Her half-squinting eyes, giving the impression that she might be near sighted, were nonetheless full of suspicion, and her lipless gash of a mouth was pinched firmly closed.

"You said Jess is dead?" she asked in a voice that was deep, sultry, and far more beautiful than her appearance.

I nodded.

"Who the hell are ya?"

"Amaryllis Saunders. I'm a guest in the house of Mr. Fish, and Jess was my friend."

She lifted one eyebrow. "If she's dead, you don't look all cut up about it."

"No, I don't," I admitted, "But I am, believe me."

"And Mrs. Thornton? You musta got the address from her—how'd she take the news?"

"With great difficulty."

Eleanor lingered on the upper step, casting her eyes back and forth. Tears gathered in her lashes, but her voice remained strong. "She was sweet on Jess."

"My condolences to you, too."

She gave a shrug, turned away, and wiped at her face with her hand. "We all gotta die, right? Look, I gotta client, and I can't just leave him. He's already paid for his hour." Her throat hitched. She took a deep breath. "Thanks for the news."

"When did you last see Jess?"

Her mouth twisted in a sad scowl. She was finding it difficult, almost impossible, to keep her composure. I noticed her pinch the back of her thigh; pain could keep the tears away, for just a little while. "Saturday night, after singing. She was happy … always was, after a good hearty sing-along."

"What time would've that been?"

"Bloody hell, I don't know … maybe midnight? Maybe one? Jess wanted to hurry home. She said her ma would kill her if she saw her sneaking back in."

"Did anyone leave with her?"

"Naw, not that I saw. But we were finished, you see, and we all left our separate ways soon after. Mrs. Thornton doesn't like us hanging about after the show; it ruins the magic, I s'pose. When I saw Jessie leaving, she was smiling and singing to herself and gay as a magpie." Her left hand clung to her right bare arm, and she kept her face down, so that the dark hair fell like a curtain over her features. "Look, don't get me thinking about Jess, alright? No man wants to pay to spend time with a crying whore."

"I understand."

She turned on one heel, but I called her name up the stairs, and she returned.

"What?"

"Where was the performance?"

Eleanor gave a shrug. "A private party. I didn't know none of the men. They was all too high class for the likes of me." The curve of her lip curled up, showing just a hint of her disgust, and revealing a missing incisor. "I thought I might catch a score, but it turns out I ain't quality 'nuff for 'em."

"They didn't like the Sing Song Girls?"

"Oh, they liked us just fine, if we were singing. But when I started chatting up one of the fellas?" She gave a sharp laugh. "They liked us best when we were sneaking out the rear door so the neighbours wouldn't see."

"What was the address?"

"I shouldn't tell," she said, "Mrs. Thornton would be right pissed."

"She might," I agreed, then gave a crafty grin, "But so would the gentlemen who planned the party."

Eleanor smirked. She weighed my suggestion, then came down a few steps. She dropped the volume of her voice, and said, "The white house on the corner of Superior and Montreal. But if anyone asks—"

"You never told me." I replied. Eleanor smiled at that. She possessed a very pretty smile, despite the gauntness of her features. She gave a sharp nod and turned back as if about to say more, then shook her head and disappeared into the darkness of the upper landing. I hurried out the door, eager to leave behind the smell of perfume and vomit and the pathetic potted fern.

Fourteen

At the corner of Superior and Montreal sat four very different buildings. One was a brick warehouse, another a tall three-story clapboard house surrounded by box hedges. From the wooden plaque above the door, it was a boarding house of high quality, run by a woman named Mrs. Mills. The third building was a shop front that had once housed a green grocer, but had long been shut. Even though a pair of low tables still flanked the entrance, ready to display fresh vegetables, the door had been sealed closed with planks and the canvas awning that had once advertised the name of the proprietor had been removed. It was an empty, sad little building, but the area was growing and attractive to a high class of investors. I doubted that it would stay abandoned for long.

On the north east corner was a squat white house, with blue shutters and a freshly painted blue verandah, surrounded by a froth of bushes. A low, white picket fence encircled the small yard. The crisp white curtains were closed. The carriage house in the back had been locked, but the gravel drive carried the twin ruts of wheels. This dwelling was inhabited by a man with money, who didn't have to rent a buggy when he went out for the day.

Neither a warehouse, a boarding house, nor an abandoned shop were suitable places for a gentleman's gathering, but this? This must be the place.

A couple of boys played with a dog in the street, and a young woman hung laundry in the side yard of the boarding house, trying to take advantage of the last rays of cold sunlight—Mrs. Mills, I presumed. She whistled around the wooden pegs in her mouth, fully engrossed in her work.

I saw no one else, so I hopped the fence and scurried around the side of the yard. The building was broad and flat, only one story high, so I had only to crawl onto a flowerbox to peer through the kitchen window.

Inside, all was dark. No candles were lit, and most of the curtains were closed. The house appeared empty. No one was home, not even a maid-of-all-work.

The latch on the back door was locked, but I found a hoe in the garden shed, and I used the flat edge of its iron blade to pop open the bolt with a soft crunch. Setting the hoe beside the door, I poked my head inside.

The air smelled of cold tobacco smoke and plum cake, as well as stale wine and dirty clothes. I wrinkled my nose at the combination. While the exterior of the house gave every impression of proper tidiness, my first impression of the interior was one of disgust and amazement: the kitchen was a mess. Towers of used plates and piles of half-eaten food obscured the counters, along with a peppering of mouse turds. Scattered across the ground were wadded linen napkins that no one had gathered to wash. I had to step over a wooden chair that lay on its side.

The next room, a dining area, was in worse shape than the kitchen. Whoever lived here cared nothing at all for the piles of clothes, empty bottles of beer and wine, and soiled table cloth ringed with purple stains. The silver plates held chicken bones, puddles of congealed gravy, and dry, stale biscuits. Clearly, these were the remains of the party only a few nights ago. I started to suspect that the family had no house staff to clean up after them, and I picked my way through the home with my nose wrinkled in disgust—not at their lack of staff, mind you, but at the sour and fetid smell.

The living room could've been comfortable, if anyone cared for it. The furniture was of the highest quality, the book shelves were full of leather-bound editions, the mantle was constructed out of thick slabs of white Italian marble. The clock that sat atop it was made of burnished gold.

But whomever lived here had covered all the tables with refuse, scattered newspapers across the chairs, and left a thick film of dust on every horizontal surface. The grate was too full of ashes to hold a fire. The clock was slow by almost three hours, and had not been wound in quite some time. I circled around the chesterfield, noting a number of stains on the horsehide. The smell was worst of all, but I soon discovered its source: in the corner, behind a palm plant that was dying of thirst, sat a full chamber pot.

The man who lived here had money but no pride, and he certainly had no housemaid. At a roll top desk by the door, I plucked through a tower of envelopes, looking for a name, but saw nothing to identify the occupant. There were no bills, no letters or correspondence, and only a few leaves of paper with random names and addresses that meant nothing to me. None of the items spoke of Jess or the Sing Song girls. I was certain that this was the location of the gentlemen's party (and what a rumpus it must've been!) but there was nothing here to lead me to her killer.

I decided to go. The thick smell of day-old turds and cold gravy was enough to turn my stomach.

Then I raised my eyes to the painting above the mantle.

The face staring down at me, rendered in oils and covered in dust, was the stern, patrician visage of Judge Carter.

"Well, I'll be," I whispered to myself.

But I couldn't imagine Judge Carter living in such a state, nor could I imagine him holding a party that would result in this sort of devastation. Nor, to be truthful, could I imagine him living a life without servants. But who would place a portrait of the old man in such a place of honor?

"You remember my father," said William from the shadows in the hall.

I wheeled on one foot and stared at him.

He stood on the threshold between bedrooms and dining room, slumped heavily against the wall. His eyes looked tired, pinched. He didn't seem angry or sharp, though the reptilian coolness remained. When he stepped towards me, his knees wobbled, and he laid one hand upon the door frame to steady himself.

"How long have you been here, Miss Saunders?" he said with a casual air, as if it was natural to find me in his living room.

"Not very long, Will."

"What are you doing in my house? Is Smithy still here?" he said. "Or did he finally go home?"

"I don't think anyone's here but you and me."

He scrubbed one hand over his face, and the two-day beard rasped under his palm. He still wore a suit, but his shirt collar was unbuttoned and he'd lost his jacket.

"You had a party on Saturday night," I said. "Jess was here." I didn't step back, but I glanced quickly to my right. There was a door there, ajar. I saw that it led to a corridor. I wondered if the front door was on the other side of the wall, and whether I'd find it locked.

"The negro girl, right?" he replied. "Yeah, she was here, squawking." He took a step towards me. "Is it Sunday?" He took a mug from the table and downed whatever it held. "Or is it Monday? It must be Monday." Then he looked squarely at me and said, "You still haven't answered my question. What are you doing here?"

I swallowed. I was not afraid of him, but I was aware that I was unarmed. Shao's knife was in the portmanteau at Mr. Fish's house, and I suddenly missed the weight of it in my hand. "Jess is dead, Mr. Carter."

"Really?" He blinked twice. "I guess that ends her squawking."

"Did you have anything to do with it?"

He laughed sharply. "Me? Hell, no. Why would I?" He rubbed his hands over his brow, then he looked up at the portrait of his father, and his eyes shone with devotion. "God, the old man'll be furious, won't he! Pompous old ass, hanging up there on the wall while we—well, he would've seen our little soiree as a frightful revelry. And now, a girl dead … damn! He'll disown me for sure." He laughed at this, followed quickly by a wet belch and a hung-over groan.

"Who else was here, William?"

He waved his hand absently, refusing to answer my question. "How did Jess die?"

"Murder."

He spat on the rug. "Little whore, served her right."

Anger sparked in my heart. I clenched my hands. "What do you mean, Will? Jess was a lovely girl."

"She wanted to be an actress, though, didn't she?" he said, "And we all know, actresses are whores."

"I thought you loved the theatre—"

"Fuck," he said as he slumped down into a horsehide chair. "Did you know why I hosted a party on Saturday? Because I was accepted into my father's club. And you know what? That means I'm a god damn gentleman now. And that means," he rose one finger to me and jabbed the air, "No more performances, no more dress rehearsals, no more meet-ups with the pretty girls back stage for a spot of fun. No more." He focused his eyes on the stern portrait and said, in a fine mockery of his father, "No more shenanigans, young man!"

"Did you sleep with Jess?"

He trained his eyes on me again, blurry but confused. "Why would I do that?" He gave a cold laugh. "I said PRETTY girls."

Reaching out to the floor, he grabbed a leg of meat that had lain in the dust under his chair, and plucked a bit of hair off before taking a bite.

"Don't look so damned sanctimonious, Liz", he said, "I never touched any of the Sing Song girls. They're all crawling with the pox, especially that Nell. God, I tell Alma I need a bit of entertainment, what do I get? Four ugly piglets." He suppressed a shudder. "They sang alright, but then Nell started chatting up the guests, so I shunted them out the door. Like I said, I'm a gentleman now." He tossed the bone aside, and it bounced over the rug. "I'm supposed to keep a level of quality."

"So I see," I replied, glancing around the disgusting room.

When William guffawed, he letting forth an arc of spittle. "You'll forgive me, Miss Saunders. I'm between maids right now," he said. "The last little minx ran out on me and I can't find anyone to take her place." William slumped down in the chair. Under his breath, he muttered, "I might have to hire a dirty little Celestial."

That clinched it. A flash of rage streaked across my vision. My hand grabbed a ceramic mug from the table. It nailed the middle of his forehead with a deeply satisfying thud, and spilled a gold shower of cold ale down his chest.

At least, I think it was ale.

The heavy mug bounced off William's skull and hit the ground, cracking into three pieces. His head jerked back, his body slumped deep into the chair. The strike could've left him dead, but a rattling moan assured me he was still alive. His exposed throat, speckled with whiskers, lay long and white and vulnerable in the dim gloom.

The knives on the table winked at me. How satisfying it would've been to dispatch this crude mockery of civility.

But I had things to do, and today, murder was not my priority.

Fifteen

I arrived at Mr. Fish's house just as a dinner of cold meats and cheeses was being served. A physician had been summoned, and Dr. Sumner had given Eddy a shot of morphine to calm her nerves. She lay in a sad, weeping heap on the couch in the parlor. Around her, the women of the neighbourhood had gathered in force, as they are wont to do upon the news of a death, and five of them bustled about the kitchen making food, sending messages for supplies, tidying the rooms, and comforting the grieving mother. I hardly recognized any of them. As I entered the front hall, one pressed a plate of food into my hands, and another took my coat to hang by the stove. I gave thanks to each and found Mr. Fish in the library, trying desperately to make arrangements for the retrieval of Jess' body and the organizing of her burial.

"The constable returned with news," he said to me as I sat by the window to eat my dinner, "They are looking for a short man in a green coat."

I swallowed my bite of cheese. "What?"

"He's already informed his superiors," Mr. Fish replied, "Bloody marvelous, to have such a lead already, don't you agree? I had my doubts, but it seems a bright man like Constable Grange may be the best man for the job."

"Did he say anything more?"

"Not to me, no," Mr. Fish replied, "But he said you were very good with identifying Jess." He lowered his head to his letters. "And he said you were very brave and only cried a little."

The nerve!

The sound of a pebble striking the window woke me from my sleep—the first good night's sleep I'd had in weeks. Groggy, I dragged myself from the creaking bed and shuffled to the window, where I had a clear view of the garden and alleyway.

A familiar silhouette stood in the moon shadow of the oak tree.

I dressed hurriedly in trousers and shirt, but waited until I reached the back door to pull on my boots. I slipped silently down the stairs and across the garden.

Shao reached out and took my hand. "Xi told me," he said. "Jess, murdered?"

"Saturday night."

"*Zao gao*," he whispered, "A robbery?"

"I don't think so," I replied as we fell into step with each other. Hand in hand, we walked slowly along the alley southward, towards the Dallas Roadway and the seashore. In the dark, there was no need for propriety. His grip felt solid, warm, comfortable. "The police assumed robbery because she had no purse on her person, but I doubt she ever did—Jess had only gone a few blocks, and didn't intend to stay out for long. But the gold necklace was still around her throat, and a robber would've taken that for sure. And there's more: she was pregnant. Four months at least."

"Who's the father?"

I shook my head. "I don't know."

"This is nasty business," he muttered, and looked askance at me. "But you look much improved."

"I was sleeping," I replied. "I ate a good dinner tonight."

"This murder … it's not dredging up old wounds?"

I looked up at him. He did not seem angry, or accusatory. He regarded me openly and honestly, and my heart warmed. "You mean, Violet's death? No. No, I am quite fine." I swallowed. "I think I may feel useful again. It does a soul good, to have a purpose."

"All you need to cure your ills is a little murder."

"I am quite a bad person, aren't I."

He did not answer, except to wrap his arms around me and kiss me on the forehead.

We walked as far as the ocean and sat for a while on the shoreline, speaking quietly to each other. A stiff, cold breeze had blown the clouds away, and the stars twinkled high above in a sky that was crisp and clear. We'd chosen a spot that was close to the scrub-covered bluffs, partially sheltered from the wind by the curve of land. He wore a sweater, I wore my wool coat, so that tucked under his arm I felt more comfortable than I had in a long time. The world was filled with only Shao and me and the wide, welcoming ocean. I told him all I knew of Jess' murder, from visiting Eleanor to my encounter with Will, and finished with a scowl. "And to top it off, the constable is taking my deductions as his own. Blasted thief!

Telling Mr. Fish that the murderer is a short man in a green coat, and that I cried when I saw the body—blast him!" I picked up a pebble and lobbed it into the sea, where it vanished with a plop.

"You're too quick to prove yourself clever, Liz," Shao laughed.

"Are you suggesting that I ought to keep my mouth shut?" I replied, insulted.

He held me a fraction tighter. "No, I'm not saying that. I'm only suggesting you practise a bit of discretion." He leaned closer, pressing his head to mine. "And as for crying … well, perhaps Grange was trying to make you sound more caring, to save your reputation from yourself."

I fumed a little over this.

"Who do you think the short man is?"

"I don't know," I replied, feeling sour. "And who's to say it was a green coat? It could've been a pair of socks, or a scarf, or any number of things … there's not yet enough evidence to jump to that sort of conclusion!"

"I'm impressed that you looked at Jess' body and could tell that she was with child. How'd you learn that sort of trick?"

"Emma Briggs shared with me a few of her secrets."

"The doctor's wife? You seemed to slip into her confidences quickly."

I gave a shrug. "I think I could count her as a friend, given time." I tossed another pebble in the sea. "She reminds me of Violet, except she's sensible."

Shao grinned, but there was a taint of sadness about the expression, too. "You have taken the whole loss of your sister with … with …"

"Enviable fortitude?" Others had said as much. "Please. You know me better than that."

He shifted uncomfortably. "Do you feel any sorrow at Violet's death?"

I lowered my chin. "Deep inside, yes. I think so." I winced at my own answer, knowing as soon as I said it, it wasn't the right thing to say. "I'm not like others. I have … deficiencies. I want to feel everything that other's feel, but sometimes, I don't know how."

"What about us?"

I raised my face to him. "I miss you. I know that." And then, before my brain even consented to admit it, my mouth said, "I love you."

"You do?"

I nodded.

He planted a kiss on my forehead and held me close.

After a while, he added, "Maybe they aren't deficiencies in your character, Liz; you've already put your fearlessness to good use. I mean, there aren't many young women who could face a corpse without being frightened or fainting."

"Well," I said, growing pensive, "Aren't I lucky."

"But you have to be careful, please be careful. We've made it this far, but I don't know what I'd do if—"

A skitter of pebbles came from behind us, sliding down the bluff. We both turned quickly in our seats.

"Hello?" Shao said sharply.

No reply.

I grabbed a stick from the beach and stood up to face the bushes. "Who's there?"

The only reply was the sound of the waves, the shudder of the wind through the leaves, and the distant sound of horses' hooves on a street far above us. Thick knots of brambles and dense ferns covered the top of the bank. I wager it would've been impossible for someone to climb down without a great amount of noise, movement, and probably curses.

Far above us, far away, the sound of hooves grew faint and vanished. James Bay fell silent. The water continued to lap at the beach and another gust of wind played amongst the leaves.

I listened and heard nothing.

"Maybe a cat," said Shao warily. He stood, keeping his eyes on the top of the bluffs.

I did not easily cast off my suspicions. "Let's walk," I suggested.

He began wandering along the beach, and I lingered a moment, but there was no further sound. I lowered the stick and followed him, skidding slightly on the loose gravel.

When I caught up to Shao, I took his hand in mine. "You know, the constable said Jess was tangled in the fishing nets off McLoughlin Point."

He looked down at me. "And?"

"Well," I said, "I can't help but wonder why she was killed there. That's a far distance from home."

Shao lifted his gaze across the black water. On the other side of the harbor, McLoughlin Point created a shadowy finger of rocks pointing south towards the Strait of Juan de Fuca. "What was she be doing there?"

"And how did she get there, after Will's party?"

Together, standing side by side, we studied the point.

"Someone took her by carriage?" said Shao.

"Maybe. But who?"

Another long pause stretched between us.

I looked up at him. "Fancy a walk?"

He laughed as he held up one foot, displaying his battered, scuffed boot. "*Ai ye,* Liz, have you seen my shoes? I'll wear the soles right through if I walk that far! Besides," he grinned, and I thought again how handsome he was, his smile flashing in the starlight, "That's a long hike around the harbor … across James Bay Bridge, through Chinatown, all the way to Bay Street, then over the Work Street Bridge—and that won't even take us half way there." He shook his head. "It'll be mid-morning by the time we reach McLoughlin Point."

"We'll hire a hansom."

"Ah, won't that inspire questions!" he laughed, "And I don't know about you, but my finances are a little slim for hiring carriages!"

I looked up the beach, casting my thoughts for any idea, when a rounded shape above the high tide line caught my eye, only a few hundred feet away. It looked like a beached whale basking in the moonlight.

"I have an idea."

He followed me and, setting his eyes upon the red skiff, shook his head. "Are you crazy? I don't know anything about boats!"

I feigned disappointment. "No? I didn't think you knew how to dance, either. You're full of surprises, Shao; I figured you might have a few more secrets up your sleeves."

"We can't steal a boat, Liz."

"We're not stealing. We'll bring it back," I said. "Now hurry, help me tip it upright, and we can carry it down to the water."

We managed to move the rowboat to the shore, and together we slipped it into the black sea. It was our good fortune to find that the owner had set the oars underneath the boat to keep them dry, and I put them in as Shao took a seat by the stern. The boat was only big enough for two, and it bobbed on the waves like a spirited pony, derelict and ragged but eager to slip away to the high seas. I held the rope at the bow, my feet planted on the shore, and leaned back to keep it from escaping.

"Will it stay afloat?"

"The only thing keeping it together is the paint," said Shao as he studied the craft for any sprung leaks.

"Do you swim?"

"I can. You?"

I shook my head. "Not really."

He furrowed his brow. "Having second thoughts?"

"No, no," I replied, "I just wanted to know: if the thing flips, will we both die, or only me."

"Are you still sure it's a good idea?"

I swung my leg over and the boat scooted away from shore, and I clumsily fell to my bottom. "Right," I said, "Let's get on our way."

With only a little fuss we soon found ourselves bobbing on the tide, each of us pulling an oar.

"Together!" he said, "Or we'll go in circles! One, two, one, two—"

As we began to work in unison, the little boat shunted along the water, and soon we were gliding across the waves. I glanced to the shore and thought, for the briefest moment, that a figure stood in the shadows of the cliffs. I opened my mouth to tell Shao, but a high wave tossed the light craft upwards. “Steady, steady,” he said, adjusting his seat so that the boat stayed level. “Alright, on my mark,” he replied, and after a pause, said, “Pull!”

By the time I could look to shore again, the beach was deserted.

Sixteen

November 1, 1898

We pulled hard but the tide conspired against us. By the time the rowboat scraped the rocks of McLoughlin Point, beads of sweat soaked my collar and the sky in the east was brightening.

"Perhaps it … would've been faster … if we'd walked," I panted.

Shao crawled from the boat and lay down on the hard stones, holding his side and struggling to catch an even breath.

"*Zao gao*!" he wheezed, throwing one arm over his face.

"Your rib?" I asked.

He nodded.

I left him to recover and climbed the rocks at the end of McLoughlin Point to survey the promontory. Like any spot that's exposed to constant wind, the shoreline was bare of lush vegetation, but a few sprigs of tough grass sprouted through the rocks and gorse bushes clung to the highest point with determined roots. White splotches of gull droppings splattered the crags, and at its highest part, the cliff loomed twenty feet or more over the tide line. Around the tip of the land, large boulders poked their noses from under the choppy water, and atop the cliff, the exposed granite bedrock provided a hard, unwelcome surface. Wherever dirt had collected, in the cracks and fractures, it was yellow-brown and full of clay. The grey Pacific Ocean stretched south and west, and as the daylight grew, a bank of woolly fog was moving offshore and obscured any view farther than a few miles. Turning my back to the sea, I looked north across fields of grasses and scrubby bushes.

Farmland stretched to the northwest. A herd of cows grazed in the pastures, and I heard the bleating of sheep in the still air. A low mist covered the land, turning the distant barns into dark square shapes against a murky gloom, but the wind now rising off the water would soon sweep it and the fog bank away. A straight dirt footpath skirted the farms and led directly north towards the barracks of a naval base on the western edge of Victoria Harbor, almost a mile away, and visible from this vantage as a cluster of stubby brick buildings.

Shao stood and stretched his side, and waited at the base of the cliff. "There's nothing here, Liz," he called up to me. "Nothing but bare trees and a couple of cows."

I surveyed the shoreline. It curved into the shallow depression of Rose Bay and, just offshore, the little hump of Work Island poked up like the round nose of a petrified hippo. I dropped my gaze to the coastline closer to us, and noticed the tips of thin wooden poles breaking the surface of the waves: these must be the fishing weirs where Jess was found. They were constructed of supple saplings, driven in precise rows into the mud offshore, and some still had nets strung between them. Three of the poles, closest to the point, had snapped off at the level of the water's surface.

I hopped down the stones to the edge of the bay.

"Do you think this is where she was snagged?" said Shao.

"They're the only ones broken, and they don't look like they'd support a person's weight."

Then, more to the landscape than to me, Shao asked, "Why, of all places, would Jess come here?"

I climbed back to the path. 'Think, Liz,' I prompted myself, "Think of it as a play, and recreate the scene. How must it have looked when her body was discovered?'

Boot prints scuffed the dirt. The marks of horse hooves marred the verge, and at first I thought this might be where she was dumped, but a closer inspection changed my mind. To start, the hoof prints were immediately across from the broken poles, the shortest distance possible from the body to the shore; I doubted any murderer would select the spot so precisely. He would drag her and dump her, and pay no attention to distance, but whomever had stopped here had chosen this spot because it was the closest to where the weirs had snagged the body.

I spotted the remains of broken netting and wood, tiny fibers that scattered the dust. I crouched down, and without touching them, saw that they overlay the hoof prints and wheel ruts.

No, I decided, this was where the police dragged her out, not where her killer put her in. I stood up and gazed across the bay, north along the shore, to the rocks and twisted, stunted trees.

"We need to find where she was dumped to the water," I said, "That might lend us a clue."

For a whole hour, we scoured the rocks, scrambling up the boulders and peering at tangles of tree roots. I saw no more evidence of anything moving from dry land to sea, other than light footprints in the thin soil of the men who checked the nets. No furrows, no body prints in the soil, no blood from Jess' wounds.

By the time the sun was a hand span in the sky, I decided this quest was folly. "God's teeth," I muttered, "There's nothing here. It's like she fell from the sky."

Shao sat on a root, massaging his sore hands. "We've been here for ages, Liz. Don't you think we ought to return the boat?"

Then I saw a group of ten or twelve men walking towards us, down the long dusty road between the farms. They wore old work shirts and canvas pants, and each man carried a woven basket of cedar bark, slung over his shoulder with a wide woven strip. Their hats were conical with a flat top, woven of bark too, and designed to provide protection from rain and sun. These were the Songhees men, of whom Constable Grange had spoken.

"Not just yet," I said.

As I walked towards them, they looked at us with surprise, and no wonder: both Shao and I were sweaty, dirty, and rumpled. But the oldest man held up his hand in a cautious, friendly greeting.

"Good morning," I greeted him.

He was guarded, wary, and dressed in a flannel shirt and patched dungarees with a cape of woven cedar bark covering his shoulders. He was perhaps thirty years of age, but with a face that was heavily scarred and ravaged by smallpox, and when he removed his hat, silver streaked his thick black hair. His mouth was broad. When he smiled, the expression was quick and cautious and swiftly hidden. Like the women selling fish along the harbor, he did not warm easily to strangers, but he was accommodating, too, and the appearance of a sweaty, salt-encrusted girl at this barren point of land was more than a little curious. The only way to find out what I was doing was to ask, plain and simple.

"Why are you here?"

"I'm looking at the nets. Are they yours?"

A palpable sense of aggression filled the air.

He spoke slowly and carefully, weighing the word. "Why?"

"I was told that a woman was found, caught in one." I pointed to the nearest poles. "Those broken ones, over there: was that where she was tangled?"

The men standing behind him lowered their gazes. A couple of them turned away. "We found her yesterday," said a young man in a blue shirt.

"It was a grim catch. It brings bad fortune." said another. "We shoulda just set her adrift." A third man hit him hard in the shoulder.

The sense of aggression was quickly replaced by one of embarrassment.

"That's no way to speak, Billy," said the oldest with the cedar cape, and he gave an apologetic shake of his head. He spoke thoughtfully, his voice low in respect. "Look, girl, we've had trouble with the law. They're saying our nets need to be pulled down, that they're a nuisance. Finding that girl just gives the officials one more excuse to rip out the nets themselves." He set his jaw. "But this, this is how we eat through the winter. We aren't about to pull 'em down, that's for damn sure."

"We're not here to remove anything," said Shao, "But Lizzie knew the girl you found."

"There's nothing more of her here. The police took it all, and broke half the poles as they did it."

"So you found her around this same hour?" I replied.

"Round 'bout the same time, yeah."

But Billy stepped forward. "Naw, it was earlier. We were up just b'fore the sun rose. 'Member, the fish boats were just heading out?"

A brief, heated discussion began, some in English and some in a lyrical, expressive language that sounded stuttered to my ear. A few of the men added their own opinions—earlier, later, before dark, after the sun was up. There were hand gestures, chins nodding, a consensus reached. The man with silver hair listened, nodding, and finally turned to me.

"Yeah, Billy's right, we saw 'em passing," said the older man. "They had their torches lit. Sparks from the boilers. Dark sky. Maybe it was closer to 5 am."

We thanked them, and Shao and I put to sea again and rowed, and this time the tide was with us. We flew across the waves as the tide began to empty the harbor into the strait. We jumped out of the boat into freezing, knee-high water and pulled the craft ashore on the Dallas waterfront almost half a mile east of where we'd found it. From the ocean, we'd caught sight of the owner, fretting about its loss, along with the outline of two police officers taking the details of his theft. If they saw us, I didn't stay to find out. We sprinted up the pebbled beach and vanished through the ferns to the main roads of James Bay before the trio of men could race the distance and catch us.

When we arrived back at Mr. Fish's home, the house was as still as a tomb. Mr. Fish had already left to attend to his lobbying, and Mrs. Garry was likely taking solace in the home of a friend, for she was reluctant to stay in the house by herself.

Coals smoldered in the oven, and I roused them into a hot fire. When the iron skillet was ready, I made us both a hearty breakfast from the larder, setting out plates of eggs, sausages, and bread fried in beef fat on the kitchen table. Together we sat in silence, feeding a hunger that had been made enormous by all of our rowing. When we'd each sopped up our egg yolks with the last of the bread, we sat and discussed the scene we'd examined, reliving each detail and discussing how a murderer could kill a woman, dump her corpse, and leave her in the water with nary a trace of blood or violence.

My heart was happier than it had been in more than a month.

"He must've surprised Jess," said Shao, reclining in the wooden chair. "Maybe it was done quickly?"

"But her wounds were not the kind that kill swiftly," I mused. "Until her head was bashed, she would've fought and struggled, and she would've bled gallons of blood."

Shao winced. I spoke too plainly for him. He'd not known Jess as well as I had, but he still felt her loss more keenly than me.

"When Violet was killed—" Shao began, then hesitated, looking uncomfortable.

"You can ask me, I don't mind." I licked the last of the grease from my fingers as I brought to mind the scene of my own sister's death. No, that's not entirely true. I brought to mind the site of Mr. Kelly's death, for Violet had been killed in my father's workshop. But no one knew that detail, and I was content to keep it that way.

I wiped my fingers on the hem of my shirt. "At the lake side, there was blood, everywhere. The earth had been churned into mud, there was so much of it! And then it had dried again in the August sun."

I did not mention that it had been Mr. Kelly's blood, and that I'd found his corpse high in the tree, hanging from a branch, his throat slit by my father.

"The truth is, Shao, that when a body is ruptured, it makes a horrible mess. We hold a lot of fluids inside our bag of skin, and once they begin to flow, it's hard to stop. So whomever stabbed poor Jess in the abdomen must've had to contend with a great deal of evidence, and yet there's none to be seen on the rocks or the soil at McLoughlin Point."

He looked a bit green at my description, but he said, "There's been plenty of rain—"

"But the dirt would've held onto the red, and the roots of the trees would've been covered. No rain would wash away such a porous surface. There would certainly be—"

I stopped. I was a fool.

"Damn!" I slammed the flat of my palm on the table. Shao jumped. "She wasn't killed there. But nor was she dumped there, either. We were looking to the land for clues, Shao, when we ought to have been looking to the sea!"

His eyebrows arched. "She washed up!"

"She was dumped on this side of the harbor, and she snagged on the nets with the drift of the tide. Think about it: it was perilously difficult for us to row across the neck of the harbor last night!"

Massaging his shoulder, he said, "You don't need to tell me."

"If the tide could keep us from moving west easily, then the pull of the water could certainly carry her. We only have to work out the pattern of the tides, and we can trace back the most likely route she'd drifted."

"Oh, that's all?" he said sarcastically.

"Come on, hurry up," I urged him. "We need to speak to someone who knows more about the ocean than you and me."

Seventeen

The shipyards off Erie Street were a gritty place, but not in a way that spoke of poverty or desperation. The men here were unfamiliar with a classical education but they were highly skilled, talented craftsmen, and they took great pride in their creations. Shao and I paused at the brick wall that separated the yard from the street, and I took a moment to assess the place. A wide expanse of gravel and sand, crossed with wooden beams and neat piles of seasoned timbers, ended at a series of wharves. A range of boats lay in docks at the edge, where a cove gave a sheltered berth from the wider traffic of Victoria's Inner Harbor: white dories, a large grey fishing boat, a bark with its rigging removed. Teams of men crawled over the larger commercial ships, while pairs worked on the smaller vessels. The sound of hammers striking metal rang in the still morning air.

"Who do we ask?" said Shao, and I could tell from the tone of his voice that he thought this a mad endeavor. He was tired, sore, and growing cranky. His sweater was damp with seawater, his pants were soaked from the waves. Neither one of us had slept much, but instead of tired, I felt invigorated. Shao, obviously, did not suffer from the same inspiration as me.

"I'm sure anyone here knows more about the flow of the sea than us." I waved at a stout, middle-aged man standing alongside a dinghy, who had stopped working to stretch his back. "Hello there! Hi! Can you spare a moment?"

The worker wandered over, and as he neared, he peeled back his red cap to scratch his bald head. He had a broad, craggy face speckled with moles, and a big nose that hooked like the beak of a hawk. When he spoke, his words jumped up and down, with an accent that was both musical and guttural—a man of Cornwall, I supposed, though he'd been living in the colonies for quite some time. He greeted me directly, but barely gave Shao a passing glance.

"Hullo, missy? What can I do for you?"

"I have an odd question, and I wondered if you might help me. Do you know much about the tides?"

He gave a great guffaw, and I saw he was missing two teeth. One had been replaced by an ivory peg, but it was the wrong size for his mouth and appeared childishly tiny next to his huge, square incisors. "Ya, that I do! What would you be needing to know?"

"The current running past McLoughlin Point—where does it come from?"

"Well, now, that would depend on the how the tides a-running," he said, "And the time of day, like."

"Perhaps, last Saturday night, close to midnight?"

He scratched his head, then turned to one of the nearest foremen. "Oi, Pete, what d'ya think about the running of the harbor last Saturday? Was she ebb tide 'round about midnight?"

The man paused and picked at his teeth in thought. "Maybe, Jory, could be. Why?"

"This lass is askin'."

"I think it might've been. Highest point was probably 'round 12:30 or so, and this time o' year, she's flowing out until the tide turns, 'round about 6 in the morn."

"See?" I said to Shao, "We struggled to cross the harbor last night because the current was flowing out to sea."

"And Jess was found about five, so she'd come from farther up the harbor."

"But how far?" I mused.

"Depends how long she were in the water," said Jory as he settled his cap onto the back of his head, "You talkin' bout the lass found down by the point? Yeah, we've already heard—news travels fast around the bay." He gave a boom of a laugh, flashing that peg tooth.

"She was last seen about one in the morning," I said.

"Cor, might've been a ways I figure, then," he said, "Though the current is strongest from the inner harbor out around the point. It can pull you right out into the strait, if you're not careful."

A thought occurred. "If Jess was dumped on this side of the harbor—"

"She'd've gone straight across," Pete nodded, then said added, "Jory here dropped his cap in the brink off the shipyard here."

"Oh, aye!" he said, "Bloody thing washed up on Work Island. Lucky me, it's one helluva ugly cap."

"That's for sure," laughed his friend. "Ugly as a cat's arse."

"So no one else had one like it," Jory added, as if this benefit had been planned. "So yeah, the lass might've come from this side of the harbor.

Wouldn't surprise me."

"These shipyards, at night—"

But Pete saw where my mind was going, and he shook his head. "We've been finishing up a number of big contracts b'fore winter, and there's always workers here," he interrupted. "I'll ask around the lads what were here, but I was working on Saturday night, and I didn't see nothing out of the ordinary."

I thanked them as they returned to their work. We began walking down Belleville Street, past the big white houses overlooking the harbor, towards the pedestrian bridge.

Before long, we reached the low stone wall that circled the new legislative buildings. The old buildings, nicknamed 'The Birdcages', had been notoriously drafty and cold, so the government had raised funds and begun construction of new buildings in 1893, and they had hired the esteemed Mr. Rattenbury to design something regal and noteworthy. He'd devised a neo-Baroque building, made of rough-hewn granite, that combined British Columbia's rich resources with the classical aesthetic of the British Empire. The Birdcages remained, but now they looked dilapidated and rustic and pathetic next to their grand replacement.

Shao sat next to me on the stone wall, our backs to the new buildings. There would be lawns here, I suppose, but for now the land between the street and the legislative building was a long tract of mud, so that the pavilions of white marble, the stone arches and statues, and the central rotunda topped with a gleaming copper dome, all seemed to squat in the dirt. We faced the muddy harbor and the long, slender James Bay Bridge. The Songhees women were just arriving in canoes, and I watched as they set up their mats and baskets of fish.

"She might've gone no farther than William's house," I mused. "It makes sense. She had no money, she needed to get home …"

He stifled a yawn. "I'm exhausted."

"Really?" I said, "We're just getting started."

He glared me in frank disbelief. "I've got to go, Liz."

"Why?"

"I'm needed at the shop, and Mr. Lim will already have a million questions why I didn't come back to the apartment last night. I'll tell him I spent the night at one of the gambling dens, that'll make him happy …" He scrubbed one hand over his eyes. "But my arms ache, my clothes are covered with salt, there's sand in my hair … and what the hell do you mean by 'just getting started'?"

"Well, I'm not going to be able to find the murderer by sitting in Mr. Fish's parlor, am I!"

Shao did not protest, as I thought he might, but instead rolled his eyes.

"What?"

"Leave policing to Constable Grange, Liz."

"And you trust him to do a good job?"

He glared at me, but he said nothing.

"You, with your short hair …"

"What's that got to do with it?"

He knew exactly what I meant, but I wasn't afraid to explain it in plain terms. "You told me the opium runners cut their hair short—in the European style, I think you called it—because the police have a habit of grabbing men by their queues to catch them when they run during a den raid. And because your hair is short, through no fault of your own, you've said the police don't trust you."

"And this has what to do with Jess' murder?"

I leaned close. "I don't trust the police, Shao. They seem to be everywhere in this city, yet still the law is broken, again and again. If my experience with Constable Grange is any indication, they're a bunch of incompetent, self-aggrandizing, backstabbing buffoons, who couldn't find their own buttocks with both hands and an oil lamp."

"*Ai ye*, Liz, could you say that a little louder?" he jabbed, then tipped his head in the direction of the walkway. "I think the constable crossing the bridge might be interested in your opinion."

"There are only two people that I'm confident can solve this murder." I tapped my finger against his chest. "You and me."

He smiled at me. Suddenly, we were partners again—not two individuals building lives in different parts of a city, separated by the gulf of different cultures. We were a team.

"When can I see you again?" he asked.

My heart soared. "Tonight. Meet me at the Ross Bay cemetery, in the Jewish quarter."

He held my hand and squeezed my fingers. Then he stood and walked briskly away, never looking back, across the James Bay Bridge towards downtown. I loved that about him. He never lingered; he was decisive. I watched as he followed the street and, eventually, disappeared in the crush of people and wagons as the city rumbled fully awake. I sat on the fence as I watched him go, and I tried to figure why Jess would not come straight home after her performance. The route from William Carter's house to Mr. Fish's would have taken Jess directly through the community of James Bay, and nowhere near the water's edge. So where did she go?

But as I pondered this, a particular tingling on the back of my neck appeared.

I do not believe in ghosts. If I did, I'd certainly be afraid of all the ones that follow me, but my father taught me that there are no spirits of the dead to haunt us. So, the shiver that crossed down my spine came, not from a goose crossing my grave or some such superstitious poppycock, but the sensation of being watched.

I did not look up. With the bevy of workmen behind me and a bustling harbor before me, I knew I was in no danger. No one would be so foolish as to attack a defenseless girl in the morning sunlight, surrounded by passersby who could come to her aid. But the longer I sat, the more certain I became. I may not believe in ghosts, but I trust my intuition.

I examined my shoe, as if something was amiss with the sole. I took it off, straddled the wall and under the guise of studying my stocking foot, I looked askance at the roadway. Everyone was in a state of movement. If I was being watched, it was not from the street. Oh! Clumsy me! I dropped my shoe and it fell into the yard. I half-turned in my seat and reached over the stone wall, casting a quick glance in that direction.

At the beginning of the row of white houses, on the other block and facing the harbor, sat a grand building. It was two stories high, with a rotunda at the far end and a glass conservatory at the side. I supposed it to be the local residence of some government official—not the premier or his ministers, for they resided in the lush homes of the Rockland neighbourhood, only a short carriage ride to the east. Perhaps it was the Speaker of the Legislative Assembly, or a successful businessman with his fingers in all sorts of government contracts. To be sure, whomever lived inside had a love of gardens, or at least the money to hire an army of gardeners. Surrounded by Doric columns and stained glass accents, the house possessed a wide verandah decorated with a wicker lattice screen. In summer, the screen would be covered with clematis vines, but in autumn, it was bare of foliage, though it still gave the verandah a bit of privacy from the wagons and pedestrians on Belleville Street.

A shape moved behind the lattice, little more than a shadow. It could've been a rug hung to dry, moving in the breeze. It could've been a man, standing still and watching me.

I pulled my shoe back on, tied my laces, and began a leisurely walk eastward along the harbor. But instead of following the road across the James Bay Bridge, I turned right, up Bird Cage Walk and towards Beacon Hill Park.

From my rambles, I knew that a small path between two houses joined Bird Cage Walk with the northern end of Carr Street. It was never easy to navigate, because the owners had used it as a place to store old crates and barrels. It was, however, a fine spot for someone of my size to squeeze through. Perhaps the debris would slow down a pursuer, and give them no place to hide. If they followed, they'd find themselves flushed into a trap.

I stared straight ahead as I walked. I dared not give the impression that I suspected his presence, but the tingling on the back of my neck remained, and I was almost certain I had a follower. There were many people about, enjoying the fine morning. Only a few of them paid me any attention, and those that did looked over my messy hair, salty clothes, and muddy trousers with a disdainful sneer. At a street corner, a nun stopped me to press a coin into my hand. She patted my head and blessed me, and reminded me that God loves all His children, especially those who are poverty-stricken and homeless.

By the end of Bird Cage Walk, I was certain I knew my pursuer's identity. William Carter would not have taken my assault lightly. If, upon waking with a dashing hangover, he remembered our conversation, he'd certainly want to even the score between us. A man of his caliber would be mightily embarrassed to sport a bruise on his crown from a mug to the head. That embarrassment would triple with the knowledge that it had been thrown by a girl.

Here was the narrow fissure. Without looking over my shoulder, I dashed down the path, under bowers of laurel leaves and leaf-bare rose bushes. The alley took me between a garden shed and an outhouse, then into the warren of crates, boxes, and cast-off lumber. I scrambled quickly over and through. My pants snagged on a nail, a sliver bit into my palm, but I wriggled past the obstacles and ran to the end of the alley and dodged left. I pressed my shoulder to the corner of the carriage shed, and looking back, had a clear view of the detritus. I waited to see William pluck his way through.

But nobody followed. I stood and watched and waited for almost ten minutes, and I won't lie, I was terribly disappointed. I peeked through the bins to the alley beyond, and it was empty. Either he'd realized I'd seen him, or I'd been too quick and lost him.

Or, I suppose, there might've been no one there at all.

EIGHTEEN

The house was quiet but not empty. Mr. Fish had returned from his morning meetings, and he sipped Earl Grey tea in his study as he pondered some stuffy pile of papers. He looked up as I came in the front door, and the expression on his face reminded me of someone standing too close to a gun blast: startled and afraid.

I suppose bad news had recently come through this very door, and he anticipated more.

"By the saints," he muttered, "Thank goodness it's just you, Liz."

"How is Mrs. Garry?"

"Not well, I'm afraid." He folded his hands, shook his head sadly. "She's taking time to collect herself at the home of Isa Simms. I can't stand that Simms woman, frightful bore, but if she can give Eddy a bit of companionship, then I suppose she's got some worth." He squared the pile of papers and said, "Constable Grange returned this morning, just after breakfast."

"He did?" I said, taking a seat on the sofa. "Why?"

"I hoped you might know. He asked after you, and said he had a few more questions for you."

"Well, I have a few more for him, too," I replied, then yawned. "But I'm afraid I ought to catch a bit of sleep, as I've been up most of the night."

"Alone?"

"With Shao."

His eyebrows arched.

"No," I replied to his unspoken inquiry, "Just walking and talking."

And stealing boats, and scouring the ground for dried blood, and dodging a stalker. But I thought it best to leave those out.

"Well, that sounds positively proper," he replied with an impish smirk, then the mirth left his expression and he said, "Do not think me presumptuous,

Liz, but do you think it's wise for a girl to be out at a time like this? There is a murderer roaming the streets." He shook his hands, dismissing his own comment. "I know, I know, I'm meddling in your affairs, and I promised I would do no such thing, but allow me at least to be concerned for your safety. Mr. Chen is welcome in this house, and provided you're discreet upon leaving, I'm happy to turn a blind eye to his visits. Wouldn't it be safer for you to meet here?"

I did like Mr. Fish, very much, and instead of being insulted by his worry, I was touched that he'd be concerned for me. God knows, with my family dead and few friends to call my own, there was hardly anyone left who would show me any compassion. "I appreciate your good sense, sir. Consider it noted."

"And promptly ignored," he read from my expression, and gave me a weary smile.

"Do you or Eddy know the boy that Jess was seeing?" I asked.

He shook his head at the question. "No, no, but it wasn't the first time she'd slipped away in the middle of the night," he replied. "Eddy was too furious to speak with Jess about it—she simply forbade Jess from seeing him, which made the girl more rebellious. I suspect he was a fellow of some means, though."

"Why?"

"The gold cross that Jess wore? He gave it to her."

I raised my eyebrows at this. "When?"

"Only a few months ago." He shook his head. "But leave these matters to the police, my dear. You're a girl of high spirits—it's one of the things I like best about you. It would break my heart if those high spirits landed you in trouble."

Perhaps it was the way his concern had warmed my heart, or maybe it was the fatigue that broke down any barrier between us, but I quickly stepped forward and planted a kiss on his papery old forehead. "Thank you, very much, for all you've done, sir."

I'd never seen Mr. Fish so flustered, and as I retreated up the stairs to grab an hour's rest, I raised a hand to my mouth to stifle a laugh.

A delicate touch on my shoulder woke me.

"Lizzie, dear," said Emma's soft voice, "Lizzie, are you awake?"

She sat at the edge of my bed, wearing a blue wool dress and fine hat trimmed with jet beads and white feathers. A muff of white fur sat at her side, and she wore a matching stole of fur around her shoulders. The sun slanted in the small window from the west, casting a warm glow over my room.

"What time is it?" I stammered, still half asleep.

"Almost three," she said gently, "Mr. Fish says you've slept most of the afternoon."

I rose to my elbows. "What are you doing here?"

She answered my question with a giggle. "Liz, why can't you stay on the main floor? It would be so much easier for me to reach you, and you deserve a bigger room than this one! At least something with a nice Persian carpet on the floor, or some artwork on the walls!" She removed the stole from her shoulders and set it with the muff, and I imagined that she must've been sweltering under so many layers, after climbing the stairs to the attic.

Emma rocked back and withdrew her hat pin, and set her hat on the bed. "Better yet," she continued, "Come stay with me, where I can jealously keep you to myself! Mr. Franklin-Milne has gone home to Vancouver, and Mr. McMurdo will be leaving soon enough for Eastern Canada, and you can have our guest quarters. A big double bed with down pillows, all for yourself, and a private entrance onto the garden." She gave a huff as she took a fortifying breath and primped her hair. "I'm sure Mr. Fish is an adequate host, but looking after the guests is a woman's responsibility, and I know I'd do a much better job than him!"

"Climbing all those stairs," I said, "You're going to bring on labor!"

"Good," she replied, laying one hand on the swell of her stomach, "I'm tired of hauling about this belly!"

I crooked myself up on my elbows. "It's too early, Emma. You're only six months along."

She smiled sweetly as she smoothed my hair back with her fingers. Her eyes twinkled. "Can you keep a secret?"

I snapped awake. "Of course!"

"Your father was a doctor, yes? You've had some medical training?" She lowered her voice. "Do I not look a little more advanced than six months?"

Her question hit me like a slap. Bloody hell, she was right.

"When you and Mason married ..." I let the question trail away, unspoken.

She nodded. "It's a good match, and I'm happy to be his wife, but yes, our marriage was a very quick affair. Thankfully, my wedding dress covered the bloating."

I threw my arms around her with a laugh. "So," I counted in my head, "November? Any day?"

"The doctors insist that I am at the end of my second trimester, but my parents are sure that the baby will be quite robust and advanced for its age." She rolled her eyes. "It will be any day now."

Eight-month pregnancies were quite common, as were seven. The medical establishment even held that a six-month pregnancy was possible, if only to save everyone's dignity. I supposed a two-month gestation might even be accepted, if the family was wealthy, powerful, and God had thrown a miracle their way.

"Then why are you here?" I implored, "Mason was right, you shouldn't be out visiting! You ought to be home!"

Her chin trembled. "But I needed to come, Liz, to see if you're alright. With the housemaid murdered, and the house in turmoil, and my goodness, it's all so dreadful!" Her mouth pulled down, and a tear spilled down her cheek. "I did not know the girl, but I know Mr. Fish and I know you, and I wanted to give you both my condolences on her loss. What a horrible affair!"

I sat up, tried to tidy my rumpled nightgown, and watched as her pretty face contorted in grief. "It is," I agreed, and wondered again why I seemed so incapable of this basic, human emotion. How could people stand to be so fragile, especially at a time when their wits were needed most?

"I heard a rumor she was pregnant, too—is it true?"

"I'm afraid so."

"Is there no decency left in the world?"

Though the question had been rhetorical, I couldn't help answering.

"I don't think there ever was."

Emma set her chin and wiped the tears from her cheeks. "Is there anything I can do to assist you or Harris during these dark times?"

"You can help me!" I said, snapping my fingers. "You can tell me something. The dark line that run from your … um, your …" Oh, hell—decorum be damned. "From your navel to your vagina."

Emma's cheeks blushed a little. "Yes?"

"When did that appear?"

She thought. "At the end of the third month, I think."

"You knew you were pregnant, though."

"Oh yes, I'd known for at least a month, maybe more. Even my belly had gotten bigger by the time that line developed; I'd had to take my dresses out a bit. It was no surprise. Why?"

"Jess must've known she was with child, then," I mused. "Perhaps her paramour did as well."

Emma leaned close to me. "What do you suppose?"

"I'm trying to figure who would gain most from killing a pregnant woman, and I can't help wonder if the answer is as simple as 'the father'."

"Oh, vile business!" Emma gasped, and for a moment, she looked remarkably like Violet, all prim and proper and repulsed by the evil in the world. "But who is the father?"

I thought back to Jess and her social circle, only to find it remarkably narrow. A man of means, with money to pay for gifts … Perhaps, as a Sing Song Girl, she was seeing a client? There was one person who would know, and I was willing to wager it was the same woman who had altered Jessie's dress when her belly began to swell.

I sat down to tea with Mr. Fish and Emma, and the two of them fell to easy gossip about shared acquaintances, but my mind was occupied with other topics. I would find the father in the theatre, I was sure of it. Jess had no other social outlets.

But for all the trysts, dalliances and shenanigans that took place behind the theatre curtains, I couldn't figure with whom Jess would've coupled. She had been so shy, so disarming. I tried to imagine her stalking and pursuing a casual affair, but found the task impossible; besides, if her boy had given her the golden cross at her throat as a parting gift or passing trinket, would she bother to wear it? I wondered if the relationship had been more important to her than to him. She'd told me once there was a boy in her heart, but she'd put aside her feelings and poured herself into singing, and I thought she'd been successful.

Alfred the bricklayer? Perhaps. Or maybe Joseph Hali'eva? No, he was married, and had never shown much interest in any of the theatre girls. The General? The mere thought made me shudder.

Whomever Jess had loved, she'd been remarkably successful at wiping him from her life.

"Is your egg sandwich off?" said Mr. Fish to my expression.

"Hmm? Oh, no! Not at all. Quite good." I stammered, covering my thoughtful expression with a smile. With Eddy in the throes of mourning, Mr. Fish had made today's tea, and I didn't wish to insult him.

"She is deep in contemplation with the murder of Jess," said Emma, but not disdainfully, as Violet might have said. Her smile twinkled. "Our dear Liz is quite clever, Harris, and I think she may be onto a clue."

Mr. Fish rolled his eyes to Emma. "Don't encourage her, Emma."

"Why not?" she replied, "Why shouldn't we encourage a young woman with such a strong sense of loyalty and justice? I think it's marvelous."

I shifted uncomfortably in my seat. It was strange, to see these two people debate the merits of my task.

"Because this is dangerous," said Mr. Fish as he checked the teapot, "Both you and I know how ruinous this could be to Liz's reputation."

"What good is my reputation, sir, if it means I must sit down and be quiet and let the evil of the world win?"

He smiled at that, a warm proud paternal smile that was mismatched to his cantankerous features. "I respect your feistiness, Liz, but our reputation is all we have of value in the world. More than wealth or land, our reputation is what sustains us. And once it's gone, it can never be reclaimed."

"I don't give a whit for my reputation."

"But you may, one day," he said. "And you'll regret casting something so precious aside so lightly." He turned to Emma. "You know what I'm saying is true. Strip away the fantasy of an adventure, Emma, and you'll see that Liz is playing a dangerous game."

Emma looked sour and chastened. "But what if she actually finds the murderer?"

"Then she may well be next to meet the edge of his knife," Mr. Fish replied. "And none of us want that."

An uncomfortable silence descended.

"I can't help it," I said at last. "It's in my nature."

"Posh," Mr. Fish spat immediately. "We all have facets of our nature that we must restrain. You are no different than anyone else in that regard."

"But, my mother's madness—"

"—Does not run through the woman's bloodline. That's a pile of hogwash," he completed.

I reclined in my chair, tipped my chin down to think on this. What if the madness had been avoidable? What if my mother's odd obsessions could've been healed, if only she'd been able to leave my father and his crushing, murderous, blood-spattered desires? Maybe she wasn't mad at all, but a woman so cruelly constrained and restricted, so wracked with guilt and stifled passion, that her mind had fractured.

"Do you think so?"

"I do," said Mr. Fish. "And you could rebuild a life here, Liz, free of your grievous past, but only if you respect and use the reputation you have." He smiled to Emma. "We are here to help you, Liz. We are your friends and we do not judge you, but ask only that you tread carefully. Can I ask that of you?"

"I suppose."

Emma leaned close. "Don't worry, Liz. Neither one of us is asking you to change. Just," and she patted my hand, "Be discreet."

Mr. Fish laughed as he lifted the teapot. "And don't get killed. Here, Liz, my dear. Let me fill your cup."

Nineteen

After tea, I left Emma with Mr. Fish and hurried along the waterfront to the downtown core. The door to Mrs. Thornton's costume shop was locked and bolted, but I continued around the corner to the entrance to the Temple of Thespis and found her inside, supervising the hanging of background curtains. She looked pleased to see me, but as she ushered me to a more private area, her expression soured.

"What do you think you're doing, scaring Eleanor halfway to death?" she hissed. "She confronted me yesterday and said there was no way she'd perform again with the Sing Song Girls, now that Jessie's been murdered and folks are asking questions." She poked one long finger into my sternum. "Folks like you!"

"I said nothing to insinuate that she was involved."

"No, but her Madam doesn't take kindly to folks sniffing around her establishment, and Eleanor's now got to thinking she's going to lose her job and her home, all in one foul swoop!"

"So you'd rather I stop asking questions, and let Jessie's killer run free?"

She grimaced. "No, of course not. But you're a busy body, Miss Saunders, and no one takes kindly to folks who stick their nose where it doesn't belong."

And in a flash, I saw something in her face: a glimmer of fear.

"Do you know who killed Jess?"

She took affront, but too much. Her expression projected too much, her eyes were too wide. After all, Mrs. Thornton had been trained for the theatre, where facial expressions must be visible to every member of the audience, even those seated in the back row. Ever the skilled thespian, she had a tendency to overact in close quarters. "Well! I never! The thought that you'd accuse me!" Her hands flew to her breasts, her fingers clasped at the hollow her throat. "How dare you—"

"I'm not accusing you," I said calmly, "But you know something. You're hiding something—"

And like a clap of thunder, I suddenly understood. What was worth more than the world to dear Mrs. Thornton? What would she lie to protect? The answer was simple. "Andrew!"

She blanched. "No, you don't understand, my Andy didn't kill Jess—"

"But Andy and Jess …?"

"That boy!" she sighed, "He's a slave to his impulses! I swear, Liz, if I had a nickel for every theatre woman who's sweet-talked him into her clutches …"

Andy was a generous man, but naive and simple. I thought of how easy it had been to influence him; I had only to ask for his help hanging curtains or moving props, and he'd leap to my assistance. Though I'd never considered it before, the trait might run a little deeper than theatre tasks. With a well-aimed compliment and a winsome smile, he'd be putty, and if a woman wanted him in her thrall, she'd find the task very simple.

"So I keep him close. A mother must look after her son," she added. "The girls would run him to the ground, take all his savings, leave him penniless."

"And the baby was his?

Mrs. Thornton slumped against the wings of the stage. "Oh, glory," she whispered, her face falling slack. The simplicity of this expression marked it as true. "Oh, you know about that."

"So did you, apparently."

She looked out over the stage with haunted eyes. "We can't talk here." She grabbed my forearm. "The theatre ghosts will hear us. They're dreadful gossips."

"Did he know?"

"Of course he knew! He might be a man and a bit slow, but the signs were all there, and growing bigger every day." With my arm in her grip, she moved towards the back exit, to a wooden crate between coils of rope. Mrs. Thornton released her grip and collapsed in the seat. "But Andy didn't murder her, Liz." She pointed at me, accentuating her words with little jabs of her finger. "I know that, not because I'm his mother and I want to protect him, but because I saw how much he loved that girl. He'd never have done anything to hurt her." The tears began rolling down her cheeks, cutting valleys in her makeup. "But Edwina Garry would never let them marry, so they were going to elope. It was all planned."

"You knew this?"

"Knew it? Lordy, I paid for the trip! Two tickets for a steamer to San Francisco, departing the 12th of November, right after we closed up *The Duchess of Padua*. This was going to be Andy's last show with us. My sister's family lives in Marin County on a little farm, and she planned to set Andy up with a house and a bit of work, and they'd have been happy, forever and ever." Her throat hitched. "All three of 'em, a beautiful family with a bright future."

Suddenly, Jess' comment that I'd overheard made sense: Andy would not be auditioning for the December production, because he'd be settling to a new life in California.

"And Mrs. Garry knew this?"

"Goodness, no! She'd never let Jess go, would she!" Mrs. Thornton spat, "Jess was her only child. But she was killing Jess by keeping her here, never letting her out, never letting her sing." Mrs. Thornton's voice caught in the back of her throat as she dabbed at her eyes with the lace of her sleeve. "The poor girl was a withering flower before she came to us, before she met Andy." At last, her fortitude broke. She let out a rattling sob and buried her face in her hands.

Alerted by the sound, two of the men came down from the ladder, and Andy came around from the back of the stage, a hammer in one hand, grabbing for the handkerchief in his pocket with the other. The purple shadows under his eyes were mournful. He looked between my face and his mother's, saw the distress in her expression, and he dropped the hammer and rushed to embrace her.

"Ma ..."

"Never mind, Andy," she said, crying fully now, unable to contain herself. She took the offered handkerchief and buried her face in it. Between sobs, she gulped, "I'm all right."

The two stagehands took Mrs. Thornton away, to her costume shop, where she could have a moment of privacy to weep. I watched her go, then turned my attention to Andy. He stood with shoulders hunched, his expression full of despair.

"I'm sorry, Andy." I said. "I'm sorry for Jess."

His throat hitched, and his eyes glistened with tears. "Thanks." Then, as his face tensed into a mix of grief and rage, he asked, "You know who done it?"

I shook my head.

The look in his eyes was murderous. "I'll kill the bastard who done it. I swear I will."

"I'm sure you would." I studied the poor man for a moment, wondering if I could use his faults against him as others had done. "You're very watchful, aren't you. You know theatre gossip that other's might miss?"

"I do?" His face brightened. "Maybe."

"I heard an argument between Jess and another woman, on the night of the dress rehearsal. Do you know who it might have been?"

He shook his head, and I believed him. "Everyone loved Jess," he said, and his chin trembled again. "She was so pretty. That's why I gave her the pretty necklace. I thought it would look best on her."

I raised my eyebrows at that. "You gave her the necklace?"

"When she told me about the baby, I gave it to her. I spent all my money on it, and she was so sad, and I thought it would make her happy again."

Poor, soft-headed, foolish man.

"I am sorry for your loss, Andy. I really am. I think you and Jess would've been very happy together."

He shuffled from foot to foot, trying to keep from crying. "You tell me if you hear anything? Anything at all?"

"I promise."

He bowed his head, and followed his mother to the privacy of her shop, where they could grieve together in peace.

Twenty

I left the playhouse by the back exit, the door that led into the alley. I'd heard Jess talking here, heard with my own ears that Andy wouldn't be auditioning for the December play. I hadn't understood what she'd meant, but now the pieces fell into place.

Jess had discovered herself pregnant with Andy's child. How Edwina would've raged! I suspected she did not know; she'd made no mention of the child, and nor had I. Jess, seeing an opportunity to escape from her mother's stern rules, had agreed to elope to California with Andy, where they could build a life together away. Mrs. Thornton had even purchased them passage on a steamer, due to depart from Victoria Harbor in November.

Andy was no longer my main suspect. He'd looked crushed and raw at the loss of Jess. He wanted to know the murderer, he wanted to seek revenge. He was not a calculating man, and I doubted Andy was capable of devious machinations; he was too simple a soul, too forthright with the truth. Unlike Mrs. Thornton's overt display of fake distress, Andy's reaction seemed fully genuine.

So if the killer was not Andy, then who?

With my head so full of thoughts, I'd almost walked two blocks before I noticed my surroundings. I stood on the corner of Broad Street and Pandora, the outer edge of Chinatown, and only half a block from the red brick edifice of Victoria's City Hall. The sky was turning from sunny to cloudy. Chinese vendors hurried to unfurl their canvas awnings so that passing customers would be sheltered from the advancing rain.

My stomach growled. I wondered if a bit of food might help me to think; I fished in my pocket and pulled out the coin from the nun and a shinplaster, a 25-cent banknote. It wouldn't buy me much, but maybe a steamed pork bun would help me figure out the gaps in the story.

At the corner of the street, a vendor with a wooden hand cart sold hearty finger-food like steamed buns, bits of braised meat, and wisps of grilled vegetables. His wrinkled face was wreathed in fragrant smoke from an iron brazier on the top of the cart, and his hands flipped the cooked buns on a bamboo platter, suspended over a pan of water. He watched me as I drew close and examined his wares. The pale white dumplings glistened in the watery afternoon sunlight. I furrowed my brow, concentrated, and said, "*Tchayng mun cha siu bao?*" My tongue tripping over the syllables. *Please may I have a pork bun?*

He laughed loudly at my attempt.

"*Ai ye!*" he exclaimed, "You are saying you want pork bun, yes?"

"Yes, please," I replied. He plucked one dumpling from the platter with a pair of long chopsticks.

"How much?"

"No money," he replied, "You give me best laugh of the day."

I thanked him again and stuffed the shinplaster back in my pocket.

"And your friend? He want one too?"

I paused, mid-bite, the sweet sauce flooding over my tongue. "Hmm?" I grunted around cheeks full of food.

"The man behind you. He follow you down the whole block." The vendor looked over my shoulder.

I turned and surveyed the crowd. People filled the boardwalks. A parade of trolleys, buggies, and men on horseback passed by.

"Where?"

The vendor peered passed me and looked around, confused. "He was there, in doorway, I don't know now. He walk so close behind you. He kept his eye on you. I thought you must know him."

Pandora was a busy thoroughfare, crowded with hundreds of men in work clothes, Chinese women with shopping baskets, children running underfoot, and dogs squabbling over bones in the road. If William Carter was following me, dressed in a workman's costume of corduroy overalls and hat, he could have easily turned his back to me and walked away. I'd never know he was there.

But if he'd followed me this far, I doubted he'd give up now.

My pulse increased, not in fear but in anticipation.

I dearly hoped to face Mr. Carter again and give him a piece of my mind. If he'd followed me here, into Chinatown, he was surrounded on all sides by those he deemed a scourge, and he would certainly be uncomfortable and out of his element.

'*Xi*,' I said to the vendor: a thank you not only for the bun, but for the warning, too.

I began walking west, towards the water, deeper into the Chinese quarter. I continued slowly, but not too slowly. I'd originally intended to return to Mr. Fish's house, but if Carter was following me, I wanted to know it. My boots took me down Pandora Street, along a curve in the roadway as it jogged towards the Johnson Street Bridge, and we passed grocers, dry goods retailers and silk merchants, crooked staircases leading to joss houses and smoky temples, and a pair of wide red doors leading to a school. The air grew sweet with incense, then savory with the fragrance of dried herbs.

I plucked my way through boxes of vegetables, between racks hung with salted fish, under hand-written signs in a language I could not read. Street vendors in grey cotton suits waved hands at me and shouted for my attention, but I was not here to shop—I paid them no attention. Would I lose Mr. Carter in the crowd of men, merchants, and wares? I slowed my pace, just a bit, to ensure I didn't. Pausing at the corner, I finished the bun and licked my fingers clean. It was almost impossible to keep from glancing over my shoulder, but I kept my eyes focused ahead. I didn't wish to scare him away. I wanted to lead Carter right into the beating heart of Chinatown.

Just past Government Street, a crack between two buildings beckoned.

Shao had called it 'Fan Tan Alley', and we had entered it from the other side, from Fisgard Street. At the Pandora end, the narrow entrance was a mere three feet wide: large enough for men to pass, but no vehicles, and certainly no mob of police officials. I kept my head down and my hands close as I squeezed through a crush of revelers, smoking clay opium pipes. Shao and I had visited Fan Tan Alley in the morning hours, when the prostitutes were sleeping and the gambling dens were closed, but by late afternoon, the whole place hummed with entertainment, anticipation, lust. Scores of patrons loitered between the buildings. I could smell the desperation on their skin, a perfume of sweat and sex and alcohol. They waited for the dens to open for a night of revelry, and they all seemed impatient.

I kept my head down. Women were not common here unless they were selling the pleasures of the flesh. When I felt a hand on my shoulder, I spat one of the few phrases I'd managed to master: "*M̀h'hóu gáau ngóh.*" *Leave me alone!*

I dipped into the shallow recess of a closed door, the same one where Shao and I had embraced, and glanced around the bricks at the way I'd come. Thick waves of fragrant smoke from the dens mixed with ribbons of steam from braziers, filling the alley with shifting silvery clouds. Through the clustering bodies of men, the drab afternoon sunlight silhouetted one figure against Pandora Street: a large, imposing man wearing a long leather coat and battered hat. My heart stuttered. He hesitated when he saw the mass of humanity crowded between the buildings.

Then he pushed in without a word of apology.

I pressed my back against the bricks, let the shadow of the doorway fall over me, and waited in silence until he passed by.

I'd been sorely mistaken; this was not William Carter. My eyes widened, drank in the sight of him with awe, committed every detail to memory as my heart thumped in my chest. He didn't see me in the gloom, and continued down the alley without a pause.

I melted into his wake. I followed him along Fan Tan so closely, I could've reached out to brush my fingers against the back of his leather coat.

On Fisgard, he paused to look both ways. Failing to see a small girl in either direction, he removed his hat, ran his huge hand through his dirty-blonde hair, and spat.

"Aw, goddammit!"

I stepped alongside him.

"You looking for someone?"

Jack Hunter did not startle at the sound of my voice—oh, how satisfying that would've been! Instead, he looked down at me, cocked one eyebrow, and cast me that wolfish smirk.

"Well, I'll be ..." he drawled, setting his battered hat back on his head, "Ain't that a corker, bumping into the Lady Amaryllis."

Jack looked exactly the same as the last time I'd seen him, back in the hot murderous days of August. He was a dirty, unshaven, weathered bear of a man, as large as a freight train and as filthy as a coal scuttle. He wore the same clothes: a duster coat that looked like it should've been burned years ago, denim work pants stained at the knees, and a shirt that may have started white, but was now the color of old newsprint. A ragged line of black stitching patched the fabric where my father had sliced it open along his side. His blond-brown hair hung down passed his collar, ragged and forgotten. His boots had not seen a shine for twenty years. There was not a scrap of decency about him, but for all his filth and unkempt appearance, his slate-grey eyes blazed. The man I knew as Jack Hunter saw all, noted every facet of his surroundings, and was rarely taken by surprise.

From the curve of his grin, it seemed he rather liked it.

"How long have you been following me?"

"Followin' you? Hah!" he laughed. "Now, why would I do something like that?" He glanced over me. "I'm here for a bit of fun, Liz. Ain't that why any red-blooded fella comes to Fan Tan Alley?"

"I ought not to be surprised to find the likes of you here, Jack." I flashed him a look of disapproval. "Or is it Jack? What are you calling yourself these days?"

"That name works just fine, sweetheart."

"What's your real name?"

"Don't matter all that much, does it?" he replied, "You know me as Jack, and I'm happy with the arrangement."

"You'd keep the alias of my father?"

He grunted at that, and his smile faded. "There's a lot of fellas go by the name of Jack. It's a good honest name, and it don't seem right for a devil like your father to go and ruin it for the rest of us."

"And I'm sure you're doing your charitable part to return a sense of honor and dignity to the name?" I needled, "You're spending your days doing good Christian work?"

"Of course," he replied, turning on one heel, "Even Jesus hung around with whores."

We began to walk along the street. I marveled, then felt repulsed, at how natural it felt to be in his company. Fisgard was mercifully quiet after the crowds of Pandora and Fan Tan Alley, and I could walk along the boardwalk with him at arm's length. He towered over me, as formidable as Goliath, but he moved with grace and stealth, sliding through the crowds as if they were made of smoke.

"Are you going to turn me into the authorities?"

He chuckled. "Why would I go and do something like that?"

"Because I killed a man."

"You saved my life," he replied, "It wouldn't be right."

I scowled at this. "So why have you been following me?"

We'd reached the end of Fisgard, and he tipped his head towards a despicable, run-down brick hovel that sat across Store Street. Above the door, a carved placard read, 'The Pelican', though I'd never seen any such bird here. The windows were boarded and covered with paper, and three or four men slumped in intoxicated slumber in the gutter. The place was low, with a flat roof and a rickety porch that hunched over the wharves and ships below; only the foolhardy and intoxicated would trust such a structure with their life.

"C'mon, Liz," Jack said, "Let me buy you a drink." Then he turned and walked to the door, trusting that I'd follow.

Which—because I'm too curious for my own good—I did.

Twenty-One

A short passage led into a musty, sawdust-strewn room. It held ten or twelve tables, but the walls were bare of decoration except for a shelf above the kitchen door, where the owner had balanced two cracked plates, along with what I first mistook to be a sleeping cat. Closer inspection showed it to be too moth-eaten and motionless to be real. No, the cat was dead, and taxidermied, and poorly done, and stared down at the drinkers with bulging glass eyes.

The only source of light in the room came from a couple of cracked windows overlooking the harbor. The single coal-oil lamp behind the bar did nothing but illuminate a shallow circle at the barkeep's elbow. He was fat, sweaty and bald, with thick lips set in a crafty scowl. When we walked in, he momentarily paused from pouring ale from a sputtering, rusted tap to size us up, and he nodded in a familiar greeting to Jack. A trio of salt-worn fishermen huddled at the table nearest the fire, sucking on clay pipes. Their conversation paused as I entered. The air stank of mildew, rancid fish oil, old sweat and wet dog fur, and I was thankful for the wood smoke that billowed out of the fireplace, if only to cover the stench. Every watery, weary, bloodshot eye in the room followed me as I trailed in after Jack, who didn't pause as he entered, but strolled in as if he knew the place intimately.

Jack looked back to me. "Watcha drinking?"

"I'm fifteen."

"I ain't your pastor. What'll it be?"

"Raspberry cordial," I said. He smirked, then held up one hand to the man behind the bar.

"Archie, give us a couple of whiskeys."

Jack settled onto a seat by the front window, shrugged off his coat and dropped his hat on the table. The neatly-stitched line snaked up the side of his shirt, and I saw that he'd tried to wash out the bloodstains, but only managed to turn them into ghostly brown patches.

The bartender limped over and set down two glasses and a bottle, then stepped back to examine me. His small, beady eyes peered from under a pair of thick black brows. "I ain't never seen this face," he said, "Who you working with, bint? Martha on Black Street?"

"She ain't working with no one," Jack replied easily as he portioned out the whiskey, "This here is my sister, Archie, and I 'spect you to be civil. Here y'are, Lizzie ma love. Drink up."

Archie laughed so hard that the wattles of his throat jiggled. "If she's your sister, than I'm the king of bloody France." He limped back to the bar, pausing to tell the other patrons that this was a woman of high quality, and they ought to be as gentlemanly as possible. This caused a great roar of laughter.

"Never mind them," Jack said. He kicked out one of the chairs at the table as an invitation to sit.

I took the chair and smoothed the hem of my pinafore over my knees. "So? Why follow me?"

He took his glass and drained it, then motioned for me to do the same. The whiskey seared my throat on the way down, and my stomach lurched in rebellion as the liquid hit my gut. I coughed, and from the distant corner, I heard the table of men laugh again.

"You saved my life, Liz," he said, and he portioned out a second glass for each of us. "But I don't trust you. You got a streak of the devil in your heart, girl, and it's bound to show up sooner or later."

"That's not a very nice thing to say," I said.

"Being 'nice' ain't never been my strong suit."

I leaned forward, leaning my elbows on the table. "What do I call you?"

"Jack Hunter."

"But it isn't your name."

"Course not." He hailed one of the barmaids with a wave of the hand and said,

"Tell me, darlin', I'm starving for a bite of dinner. Whatcha got to eat?"

I figured she was the same age as Violet. She was neatly dressed in a corset and brown skirts, her pretty face plastered with make-up. She smiled at me politely, but turned on her charm for Jack; a playful giggle, a saucy hand on her hip, a full view of her cleavage. She knew well enough where her tips came from.

"Bit of cheese, some oyster stew, a nice joint of some sort of meat," she said, "Let me see what I can find ya that ain't gonna leave you gagging, sweetie."

He grinned and studied her rump as she walked away, through a door into a kitchen—that lascivious, lecherous grin that cause the crinkles around his eyes to deepen. Eventually he returned his attention to me. "My heart was warmed to see you and Mr. Chen on the beach last night, still keeping company."

"He's been working a decent honest job," I said, feeling defensive.

"He knows what you did?"

I lowered my chin, looked to the floor.

Jack laughed. "I didn't think so. Whatcha told him, Liz? Ain't he been wondering why you're on your own? Surely someone's asked questions."

When I spoke, the words were sharp, clipped and forceful. "My father has gone to Europe on holiday," I said. "He will then return to London to buy us a house, and send word when he's ready for me to join him. I felt it best to stay here and make sure that Shaozhu's injuries healed."

His sharp eyes ranged over my face, cataloguing my determined expression. "Really, now." The barmaid returned, slapping a plate of pungent cheese and stale bread between us. Jack thanked her and told her to stick it on his bill and, as she left, he said, "And they bought it, huh?"

"It's the truth."

"We both know it ain't the truth."

I winced. "It's the truth I need everyone to believe while I figure out what to do next." I took my glass in hand. "If you say anything to Shao, or Mr. Fish, or—"

"Aw, hell, what am I gonna say? Ain't none of 'em gonna believe me over you—I'm a drunk and a cheat and a thief, Liz, while you're a daughter of high society. I start telling tales about how you stuck a hunting knife through your own father's goddamn neck, and I'm likely to be locked up for breaking the peace." He swallowed the contents of his glass in one gulp. "B'sides, Liz, I owe you my life. I haven't forgotten that." He slammed his glass down. "So you'll go back to England when it suits ya?"

I shook my head, shrugged limply, said nothing.

"You oughta go to yer grandfather in Wiltshire."

"He wouldn't want me," I replied, "You told me he thinks I'm a soulless monster. I wrote him a letter, but I don't expect a reply." I took another sip of whiskey. "I'm on my own, Mr. Hunter, and I don't know where I'm going next, but I'll figure it out."

"Shit," he muttered, "He's the only family you got left. He'll take you in, 'cause it's his duty, and yer his kin." Then he looked out the window, a wicked smirk on his face. "Yer whole goddamn life is falling down around you, and you don't even have the good sense to ask for help? Maybe you aren't a soulless monster … just a stupid, pig-headed one."

I pushed down my rage and insult, turned my face to stone. "Ask for help? From you? I'd never stoop so low." I bared my teeth. "Maybe my world is falling apart, Mr. Hunter, but you're the sole reason my life is in pieces."

"I beg to differ, Liz." he said. "I'd say it was ruined the day yer pa ripped up his first whore."

We stared at each other across the table, and his face was thunderous; for all his levity, he did not like me, and I certainly did not like him.

"You're a cold, calculating devil-bitch," he said. "I can see it well enough in your dead eyes: you're gonna turn out just like the good doctor. Goddamn it, I shoulda killed ya when you begged for it."

If he'd struck me with a closed fist, I would not have been as winded.

"I'd never kill anyone—"

"You already did," he warned.

I closed my eyes for a moment, tried to compose myself. "I'd never kill anyone *who didn't deserve it*." I took another drink and thought of how to phrase my next sentence. The whiskey seared my tongue and tasted foul, and helped me focus my thoughts away from how much I wished to throttle the man. "I understand that this must seem strange to you," I began slowly, "But I did what had to be done, and I feel no remorse for my actions. My father was going to kill you. He had killed many times before. He needed to be stopped."

"But … not even the smallest regret?"

I ran my finger along the table's wood grain, felt the grooves where men had dug their knives into its surface, scratching rude words. "I miss my sister, Mr. Hunter. I miss my father and my mother—but I miss the memories of how I knew them, not the people that I discovered them to be."

"I miss my mother, every god damned day, even though I know she were a cheap prostitute."

"Your mother chose to sell sex to pay for a roof over her head. She didn't kill defenseless girls to satisfy a selfish urge. It's a little different."

He tipped his head to accede to my logic.

"You're an unconventional girl, Liz."

I'd had enough of his company. I knocked back the rest of the drink and slammed down the empty glass. "My mother was a Sapphic and my father was a blood-thirsty beast; I can not help but be unconventional."

He paused, scowling.

Then he gave such a booming, boisterous laugh that other patrons paused and the bar went quiet. They cast suspicious glances to each other, and as conversations resumed, Jack leaned forward and said, "So if you ain't running back to yer kin, what're you gonna do next?"

I had the fleeting impulse to lie, but I said, "I don't know. Shao's starting to ask questions; I don't think he believes me anymore. Emma Briggs has offered me a room in her home until Father sends notice, but she's too clever to fool for long. Both you and I know, a letter will never arrive. Mr. Fish has been very hospitable, but I can't stay there forever, and with the death of his housemaid—well, frankly, I can't just leave at a time of mourning. That would be poor etiquette, don't you think?"

"I'm not the sort to ask about etiquette, Liz," he smirked, "And I don't think there's much been written about what to do if there's been a murder in the house."

"I feel I ought to stay and help Mr. Fish, at least until justice is served."

"Who done it?"

"I don't know."

"But you got a theory."

"I'm putting the pieces together, yes."

He leaned forward, fixing me with his sharp eyes. There was enough of the wolf about his features that I recoiled. "You're good at figuring, ain't ya."

"I suppose." I thought of the scraps of newspapers precisely organized in the jewelry box and my obsession with understanding the past. "How else will I ever find answers, if I don't go after them myself?"

He heard the depth to my reply, and said, "You ain't exactly talking about the housemaid now, are ya."

How much do I dare tell him? I hated him, I hated what he'd done to my family—he'd torn us apart by casting a bright and shining lamp upon my father's indiscretions. If he'd never come to Cumberland, Violet would still be alive, and so would the gentleman Dr. John Saunders.

A small voice in my head reminded me that would not have been a good thing.

"You said I'm going to turn out like my father," I said, "But I want to know who he was, and why he killed so many women." And swallowing quickly, I added, "I want to know how I can avoid the same fate."

For a moment, he regarded me thoughtfully, taking a drink.

I cursed myself for telling him the truth. I didn't like feeling so vulnerable; I ought not to trust him.

But it was so satisfying, to be honest after months of lies.

He plucked up the bottle, filled my glass again, and said, "Y'ever heard of blood-guilt, Liz?"

I shook my head.

Jack reclined in his chair and took a swig of his drink, watching me over the rim of his glass. "The ancient Greeks thought there were no greater crime than killing your own kin, and them that slaughtered their own family were cursed by the gods. Just like Tantalus and Orestes, there ain't nothing can be done to save a blood-guilty soul from hurting everyone they touch, save for purging their sorry state with rituals and sacrifices to the heavens. So I figure, it's just a matter of time before you hurt the people around you; it don't matter what you find out. You'll kill again, Liz, 'cause I wager you can't help yourself."

"You're the last person I'd expect to quote Greek mythology, Jack."

He drained the glass and slammed it down on the table. "Well, lookin' at you? With your skinny little arms and freckled nose? You're the last person I'd expect to be a murderer, sweetheart."

I thought over his words. "Is that why you're following me? Because you think I'll kill again?"

"Someone's gotta keep an eye on you."

"Have you been following me since I arrived in Victoria?"

To my surprise, he shook his head.

"Naw. I figured you were gone back to England, sweetheart, and my opportunity was gone. But then Fate gave me a helping hand: you dropped by The Siren's Rest to chat with Nelly." He smiled, but not a licentious smirk. It was a warm, caring expression that I'd never seen him wear before. "She's a particular friend of mine."

For the first time, I let the expression of shock and surprise cross my face, and he took open delight in it, but I didn't care. "You and Eleanor McCloud? Bloody hell, she knew Jessie! They performed together! What do you know about the Sing Song Girls?"

He shrugged. "Only that Nellie's busy on Saturday nights, making a bit of bob and pretending she's an actress." Under his breath, he added, "Goddamn silly notion, that is."

I felt the surge of anger return. "Why is it silly?"

"She's a whore," he said plainly, "No use pretending to be something you ain't."

I stood, unsteady from the whiskey. "By that logic," I leaned over the table and whispered, "I'm a killer, Mr. Hunter. No use pretending otherwise. And nothing you do can stop me."

I strode out with my head held high.

Twenty-Two

Fueled by a dizzying mix of rage and hatred and adrenaline, I made it halfway down the block by the time the whiskey caught up with me, and I slumped into the doorway of an apartment with the world spinning around my head. I might've vomited into the gutter then, I don't know. It's a bit of a blur.

A young Chinese woman in a black silk dress stopped and offered me a gloved hand. "You alright, miss?"

"I feel unwell," I said, "Can you point me in the direction of Mr. Lim's apothecary?"

She helped me down a street and around the block, before delivering me with a brief explanation in Cantonese to Mr. Lim. He gave me a pitying look, then he guided me to a wooden chair in the corner by the window. My face had broken out into a cold sweat.

Mr. Lim studied my face for the root of my illness. "Strong tea for you," he said as Shao emerged from the cellar. The older man patted my cheek before hurrying to put the kettle on to boil.

"Liz!" said Shao when he saw me, and he held his palm to my clammy forehead. "You look green! Are you sick?"

"No." Belch. "I've been drinking whiskey."

Shao looked unimpressed. "Why were you drinking whiskey?"

"Because that's what Jack ordered."

His face dropped. "What!"

"He's been following me. Now, just wait, don't get angry—" I gave a cough, another belch, and a groan as Shao returned to my side. "I don't think he means you any harm. Oh Lord, I don't feel good …"

Shao said nothing but his hands had balled into fists. His eyes blazed. I could see the thoughts written plainly on his face.

"He saved your life," I reminded him.

"He's a bastard and a cheat and he knows more about Violet's death than he lets on," Shao spat.

"Calm down—"

"Don't tell me to calm down, Liz! Was he following us the other night? At the beach?"

"Yes."

"*Zao gao*!"

Mr. Lim pressed a clay cup of tea into my hands, and then handed a second cup of tea to Shao. He asked a calm, smooth sentence in Cantonese, and Shao shook his head discreetly. Mr. Lim patted one hand on Shao's shoulder and retired to the back of the store, where he'd been sorting his accounts at his desk.

"He asked if you're in trouble?" I said quietly.

"No, he asked if you're my girlfriend," he replied. One corner of his mouth kinked up in a grin. "Same question, really."

We moved to a small balcony in the rear of the building, with a restricted view of the brick alleys, piles of refuse, and roosting pigeons. The sunshine of the late afternoon had long since disappeared, to be replaced with a light evening rain, but we found shelter under the cover of the wooden balcony that hung at an angle above us. The fresh air did wonders for my lurching stomach.

"That's not the only news I have for you," I said as we sat and sipped the tea. It was strong but flavorful, a deep jade color with flecks of black floating on the surface, and it tasted of citrus, peppermint and caraway seeds. I ought not to drink anything strong, it suits me poorly, but the tea soothed my stomach and cleared my head. I'd need this recipe from Mr. Lim for any future endeavors, I thought as I took a mouthful, savored it, swallowed. Then I said, "The father of Jessie's baby was Andy Thornton."

This meant nothing to Shao, so he gave no surprised reaction. Instead he asked, "This Andy Thornton … he knew?"

I nodded.

"And you think he killed Jess?"

I shook my head. "From what I understand, they were preparing to elope, and from the stricken look on his face—no. I believe he didn't do it."

"Mr. Kelly loved your sister, too," Shao reminded me. "That didn't stop him from strangling and stabbing her."

I turned my face away from the lie.

"Sorry," he said at my reaction, "I didn't mean to bring up bad memories."

How I wanted to tell him then, the truth of the situation.

But the moment was fleeting, and before I could admit my deception, he said, "We still haven't found the location of the murder."

"It must be somewhere along the waterfront on the east side of the harbor," I replied, draining the last of the tea. "But I don't know anything more than that. I can't figure for the life of me, why Jess would leave William Carter's house and go west, rather than east, straight home to Mr. Fish's."

"How's your stomach?"

"Better, thanks."

He took the tea cup from my hand, and returned in a moment with a satchel slung over his shoulder.

"What's in the bag?"

He glanced down at it. "If we're on the hunt tonight, I'm bringing food," he replied, "And just in case we go boating again? A change of clothes."

By the time we reached William Carter's house, the shops were closed and people of quality were safely home, stoking their fires and lighting pipes and finishing their puddings. The streets of James Bay were deserted. The light rain had turned to a cold mist that gnawed on your bones, and through the thick soupy darkness, I heard foghorns blaring across the water. Victoria, on a chilly autumn night, was not a place of comfort.

The lamps in Will's parlor were lit. I peered through the window to see him with his back to the front door, hunched over his writing desk. A half-empty bottle of sherry sat next to him. He scribbled in short bursts, composing a letter. The room still looked frightful. I wondered if he'd bothered yet to dump out the chamber pot.

When I returned to the street, Shao whispered, "This was the place? No wonder Mrs. Thornton wanted to keep it a secret. This isn't the kind of person you'd expect to hire girls."

"They weren't prostitutes."

"But they might as well have been." He looked around. "A gentleman's soiree is no place for a proper lady."

"Listen to you, all fussy and fancy!"

He peered over the fence, where a line of rose bushes had lost their last blossoms. "It's the truth, Liz. Anyone who saw them leave, especially after midnight, would assume the worst."

We skirted around Carter's yard and entered the back alley. The rain was starting to fall harder now, so we took shelter under the eaves of the carriage house to wait out the worst of it. Our vantage gave me an opportunity to study the yard again. Will had fixed the lock on the back door, but hadn't bothered to return the hoe to the shed.

"Nell said she saw Jessie leave out the back door, looking merry."

"Which way did she see her go?"

"Well," I peered around, "Nell said Will didn't want anyone to see them come and go, so they left, one by one, by the alley. If I was Jess, I'd have gone east; that would've been the fastest route home." I looked down the alley. It was pitch black, and so dark that I couldn't see the ground. The closest illumination was the distant pin prick of light coming from the lamps on far-off Oswego Street. "Gods teeth," I whispered, "I can barely see!"

Shao peered over my shoulder, down the tunnel of blackness. "She was pregnant."

"She wouldn't wish to fall."

"Exactly," he said.

I turned west. Because Carter's house was the first in the block, it was only a short distance to Montreal Street. Even with the rain, it provided a far more welcoming sight.

"That explains why she went towards Montreal Street," I said. "Maybe she decided to head as far east as St Lawrence, just to avoid Carter's neighbours?"

The rain had begun to ease. A star peeked through the clouds above us. "Come on," said Shao, "Let's see if we can think like Jess."

We left the shelter of Carter's yard and began strolling, up the alley and southwards along Montreal, but only for a short distance. The street was predominantly well-to-do houses; on a Saturday night, there might have been cabs driving from home to home, and there certainly would've been nosy matrons looking out of upstairs bedroom windows. Jess knew the whole of James Bay, and she would've been attuned to what areas would be highly visible.

But, if we turned right on Superior and walked one more block to St. Lawrence Street, the homes gave way to brick warehouses. After business hours, this thoroughfare was as deserted as a tomb. I supposed that, after midnight on a stormy Saturday, not a soul could be found here.

"The street would've been quiet, just like tonight," I said.

"She might've taken this route," said Shao, "It's well-lit, and the eaves would've provided shelter from the rain."

So I walked close to the building, under the shadows cast by the roofs, and tried to imagine that I was Jess, heading home after a night of singing. I imagined I must be pleased with myself—singing always left her in high spirits, Mrs. Thornton said—but she would've been tired too, and perhaps a little disappointed by William Carter's dismissive attitude. I'd have felt secure in the privacy of the warehouses, rather than frightened to be alone. We almost reached the end of the block, and my eyes noticed a small hump in the road: the rise of a little bridge, crossing a small creek.

"Look," I said, stopping in my tracks.

St. Lawrence Street hardly paused at all, the bridge was so small. On the landward side of the street, the warehouses reached right to the edge of the water, so that it gave the impression of a moat between two brick castles. On the ocean side, wooden shacks clustered together along a muddy shore.

The soil here was soft. A few clumps of rock stuck up like rotten teeth, and the whole place smelled of decay. With all the rain, the watercourse boiled with a swift current, and the sound of the water rushing against the bricks and the bridge posts sounded like trolls grinding bones into bread. I figured this water must drain from swampy Providence Pond, a little cesspit in the middle of James Bay—but this required no great leap of deduction on my part. There were simply no other lakes or springs in James Bay, and the stream emptied into a small murky cove called Major Bay, only a few hundred feet from the bridge.

Major Bay formed part of the harbor's edge, and anything tossed over the bridge would float down the river, into the harbor, and out to sea.

"This is the place."

"You sure?" said Shao.

I thought of how the scene must've played out: Jessie, crumpled to her knees, clutching at her stomach, the murderer stabbing a sharp tool into the soft meat of her belly, the cries for help going unheard in the industrial area. In frustration, fearful that the noise would alert a nearby guard or watchman, the murderer grabbed a stone or brick, and smashed it down on the back of the woman's head.

I looked around. At the edge of the roadway sat a pile of loose bricks. It would be easy enough to grab one, use it to silence the victim, and toss into the water.

I fished through my pocket and found another shinplaster, rumpled and soft. I rolled it tightly.

"What are you doing?" said Shao.

From my jacket pocket, I withdrew the small tin tube of lucifers. I shook one into my hand, and it made a satisfying crack as I flicked it against the brick wall, flaring into a fierce little flame. The shinplaster lit quickly, and the circle of light widened a bit; it was hardly a candle, but it was better than nothing. Protecting the flame from any breath of wind with my cupped hand, I looked across the ground for a hint of a scuffle, but the cobblestones yielded nothing.

"It was raining heavily that night," I said, more to myself than Shao, "Jess would've walked under the eaves, avoiding the rain."

"But on the hard surface of the cobblestones? The rain would've washed away any blood," said Shao. "You'll never find the exact spot."

I cast my mind back to another night, more than a month ago.

The arc of the knife slashing down, the spray of blood rising up. I'd seen it before.

"This is the exact spot." I said.

"How can you know for sure?"

I aimed the light upwards, into the eaves.

There, protected from the rain, were long thin trails of blood droplets, a bright red against the white plaster.

Twenty-Three

THERE is one wretched thought about the Whitechapel murders, and that is the ease with which murder may be done when it is contrived with an average amount of skill and forethought. It is the appalling clumsiness of most murders which puts authority on the trail. Murders done in passion or from greed or by a robber caught out in theft usually leave a broad track behind them. Here there are not only murders, but a murder plan thought out and executed by that most dangerous of assassins, a cunning maniac. MOREOVER, the assassin has chosen the easiest form of crime by picking on victims who become his accomplices. The murdered women have been as anxious to avoid the eye of the constable as the murderer. Both have conspired together to watch him out of sight and hearing, and so diminish the chances both of interruption or rescue.

The Star, Tuesday, October 2, 1888

Shao, looking directly up, whistled low.

I pointed out the trajectory of the blood. "Every time the murderer flung back his hand to stab again, he left behind a trail of red spatter," I said. "See? One, two, three … maybe four lines. That's consistent with the five stab wounds in her stomach. The first stab would've gone in clean." As I counted the last, the shinplaster fizzled in my fingers. The light died, I gave a yelp, and stuck my fingertips in my mouth.

"*Ai ye*," he muttered, still looking up.

"And the bridge, right there," I continued, "Easy enough to dump the body over. Buoyed up by her wool jacket, the water would've carried her out to sea. The murderer probably thought she'd never be seen again."

"So the weapon?" said Shao, studying the dark eaves again. "What do you think it could be?"

We cast about the street, looking in the gutters and the alleys, but found nothing except lumps of horse manure and a dead rat. When we met again on the bridge, an hour later, Shao leaned against the railing next to me and trained his sight towards Major Bay.

"Maybe he took the weapon with him." I said.

But Shao shook his head. "If the murderer hoped to get rid of Jess by water, maybe he did the same with his knife?"

We both stared down into the murky waters flowing out of swampy Providence Pond, knotted with sea grasses and thick with mud.

"Ah, well," I said helplessly as I shrugged off my coat and kicked off my boots.

"What are you—"

"If it's down there, we ought to find it." I replied.

Shao took my coat but said, "It's freezing cold, Liz, and you'll never find anything in the dark."

"The clouds are parting, there's still a good moon, and I'm not going in completely blind." I hurried to the alleyway and picked up the dead rat. It was heavy in my hands, rigid with rigor, and I wondered how different from the weapon's weight it might be. When I returned to the bridge, I heaved it over my shoulder and gave it a good fling, straight towards the harbor. The rat hit the surface with an ungainly splash.

"There, by the little bush. That's where I'll start."

"You're crazy!"

"Yes, but soon I'll be crazy and cold, so keep that coat handy."

I skirted down the edge of the bridge and picked my way along the slippery embankment until I reached the small bush, which had taken purchase on the bare soil at the edge of the water. The stream was not too deep, but it was moving more quickly than I would've preferred. I waded in to my thighs. The temperature made me gasp.

When I ducked down to put my hands below the water, I made a sound not unlike a punch to the gut: less of a cry, and more of a throaty exclamation of surprise, gusting up from the bottom of my lungs. I held my chin up as high as my neck would allow, but the water flowed around my chest and shoulders, and splashed merrily against my throat. Between my extended fingers, the mud felt silky, thick, sensual and cool. I came upon something hard, but my excitement was soon squashed when I brought the object to the surface.

It was a rusted iron spoon.

"Damn," I muttered, tossing it to the shore.

I continued towards the center of the stream, and now I had to put my head underwater to reach the bottom. Every dive took me into silent darkness. The silt brushed my cheeks and my hair swept towards the sea, and I kept my eyes closed, preferring the intimate exploration of touch. I found a number of items: three horseshoes, a little pail with a hole in its bottom, a few iron nails, a wad of fabric that might've once been a bit of tarpaulin. Each joined the spoon on the shore. Soon, I'd gathered a little pile of trash. I even found the rat again, which gave a moist splat when I tossed it back to land.

"Anything?" shouted Shao from above.

My teeth chattered. "Not yet."

"Maybe I'm wrong," he replied, but I don't think he believed himself. He only wanted me out of the water before I shivered to death.

"Give me a minute more," I said.

I dived again, down into the stygian black, where the water washed away all sounds and my ears pulsed against the cold. My freezing hands felt like they were burning, my cheeks ached, my jaw clenched painfully. I knew I couldn't stay in much longer, but I buried my fingers again in the mud, sweeping along the bottom against the pull of the current.

My smallest finger touched something hard.

I rooted again, and pulled out an object that was thin and metallic. My heart beat a little faster. This was it. It must be. Long, cold, with a tip as sharp as an awl.

When I broke the surface, I was about to shout in triumph when voices caught my ear, and I swam into the shadow of the bridge.

Shao was not alone.

"—at this hour, hey?"

I heard hard soles rap against the bridge deck.

Shao made his reply calmly, but slightly stilted. "Walking, sir."

"In this neighbourhood? Where were you walking to?"

"No English, sir."

"Like hell," the man growled. I peered up to see a burly police officer thumping the end of his baton against Shao's chest. "Short hair, hey? You running a delivery?"

Shao shook his head.

"You've got your papers with you, then?"

The officer sheathed his baton. I heard the flip of the documents, the grunt of the officer as he tried to read by the low light. "Cor, can't read this damn thing—well, we'll see what you remember down at the station, Jim boy. Come with me." He thrust the paper back to Shao. Then he picked up his bull's eye lamp with one hand, and grabbed Shao's collar with the other, pushing him roughly forward. "A night in a cell does wonders."

My teeth no longer chattered, I'd ground them so tightly together. I took the thin object and tucked it into my stocking, along my thigh. Then I swam to the shore and, grabbing the scrap of tarpaulin, called out, "Have you kept my coat dry, young man?"

I rounded the side of the bridge to find the two men, both surprised to see me. I hurried towards them, muddy water streaming from the hem of my dress, my ginger hair a tangled mess of grass and silt.

"Well? I know your English is bad," I prompted, "But my coat—do you still have it? Oh, thank goodness! There it is!"

Shao raised one eyebrow and held it out.

"Miss, what are you—"

I faced the officer. He held up the bull's eye to examine me with its glare.

"What an evening, sir! Glory be, did you get caught in that great gust of wind?"

He stammered a bit.

"I was walking home from an evening of teaching piano, and that wind caught my scarf and OFF IT FLEW!" I made a great theatrical gesture, one worthy of the Yates Street Players. "And goodness, it's my mother's scarf, and if you only KNEW the trouble I'd be in if I did not bring it home! And this young man here," I gestured to Shao, "He saw my distress and held my coat while I went in to fetch it! Look at it! Ruined!" I held out the tarpaulin, so thick with mud that it could've been canvas or a fine weave and no one would be the wiser. I gave it a disheartened shake. Bits of mud flew in all directions.

The officer, mindful of his spotless uniform, released Shao and took a few steps back to avoid the spray. "Yes, I fair say your mother will be furious!"

"And my dress—I'll be in such trouble!"

He rounded on Shao. "Why didn't you go in? God damn, boy, where's your sense of chivalry?" Then, giving up on Shao's ability to understand, said to me, "It's far too late for a lady to be out!"

I seized on his warning with relish. "You are absolutely correct, this is no fit place for a young woman to be walking at this hour!" I laid one grimy hand on his sleeve. "Would you walk me home, officer? My father would be so very pleased; I'm sure there would be a letter of commendation from him for your help."

He looked between Shao and me. "You get back to Chinatown, hear?" he shouted at Shao.

I raised my voice a little, too. "Thank you! Thank you for your help! You were most gracious!"

Shao gave a clipped nod.

"Come by my father's piano business as soon as you can. The name is Ross. It's in the Jewish quarter. I'm sure I can find suitable payment for your trouble."

He looked at me like I had lost all my marbles, then the corner of his mouth kinked up in a slight smile. Shao gave another nod, and shoved his hands in his pockets as he walked briskly away.

For eight whole blocks, I received a long list of stern warnings about the perils of the city to those of the fairer sex, and Constable Pickering was most insistent that he walk me to the front porch of the house, though I would not let him knock on the door. This was absolutely necessary, for it was not Mr. Fish's door—I had guided him to a modest residence on the north side of Beacon Hill Park, a suitable size for a piano merchant and far from the Jewish quarter of Ross Bay cemetery.

I bid him farewell and waited until he was out of sight before dashing off the porch and into the lovely secretive oak groves that wreathed Beacon Hill. The wet dress stuck to my body and the water made me cold, so I took shelter under a bower of ferns to strip it off. Then I wrapped the dry coat around my bare body, and the warmth it gave me was delicious. I wrung as much water from my smock as I could, appraising the damage. Only sodden, it could be saved; I slung it over my elbow, and dropped the scrap of tarpaulin under a bush—it reeked of swamp mud and dead rat.

Oh, wait. Another sniff of my fingers proved that it was not the tarpaulin that smelt of rat, but me.

Wearing only the coat and my stockings and boots, I skirted the bottom of the hill and ran as fast as I could to Ross Bay cemetery, a long strip of meadow that followed the curve of the sea, separated from the beach by a narrow boundary of dirt road. The exercise warmed me a little, and by the time I reached the graveyard's low stone fence, a rosy flush had risen to my cheeks and my hands tingled.

Ross Bay was the resting place of the elite. To be laid out here was an accomplishment of which the dead could be proud. The frontiersman Billy Barker had been buried here only a few years ago, as had Amor de Cosmos, the most wonderfully-named journalist to ever grace the Earth. He'd been the second premier of the province, but he was not alone: premiers James Douglas, Andrew Eliot, and brothers Alex and Theodore Davie were laid out in this graveyard, too, as well as a parade of surgeons, mariners, politicians, entrepreneurs. They lay alongside each other, arguments forgotten, their flesh now quietly feeding the noble oaks. Under the tranquil trees, with the moon casting its silver glow over the branches, it was easy to grow reflective on life's transience. Ozymandius would've fit in nicely.

Robert Dunsmuir, the man who hired my father, lay here, too. I stopped and rested at his marker, a great square granite pillar topped with a statue of an urn, draped with a mourning shroud.

Dunsmuir had known my grandfather's friend, Mr. Wadham Diggle, and through that connection, my parents had secured a future in Canada. Dunsmuir was a wealthy man with connection and influence around the world—his network of British Columbian coal towns provided fuel for the ships and factories of the Empire. He'd begun his career as a miner, making only a few dollars a day, but when he died, he was the richest man in all of British Columbia. Dunsmuir had been an industrialist of boundless ambition, shrewd business sense, and hard-headed practicality.

But I had never seen him, nor my father met him, for Robert Dunsmuir died in 1889, the same year we had come to Canada.

'How strange,' I thought, 'That this man who changed the course of my life should lie here under my feet.'

A soft footfall on the grass caught my ear, and Shao whispered, "I wasn't looking forward to a night in jail."

I melted into his embrace. "Claiming to speak no English? You speak better English than Cantonese!"

"It buys me time," he explained. "It's always better to understand more than they assume."

I pressed my lips to his.

His hands were everywhere, and I felt the shiver race across his body as he discovered my nudity. A low laugh escaped his throat. We sought privacy under the trees, and Shao laid me upon a bed of moss and fallen leaves. I fumbled at his pants, and we became a tangled lump of limbs and giggles between the mortuary statues and mausoleums.

Shao warmed me up the best way he knew how.

When we were finished, we lay in each other's embrace at the roots of a majestic Garry oak, my coat thrown over us. He planted light kisses on my forehead, and I snuggled under his arm, but my thoughts had returned to Jess. We hadn't bothered to remove my stockings from my garter belt, and I slipped my hand down the outside of my thigh to find the long metal object still hugged tightly to my flesh.

I withdrew it and held it up to the moonlight.

Shao glanced down at the object in my hands.

"A screwdriver!"

"Apparently," I replied.

Together, we studied it. The screwdriver had not been in the mud for long. Its iron shaft was neither rusted nor encrusted with dirt, and the wooden handle had not cracked or rotted, though it was sodden through from days at the bottom of the creek. The handle was polished smooth by years of hands gripping it, but it was a serviceable tool. The tip was sturdy and, from the way it shone, it had recently been sharpened. No workman would toss this away.

"That's what stabbed Jess?"

"Yes," I said, studying its handle.

"How will you ever find who owned it?" he asked. "It looks like a million other tools, and the whole area is industrial. One of the shipyards, maybe?" He held me a little more tightly. "Honestly, Liz, it could've been anyone."

"But it wasn't anyone," I replied thoughtfully, "It was someone with a motive."

He looked at me askance.

I sat upright. The coat fell away and the cold air felt like a slap on my naked breasts. "Whoever grabbed this tool had crossed paths with Jess. That narrows down our suspects."

"Why yes, from millions to hundreds," he replied, pulling up the coat to cover me again. "And we still need a motive. Without that, we don't have chance to find a solid lead."

"Green fabric. A screwdriver. The location of the crime. A pregnancy and an elopement." I considered how they must fit together, then said, "No, we don't have enough yet. But we will." I leaned forwards. "I still haven't spoken with Greta Braun or Maude Mawson, and they may have information. I'll find them tomorrow and ask them about the night Jess went missing." I reached up and kissed him, and said, "Can I ask you a question?"

"Of course," he replied, still studying the screwdriver with a scowl.

"When Mr. Lim asked if I were your girlfriend, you said no. Why?"

"It's complicated, Lei Zi."

"Try to explain," I pressed. "I have all night."

"No," he laughed, "I mean, if you're my girlfriend, it's complicated. Mr. Lim has been kind to give me a job, but if he knew about us … well, it's like Jess and Andy, isn't it. No one wants to upset the order of things. It's difficult enough for us to be friends." He had looked so contented before, and now, his expression of sadness seemed all the more poignant for the comparison. "If people knew we were more than friends, there would be questions, disapproval, and they would scorn us and suggest politely that we part ways. Mr. Lim is a good man, and I know he wants me to settle down and stay with his business. He's been so kind, and I don't want to disappoint him." Shao gave a rueful chuckle. "He's been introducing me to all sorts of girls: Xui Li, the daughter of the butcher, and Qaio Ying Ma, the laundress on Herald Street."

"You're interested in them?"

"No!" he laughed, "But Mr. Lim's starting to wonder why I'm not pursuing a girlfriend." Shao studied the screwdriver again, but this time, a smile played across his mouth. "It's made me think about my future, which I never really considered before. When I lived with *jiu fu*, I never thought much farther than surviving my next shift in the mine. Trying to pay my head tax, I never dreamed of saving money or building a business." He smiled again, and now the light of hope illuminated his face. "Liz, I never considered that there could be more to my life. But now that we're here, and Mr. Lim is offering me so many opportunities, and maybe there's more I can accomplish … well, I'm starting to think that Victoria could provide everything I need."

"Could Victoria be your home?" I asked. "Have you found a place where you belong?"

He thought for a long time.

At last, he said, "I love you, Liz."

I kissed him.

"That isn't an answer, Shao."

"I don't think I have one," he admitted. Then, after a pause, he said, "Maybe yes, Victoria is a place I could call home." He looked down at me. "And some things need time before they can be said. Maybe we can be open with Mr. Lim about our relationship, once he's come to know us and accept us."

"You think so?"

He held me a little closer and closed his eyes. "Maybe this is a place we could call home, together."

I raised myself up on one elbow. "What?"

Shao paused. Then he took a sharp breath and wrapped his fingers around my hand.

"Liz, would you consider marrying me?" Then quickly, he added, "Not now, not right away. Give us a year or two, and we can live above Mr. Lim's shop for a while, and wait until you're a little older, and maybe finish your schooling, but we could build a business here, and it would be difficult and there would be challenges and I can never offer you a comfortable life but, well," He paused to take a breath. "Would you?"

I stared at him, wide-eyed.

"I … I …"

"You're going to say no."

"I'm going to say, I wasn't expecting this!" My stomach lurched, but I didn't think I could blame the whiskey this time. He was so earnest, his eyes searching my face for any hint of my acceptance. I realized he'd been mustering his courage to ask, but there had never been a moment more perfect than this.

I'd missed him, and I'd thought he'd been leaving me behind, but all this time, he'd been building a path for us to follow, together.

"God's teeth, I love you," I whispered.

"You sound amazed by that."

"I am," I admitted. Jack could accuse me of being a heartless monster, but every minute I spent with Shao was evidence to the contrary.

"Don't answer me now," he said, letting go of my hands. "Just, promise me you'll consider it."

"I will."

"I suppose I'll need to ask your father for his permission," Shao said. "That won't be easy."

"No," I agreed, "It won't."

"But we can be happy here, together," he said. "I know it."

I kissed him again, just to keep him quiet while my mind raced.

Twenty-Four

November 2, 1898

At the corner of Ross Bay cemetery, we parted ways furtively like thieves, with a quick kiss under the shadows of an oak bower. I wanted time to consider Shao's question. I insisted I walk home alone.

No, to be truthful, I was not quite alone: the milk wagons had started to clank and clatter along the streets. Roosters in back yards had begun to crow, and a few dogs barked a warning as I passed.

I held the screwdriver in one hand, my sodden dress in the other. The weight of the weapon dragged at my tired arm but I was unable to consider the scene of the crime or the identity of the murderer. My mind was a muddle. Holding the tool, I wanted to plunge it into something, if only to release the confusion that coursed through my addled thoughts.

Oh, Shao. Why did you have to ask me?

I was sure I loved him. There was no other fact of which I was so certain. But I'd come out tonight to find a murder scene, and I hadn't expected a proposal, and I promised myself I would not hold him to it. If the moonlight and our congress had cluttered his good judgment, I'd understand. A marriage between us would be no easy endeavor, and if he reconsidered his offer after a good night's sleep and a healthy breakfast, I wouldn't be surprised, insulted, or angry.

Maybe I ought to be angry, I thought as the end of the block. He's put me in a most precarious position. If I refuse, he won't understand why—he'll think I'm dissatisfied with him or the future he could offer me. He'll think any reason I give him is a lie to cover a more sinister one: that we are not of the same race, and such moral discrepancies are not allowed.

This, of course, would be utter poppycock.

I stopped at the edge of the sidewalk, considering.

Why *would* I refuse him?

'He doesn't really know me,' I thought, 'He doesn't know what I'm capable of; he doesn't know what I've done.' I looked at Mr. Fish's house from a distance. 'Can I lock all of that away and be a normal person?

Maybe I could, but I felt a little sick about it.

But I loved him. I really did. More than any other emotion—more than grief, or regret, or fear—I knew that what I felt was love for Shao.

And for a heartbeat, I allowed myself a moment's liberation to wonder: could I be happy here with him? Could I abandon all my questions about my family and bloodline, forget all that had happened since the death of my mother, set my eyes to the future, and build something beautiful and prosperous with Shao? Would he want me still, if he knew I was a murderer?

Maybe there was no need for him to ever know. I simply leave that part of my life behind, too.

I was very cold, very tired, but I barely noticed the discomfort. I only registered the confusion that had become a fist squeezing my heart. Then I said a name, out loud, and the sound of it was like the peal of a bell from a distant harbor, calling me through the fog.

"Mrs. Lizzie Chen."

Perhaps.

When I returned to the house, I boiled water on the kitchen stove for a hot bath. I lay for a long time in the scalding tub, letting the heat seep into my bones and chase away my concerns. After I toweled dry, I washed out my dress in the soapy water and hung it from a peg behind the stove, hoping it would dry quickly, then I ate a little bit of cold roast chicken I found in the cooler and retired to the attic. I stashed the screwdriver in my satchel, hanging from the bedpost, and I lay on my cot for a long time, resting and thinking.

He was intelligent, generous, handsome. He brought me happiness. He made me feel like I could be a good person.

I couldn't imagine my life without Shaozhu; I couldn't imagine what I'd become, without him.

Twenty-Five

By the time I awoke in the late afternoon, my black frock was dry from the heat of the stove, and because the house seemed to be empty, I dressed in the warm kitchen. Swimming in the stream had ruined my stockings—they were quite beyond hope—so my legs were bare and cold, but I found a pair of men's black socks in the laundry hamper that would, at least, keep my feet warm. I fetched an apple from the larder and a bit of rye bread from the pantry, which served nicely for lunch, and in Mr. Fish's office, I pulled out a city directory.

I ate as I leafed through the pages, looking for a name. There were very few Brauns listed in Victoria. One lived out by Oak Bay, and another lived in Ferndale. A third lived in the downtown core: a Mr. Bertrand Braun owned the tobacco shop on Government Street. Considering it was only a few blocks from the Temple of Thespis, I figured this was the most likely place to find Greta; she would not have joined an amateur theatre club if it were located too far to walk.

"Oh, you're here," said a weary voice. I turned in my seat to see Mrs. Garry coming from the basement stairwell, carrying a wicker basket of laundry in her hands.

"I am, yes," I said, and I wasn't quite sure what more to say. I'd rarely seen the woman since the death of her daughter. She looked terrible. Her skin was waxy and unwashed, her hair unkempt, her eyes as dull as stones. I wondered if this is what I ought to look like, having lost my entire family in the space of seven months.

"Mr. Fish says you've been coming and going, and I ain't been myself for the last few days," she admitted. Her voice was hollow and distant as she said it, as if giving apologies for someone quite separate from herself. "The state of the house has been deplorable. The dusting's not done, the fire grates ain't been cleaned, and the sheets on the beds—"

"I have no complaints," I stammered, "And I will help out where ever I can. Let me do the washing today! Take ease and rest, Mrs. Garry. Surely at this time of mourning—"

But the mere mention caused her to choke and strangle a sob. "I got to do this, miss. It's my responsibility."

And clearly in her face, as if she'd said it aloud, I saw that the housework was all that bound her together. She must keep busy, or she would crumble to pieces.

"Can I ask you a question, Mrs. Garry?"

"I s'pose," she said.

"You said that Jess was seeing a boy … do you know who?"

She shook her head. "Naw, I never knew his name. But she was sneaking out here and there, I figured it must be some silly romance. She was such a … such a silly …" Her throat constricted, and she didn't bother to finish the sentence. Instead, she took a long breath to steady herself, and clung tightly to the laundry. "Miss, you've been very kind, but you shouldn't be getting entangled in this. The theatre ain't the place for an upstanding girl."

"Thank you for your concern."

"I mean it, now," she insisted. "You keep with your match girl reading, and your medical books, and you leave all these ridiculous follies behind." She gave a motherly harrumph, as if to say she would listen to no further arguments from me. "They're liars, miss. It's what they love to do. How can anyone trust an actor, when they spend all their waking hours perfecting their talent to lie?"

I wondered if Andy was a better actor than I gave him credit.

"That's a harsh assessment, Mrs. Garry."

Her face tensed. "They stole my daughter away from me," she spat. "I could say a hell of a lot worse."

I bid her farewell, but she barely heard me and returned to her washing with as much liveliness as a woman asleep. Once she was gone and I was finished my lunch, I pulled on my coat and slipped from the house. I had to walk briskly through James Bay, to keep my bare legs from freezing in the wind.

Government Street was a wide, busy thoroughfare, cluttered with pedestrians, trolleys and cabs. I hurried along the boardwalk, under the wide awnings that sheltered a series of dry goods merchants, and passed a tin smith shop, where a flurry of loud pings and bangs drowned out any conversations on the street. On the corner, next to a tea house, I finally arrived at the address from Mr. Fish's directory: a small, compact establishment under a crisp green awning. The sign above the yellow door proclaimed it to be a 'celebrated purveyor of fine products from all countries of the globe'. The leaded window offered a luxurious display of cigars, shaving brushes, wooden-handled razors, white clay pipes, and enameled boxes. Their colorful artwork provided a whole circus of pigs, horses, soldiers, ships and washerwomen on parade across the window ledge. I'd never seen such a riotous collection of things.

I pushed open the door. Inside, I found the shop crammed with patrons. The high suffocating shelves carried a countless multitude of quality goods. The place was too crowded for my liking, to be sure, but the friendly, comfortable smell of warm cigars, loose leaf, and pipe smoke greeted me and welcomed me. I moved amongst the customers, examining the wares.

A stately man with slick, dark hair stood behind the glass counter. He wore an expensive black frock coat and grey paisley tie under his long white apron, crisp, clean, and freshly laundered. His features were as severe as the blade of a knife, and the points of his waxed moustache looked dangerously sharp. "We will not be affected by these outrageous taxes currently being raised by the American Congress, I can assure you," he told his customer, a rugged looking chap with grey hair and grizzled, tangled beard. "The Spanish War is a decidedly south-of-the-border problem, Mr. Duke, and I can promise you, our prices will remain as they always have: quite reasonable." He leaned in close and dropped his voice. "There is no need for stockpiling."

I admired the items in the case, listening.

"I'm not about to be left out in the cold, I promise you," said the weathered Mr. Duke, "If I find the price starting to rise, I'm not gonna be happy."

The tobacconist looked suitably offended. "I endeavor to keep my patrons well-stocked, sir! And always at the most reasonable prices!" he insisted.

"Reasonable?" said Mr. Duke. "I can get twice as much for the same coin in Seattle."

"And you'd trust cheap tobacco? Believe me, you can get an old knacker for cheap at the glue yard, but it won't carry you as far as a thoroughbred! Smoking is a fine way to soothe your respiratory ailments and ensure a healthy complexion. This is a matter of good health, sir, and you can not put a price on that." He noticed me, and said, "Can I help you, miss?"

"I'm looking for Miss Greta Braun," I said. "Do you know her?"

His face brightened. "That would be my daughter." Then he gestured to a young boy unloading a crate to a shelf and said, "Simon, run upstairs and fetch Greta."

It took only a moment for Simon to return, with Greta close behind him. She looked confused, then displeased, to see me. She led me to the quietest corner of the crowded shop, where she crossed her arms and said, "Why are *you* here?"

"I wanted to ask you about the night Jess died."

"Well, I don't want to talk about it, and I certainly don't want to talk about it with you," she said sourly. "Jess was like a sister to me."

I rolled my eyes. "I know we haven't always agreed—"

"It's not that, Miss Saunders," she said, "You ought to keep your nose out of other people's business. I don't want to meddle in things that aren't my affair."

"You think Mrs. Thornton will disapprove?"

She gave a little huff, and I saw how the severity in her father's face matched her own. "It's not decent, Miss Saunders. Although," she added, looking at my bare legs and wool socks, "You don't seem to have much sense when it comes to decency. You and Nell would get along like a house on fire."

The name came out in a sneer. "You aren't fond of Nell."

"None of us are," she replied. "Nell always ruins a good thing." She growled and leaned her shoulder against the wall, and dropped her voice lest her father heard. "You know, with all her … propositions. Take last Saturday, for example: we were having a fine time, until she decided to improve the quality of her clientele. Mr. Carter was furious! He smashed a tureen and threatened to teach her a lesson if she didn't get out of his house."

"But you had no objections to Mr. Carter's behavior?"

She squinted in confusion. "Why would I?'

"The squalor of his home? The tone of his dismissal?"

Greta laughed. "I'd never claim he's a nice person, but he's a gentleman, so who am I to judge?" She cast me a patronizing glance. "Don't tell me you're so naive, Liz, to think a gentleman's status guarantees him to be kind, or thoughtful, or clean."

"No, I'm well aware of that."

"Well, Mr. Carter paid for our singing, and it was poor form for Nell to solicit his guests," she continued. "She chews nickels and spit nails, that one, and she could've ruined our chances of ever singing again with her presumptions."

"But the Sing Song Girls are no more."

"So Jess ruined it by going and getting murdered," Greta looked genuinely sad, but I wondered if it was for the loss of Jess, or the loss of future invitations to gentlemen's parties. She dabbed at tears that had formed in the corners of her eyes. "Too bad for that. It was fun while it lasted."

"But you aren't sad for Jess?"

"Of course I am," she snapped. She spoke more loudly, and a few of the customers looked surreptitiously at us, then moved away to give us privacy.

I knew it to be false, though: their eyes were riveted too closely to the products on the shelf, and I doubt any of them were reading the labels.

"Did anyone leave with her?"

Greta shook her head. "Not that I remember."

I waited as a crush of patrons moved past, once again giving Greta and I a bit of intimacy in the corner. "This may seem like an odd question," I began, "But do you recall, were any of the men in attendance wearing a green coat?"

She blinked twice. "I … I don't know. Perhaps."

"Perhaps a workman? A gardener, even?"

"It was midnight! There weren't any workmen around," she replied. "The guests were all decent men. I don't even remember many of them being overly drunk; well, perhaps William Carter, but he's never been known for staying dry when there's an open bottle on the table. We'd been hired to sing, but nothing more." Greta twisted her face in disgust. "So when Nelly tried to work her charms for a few extra dollars, we were kicked to the alleyway. But Jess left before I did, and Nelly left after me. Who knows? Maybe one of the men accompanied her home."

"What about Maude? When did she leave?"

"After me, that's for certain."

So Jess left first, then Greta, then Nelly and Maude. Yet neither Greta nor Nelly had seen anyone leave with Jess; I briefly entertained the thought that her murder had nothing to do with the evening performance, but couldn't shake the suspicion that they were somehow connected.

"Thanks for your help, Greta." I said, still thinking, paying little attention to her look of disdain. "Do you know where I can find Maude?"

"She lives with her parents on Cook Street, but she works as a laundress at the Driard Hotel. You'll probably find her there."

I turned to the door but Greta stopped me, laying her hand on my elbow. "Miss Saunders? You asked if any of the men had a green coat … Now, I don't know about the men, but Nelly has one."

"She does?"

"Yes, a lovely felt coat, deep green, like the color of ferns. Does that help to you?"

I paused.

"Yes, Greta. Yes it does. Thank you so much."

I bid her farewell but did not immediately go to the Driard Hotel. Instead, I made my way to the Siren's Rest. A brief knock on the door brought the same peg-toothed, thin-haired woman to the door. As before, she was ever so happy to see me.

"What choo want?" she spat, "You ain't here t'upset Nelly 'gain, are yeh?"

"Is she here?"

Those watery eyes rolled like marbles in their loose sockets, darting to either side of me and full of suspicion. "Course she's here, but she's busy with a johnny, so screw off."

"I'd rather wait."

The woman's voice pitched upwards. She was only slightly taller than me, as gangly as a rake, but her spindly fingers and cracked nails bit into my left wrist like talons. She had a surprising, wiry strength. "No you ain't!" she squawked, "You're gonna scare away business!"

"I know that Nelly's time is worth money," I began, prying her fingers from my wrist, "And if it's so damned important, I'll pay."

This stopped her. "How much?"

"What's Nelly's rate?"

She narrowed her eyes. Her expression became that of a hungry ferret. "A dollar a gambol, and you're out in forty minutes."

I pulled the coin from my coat pocket. "This is all I've got," I said, pressing the money into her hand. "I'm not in for a gambol, and I only need ten minutes."

As I suspected, seeing the money and feeling it in the palm of her hand made it too difficult to refuse. True, the coin was worth a fraction of her asking price, but it was real and solid in her grip. She didn't want to let it go.

"Right. C'mon up, girl."

We mounted the steps to the upper floor of the building, where she led me to the second door on the right. I heard grunts from within. She gave a light tap on the door—two raps, then a pause, and two more.

Then she led me next door and ushered me inside. The walls were brindled with black mold, the metal bedframe was thin and rusted. The sour stench off the mattress was enough to make my throat hitch. Faint light came from a single square window that had been swabbed with a greasy rag, leaving it streaked and spattered, and the room was cold, draughty, and dismal. The only sense of comfort came from a brown rag rug on the ground, but the glimmer of movement amongst its fibers betrayed the fleas and bedbugs that lived there.

"Wait here," she ordered, "Nelly'll come to you when she's done."

I nodded my understanding and she left.

The grunting that came from behind the thin wall sounded like a couple of pigs wrestling over a corn cob. Eventually the sound mellowed into some pleasure-filled groans, and I heard the squeal of bedsprings and a girlish laugh.

"C'mon, give us another romp, Nell my love," said a man's voice. Nelly clucked her tongue in reproach.

"You talk with Mavis about another session. The next fella's already here, and I ain't have no one budging in line," she replied. I heard a sloppy kiss, a creaking door, and the padding of bare feet on the wooden floorboards.

The door opened. There stood Nell in a threadbare nightgown, her dark hair hanging down around her shoulders. Her mouth fell open in a perfect circle.

"Hi, Nelly."

"Holy hell, what the fuck are you doing here?" she yelped.

I gave her a beaming smile. "I'm your next fella."

Twenty-Six

I sat on the end of the bed and Nelly paced back and forth, but the little room was hardly more than a closet, so the best she could manage before having to turn was three steps.

"God damn, you know Mavis ain't happy to have you here!" she whispered, afraid that the thin walls would hear and repeat whatever she said. "You're gonna get me in shit again!"

"That's not my intention," I replied. "But I was passing by and I had a few questions that don't have answers."

"Aw, god damn, I told ya all I know."

"Do you own a green coat?"

She stopped her pacing abruptly and raised one eyebrow. "Maybe. Why?"

"Not many people own green coats. They're quite rare."

"Well, ain't I a lucky one, then?" she laughed. "Must be the Irish in me. Always gets me outta scrapes and jams."

"Can I see the coat?"

"No."

"Why not?"

"What you want with it, Ms. Saunders?"

I decided to try another line of inquiry. I thought for a moment, pulling up my wool socks; the room was quite cold, and a strong draught came up through gaps in the floor boards, directly under this blasted dress.

I reached into my satchel and pulled out the screwdriver, and held it out to Nell. "Have you ever seen this before?"

"What would I need with one of those?" she said.

"You see many men from all stations—I figured the mark on it might look familiar, and remind you of one of them."

She took it and peered at the mark. "Well, these ain't exactly the kind of tools they show me," she said with a laugh, "But what is that on there?

A bird?"

"I think so."

"Looks like a magpie," she replied. "A cheeky little bird with a pretty tail." She flipped it over in her hands a few times, then handed it back to me. "Sorry, never seen anything like it."

I put it back in my bag. "Do you know a man by the name of Jack?"

She started to giggle. "More than I'd like!" She sat down on the bed next to me, and tipped her head towards the entrance. "Almost every prick that comes through that door is attached to a man callin' himself Jack." She laughed again. "Big, little, young, old, hairy, bald, all the bloody same, if you please; none of 'em have a speck of imagination! Just once," she said, shaking her finger in the door's direction, "Just once I'd like a Rudolph or an Ivan. Jaysus, anything with a little class!"

I grinned.

"Tell me, Liz, what's this all got to do with Jess?"

"Did you know that Jess was pregnant?"

Nell lowered her face. Greta had seemed so cold, so distant and angry, but Nell spoke easily and fluidly; her rough demeanor was a coat of armor protecting a caring, helpful personality. I found myself warming to the woman, to her high cheekbones and bony hands, to her melodious voice, to her demands for something better than a flea-infested room. We sat next to each other on the bed like we'd known each other for a long time, our shoulders touching. "Poor girl," she said quietly, and took a deep breath to stifle a rising sob. "I knew she was with child. She was in a bad way, and she asked me if I knew how to get rid of it."

"What did you tell her?"

Nell looked scandalized. "I never told her a thing!" She dropped her voice. "There's a man down by the bridge who performs the service for a fee, but I'd never send Jess to a place like that! Too many girls come out scarred or dead! And to be honest, Miss Saunders, I didn't get the impression that Jess really wanted to get rid of the baby; she was just afraid. You know, that first moment when you suddenly realize you're gonna be a mother? That there's gonna be a human life coming out of your body and into the world?" She patted my knee with her hand. "Ain't no woman doesn't feel a little scared by that power."

"I never thought of that."

"Well, you ain't a mother," Nell said.

"You are?"

Her thin mouth drew up in a wistful smile. "I got a little boy, he's three now. He lives with my sister up in Duncan's Crossing." She looked down at the floor again. "His name is Georgie, but I ain't seen him since he was a wee babe." She sat up straight and wiped the corner of her eye with the tip of her fingers. "Look, Jess asked for a doctor, but I wouldn't dare send her to one, and when I saw her that last Saturday, she told me she'd changed her mind. She said good things were a-coming, and she wanted the baby." Nell held up one finger to stop my question at my lips. "I asked who the father was, but she stayed mum. Jess had a bright future, she did. Someone stole that from her, and I hope they find the goddamn cur, and string him up high."

"Are you sure I can't see that green coat?" I replied.

Nell had dropped her suspicious nature, but she shook her head. "I'd show it to you if I could, but the fact is, I got rid of it a few weeks back. The sleeves were threadbare in the elbows and it was missing most of its buttons, and it didn't keep out the wind."

"Where'd you dump it?"

"I handed it over to Mrs. Thornton. I figured she could use any of the good pieces of fabric for costumes."

"Thanks, Nell. I appreciate it."

"You're welcome, Lizzie. I want justice just as much as the next—" She slammed to a stop. "Lizzie? And you said you were looking for a guy named Jack!"

"Yes."

"Big guy, American, missing a finger?"

"That's him," I said, "You know him!"

"Hell, yeah, I know him." She laughed. "He's got deep pockets, that one! Here at least twice a week." The mirth left her face, replaced by pity. "But sore troubled, he is, poor fella."

"Troubled?"

"You know the kind: drinks more than he ought. And after he's been in his cups, he's not always up for a romp, if you get my meaning."

I shook my head.

Nelly clucked in her throat. "No, I guess you don't." She thought a moment before answering. "Most fellas come to the Siren's Rest for a bit of fun, but some would rather spend the money and just have the company, y'know? They don't need sex. They just want to …" She thought for a moment, then said, "They want to not be alone."

"Not be alone?"

She smirked. "When he's been drinking, that's Jack. He shows up on our doorstep a right mess, and he just wants to lay quiet with a woman's arms around him. It's the easiest bit of bob to make, so I don't mind! And lordy, when he falls asleep …" She laughed and tapped her finger against the center of my chest. "Well, that's how I know you!"

A shiver crossed my spine. "Me?"

She leaned in close. "He talks in his sleep. He jabbers on about all sorts of things!"

"He does?"

"Oh, yeah," she nodded, "The deep sea swallowing up people, forests full of devils, a man swinging high up in a tree. He calls for his momma, he calls out for someone named John. He talks about a knife ripping down through the darkness, and someone coming to kill him." She grinned. "Lord, his yarns are right fascinating! I could lie there all night and listen to his stories!"

Ice water gushed through my veins. I fell the blood blanch from my face. I gripped the bed in strong finger to keep my hands from shaking. Nell, oblivious to my shock, threw me a sly grin.

"And I must admit, Lizzie Saunders," she said in a whisper, "Late at night, when he's dreaming his deepest? He howls out for you."

TWENTY-SEVEN

I fled from the Siren's Rest with my heart in my throat, furious as a wet cat. The sun had recently set and the clear sky was a deep, luxurious purple, with the first stars appearing as crisp, white diamonds. I clenched my hands in my pockets, I ground my teeth, I thought about what I must do. I stalked Wharf Street and watched the shadows, waited in doorways, assessed every man that passed by. Businessmen in bowlers, sailors discharged from ships, men leading pack mules that had been loaded with gear for the gold fields, lumbermen in plaid shirts and wool jackets—I watched them pass, and none paid any attention to me.

Close to midnight, I saw Jack step from a bar on Yates. He pulled his collar snug around his throat and hunched his shoulders against the cold wind that rose from the harbor. I fell into step behind him with half a block between us.

Furious, I followed him along the boardwalk, staring daggers at his back. He had revealed my secrets to a stranger, and he didn't even know it.

Jack greeted a few roustabouts on the corner. I heard him promise to pay one of them what he was due, maybe next Monday, and then he continued on his way. His heavy boots thumped on the planks, and at one point, I heard him whistle at one of the ladies strolling along Government Street. She blew him a kiss back but he didn't stop to pursue her propositions.

I followed him along Government Street and across the James Bay pedestrian bridge, and eventually as far as the alleyway leading behind Mr. Fish's fine residence. From the shadows under an oak tree at the street corner, I watched him settle into a place of his own hiding: a nook next to the garden shed, where the fence met the outbuilding. A small pile of trimmed firewood made a comfortable seat, and the light of the moon cast a shadow over that part of Mr. Fish's yard. Reclined with his back against the shed, the darkness hid him well. The spot provided a clear view of the house and most of the grounds, and a straight line-of-sight up to the attic window. He could see when my bedside lamp was lit, and if I was standing close enough to the glass, he might've been able to catch a glimpse of me.

Half-hidden behind the oak, I studied the pool of shadows where he lingered, watching the watcher. I was livid. Hearing Nell speak so openly about fragments of my life, even if she didn't understand the larger picture, had ignited a fire in my gut. I hated the destruction that Jack Hunter had brought into my world, but even more than that—I hated that he knew so much about me. He made me vulnerable.

I ought to kill him, I thought. *Right now.*

But I had no weapon. I could not throttle him; as I flexed my hands, I wondered if they were even large enough to encircle his neck. Shao's knife was in my attic room, but I dared not go into Mr. Fish's house while it was being watched. I had so very much to do, and killing Jack Hunter had not been in this evening's plan.

Jack propped up his feet on the chopping block, folded his arms, and gave every indication that he planned to stay for a while. Good. Let him watch my window. I was on my way to the Driard Hotel, to speak with Maude.

Everyone knew that the Driard was Victoria's grandest hotel. The doors had recently opened in 1892 and the whole building gleamed, new and bright and shining, on the corner of View Street and Broad Street. It was the pinnacle of modern luxury, with a stunning brick edifice resplendent with arches. Iron filigree outlined the large windows, over which the cast iron spandrels provided support and decoration. The Romanesque facade was a deep, seamless red, with black highlights and grey stone columns. Even the mortar between the bricks had been tinted a matching red, so that the overall effect was one of seamless elegance. The architect, an ambitious and talented Englishman named Francis Rattenbury, had drawn on his love of European architecture when he'd designed The Driard, and it would have fit comfortably into the skyline of any European city. Rattenbury's designs could be found throughout Victoria, including the new parliament buildings, and his vision was shaping this city's appearance, but many thought the Driard was the most luxurious and refined of his plans. At six stories high, the Driard towered over its neighbours, like a majestic queen holding court.

I watched the main doors from across the street. Women in fur stoles and men in suit jackets and top hats arrived in hansom cabs. A rare few left on foot, strolling only as far as the fine restaurant next door. Clearly, the caliber of clientele at the Driard were not prone to be pedestrians. A small army of bell hops, dressed in burgundy uniforms, hurried about the lobby. They pushed brass carts loaded with towers of leather luggage, they delivered letters and packages to cabbies, and they shooed away beggars from the front door. In my present attire of rumpled black frock and naked legs, I knew I would not be welcome. Perhaps the side door would suit me better. Certainly, it would inspire fewer questions.

A small alley ran behind the hotel. There, under a grey stone arch, I found a door that had been propped open with a stone, and it led into a hot, steamy, greasy kitchen, where white-garbed cooks chopped meats and yelled insults to each other as they created meals for the upper class. On a stool next to the door sat a young Chinese man with his hair pulled back in a queue, peeling potatoes. He looked up to me as I drew close, and before he could say anything, I greeted, "*Ni hao.*"

"*Ni hao,*" he replied, with just the hint of a question. Then, in English, he added, "We've got no rags or scraps tonight, kid. Come back in the morning."

"I'm not begging," I replied, "I'm here to speak with one of the laundresses, named Maude. Is she here?"

He perked up at the mention of her name. "She is," he replied, "You one of Mrs. Thornton's girls?"

"I suppose," I said, "I run errands, if that's what you mean."

"Naw, I meant the singers. I know Maudie's a singer—thought you might be too."

"No one wants to hear me sing!" I laughed, coaxing a smile from him. "In fact, I bet I could make a fair wage if they paid me NOT to sing."

"Well, the laundry is downstairs," he replied. "Follow the staircase, just through that doorway there."

I followed his directions, descending a stone staircase into a cavernous basement, where I found three young women sorting laundry into massive wooden vats. When I spoke Maude's name, the nearest one raised her head, and I recognized her square jaw, dark hair and deep brown eyes. Her body was made of slender limbs and creamy skin, and when she stood to wipe the sweat from her brow, she moved with a dancer's grace. Place her alongside Greta's sweetly cherubic face, Nell's saucy demeanor, and Jessie's shy allure, and I imagined that the four Sing Song Girls, standing together on stage, would have commanded any man's gaze.

She left her co-workers and joined me in the stairwell. "How can I help ya, miss?" she said.

"My name is—"

"Liz Saunders. Yeah, I know who you are."

"You do?"

"I've seen you around the theatre, and Nelly gave me fair warning yesterday that you'd be coming to visit me. She says you're hot on the heels of Jessie's killer," Maude said, although there was a note of dismissal to it, "I doubt anyone's going to catch him, love, and especially not you."

I frowned at this to hide my surprise. "Why not me?"

"Well, just look at ya! Sorry, girl, but it's true. If the police can't find him—and they won't—what hope have you got?"

"I have a great hope, Maude. I have very few friends, but I counted Jess amongst them, and I'll be damned if I let her murderer walk away from his crime." I leaned against the wall. "Are you content to let things lie as they are?"

She shook her head. "Of course not. How can I help?"

"Were you and Jess amicable?"

"Oh, more so!" she gasped, "She was one of the Sing Song Girls, and that's a strong bond, right there! I loved her like a sister!"

Her words caused me to startle; I'd heard them before, with the very same inflection. "Greta said that, too."

Maude thrust out her chin, set her fists on her waist. "Did she, now?" she said with no small measure of surprise, "Well, I suppose we forget our troubles in death, don't we."

"So Jess and Greta didn't get along?"

"They were professional enough," Maude said. "There was a taste of competition between them. Sometimes Jess was jealous of the attention that the men gave Greta. When she cleans up and wears a pretty dress, she looks as innocent as an angel, you know. All the men loved that."

I stamped my feet a little, and noticed a coal grate in the corner. "Would you mind terribly if we stood over there, Maude?" I asked, "My legs are quite cold."

"Well of course they are, you've got no stockings," she said with a measure of wonder. "Whatever possessed you to go out with bare knees, girl?"

"I ruined my stockings yesterday," I replied. Oh, the heat from the fire was delicious! I hadn't realized how cold I'd been until now. I stood next to the grate and raised the hem of my skirt, just to let a lovely warm draught gust up to my thighs. As Maude watched me rub the blood back into my calves, I said, "Did Greta know that Jess was pregnant?"

From the cold sweat that crept over Maude's brow and the way she slumped against the wall, it was clear that this was news to her. "What?!" Tears welled up in her eyes. "Oh, Lord!"

"I'm sorry, I thought you must've …"

"No! I didn't know!" She shook her head in shock, "And the father? Who was he?" Before I could answer, she said, "Sweet mercy … it was Carter, wasn't it!"

I blinked twice. "Sorry?"

"That damnable man," she repeated through clenched teeth. "William Carter. The fella who owns the building."

"I know him, yes," I stammered, "But, why would you think it's him?"

She looked disgusted. "You've heard the gossip, right?"

I shook my head.

"How he gets his kicks?" she said, "Having his way with the girls backstage, and not always with their consent?" Maude spat on the floor. "There were rumors he'd sullied Jess, but she was too timid to say anything in her defense." She shook her head slowly. "Poor little Jess, pregnant! I can scarce imagine it! She was so shy, so quiet … I mean, I could've imagined Nell knocked up, but Jess? She never said two words to a fellow, never mind getting herself in a family way!"

I thought on this for a moment. Andy had been clear: the baby was his. Carter had been equally clear: he hadn't fancied Jess. Perhaps I ought to speak again with him, just to make sure.

To Maude, I said, "The night you performed at William Carter's house, when did Jess leave?"

"She left first. I saw her go."

"And Nell? Or Greta?"

Maude shrugged. "I left after Jess. I had work sorting the laundry for Sunday morning, and I needed to get back here to the hotel before the matron noticed I was gone—she doesn't approve of my singing, you see."

"So you left Carter's house second?"

"Yeah. See Patsy, there?" she said, pointing to one of the women, "She can tell you, I was back by midnight. I fair ran the whole way, but I made it in time for my shift."

"That she was," chirped Patsy, a plump girl with lips too generous to be comely. Her mouth seemed to overtake her whole expression. "Maudie came flying in, sweaty like a greased pig, mind, but she was here."

"Greta told me that Nell left second, right after Jess."

"No, she didn't," Maude replied, scoffing at Greta's mistake. "I know! Nelly was still at the piano, laughing with the Judge's son. I asked her if she wanted to walk as far as town with me, and she waved me off, hoping to snag herself a boy."

My mind seized onto the discrepancy in Maude's story: who had left first? Greta, or Nell?

"Oi, Maudie, you coming back?" shouted another laundress, a middle-aged woman whose face was covered in patches of red; her skin did not like the borax in the air, or the moisture, or the heat. She took the opportunity to stretch her back. "Or can we all take a break from the washing up, m'lady?" Patsy laughed, and not kindly.

"Only a few more questions," I began, "How certain are you that Carter had his way with Jess?"

She shrugged. "As certain as ya can be about theatre gossip. I mean, Jess never said two words about it to no one. But Alfred told me that Mr. Carter was bragging to some of the stagehands, and Andy was angry as hell that he'd talk about Jess like that, saying nasty things. Andy's such a sweet guy, y'know? I don't think he could bear the thought of anything crude taking place in his beloved Temple of Thespis."

"Andy came to Jess' defense?"

"He was her knight in shining armor, he was," she said sweetly. "Most of the time, I just think Andy's a bit, you know …" She touched her finger to her temple. "But he showed real gentlemanly qualities, like. He didn't want a friend getting a tarnished reputation, I suppose."

Would he go so far as to marry her, though, if a tryst with Mr. Carter had left her pregnant? I supposed he might.

"You've given me lots to think about." I dropped the hem of my skirt and gave my knees one last rub.

She watched me with crossed arms. "Oh, you pathetic little waif … Wait one minute," she said, and scurried to the far side of the basement, where long lines crisscrossed the high ceiling. Laundry of all sorts hung there: sheets, pillow casings, garments, table linens. A large iron stove in the corner provided waves of heat and dry air that made the laundry sway, and Maude disappeared for a few moments among the billowing fabrics, returning a moment later with a wadded bundle in her hands.

"I can't bear to see you go back into a November night with naked knees," she hissed. "It's uncivilized." She pushed the stockings into my hands. "These belong to one of the guests on the sixth floor—she's got so many pairs, she'll never miss them. Go on, put them on, you've got a belt on to hold them up, haven't you?"

"Thank you!"

"They're French silk, so take good care of them, hand wash in cool water only," she said as I kicked off my boots, "And if anyone asks, I never gave them to you."

They were a fine pair, made of opaque black silk and only a little worn around the toes. I'd never felt anything so exquisite. I was used to knitted wool, which bunched at the knees in an itchy and uncomfortable manner. The silk was sheer, smooth, and held the warmth to my skin like the palm of a hand. I clipped the beautiful fleur-de-lys lace hems to the suspenders of my ragged garters, and heard the other washerwomen giggling at my impropriety, but when I slipped the socks and boots over my feet, the stockings hugged my legs like a second skin.

Maude stepped back to admire them. "You take good care of them," Maude said, "And they'll last a lifetime."

"I'll never go swimming in these," I said, and Maude adopted a confused expression, "I promise."

Twenty-Eight

I returned before midnight and entered through the front door. The house was very quiet, but a light under Mr. Fish's door led me to believe he was still awake, perhaps lying in bed and reading. I gathered a bit of dinner from the leftovers in the icebox, and my suspicion was confirmed when he came into the kitchen, wearing pajamas and robe and holding a newspaper in his hand. I bid him good evening around a mouth full of food—even cold, the roast beef and pudding was delicious.

"Edwina is still in a poor way," he said as he sat opposite me, "The dinner came from Mrs. Milliner, next door."

"It's quite good," I replied. The lines of his face were tense, and I asked, "Are you angry at me?"

He shook his head. "I am concerned. You're like a mouse, my girl. You come and go of your own schedule, very quiet, and I never know where you'll be. Given the circumstances, it worries me."

"There's no need," I replied. "I'm quite capable of looking after myself."

"I'm sure you are," he said as he took a seat at the table. "Liz, have you given any thought to what you will do?"

I slumped in my seat. "It's been on my mind lately, yes."

"Your father has not yet contacted you."

I looked up at him, tried to judge his thoughts. Did my eyes betray me?

Mr. Fish watched me with the same sort of cool appraisal. "You must be concerned for his well-being."

I shook my head. "He is also very capable."

He folded his hands, weighed his words. "A person, when they eagerly await a letter, tends to watch the mail box and wait for the postman's steps by the door. You, my dear, show neither of these tendencies."

"The letter will arrive when it arrives," I replied. "Whether I pine by the door or not, it won't travel any faster."

He harrumphed at my logical reply.

"What if the letter never comes? Have you thought of that?"

I took another bite. "I have," I admitted. "I'm not well suited to school, and I've never been fond of convention. I wake at odd hours, I'm up all night, I don't do well with figures of authority, and I study what I choose. Do you think any school mistress would welcome me into her classroom?"

The question lightened the mood. Mr. Fish chuckled. "You're a bright girl, Liz. You could excel at whatever you put your mind to."

"And what about my friendship with Mr. Chen? It won't serve me well if I wish to remain in polite society." I toyed with the beef. "I suppose a career as a socialite is not an option."

"No, it isn't," said Mr. Fish, "But was it, ever?"

I shook my head and wrinkled my nose.

"And this theatre nonsense," he continued. "And your ghoulish fascination with Jack the Ripper. And your visits to the morgue. And running about, trying to find Jessie's murderer—dear God, Liz," he said, sounding exasperated, "I don't know what to make of you! I worry you're putting yourself in harm's way."

"I appreciate your concern," I said.

"But you'd rather I keep it to myself," he finished.

"I feel like I'm close to figuring out what happened to Jess, but I'm missing only a piece or two," I said, "Just give me a little more time, Mr. Fish, and I'll deliver the murderer to justice."

He leaned close. "But Liz, it's not your responsibility," he said, weighing his words. "You put yourself in danger, and you put me there, as well."

"What do you mean?"

"I mean," he said tartly, "That I've spent decades constructing a careful facade around my household, and many of us take advantage of the liberties that such a facade provides. But the neighbours are starting to whisper, starting to watch. You come and go at all hours. You pay no attention to propriety. You've stayed away from church for well over a month." He reclined in his chair, tapped his fingers against the tabletop. "I hate to put you on a leash, Liz, but if you continue to brazenly flaunt my hospitality, you'll destroy my reputation along with your own."

I scowled at him. "It's not my intent, sir. I do appreciate all you've done for me and Shao."

He pressed the heel of his hand to his brow. "I am old and crotchety, Liz, but I haven't forgotten how much fun it was to be young." He tried to muster a smile, and found the task difficult. "I'm worried for your safety, above all other concerns."

"I will be more careful," I promised. "But I'm so close to discovering what happened to Jess."

"Any suspects?"

"None, I'm afraid, but certainly I've uncovered a number of suspicious people, along with a few motives." I took another bite and said, "I doubt the police have gotten so far."

Mr. Fish looked sour. "They're sniffing around, my dear, and they're looking for you."

"Really?"

"Constable Grange was by again today, asking after you. I didn't dare tell him you'd gone to Chinatown." He leaned close. "Be careful, Liz. I could not bear to lose you."

"I won't be lost."

He stared at me from under his grey brows, looking wholly unconvinced. "Does nothing frighten you?"

I shook my head.

"Fear is not something to be ashamed of, Liz," he said. "It keeps us from peril."

"I know," I replied, "This is not some misplaced bravado. I have only rarely felt fear, and my utter lack of good sense used to vex my sister to no end." I took another small bite, swallowed, and added, "I've long suspected that something is fundamentally awry with my emotions, sir."

"Does Mr. Chen know?"

I nodded.

He stroked his chin with one long finger. "Well," he said after a moment's consideration, "At least he'll have the good sense to watch out for you, when you aren't watching after yourself."

"I'm fortunate to have so many guardian angels," I replied. I briefly glanced out the kitchen window, to the dark shadows by the woodpile, and thought there might be a few guardian devils in the mix, too.

He bid me good night then, and left me to finish the food. Then, I climbed to the attic. I closed the curtains and stood between the window and my lamp to remove my dress. The coal oil lamp casting my shadow across the pale fabric, and anyone looking from the alley below would see that I was preparing for bed. As I hung the frock over the mirror in the corner, I cast a quick glance at my reflection: skinny, small, and bony, made of straight lines hanging from freckled shoulders, with a head of untamable hair the color of cinnamon. Violet had been only a few years older than me, but she'd had curves to enhance her feminine allure; she could attract any boy's eye with a wink and a smile. I certainly wasn't interested in flirtation, but I couldn't help wonder if I'd ever grow into a womanly form. I turned, studied my reflection, pursed my lips in thought.

Violet had possessed comely arms and a graceful neck to flaunt, but all I had to show were wiry muscles, lean arms, and thin legs.

'But,' I consoled myself, 'Shao's never complained.'

God's teeth, a marriage proposal. What was I supposed to do with that?

I took my nightgown from under my pillow, pulled it on over my head, and buttoned it up.

I loved the idea of living here with Shao, I truly did. I could see the possibility of a happy future together, but only if he never knew the truth of what had happened. I wondered if I could leave my family's past behind, when it had only recently been so fully revealed to me. Could I abandon my pursuit of knowledge? Could I let go of the past?

I took the tin jewelry box from the dresser. The lid squeaked when I opened it. The newspaper clippings felt frail in my hands, but I knew there was great power in them. They resonated with information.

My father, Doctor John Saunders, had killed women in gruesome ways. He had taken delight in their suffering. He had been an evil man.

But I didn't have to be evil, too. As I leafed through the papers, I refused to believe the mythological blood guilt nonsense that Jack spouted. I mean, what did the Greeks know about justice anyway? I was free to choose my own future; I didn't need a toga-wearing philosopher, dead for thousands of years, proclaiming that I'm a danger to all around me! I ground my teeth as the words spun through my fingers.

I made my own decisions, damn it. Perhaps my father had a horrid compulsion, but I was stronger, better than that.

I took the clippings to the lamp and held them over the open flame. They caught quickly, and I set the burning bundle into the tin box. I watched the corners curl into black ash, the lines of print turn into smoke.

I would marry Shao. I would take his name and leave behind my own. The legacy of my father's deeds was finished. History would forget him, and so would I.

My eyes flashed to the window.

When the fire had died and only dust remained, I blew out the lamp, but I didn't remove my stockings or socks, and I didn't crawl into bed. Instead, I slipped downstairs and glanced out the kitchen window. To my satisfaction, the figure sitting in the shadows stood up, stretched his arms above his head, and made to leave.

I snatched my boots from their spot by the front door.

Twenty-Nine

Outside, the night had grown quiet, frosty, and clear. It was as cold as one would expect in November but there was very little wind, so the ribbons of chimney smoke prowled like sinister wraiths between the houses. The naked oak trees idly reached their branch fingers to the sky. I was too engrossed in my own thoughts to care much that I wore only a nightgown, stockings, and boots. Anyone in their right mind would be freezing, but I was like a hound on a scent. Nothing could distract me.

I followed Jack as far as the Dallas. I saw him slip over the side, down through the thin trees and ferns, and heard his heavy footsteps crunch on the gravel beach, far below. By the time I reached the embankment, he'd stopped to sit on a log close to the edge of the water. His back was to me and he looked out to sea.

I hesitated, knowing my own footsteps would be loud on the gravel.

Then, over his shoulder, he yelled, "You think I don't know when I'm bein' followed? C'mon, girl, I'm waiting."

Blast it.

I plucked my way down the cliff. "What tipped you to me?"

He turned to look at me as I approached. "In all the nights I been watchin', you never go to sleep b'fore midnight."

I sat next to him on the log.

"You've been telling my secrets, Jack."

He feigned offence. "What?"

"You talk in your sleep about my father," I replied, "Nelly told me."

"Well, how'm I supposed to fix that, hey?" he replied with a broad grin. "B'sides, who believes the chattering of a drunk man, dozing off the effects of whiskey? She thinks they're just nightmares."

"But nightmares draw their inspiration from the waking world."

He grew quiet, less jovial. "We both seen things that would give anyone a fright."

I thought of Kelly's body, hanging in the trees and pecked by ravens, and the crusted rope of Violet's intestine, laying across the surgery table. And more arresting than those, I thought of the humid interior of Father's surgery, painted crimson with dried blood.

"Y'ever tormented by bad dreams, Liz?"

"I hardly ever dream."

"You don't feel guilty about that night?"

I glanced up at him. "Guilt? I'm afraid not."

He withdrew, just a fraction, and a sneer of revulsion crossed his lips.

"Does that surprise you, Jack?" I asked. "You said before, I'm a child of the devil." I folded my arms across my chest; it was cold by the shore, and no longer focused on the hunt, I'd started to feel the autumn chill cut through the flannel of my gown. "I have no emotions, I'm sinister and vile and twisted. You've already told me, you're following me because you think I'm going to kill again."

"Well? Would ya?"

I narrowed my eyes. "Perhaps," I said slowly, "If I thought my secrets were being told."

Jack looked down at me. His shoulders tensed, his jaw set, and he narrowed his eyes and drew up, defensive. He studied my face for a heartbeat, then his scowl melted away and he laughed. "Look at you, sitting there in your nightgown, seemin' to all the world like an innocent lamb, then going and threatenin' me. Me! I bet, if I felt so inclined, I could crush you with one hand."

"Do you think so?" I taunted, and the air around him shimmered. The prickling warmth of anticipation skittered up through my skin, the world grow sharp and defined. I almost thought I could hear his heart beat a little faster in his chest. "Is that why you've moved a few inches away, Jack? Because you know I'm so dreadfully helpless and frail?" I grinned, and I knew my eyes had grown dark and flat and sinister.

He hunched down and scowled at me.

"Mr. Chen needs to know what you are."

That snapped me out of my focus. I replied so quickly, my voice cracked. "Don't you dare!"

"For his own safety, of course," Jack continued. "What do you think he'd say, Liz, if I told him what you did to yer own pa?"

"He'd say you were a liar!"

"Ah, that's got you all snappy," he mused to himself. "I dare say, I found yer Achilles heel."

His carefree, blithe attitude was infuriating. I balled up my fist and punched him in the shoulder. It was rather like punching a sack of potatoes. Jack just laughed.

"C'mon, Liz, I ain't wanting to fight with ya." This was said with a playful smirk, and as a concession, he said, "I do think yer dangerous, I'll admit it, and I sure the hell ain't falling asleep in your presence! I seen what you did to someone you loved—Jesus, what would you do to the likes of me, someone you goddamn hate?" He laughed again.

I despised the sound of his mockery. I grabbed for a topic that would wring the mirth out of him.

"Tell me what you know about my father."

Sure enough, the laugh died on his lips. His eyebrows arched; this request was clearly a surprise. "You knew him better than me."

"I don't know about that," I replied. "I've been collecting newspaper articles, reading whatever I can about the Ripper, and they leave me with more questions than answers."

"You and everyone else, girl," he muttered. He took off his jacket and swept it over my shoulders. It covered me completely, like a tent, reaching all the way to the ground. It smelt musky and wild, like horsehide and pipe smoke and sweat, and the fragrance was not completely unpleasant.

"How did you find out about him?"

Jack looked to the stones, shuffled his boots through the gravel. "I told ya, it was the spring of '89. My step-mother had kicked me to the winds, and I didn't have no where else to go, so I caught passage on a steamer heading from New York to London. I remembered little bits of my childhood, and I recalled that my ma, she used to work the streets around the Three Bells, so I made my way through Whitechapel, asking after her." He dipped his head down. "It didn't take long to discover what happened to her. Everyone knew her name."

"You wanted to seek revenge?"

"The broadsheets had published her picture, y'know," he said quietly. "What he done to her … what he done to her beautiful face …" Jack's hands gripped his knees; even the stump of his ring finger dug into his flesh. "It was the only photograph ever taken of my ma, and it's the only image I have to remember her, and it's a god damn travesty. So I started talkin' around the streets, listening to everything that the street arabs and the whores had to say. The cops, they were too high and mighty to listen to what them women had to tell them, but who's gonna know better than the bints and beggars living every day on those streets?" He shook his head in disgust. "All of the police, hamstrung by their squabbling. So many folks wanted the glory of bringing the Ripper to justice, they were too busy fighting over scraps to ever catch him."

"What put you on my father's trail?"

He grinned. "A girl named Doxy. She was nine, maybe ten. She lived in the alley behind the Bells, and she remembered my ma. I used to be a street arab, y'know; I remember what it was like, scratching a living from the gutter. I bought her trust with a new pair of shoes, and she told me that my ma had picked up with a fine gent who rode a hansom with a logo on the side. Doxy drew me a picture—a right little genius she were with a pencil, I tell ya. It took me a few weeks to figure what the logo meant, but eventually I found it: the seal of a gentleman's club. From there, it was easy. One man had left under questionable circumstances, the summer b'fore."

"John Saunders."

Jack nodded. "I heard he'd gone to Wiltshire, so I followed. It wasn't difficult. Your father wasn't all that skilled at hiding his nature—that was your mother's talent."

I bowed my head, seeing my mother's obsessions as a tool instead of a weakness. She spent so much time watching him, hiding him, keeping anything from him that might trigger his murderous lusts, that she went mad.

"And your mother," I began, "Who was she?"

A sadness crept into his expression; I felt it, more than saw it. "Just another nameless slash, worth nothing to nobody 'cept fer a tumble in a doorway."

"She was obviously worth more than that to you."

He cast me a fierce glance. My comment struck too close for his comfort.

"I remember, the jar you picked up had a label," I continued, "It read, 'September 30, 1888'. Now, from what I've read, two women died that night: Elizabeth Stride and Catherine Eddowes. Which woman was your mother?"

He cast me a sideways glance and smirked. "You have been doing yer studies, haven't ya … Put yer goddamn clever brain onto something more useful, Lizzie Saunders. That ain't none of your business."

"Why was my father … the way he was?"

"I can't figure that, Liz."

"Was it a quirk of his biology, or did something spoil him?" I asked, more to myself than Jack. "Am I destined to follow him?"

We sat together in quiet contemplation. It felt very good, to speak so openly with someone, even if it was someone I hated.

"Hiding my nature from Shao …" I began. "It's ripping me into pieces, Jack."

"Interestin' choice of words, Liz," he replied.

"I can't keep looking into the past if I want to build a future here," I said.

"I think I have to leave all my questions behind, and accept that my father and mother were never the people I thought them to be. In the official record, Violet was killed by Alexander Kelly, who then tragically took his own life. Dr. Saunders has returned to England, and will never again set foot upon these shores. That is the truth I need to cling to, if I ever want a normal life." I looked up at him. "I am reformed, Mr. Hunter. You have nothing to fear from me, because I choose never to follow in my father's footsteps."

"You really believe that you can simply say that, and abraca-fucking-dabra," he snapped his fingers, "You're cured?"

I smiled at him. I'd wanted to kill him earlier this evening, but I realized that, if I truly wanted to be a good person, I ought not to do such things, and there was no better time to commit myself to a reformed life than right now. I could be just as safe if Jack Hunter were far away, free to pursue his own future with impunity, and our paths never destined to cross again. Did I believe it to be so simple?

"If I am ever to lead a fruitful life, I must." I shrugged off the massive coat and returned it to him. "Good night, Mr. Hunter."

"That's it?" he said, "I'm getting dismissed?"

"There's no reason for us to ever meet again; I assure you, I am done with blood and gore, and justice has been served for all of those women—your mother, all the rest—that my father so horribly dispatched. I urge you to go and lead a happy life, sir. Your quest is finished."

He raised one eyebrow. "I don't know …"

"Don't you want that?" I asked. "It's as easy for you to leave, right now, as it is for me to commit myself to a life of non-violence."

"No, it ain't."

"I must believe it is, if I hope to succeed."

He looked skeptical as I stood up.

"Good-bye forever, Jack."

Without another word to him, nor even glancing to see his expression, I turned on one boot heel and strode across the gravel beach, heading home.

Thirty

I felt quite satisfied with myself as I walked along the Dallas towards Mr. Fish's house in my nightgown and boots, my hair unbound, swinging my arms and almost whistling. Yes, I was quite cold, but I also felt liberated, like I'd sliced a great weight off my back. If my leather boots hadn't been so solid and heavy, I might've been able to push away from the Earth and fly.

But I hadn't gotten very far when a steely hand wrapped itself around my wrist.

"Jack, there's no need for us—" I said, turning to confront the form and face of William Carter.

Whatever handsome qualities he'd once possessed were now obscured by my memory of his filthy, rude and deplorable manner. Maybe other girls would've been willing to forgive him, but not me. I did not trust him, no matter how warm his smile or genteel his manner. He looked at me now with a jaunty grin, and it held no fondness. His grey suit jacket had a crust of spilt food on the collar and a rent under the sleeve, as well as a purple wine stain on his lapel that matched the bruise on his forehead. He smelled of alcohol, but he was not drunk. He stood quite straight, and his grip on my wrist was solid.

"Mr. Carter," I said, "What are you doing here?"

"I could ask the same of you, Miss Saunders," he leered, "Meeting with a suitor by the sea?"

I nearly choked at the idea. "No, Mr. Carter, most certainly not."

"I was walking home from a party, and what should I spy upon the beach but two people together, enjoying a tryst! I can not tell you how surprised I was to recognize one of them as you." His lips peeled back from his teeth. "And in such a shameless state of undress!"

"So surprised that you felt it prudent to stop? And watch? And wait for me?" I needled. "And only reveal yourself to me when I was vulnerable?"

"I wonder what Mr. Fish would say of such behavior," he mused. "I wonder if he'd cast you out."

"Mr. Carter," I said, "Mr. Fish is a gentleman. He would do no such thing."

"Let's tell him, shall we?" he leaned in close, his hand tightening around my wrist. "What if I told him I'd discovered you, your stockings down and your nightgown filthy, rutting like a cat in heat with some gutter snipe? What did you say your lover's name was? Jack?"

That thought did cause my throat to convulse. "God's teeth, not for all the stars in the heavens! You are QUITE mistaken." I tugged at my hand. "I insist you let me go immediately."

Carter's eyes ranged up and down my body. "I hear you're still asking questions about Jess."

"I am."

"It's none of your concern, Miss Saunders," he warned.

"And what I do with my time is none of yours," I replied.

"Now, now," he tutted, "You're going to get yourself in trouble, if you persist." His grip tightened a fraction around my wrist. "Already there have been whispers of gossip that I had hired women in my home, and my father is most dissatisfied." He leaned closer, and his breath smelt sickly syrupy sweet, like sherry. "As am I."

I pulled away as far as I could. I was not afraid of him, but I was growing annoyed at his restraint. "Are you threatening me, Mr. Carter?"

"Absolutely, Miss Saunders," he replied. His eyes flashed, his tongue darted across his lips like a man confronted with a luscious dessert. When he bared his teeth, a leaf of parsley darkened his gums. "If I'm going to tell Mr. Fish that you've been romping, you'd better look the part, hey?"

He pushed me hard with his free hand and tossed me down, into the ferns along the embankment. The quickness of his action took me by surprise. I hit the ground so hard that my teeth clacked, but I was onto my feet by the time William had waded into the underbrush. He wanted a bit of privacy as he began to unbutton his green trousers.

Green.

Blast it, I thought, I'd forgotten his outfit the night of the rehearsal. Here was the green I was looking for!

And as the shock ricocheted through my mind, he was upon me, grabbing my arms again in his hands. He was not as large as Jack, not as nimble as Shao, but he was built as solidly as an ox, and I wager he carried more than twice my weight. He pushed me up against the side of the hill, and I pushed back, which only seemed to excite him further.

"Hold still!" he demanded.

I, of course, did not.

He held down my wrists with one hand, threw his arm across my chest to pin me to the dirt. "Mr. Carter," I snapped, "You do not wish to do this."

He was panting, eager, rubbing himself against me. I felt the bulge in his trousers, the sheen of sweat rising to his skin, his humid breath against the skin of my neck. "I'm going to give you a right frig, you little whore," he panted, and the words excited him more than my protests. Holding both my wrists against the ground with one hand, he fumbled with his other hand to free his member from his undergarments, then began to pull up my nightgown. I ceased struggling; it would do no good. His fingers clutched at my stockings. I heard them rip as the silk gave way, splitting down my thigh.

Time slowed. I took a deep breath and studied his face: the flush of purple that had crept up from his collar, the way his brow had furrowed in concentration, the glisten of spit upon his lips. The edges of him shimmered, the world around us grew dark. I studied every hair and pore, the foam collecting at the corners of his mouth, the bulging hunger in his dilating pupils.

I took a deep breath. The world stilled, as it does before a thunderstorm. I felt my heart drum strong and steady in my chest.

"C'mon, give me a bit of a fight, you little cunt, you dirty wagtail," he hissed, "I'm going to stick my cock so far up your notch—"

"That's enough, Mr. Carter."

Perhaps he thought I was leaning in for a kiss, I don't know. He looked thrilled as my head drew close to his. His eyes gleamed.

I clamped my teeth around his generous nose and bit down.

He howled. I felt the breath of his nostrils burst into my mouth as I sawed my incisors over flesh and cartilage. The bright copper taste of blood warmed my tongue. The blood was delicious, it moved and lived, it throbbed down my throat. My heart soared with joy. He struggled backwards but I did not let go; my jaws locked themselves around his face, I clasped the back of his head with both hands, the starched ruff of his hair rasped between my fingers. I pulled and pried at the appendage between my gnashing teeth as the skin stripped away from the bone. I felt and heard the crack of the septum as it gave way. The howls became more primal, wilder and wilder. Now he was beating at me with both fists, rolling away from me, clutching at his face, trying to wedge my teeth from the mess that had been his nose.

I snapped out of my revelry at the sharp blast of a whistle from the street above.

When I released him, Carter skidded backwards down the embankment, screaming in horror as dark, hot blood gushed from the center of his face.

I spit out a knob of flesh as big as my thumb.

He was still howling as I crawled out of the ferns and stood at the side of the road, and when the police officer trained his bull's eye on me, I saw him stumble back in fright. I suppose I must've looked a mess: my nightgown smeared with black dirt, my stockings ripped and sagging at my knees, the circle around my mouth and chin painted a vibrant red. Somewhere behind me, down in the ferns, the wild primal screaming continued.

"Good evening, officer," I said.

Thirty-One

Between the two of us, I'm not sure who appeared more startling. Carter's frantic eyes peered out from behind a crimson-splattered handkerchief, pressed hard against his face in an attempt to staunch the bleeding. I had not been provided with a cloth, so my face was still red with blood, although it had dried and started to itch. The officer hailed a passing milk cart, and the three of us—along with a reluctant driver, who dared not grumble openly but sat dour and hunched over the reins—went swiftly to the imposing, brick fortress of Victoria's City Hall, where the headquarters of the Metropolitan Police Department occupied a portion of the lowest floor. The officer led us through a side door, down a crowded corridor, into a window-less holding room where the nocturnal scourge were brought for arrest or questioning or processing. No matter how high or low their station, every scoundrel, pick pocket, counterfeiter, drunkard and temptress watched us pass with wide, curious eyes.

"Stay here," said the officer, leaving us in a small recess, furnished with two wooden chairs. A small selection of oil paintings decorated the walls—a seascape, a portrait of the Queen, and a pastoral scene with a surplus of sheep. When the officer left, I briefly wondered if Carter would try to attack me, but a younger officer and a matronly nurse joined us almost immediately.

The nurse came directly to me, but I shook my head. "Not me," I said, pointing to Carter. "Him."

As she attended to his injuries, the first officer returned with a familiar man in tow. Constable Grange looked polite and congenial, but with a particular tension around his shallow eyes that told me, he was not pleased to see me. The blotches on his skin seemed a little more ruddy, and under his pale moustache, his mouth was a thin, pinched frown.

"Miss Saunders," he greeted, "Can I offer you something to make yourself more presentable?"

"Yes, thank you," I said. "A washcloth and a robe would be very helpful."

"Go on, Cole," he said to the younger officer, and once he'd left, Grange sat down next to me on one of the wooden chairs.

"This is a nasty mess, isn't it."

"Yes, sir."

Carter bellowed, "The liddul slut bit off my god dab doze!" And he screeching in pain again as the nurse replaced the cloth with a fresh, steaming-hot towel.

"Oh, this is quite bad," she clucked to Grange. "We best get him to hospital."

Grange gave a nod and the nurse tried to usher Carter out of the room, but he refused to go easily. He brandished his fists, spat blood, and cursed as wickedly as a miner. Two more officers arrived to help, and the crowd of them scuffled around the room like dance partners, trying to subdue him.

At last, they restrained him, and he rolled those wild horse eyes in my direction. "I'll kill you!" he sputtered at me, and the threat sounded muffled and flaccid from behind the towel, "I'll god dab kill you!"

I studied the green trousers. "May I?" I said to Grange, who in confusion, gave me a clipped nod. I strode over to Carter, now restrained between two officers and, seizing the pocket of his trousers, gave a sharp tug and ripped it off.

"Stawp! God dab it, she's god dab crazy!" he screamed.

"Payment for my ruined stockings," I replied.

They dragged him away. I found myself alone with Grange in the waiting room, with the door open to the busy hall. The only evidence of Carter's presence was a spatter of red drops across the wooden floor. The younger officer named Cole returned with a warm washcloth and a woman's silk kimono, scarlet and gold, which I assumed had come from the storming of a brothel. I took it with appreciation.

Cole said a few words in Grange's ear. Then, Grange turned to me and looked me up and down with a stern shake of his head.

"Mr. Carter wishes to press charges against you for assault," he said.

I gave his comment the attention it deserved: I ignored it. "Are you still seeking Jessica Garry's murderer?" I asked as I scrubbed the dried blood from my chin.

"Of course."

"I'd like to speak with you in confidence, Constable, and I wondered if you had a moment to—"

"Miss Saunders, did you not hear me? Mr. Carter wishes to press charges."

"So?" I replied. "I was defending myself from his unwanted advances."

This flustered Grange. He said, "If you wish to talk about Miss Garry's murder, you can make an appointment with me; I may have an hour to spare next week. But for now, I think we ought to deal with the problem at hand."

"Jess's murder came first," I said, "Therefore, we will speak of it now, and leave Mr. Carter's ridiculous accusations for your spare time."

His eyebrows arched up at my tone, then drew down in confusion. "You're not afraid of his threats upon your life?"

"Do I look concerned?"

"But Miss Saunders—"

I narrowed my eyes. "The people of Mr. Fish's fine residence are eager for any advance in the case. I wondered if you might be able to share your latest findings?"

For a moment, he considered my request, and the deepening curve of his scowl showed plainly that I perplexed him. Between those papery ears, his mind labored at a furious rate. At last, he gave a frustrated sigh of defeat.

"There's not been much, I'll admit," he said, "It may simply be an unfortunate burglary."

"Perhaps her case is not of great importance to you?" I said loudly.

He looked affronted, embarrassed. "Miss Saunders, that's not true—"

Faces from the crowd in the corridor—officers, ne'er do wells, criminals, prostitutes, and likely Grange's immediate superiors—turned towards the rising pitch of my voice. "She was my good friend, sir, and as I have very few of them, I dearly hope you are not pushing her case to the back of your desk. She deserved better than that."

"Of course, of course!" he said, "But please miss! Quiet yourself!"

"Mr. Fish, that esteemed gentleman with ties to our government and, who I've heard, has met the Queen on occasion, would be greatly unimpressed with this city's inability to—"

His face had turned red. "Come with me."

I was immediately ushered into one of the inner rooms, away from curious eyes.

"Look," he began, shutting the door behind us. "There's been very little to go on." He stopped. "Has Mr. Fish really met the Queen?"

I shrugged. "Maybe. Who knows? But I wanted to speak with you in private."

He flushed. "Are you completely mad?" I know I bristled at the suggestion; I couldn't hide it. But before I could reply, Grange retracted himself from that line of questioning and instead proclaimed, "I'm a very busy man!"

"But not busy enough, if you haven't found any leads on Jess' murder," I replied.

Grange leaned forward, affixed me with a fierce gaze. "I am trying to help, but it's not a simple process. Do you think people welcome the police into their family's private sphere?" His frustration showed plainly. "Every question I ask breaks that sanctimonious boundary, Miss Saunders; even your good friend Mr. Fish tells me little and obfuscates the truth. I ask where you have gone, and he gives me an answer that leads me in circles!" He shook his head. "How am I supposed to apprehend a murderer if no one, not even those seeking justice, will answer my questions?"

If his speech was meant to humble me, it was successful, but I didn't let it show. Instead, I brandished the scrap of fabric torn from Carter's trousers. "Where is the thread of fabric taken from the body? You must have it still."

He shook his head. "Of course not. Why would I keep such a thing?"

A cold, clammy feeling dripped through my stomach.

"You destroyed it?"

He offered me a chair with one hand, as he himself sat on the opposite side of the desk and removed his hat. "No, I didn't. But I don't carry the bits and pieces of every investigation with me, wherever I go. You think Carter may have a connection to her death?"

Great relief flooded through me. "His relationship with Jess is more complicated than I thought," I admitted. "Where's the thread? We must compare the two."

"The box of items found on Miss Garry's person is still at the morgue, I believe. Doubtless, the thread is there. Leave the fabric with me, and I'll compare them myself."

"Absolutely not," I snapped, and I scolded myself for letting such a key link between Jess and the murderer remain in the hands of these buffoons. "Am I under arrest, Constable?"

"What? Of course not! Until Carter files a formal complaint, I have no reason to keep you."

I stood quickly and made to go.

"Wait a moment, wait a—Miss Saunders! Wait!" he stammered as I left the room. I'd already walked halfway down the hall before he caught the sleeve of the red kimono. "Miss Saunders, I implore you to cease your meddling. It's not safe. This city is no easy place for a woman to walk about, free and easy, never mind a girl of your youth and inexperience! You put yourself in danger." His face softened; I saw genuine concern in his features. "Please, Miss Saunders … I do not wish to find your body in the same state as your friend."

"You know nothing about me, Constable, nor that of which I am capable," I replied.

Grange arched both eyebrows at my impertinence. "I know you'll thrust your hands into corpses and bite off gentlemen's noses."

"If you will not find Jess' murderer, then the task is left to me."

My reply caused him a moment's pause. "A girl your age ought to be in school, Miss Saunders, not play-acting with theatre folk or loitering in Chinatown."

"What do you know—"

"When I spoke with Mr. Fish about Miss Garry's habits, yours were also discussed. He is very concerned for your safety." Grange released my coat sleeve, dropped his hands to his sides. "As am I."

Conflicted, I found I'd lost my tongue. Should I be angry at his presumptions, or touched by his concern? He'd gotten under my skin by claiming credit for my observations, but I wondered if he was, perhaps, not such a terrible person. He was young, new to the force, fighting to carve a place for himself in this institution, and he had the ability to take my observations farther through the legal system than I ever could. I was only a girl; would anyone listen to my theories? Sharing those same theories, his voice carried more weight and travelled farther. Yes, he had stolen my observations, but only because he saw merit in them, while others would have dismissed them as the fanciful ravings of a lunatic.

At last, I said, "The city is full of dangers, I'll agree. I'll take your warnings to heart, Constable, but under two conditions."

He smiled. "Yes?"

"One: you are prepared to arrest Jess' murderer on my advice, and give her the justice that any innocent victim deserves, regardless of her race, station or creed. Can I expect that of you?"

"Of course!" He frowned in all seriousness; this was a pact, and he would not brush it aside lightly. "And the second?"

"You will fetch a cab and escort me home."

His frown relaxed, his mouth curved into an awkward smile.

"With pleasure, Miss Saunders."

In the late morning, when I woke, the first thing I saw was the tin box full of ashes next to my bed. The air in the upstairs room smelt faintly of cold smoke.

I cursed my impulses, then reminded myself that it was all for the best, but my resolve to abandon my questions about the Ripper had put me in a sour mood. Plus, my jaw was quite stiff, and I had no stockings to wear.

I was short of temper with most everyone I met.

I walked briskly to Chinatown, keeping an eye over my shoulder, but I saw no hint of Jack or William. For that I was grateful. Carter must be languishing in a hospital, I thought with satisfaction. Jack, I hoped, had taken my words to heart and vanished.

THIRTY-TWO

November 3, 1898

I sat on a stool in the corner of the shop as Shao sorted deliveries into their glass jars. I loved watching him work. He was meticulous. He wiped the counters after opening each box to clear away anything he might have spilt while pouring, but he was too careful to spill even the smallest wisp of root or grain of powder. The store was empty except for Shao and I, but while there were rarely any customers before the lunch hour, there was always much to do. Mr. Lim worked in the basement, and we could hear him muttering to himself downstairs, searching through crates for supplies to refresh the stock on display.

I sipped tea from a blue pottery cup that had no handle. My body was sore and bruised from Mr. Carter's assault, but the tea eased the aches and relaxed my muscles. It tasted like licorice root and left the faint prickling sensation of an exotic spice on my tongue.

Maybe it wasn't just the tea. Being in Shao's presence relaxed me, too, and when we spoke of murders and intrigue, I found my deductions moving in new, exciting directions. My mind was not a whirlwind in his presence. Instead, it became a gust of sea air, the kind that pushes tall ships forward. I took another long sip of tea, savored it, and studied the slip of green fabric on the counter before me.

"I still can't believe the constable let you rip that from his trousers," said Shao without looking up, smiling.

I heard heavy footsteps on the wooden stairs and the wooden floor. "And here are still more," said Mr. Lim as he set a series of boxes on the counter beside Shao. To me, he said, "I do not know what I would do without your friend."

"Me, neither."

"Be quiet, both of you," said Shao, concentrating as he poured a fine brown sand into a narrow-necked flask. "You'll make me slip."

Mr. Lim threw me a smile that squeezed his face into a knot of merry wrinkles. "How do you like the tea?"

"Quite good, thank you."

He and Shao swapped looks, and Mr. Lim said, "I need all of eastern wall refilled, and then, three prescriptions to fill and deliver."

"Yes, sir."

"And this," he said, pushing a note across the counter. "Take this to the laundress, Jiahui, very discreet, when all else is done." Before he returned to the basement, Mr. Lim patted my shoulder. "You are sleeping well?"

"Very soundly."

"But how much?"

"A full hour, every night."

He shook his head and clucked in his throat. This answer did not satisfy him. "The winds are moving about your liver, Lizzie; your body struggles to find balance." He looked at me a little more closely. "For a long time, I think."

"Perhaps you're right."

He nodded thoughtfully. "Shao can help you. He knows much about the pernicious winds." Then he said something quickly to Shao, in Mandarin, and because Shao had been teaching me phrases in Cantonese, I could only guess at the meaning.

As Mr. Lim disappeared down the stairs, I said, "He wants you to heal me?"

Shao stoppered the vial and put it aside. He wiped his hands on his apron. "You don't sleep very well. You're too focused. You need to relax."

"How can I, when I'm so close to discovering Jess' murderer?" I said, and I tried not to smile eagerly, but failed. I took another long sip of tea, felt the bitter tickling sensation on my tongue, and watched as Shao pocketed the letter. "Is this woman … Jiahui … someone that Mr. Lim hopes you'll find comely?"

He smirked. "No."

"But delivering secret letters?"

"It's not what you think."

"And what am I supposed to think?" I teased, "Discretion has been ordered!"

Shao looked to the basement steps, then back to me. "Come here," he said, and took my hand in his.

We descended the steps. The basement was a cavernous place, stone-lined with a dry dirt floor and very dim. The tall stacks of wooden crates became high walls, creating little aisles and rooms, where I could see the flickering of tallow candles. I heard Mr. Lim talking to himself again, far in the back of the chamber, where the strong, cool light of an oil lamp glowed through the cracks between the boxes. Shao looked back to me and held his finger to his lips.

He guided me around the first wall of crates. A pallet on the floor held a straw mattress, and there lay a man on a blanket, sleeping soundly. Next to him was an opium pipe and a mug of tea, similar to my own. His soft, relaxed face held the expression of a peaceful dreamer.

"This is Jiahui's husband," Shao whispered in my ear, his breath tickling my cheek, "He sends her a letter every day to tell her he misses her."

I looked around, and realized that there were more men here—five or six, perhaps, though I could not see them all. They slept soundly in their little rooms made of wooden crates. I understood, then, that Mr. Lim was not talking to himself in the basement, but asking questions of his guests. The man on the floor gave a groan, and rolled over, opening his eyes a mere crack to see Shao. In a sleepy, cotton-swaddled voice, he asked a question. In stilted Mandarin, Shao replied.

I stared at the opium dreamer, and my surprise was so complete that I did not realize, until his hand was on my elbow, that Mr. Lim had joined us.

"Come upstairs, Lizzie," he said in a voice that was friendly but wary. "Let us give them peace."

We returned to the main floor. Mr. Lim carefully closed the door to the basement. He looked at me, then Shao.

"Liang asked you for more opium?"

Shao stood with his back very straight, but his head bowed in respect. "It's too soon. I won't give him more until tonight."

Mr. Lim nodded in approval. "Good boy."

"You're running an opium den?" I asked carefully, aware that I'd been made privy to something clandestine, but not sure what.

The old man shook his head. "They are sick. These people need medical help that others will not give them."

I listened, I heard, but it took a moment for me to understand. "They have leprosy?"

Mr. Lim gestured for me to sit on the stool again. "It starts as a patch of numbness on a hand or a foot. It does not need to go much further. If the disease is caught early enough, there are traditional remedies that will help soothe their pain until the body grows strong and healthy. But people are afraid they will be cast out and shunned, and so they hide it away, and because of this, the symptoms grow worse, disfiguring, and incurable."

"I heard of the lazaretto on the island, but I thought—"

Mr. Lim's expression barely changed, yet the rage that charged through his black eyes was so powerful that I recoiled; I would never have thought this kindly old pharmacist contained such anger. "You have been told there is no cure. You have been told that they are contagious and must be condemned to die."

I nodded.

"No one knows why some people become lepers, while those who live alongside them do not. It is a strange disease, but I believe the … what is the word …"

Shao spoke. "Stigma."

"Yes, yes, steeg-ma. The steeg-ma of the disease is worse than the disease itself." He smiled. "You are concerned for Shao? I see it in your eyes, but I assure you, there is no need to worry. He is perfectly safe here; he will catch nothing."

"But if the police knew about these patients?" I said. "What then?"

Mr. Lim smiled again. "It is a risk, but only one of many for us. If the police want to shut us down, there are other ways." He nodded his head towards my cup. "Drink your tea, Lizzie, and do not be afraid for your friend Shao. And you, my boy," he turned to Shao, "There is much work to be done."

Mr. Lim returned downstairs and I sat in quiet contemplation, feeling thankful to know that Mr. Fish's assessment had been right: here were people working quietly in the background, trying to make all right. Shao left me to my thoughts as he returned to work. With a copper funnel, he poured a box of white granules into the jar, then set the jar on the shelf, arranging it so that the paper label was squarely displayed.

"He is a very good man, isn't he," I said.

"I told you, I'm fortunate to know him," said Shao. "Mr. Lim was an esteemed doctor in Canton, and he has a high reputation here, and a network of friends who owe him many favors. He's very respected."

I leaned my elbows on the counter as he worked, watching. The white granules glittered in the lamp light, but the label was written in Chinese characters. "What is that, in the jar?"

"Powdered foxglove root."

"What does it do?"

"I add it to tea to nourish the yin, the feminine essence, of a patient's kidneys."

I pondered this for a bit. Mr. Lim had prepared this tea for me, and the glance he'd exchanged with Shao now took on new meaning. "This tea …" I began, "I haven't had it before."

"No, I suppose not," he said, but he didn't look at me.

"What did Mr. Lim put in it?"

He cast me a guilty expression, as if he'd been caught stealing a cookie. "Only good things."

I raised one eyebrow.

Shao leaned on the counter opposite me. The jig was up, and he knew I could not be dissuaded. "He made it to calm your mind. You've been running around the city at all hours of the day and night … I thought you might need it to help you relax."

"You're sedating me?"

"No, nothing like that," he laughed. "It won't put you to sleep. It only …" He thought for a moment, "It will ease your spirit. And perhaps make it easier for me to follow your leaps of logic." He glanced at the cup. "A little dried marigold flowers, some jasmine flowers, and a single grain of opium. You'll be fine."

I took another sip. I'd never tasted opium before, and I wondered if that was the bitter flavor I detected. "It's not working. I don't feel at all relaxed."

He shrugged and said nothing.

"Aren't you afraid of catching the disease from the men downstairs?"

"No." He smiled. "A few of them will stay for a couple of weeks, but most come and go in a matter of days. They don't all have leprosy: sometimes it's only the flu, or a cold, or a headache brought on by stress. They come, regain their health, and leave again."

"Mr. Lim seemed unconcerned that you showed me the basement."

"Well, Mr. Lim suspects things between us are not merely platonic," he replied. "He knows I trust you. But," and here he stood, and stretched his arms above his head, "He's afraid that your meddling will get you in trouble, and by extension, me."

"My meddling? Is that what he calls it?" I frowned. "Mr. Fish is afraid I'll ruin his reputation, too."

"These are men who have sacrificed much to build positions that protect their interests," said Shao, "I don't blame them for cautioning you. Your unconventional ways could destroy everything good that they're doing."

Shao was only a few years older, but his experience with the world was much broader, and sometimes he seemed so much wiser than me. Shao's council was humbling.

"I'll be more careful," I said.

"Good," he replied. "You can't simply bite the nose off anyone who gets in your way."

"You heard about that."

"Who hasn't?" he said. "William Carter owns a number of buildings downtown, and his father is a judge. Mr. Lim says neither one is to be trusted. You might be in more trouble that you guess."

"I was defending myself!"

"I know," he replied. "But Carter claims you attacked him when he tried to escort you home."

"From what I've heard through the theatre, I'm not the first girl to claim that Carter's affections were unwanted," I said, "I think he may have raped Jess and left her pregnant."

"And you think he killed her?" Shao asked, "He was at his own party on the night of the murder. He has a house full of alibis."

"Maybe Carter was in cahoots with someone," I continued. "He might not have stabbed Jess, but maybe he hired someone to do the deed."

"Who?"

I shook my head. "I don't know."

Shao held out his hand. "Let's see the cloth from Carter's pants."

I moved it to the counter between us.

He studied it, then asked, "You're certain it's the same? You only glimpsed the fiber on Jess."

"How can I be certain?" I replied rhetorically. "Look, it's not a common color. That's what makes me wonder. He's the only man I've ever seen to wear green trousers."

Shao's expression changed. His eyes brightened. "Of course … yes. It's not common at all." He grinned. "Do you know why it's not a common color?"

I examined the fabric. It shimmered, a forest-green shade, smooth and silky. "Because it makes you look like a peacock?"

He laughed. "You're too young to remember."

I scoffed at the comment. "I'm not that much younger than you!"

Shao opened a cupboard and rooted through shelves of glass bottles and vials. "I'm old enough to remember Scheele's Green," he said, and when he saw my blank look, he explained, "It's a green dye that was used to color everything from fabric to food to wallpaper. It was bright, vibrant, but it's made of arsenic and it's highly poisonous. It gives off vapors that will kill you, if you stay in contact with it long enough. People don't trust green anymore, and that's why it's not often used for fabric, and that's why it's rare. Ah, here!" He withdrew a small, oval glass bottle from a drawer, uncorked the top, and poured a tiny pyramid of white crystals into a shallow dish. "Let's have a look."

"What is that?"

"Smelling salts," he replied, carefully pouring a drop of my hot tea into the dish. Instantly, a powerful, sour smell filled the air between us; I coughed and tears came to my eyes. "Don't breathe too deeply. They contain ammonia," he continued, stirring it with a small glass pipette as the salts melted. Shao appeared utterly unaffected by the crisp chemical scent. He gestured to the scrap, "Scheele's Green wallpaper still hangs in old houses, like the run-down tenements of San Francisco, and if a place had green wallpaper, my uncle taught me to check for poison."

I watched as he took a dropper from a drawer.

"If we put a bit of this spirit of ammonia on the fabric ..." he began.

Where the liquid hit the fabric, the green turned a vibrant blue.

"There you go." he said. "There's arsenic in Carter's trousers, and a lot of it, judging by the hue."

"Remarkable!"

"Chemistry, alchemy, pharmacy," he replied. "All flowers from the same root."

He placed a few crystals of smelling salts into a square of wax paper. "If the thread turns the same hue, you'll have a good idea that they came from the same garment," he said, handing the square of paper to me.

"I need to go." I said, standing and stuffing the paper envelope in my pocket. I was eager to test his theory, ready to bolt for the door.

"You're right," he replied thoughtfully, "The tea did nothing."

And with that, I was gone.

THIRTY-THREE

I'd barely reached the edge of Chinatown when I heard my name called out, "Lizzie!" and a horse cantered towards me out of the flow of traffic. The rider was none other than Mr. Fish. His hair stuck at all angles, his grey felt bowler had been crushed flat; he'd been holding it fast to his scalp with one hand, and clinging tightly to the reins with the other. The horse, a long-legged black gelding with a white blaze along its muzzle, gave an indignant snort as Mr. Fish struggled to halt it alongside the boardwalk.

"God's teeth!" I said with surprise, "I didn't know you rode!"

"I haven't in years," he said, snapping the reins to keep the prancing, snorting, whinnying animal under control. A fine sheen of perspiration covered its black hide. Upon closer inspection, Mr. Fish had developed a sweaty sheen, too: the armpits of his shirt were damp, his hair was plastered to his brow. "This monster is Mason's horse—stand still, you devil! But I needed to find you, Liz, and this seemed the fastest way, and I thought you certainly must be somewhere in this neighbourhood." And to the horse again, he demanded, "Stand still!"

"Why would you need me?"

"Emma's in her time," he said. He slung one long leg over the saddle and dismounted onto the boardwalk. "The midwives say the baby could come at any minute, and she's calling out for you, Lizzie. You must go to her immediately."

"Surely I'm of no help in a situation such—"

He completely ignored me. "Do you ride? Of course you do. What a stupid question." He thrust the reins into my hands. "You're Lizzie Saunders, Lady Adventurer. Go on, then, girl."

This creature was not the friendliest of horses. It peeled back its lips and tried to bite Mr. Fish as he held its bridle, struggling to keep its head still as I climbed into the saddle. For all of Mr. Fish's confidence in my abilities,

I was not an experienced rider, and I'd rarely been on the back of a mount. The last time I'd ridden a horse was over a month ago, when I'd stolen Mr. McGregor's mount, and at that point, I'd been focused completely on catching up with Jack and my father, leaving all my doubts behind me. I'd kept my seat in the saddle more out of luck than skill. I had no training, few opportunities around livestock, and had spent most of my life using my feet or a carriage.

The horse seemed to sense my apprehension. It skittered to one side. I felt its muscles bunch under my thighs, preparing to buck me off.

"Can you do this?" said Mr. Fish, suddenly realizing my predicament.

"Let's find out," I replied, holding tightly.

The animal wheeled around, screeching, and tore the reins from Mr. Fish's grip. If he said more to me, I didn't hear it. The black beast and I were off like a comet, tearing through the streets of Victoria, whirling like leaves on a winter wind. I believe I may have screamed then, although I was hanging too tightly onto its mane to notice.

We dodged a trolley, too close for my comfort; judging by the terrified faces in the window, too close for their comfort as well. The beast put its head down and charged. We raced along Yates and Harrow, hooves clopping on cobblestones, and when the paving turned to plain earth, we tore clods of dirt from the ground. At one point, it leapt off the street and onto the boardwalk. The thundering of its hooves on the boards mingled with the screams of pedestrians, and the air was filled with parcels and petticoats and fine hats. There was a moment of silence as we vaulted back into the street, all four hooves in the air, and then with a teeth-clattering thud, we were once more racing between hansom cabs and oxen. We must've traced a wicked pattern through the downtown core, around corners and past City Hall, through districts I'd never seen. We passed tenement houses, warehouses, docks. We tore across a park, vaulted a small fish pond, thundered through a series of vegetable gardens, leapt a fence. We left a trail of scattered chickens, frightened ladies, and cursing men behind us. I clung to the horse's neck and squeezed its body with my knees as the stirrups jangled uselessly. The wind pulled at my hair and the beast tossed its head and soon the tall buildings became flat warehouses and small homesteads and the roads became weedy paths of dirt and the wind roared in my ears. It seemed to me like we'd travelled for miles as we galloped pell-mell towards God-knows-where.

Somewhere along the way, I started to enjoy myself immensely.

And then the world sharply turned upside down. The beast, of whom I had no control, gave an abrupt turn to the left. I, however, remained on our original trajectory. Before I even knew what had happened, I was on my side in the mud.

For a moment, I was breathless. Then I groaned, tasting dirt.

The rhythm of hoof beats vanished down a side street, towards open fields and farms. Mason's horse, now free of its meddlesome rider, raced away.

I heard footsteps. There were hands on my shoulders, patting me on my back, helping me to sit. "Cor, miss, you alright?" said a young boy with a freckled nose.

"I'm not sure," I said. The bones of my spine popped as I moved. Stars speckled my field of vision. My bruised body moaned in pain.

I gave another groan. I'd rattled my brains loose with that fall.

People emerged from the houses. "She was riding a wild horse," said one woman to another, "Did you see that?"

"Wretched animal, ought to be shot," said a man.

They gathering around me, asking where I was hurt, wondering if any bones were broken. I closed my eyes against the bursts of pain in my skull, and I heard more hooves pulled to a stop and footfalls as someone dismounted.

Strong hands pried my own hands from my face. I blinked my eyes open to see Jack crouched before me. "God damn it, girl," he growled, "Were you trying to ditch me, or just get yourself killed?"

"Jack?" I said shakily, "What are you doing here?"

"Well, you know who I am, that's a good sign," he replied, tipping his battered hat back on his head. "You've gone and given yourself one hell of a knock."

"I'm fine," I protested. I tried to stand, but my body didn't quite agree. One knee buckled and fresh stars appeared.

"Yeah, that's why yer eyes are doing goddamn pinwheels in yer head," he muttered. Then, much to my surprise, he picked me up in his arms. I found myself effortlessly carried to the porch of the nearest house and set gently down on the steps. "Sit here for a minute, get yer bearings. How many fingers am I holding up?"

I looked at his hand. "Four." I squinted. "Well, three and a half."

He did not look amused.

"Well, the fall didn't knock the sass mouth offa ya. I s'pose that's a good sign."

Now that I showed no evidence of injury or drama or imminent death, the crowd began to disperse. Two of the boys took off in the direction of the black horse, to follow it and try to collect it and ask for a reward.

My own brain started to function again. "How'd you find me here?" I asked, then noticed a plump, stout-legged chestnut mule with no saddle standing in the road behind him. It had the long reins of a wagon-horse, and I could see the marks in its fur where the wagon-train had been hastily undone. "You stole a mule?"

"Well, I wasn't gonna let you slip away," he replied.

"Aren't you resourceful."

"What possessed you to get on that goddamn thing?" he replied. "From the looks of it, you ain't no rider!"

"Mason's wife, Emma ... she's gone into labor. She's asking for me." The mention of my task roused me faster than a bucket of cold water. "I've got to get to her." I stood, still wobbly but better than before. "I'll take the mule."

"What, to pitch yourself headlong into a ditch again? Hell no!" He gathered up the reins and led the mule to me. "C'mon, I'll take ya."

I stood, intending to mount from the porch, but before I could climb it, Jack seized me about the waist in his large hands and slung me up without effort. I had the fleeting suspicion he could carry me to Mason's house, all by himself, and barely notice the burden. Then, using the steps, he took his seat behind me, and nudged the mule into a lazy, rolling trot with a slap of the reins against its rump.

The last time I'd felt Jack's arms around me, he'd hauled me from a bar fight. The time before that, he'd pressed a knife to my throat and threatened to kill me. It was very strange, to be honest, to feel any sort of security from his embrace. He held the reins lightly in one hand while the other arm encircled my waist to keep me from tumbling off, and it took me a few moments to gather my wits enough to speak.

"We can go faster," I said.

"You had a saddle on that devil, and you still went flying," he said. "No way, sweetheart. This is as fast as we're gonna go."

"At this rate, she'll have had the baby by the time we get there."

"She'll have the baby when she has the baby, Liz. Whether or not you're there, ain't gonna change a thing."

"What do you know about childbirth?" I replied.

He chuckled, and I felt the rumble of his laugh through his chest. "I grew up in tenements, and I've spent my time working as a bouncer in bawdy houses from here to Chicago. Trust me, I seen my share of squawlers comin' into the world."

"You're an odd man, Mr. Hunter," I replied. "What's your real name?"

"Ain't none of your concern."

I frowned. "I told you to stop following me."

"I did. For 'bout ten minutes."

"But?"

He gave a rather hopeless sigh. "Not long after you left, I heard a whole hell of a lot of squawking, and I figured I'd better get you outta trouble. And by the time I got there, I saw you accompanying the police into a cab, all covered with blood that weren't yer own." His grip tightened around my waist and he nudged the mule to a faster clip. "You'll forgive me if I say, I ain't gonna put much stock in your promises of clemency, sweetheart."

"Mr. Carter deserved it."

"Did the cops agree?"

I sulked. "No. I've agreed to return next week to speak with Constable Grange about Mr. Carter's charges."

"You don't sound so pleased with the arrangement."

I shifted in my seat to look back at him, at the underside of his grizzled chin. "I don't wish to waste time with Mr. Carter's childish whinging. I may have a lead on Jess' murder and the constables haven't got a clue. I need to test a theory of mine."

"You got a knack for it," he said, more to himself than to me. "Makes sense, I s'pose."

"A knack? For what?"

"The cops don't know what to look for, 'cause they think like lawmen. You, on the other hand, know exactly what to look for." He nudged the mule around the corner and up Cook Street. "You, sweetheart, think like a murderer."

"And that's why you're following me," I replied sourly. "Because you think I am a murderer."

"I know you are," he replied.

"If I'd let him live, he would've killed again and again. You know it, as well as I."

"True."

"Then why don't you trust my judgment?" I said. "I could've killed Mr. Carter, given a few more moments and a sharp stick, but I promise, I am reformed. I will not kill again, Jack. I promise."

"See, Liz, that's where I don't believe ya. You got yourself a taste for blood now, I think, and the time will come when you need to satisfy that hunger again." He tightened his arm around my waist, and suddenly, it didn't feel so protective. "And when that day comes, I'm gonna be there to stop you."

I shifted in my seat. "Release me."

"What, so you can fall in the street again? Naw. You just sit tight, Liz, and I'll get you to Mason's house."

"Let me go!"

I struggled against him, but he was as unmovable as a mountain. I would never match him in brute force.

He must've had the same thought, because he laughed. "Sit still, Liz, before you embarrass yourself."

"I could scream," I hissed. "I could yell for help."

And without another word, he smote the mule on the rump and we were off at a brisk canter.

"Go on, yell to your heart's content," he replied over my shoulder. "But your friend Emma is waiting for you. And trust me, I can getcha there faster than you can alone."

"I don't trust you," I spat. "I don't trust you at all."

"That's a girl," he laughed. "Now you're thinkin' straight."

A mule is a different sort of ride than a horse: solid, straight-forward, stable. We clopped up Rockland Avenue, between a parade of glossy lacquered cabs and fine-boned horses, as the street rose up from the working districts and into the stately, hillside homes. The mule flopped its long blond ears, nickered and snorted its cumbersome roman nose, and carried us without pretentions through the iron gates of Dr. Brigg's residence. We reined to a stop under the portcullis to the main door. There stood Feng Soo, waiting for my arrival. He widened his eyes but he was well-trained in his profession, and a good butler shows no hint of surprise.

"Upstairs, miss," he said as I dismounted.

I rushed to the door, then paused on the threshold to look back at my chaperone.

"Thank you, Jack." I said.

"I'll wait here for ya," he replied.

"There's no need."

He tipped his hat. "You let me decide that, sweetheart."

I heard a horrible cry from the upper floor, and I left him without another word, thinking only of poor Emma. I found her in the bedroom, spread out on sheets and towels, her face awash with sweat and her hair unbound.

"Oh, Liz!" she cried as she saw me, stretching out her arm, "Hold my hand!"

There were two men standing in the corner of the room: Mason Briggs, struggling to appear calm, and the youthful, portly Dr. Collins, who I'd met a month before. A small retinue of women had assembled, as well: midwives and nurses, no doubt, for they all looked calm, collected, and focused on the task at hand. One woman, an old matron in a brown cotton dress with the bearing of a major general, carried a tin pan of water to the bedside table. A few sprigs of lavender floated on the surface.

"Use this to wash her face," she said to me. Then she looked a little more closely at me and said, "You'll be quite alright with this? No fainting?"

"No, ma'am," I assured. "My father was a doctor."

"Good. You'll be more useful than the men."

But I was used to corpses and autopsy, not childbirth. The blood and the gore was of no consequence, but I was quite unprepared for the noise. Emma's screams were not the collected sounds of a woman startled, but the shrill animalistic bellows of a creature in agony—rather a lot like William Carter had sounded, I reflected. She held my hand, crushed my fingers in her grip.

The matron examined Emma under the sheets.

"Good, my duckling, good," she encouraged.

And Emma screamed again, bore down, turned a horrible shade of red.

I heard a deep, strangled cry from the corner of the room, and then Mason fled, his skin ashen. The midwives chased Dr. Collins out after him.

Time had no meaning. I think the sun went down, for when I looked out the window, it was suddenly dark. The sky was sprinkled with stars. Men gathered in the garden, and their pipes glowed like little orange lanterns in the distance. Mason sat on the flagstones at the edge of the patio. His cradled his head in his hands, the curve of his shoulders shook. The others politely ignored him. He'd been unable to keep up the bearing of a gentleman, but the men wouldn't bring attention to his failing, for he was respected amongst them.

I turned back to the birth: the rolling waves of screaming, the long moments of panting, the sweat and the water, the blood and the white sheets. At some point in the night I removed my coat, although I'm not sure when. The pain came in rising mountains, and in the moments between the agony, I sat alongside Emma and stroked her hair with my hand.

"Good of you to come," she said at one point.

"I nearly broke my neck on your husband's wild horse," I smiled.

She looked at me piteously. "That terrible beast! You had to walk?"

"No," I said, "I came on a stolen mule."

Emma laughed at that, thinking I was teasing her. "So funny," she whispered, "I could not bear to lose you."

I studied her flushed face, peppered with beads of moisture. The dark room shifted and moved with the women around us, but they disappeared into the background as I turned all my attention to her.

"Lose me?" I asked.

"I dread hearing the news that you are leaving." Tears welled up in her eyes. "When your father calls for you …"

I thought hard about my next words, but I knew they would give Emma comfort, and in the close, intimate circle of the birth chamber, I felt no hesitation to share my thoughts with her. I leaned close and said, quietly, "Emma, I have been propositioned."

Her eyes widened.

"Goodness! You have?"

"I love him, very much. I know I do," I said, "My father will never call for me, Emma. I know that without a doubt, and I must plan my future. And I think," I braced myself to admit it, as if saying the words made my path concrete, "I might accept this man's marriage proposal and stay here in Victoria forever."

Her fingers tightened around my hand. "So wonderful! I had no idea! I want to meet him! I must tell him how very lucky he ..." Her comment trailed away. She closed her eyes, the red flush to her face returned, the pain was coming again. "Oh, Liz," said Emma in a thin voice, "I feel ablaze."

I bathed her face with the cloth and lavender water. She glowed with life.

"You look beautiful," I assured.

She gave a fierce bark of a laugh. "Liar," she replied, "I'm a damn bloody mess."

I knew it must hurt a great deal, for Emma to speak so candidly. "A beautiful bloody mess, then."

Emma looked as though she might laugh, but then her mouth opened wide as a tunnel and out came a scream, as wrenching as if she were being pulled in two. "It burns!" she cried, throwing back her head. I heard a moist suckling sound.

"It's coming now, duckling," said the matron. "Save your breath and bear down."

Emma pushed, heaved, strained. The bones of my fingers ached under the crushing pressure of her grip. I tried to pour my own strength into her, give her whatever I had, and I felt the trickle of sweat down my neck and back. She wailed, the breath erupting from the depth of her belly, her dry throat cracking with fatigue.

"Push, duckling!" the matron demanded, "Don't stop!"

Emma's face shifted away from pain; she was no longer delicate, but determined. The tendons leapt under the clenched curve of her jaw. I saw the pulse of her carotid artery along the side of her neck. She fought for life—for two lives, really—like a captured tiger, and her clawed fingers dug deep into the mattress like a predator's paws clasp the haunch of its prey. Men are always fond of reminding us that women are the weaker sex, but watching Emma now as she ripped a new life from herself, I saw clearly that they were mistaken: she had a core as strong and unyielding as a mountain, and an ability to tolerate such pinnacles of agony that a man would be begging for death. No matter how sweet and delicate she seems, every woman holds in her heart an ocean of strength.

The moist sound of tearing flesh filled the room. I smelt blood, saw a gush of scarlet and purple, heard a tide of moisture slap against the wooden floor. Emma sobbed and collapsed back in the pillows. Her face turned ashen, the room fell quiet. Her skin glistened with sweat, and as I leaned close to wipe her brow, the lusty cry of a newborn broke the stillness.

Emma's eyes closed, but the corner of her mouth showed the ghost of a smile. It was tired, victorious, battle-worn, triumphant.

"Fetch the father," said the matron to me, holding up the squalling bundle. She set the child to Emma's breast as the midwives began to sing a happy tune, a victory song, and she whispered in her ear, "Congratulations, duckling. You've earned yourself a good long rest."

Thirty-Four

They named her Violet May.

I thought she was quite ugly, all purple and misshapen by the ordeal of being born, but I didn't say that; instead I congratulated the new parents and took my leave quietly. Now that Emma's screams had stopped, the house had grown very quiet. The staff and visitors seemed quite overwhelmed by the afternoon. Mason's houseguests had retired to their rooms hours ago, and the midwives silently scoured blood spatter from the bedroom floor with a wash of borax and vinegar. Two women had helped Emma into a guest room, and they busily bundled the soiled bedding to be burned. I decided it was best that I go.

But before I reached the front door, Mason caught up with me. He said nothing, but abandoned all decorum to embrace me warmly. Tears of joy glittered in his eyes. I held his hands and made him promise to let Emma rest, and only send word to me when she was strong enough to endure a visit.

Feng Soo held the door open for me. I bid him good-night, and he touched my sleeve as I passed.

"Your companion," he said, "The man you arrived with?"

My heart sank. "He didn't stay, did he?"

Feng Soo shook his head. "He tell me, he will wait for you at whiskey place. This means something to you?"

I pressed my palms together. "*Xie xie ni hen duo,*" I replied.

"You are very welcome," Feng Soo replied. I thought I caught a hint of amusement behind his tired eyes. "Your accent is terrible."

"I'm working on it," I replied. "Go, get some sleep. You look exhausted."

The mule was gone and I saw no evidence of Jack, but I didn't believe that he would do precisely as he said—he was obviously quite skilled at trailing me, and he might have given me a location as a ruse. Perhaps he was waiting in the shadows at the gate. I scanned the gardens but saw nothing strange, and I headed back to the downtown core, my task still unfinished.

The hour was very late … or was it very early? I could easily descrbe the time as late, the streets were empty, the bars long closed and the hotel lobbies shut. But I could also say it was too early in the new day to warrant a milkman delivering goods or a bakery open. Either way, early or late, the city was deserted. A gauzy layer of clouds covered the stars and a light drizzle had started. The roads were muddy, piebald with puddles.

I yawned. My boots dragged. The weariness of the last few days was catching up with me, but I wasn't ready to return home. Mr. Fish wouldn't be waiting for me, knowing that I was with Emma.

I crossed the empty streets towards St. Joseph's Hospital, where the Sisters of St. Ann provided care for patients. I'd been here once before, to identify Jess' body, and at night, the place projected a more sinister air than in the daylight. The large, white-stone building had towers and pillars like a fairy-tale fortress, four-stories high with the tallest bell tower in the middle, and the grounds were surrounded by a low stone wall with iron gates. In the yard, the skinny, leaf-bare branches of the cherry trees scratched at the sky like insect legs. I slipped easily over the gate. The black trees seemed to be holding their breath, waiting for me to lower my guard before snatching me up in their limbs. I didn't bother to go to the front doors. They'd be locked at this hour, with a watchful nun on duty.

Instead, I wandered around the building and discovered a kitchen window on the ground floor. When I tried it, I discovered its latch not fully closed.

I passed easily through the empty kitchen and into the hall. Upstairs, the hospital was noisy and alive with activity, but in the basement, with the laundry and kitchen and morgue, all was calm. I slipped effortlessly through the corridors, keeping alert for the sound of footsteps on the hard floor. Only once did I hear another living body, the hard heels of her shoes clicking on the white ceramic tiles, but I slipped into a closet and waited until the nun had passed.

The morgue was exactly as I remembered it: clean and large, but dimly lit with a single electric bulb that snapped to life when I pulled the cord. Three bodies had been laid out under sheets, but when I peeked under them, I saw that none were Jess. I assumed my friend must be behind one of the wooden doors, each with a little brass plate marking a letter: Shelf A, Shelf B, and so on, all along the farthest wall.

But I was not here to look at the corpse. In an adjoining room, I found a number of boxes, neatly stacked. A quick search through them turned up

Jessie's familiar coat. Here, too, was her golden cross, her shoes, her dress. Loose about the bottom were the mundane contents of her pockets: a few coins, a small sewing kit, a bent hair pin. And then, in the corner of the box, I saw what I'd come for: the brown paper envelope holding a single, precious thread.

I moved back into the main room. The light was better here, and I would need to see well for this test. Between two of the sheeted forms, I pulled an empty gurney to a spot directly under the light bulb. I hadn't spent much time in places with electric contraptions, and the filament sizzled above my head like an angry wasp. I'd heard that light bulbs were prone to bursting, and wondered how much time I had before the glass globe turned into a small, suspended bomb.

I found a small dish in a cupboard, and a bit of water in a ceramic pitcher on a table by the door, and a pair of tweezers in a drawer. The powerful ammonia scent filled the room as I dissolved a few grains of the salt, and I blinked back tears as I dipped one end of the green thread into the liquid.

I set the thread down on the gurney and watched.

And watched.

And watched.

Nothing happened.

I took the scrap of fabric from Carter's trousers and laid it next to the thread to compare the two. Carter's fabric was a deep forest green, but as I used the tweezers to pick up the thread, I saw immediately my mistake: the thread was brighter, more yellow than blue. And without the presence of arsenic in its dye, I was certain they were not a match.

Not the same fabric, not the same clothes.

Mr. Carter had not done the nefarious deed, after all.

I walked to The Pelican with my mind in a tangle, and pushed my way through the rough-hewn door, into the small, cramped brick pub. If the city was quiet, it was because the rogues and vagabonds had taken shelter in a place like this. The Pelican was crowded with men in brown coats and bowler hats, drinking and playing cards to pass the time. The thick, acrid smoke of cheap tobacco hung like a fog in the close heat. I stood in the doorway, and the men stared unabashedly at me.

"Oi, it's the Queen of Bloody France," shouted Archie the barman. "C'mon in, your majesty, and close the bloody door. You're letting out all the good heat."

As the door closed behind me, I took one last gulp of fresh air. Then I pushed through the chairs and drinkers, ignoring the conversations and hoots and calls, the cruel laughs, the stench of vomit and dog shit, the propositions for a bit of fun. I drew up to the bar, and would've set my elbows upon it, if I'd been tall enough.

"Where is he?"

"Who?"

"Jack."

"Half the blokes in here go by that name," he said, "But I know for a fact, that fella over yonder ordered up a bit of chicken pie for you, should you come a-stumblin' in." His weasel grin widened as he added, "M'lady."

I turned towards a small, round table in the far corner, next to the iron stove. There sat Jack, his jacket off and his hat on the floor, a half-full glass in his hand, and his boots propped up on an empty chair.

"You are here," I said as I approached, not bothering to hide my surprise.

"Hell, yeah. She coulda been screaming for days. I wasn't about to wait out in the cold when there's a perfectly good fire and a bottle of whiskey waiting for me." He gestured to the opposite chair. "Sit. You gotta be half-starved."

A bowl was set before me, filled with perfectly awful-looking slop. I took up the greasy spoon and began to devour it.

"Did she live?"

I nodded. "Healthy baby, too," I said around a mouthful of gristle. "Mason looked thrilled to have it finished." I sopped up the grease with a bit of crumbly bread, held together by specks of mold. "This is absolutely terrible stuff, isn't it."

"Doesn't seem to be slowing you down none."

"I haven't eaten in ages," I said, taking another spoonful. "I feel like I could eat a horse." I paused, looking at the stew. "I probably am."

"Down here by the docks? More likely cat, I wager," he said, and set his boots on the ground. He waved to the barman, who sent over two mugs of ale.

I ate a few more bites, and now that my hunger was sated, the rancid taste of the meat was becoming more noticeable, less tolerable. I set down the remains of the bread. "I've got something to ask you, Jack." I said.

He scowled at me over the rim of the glass. "What?"

"You spent most of your life hunting my father; you are not a man to let go of obsessions easily." I took a breath, sorting out the best way to phrase my request. "If I could promise you—swear on my heart's blood—that I will never kill again, would you leave me alone?"

He shook his head. "Nope."

"What if I could assure you that you didn't have to watch over me? That someone else could fulfill that role?"

This piqued his interest. "I assume you're referring to Mr. Chen?"

I nodded.

"There's no guarantee he'd do that, kid. He's got his own way to make in the world."

"He asked me to marry him."

Jack nearly choked on his beer.

"What?"

"You heard me."

"Yer goddamn fifteen—"

"Sixteen next month."

"And he's Chinese—"

"I don't care."

"But other people will, goddamn it!"

"I told you, I don't care."

He gave a growl. "He don't know what you are."

"If I marry him, I would never endanger our union with any impulse, obsession, or urge," I continued, "And you can go away, leave us forever, secure in the knowledge that your job here is finished."

"You'll tell him what you done?"

"Never."

His scowl deepened. "You willing to give up your station in life for love?"

I looked around at the filthy bar. "All this? Oh, yes."

Jack curled his lips in disapproval at my blithe attitude. "No more teas in fancy gardens, no more silk stockings, no more nights at the theatre, no more travelling in first class circles. No matter how forgivin' your friend Fish might be, when it comes to marriage? He'll have to cut all ties with you. You'll be a goddamn pariah … worse than a goddamn leper."

I bristled at that.

But Jack saw my reaction, and leaned forward. "Briggs? Fish? Emma? They'll all hate you. They'll look down on you as if yer goddamn vermin."

I lowered my gaze. I knew what he said was true, but I didn't want to give him the satisfaction of seeing my regret.

"Yer friend, Jess," he began in a low whisper, "You figured out yet who killed her?"

I shook my head.

"When you do, I lay any money down that it was 'cause she moved outside her circle. She was black, Thornton was white, and mixing outside the race ain't tolerated, no how." He looked at me askance. "They'll come after you, Liz. Mark my words."

"Let them come," I snarled back. "Let them try."

He paused, studied my face, saw the determination in my eyes. "See?" he said, "That's what I'm afraid of."

I licked the last of the slime from my fingers, and wiped them clean on the hem of my skirts. "Jess's murder wasn't just about race, Jack. Whoever killed her tore her open. There was rage in those wounds." I fished in the satchel and brought out the screwdriver, setting it on the table between us. "This is what did the deed, and not many people carry a screwdriver on their person, so I figure this was not a spur-of-the-moment killing, but planned."

He picked it up. "You're carrying around the murder weapon?"

"What I'm trying to say, Jack, is that maybe race was a factor, but it was not the only factor. She was pregnant, she was leaving town, and someone was eager to stop both of those things from happening."

"You can't just carry around the god damn murder weapon!"

"You aren't listening to me," I insisted. "I thought it was Carter, but I was mistaken—he's an ass, true, but that doesn't make him a killer. Andy and Jess were supposed to take a steamer ship to California, to start a new life together. Who would stand in their way?"

"You're looking at this the wrong way, then," said Jack. "Maybe the question ain't, "Who wanted to stop Jess?', but 'Who wants to keep Andy here?'"

I hadn't considered that. I sat back in the chair, chewing on the thought.

But Jack wasn't so introspective. He shook the screwdriver at me. "You need to give this to the cops!"

"So they can stick it in a box and forget about it?" I snapped, "Hell, no!"

Archie the barkeep had crossed the room, sidling next to our table to take my empty bowl, and he stared at the screwdriver in Jack's hand.

"Oi, everything all right here?" he said.

"Yes, it's fine," I snapped, taking the tool back, "He isn't threatening me with it, if that's what you mean."

"Good," he replied, then he squinted a bit at the tool. "That's the mark of the magpie, that is."

Both Jack and I turned to him. "You know it?" I said, holding the handle out for him to examine.

He looked it over again, more closely this time, but gave a short nod when he saw his first assessment was true. "Oh, sure I do," he replied. "Bloke who owns 'em comes in for lunch, every now and again. Right fine lad, he's done some fix-up work for me, on occasion. You leave that with me, and I'll be sure to get it back to him."

"I'd rather return it myself," I said crisply. "What's his name?"

The barman thought for a moment, scratching at the back of his neck. "The lads call him Handy Andy," he replied. "But I think his family name is Thornton."

Thirty-Five

I raced out of The Pelican, and from the sound of chairs shunting across the floor and doors slamming, Jack wasn't far behind me. "Wait, Liz!" I heard him shout, "God damn it, wait!"

He snatched me up around the waist and lifted me off the boardwalk, so that my running gait became two feet kicking in the air. Then he plopped me down with my back against the brick facade of a warehouse, so that his great bearish body became an impediment between me and my goal.

"What're you gonna do?"

"Get out of my way," I demanded.

"Not until you tell me what you plan to do."

"If this is Andy's, I need to know," I replied.

"I ain't leaving you to confront Thornton yerself."

"Then come with me," I said, and I could barely believe I'd said the words to invite him, even as they came out of my mouth. "Just get out of my way."

We ran three blocks to the Temple of Thespis, and the sun was only a faint glow on the eastern horizon when we reached the door to the theatre. It was locked—not unexpected at such an early hour—but before I could suggest we move to another door or window, Jack slipped his hand into the inner pocket of his coat and withdrew a small black leather case, much beaten and misused. From it, he pulled out two instruments: a battered, pitted hair pin made of iron, and a slip of metal which, in the low light, I judged to be a pen knife with a tortoise-shell handle. Upon closer inspection, I saw that top inch of the blade had been bent at an 80° angle.

"Keep yer eyes out for a cop," he said to me. He crouched before the door handle, aiming his full attention on the lock.

Jack had picked the lock to my own home, but I'd never seen the trick done, and he set to work at it with great efficiency. The spring clicked and the bolt slid across. The door popped open with a faint squeak. He replaced the leather case and tools into the inner pocket of his coat, and he held the door open for me as we entered the theatre.

The lobby was as quiet as a cathedral. Even as my eyes adjusted to the gloom, I could barely see anything more than faint shapes, but the snap and hiss of a lucifer brought with it a faint glow of light. Jack, by the door, held up the match and by its illumination located a small lamp on a nearby table. He quickly turned the screw, set the gas free, and lit the wick.

"That's better," he said, placing the lucifer tin back in his pocket.

"What else have you got hidden in there?" I said.

"All a man needs to make his way in the world," he replied cryptically, and holding the lamp aloft, he entered the theatre.

The light spread out through the cavernous hall. We became two small figures in an immense vault of blackness, moving slowly towards the distant stage. I dared not speak to him; the sound of our voices would echo through the building, and as Mrs. Thornton had warned me, the theatre ghosts are always listening. I followed the lamplight as he mounted the stage, then moved through the set pieces for *Padua*: the cut-out cathedral, the fruit-seller's wagon, the Italian fountain. The shadows cast by the lamp leapt into gothic figures against the far walls. Then he disappeared backstage, with only a faint glow left for me to follow.

We found the toolbox to the rear of stage right, alongside the wooden ladders for hanging curtains. This was no portable tray, but a set of drawers constructed for durability and strength, made to keep a workman's tools safe in his shop. It was as high as my waist and almost as long as my body, square and serviceable, and like the crates of tarpaulin, the rolls of canvas, the ladders, or the coils of ropes, I must've passed it a million times while working backstage, never giving any thought to it. The tool chest had three columns of narrow drawers, each one a few inches high and two feet long, with black iron pulls. The wood was pitted and waxy, polished smooth in some places with the passage of time. I opened the top drawer and, inside, found neat rows of chisels, mallets, awls and clippers. Not all of them boasted the magpie stamp, but many did. They were old, well-used, but also well-loved.

The second middle drawer carried a suite of screwdrivers. I took them out, one by one, and lined them up on the floor, smallest to biggest.

For the most part, their varying sizes fell into a discernable pattern, each one a half-inch longer than its neighbour. But the size skipped a full inch between two of the tools, exactly where I predicted it might.

Jack watched me sort the screwdrivers. "That ain't exactly proof that Thornton's guilty," he said. "The box ain't locked. Anyone coulda grabbed it and hidden it under his coat, and taken it with him."

"Yes, but—"

I never finished my sentence. Behind Jack, a swooping motion in the dark stopped my breath, and I cried out a warning as I heard a whoosh, followed instantly by Jack's shout of surprise. He dropped the lamp. It clattered against the floor. Jack threw a punch into the shadows towards his assailant, and I heard the smack of his fist against a face, along with a startled cry. The two bodies scuffled back onto the stage, and when the assailant dropped his weapon, a length of planed wood clattered across the floor.

I grabbed for the lamp, snatching it off the floor before the oil could escape and cause a fire. I heard the fight more than saw it: grunts, bodies falling, the smash of props and set pieces. A voice cried out, and I recognized it before I had a chance to hold up the lamp and cast a wider circle of light.

"Stop! Stop!" begged Andy, "Sweet merciful Lord!"

By the time I reached them, the fight was finished: Jack had his knee on Andy's throat and one arm raised above his head to throw another punch.

"Stop! Stop! For the love of—" His eyes, drawn to the light, fell on me. "Lizzie? Oh, Liz! I didn't know it was you here! I thought, a burglary, or a drunk looking for a place to sleep, or—"

"Get off him, Jack," I demanded, "Andy, sit up. Are you badly hurt?"

"Him? What about me?" complained Jack as he stood, massaging his right shoulder. "He hit me with a goddamn piece of lumber!"

Andy curled into a seated position with a painful moan, and his right eyelid had started to swell. He looked deflated, defeated, and much abused. "I came in early to strike the set, I can't sleep, and I thought I'd get some work done, and I saw the light—"

I crouched before him, noticing a speck of blood beading at the corner of his lips. "I wanted to look at your tools. I didn't think anyone would mind."

He shook his head, but absently, as if he was just waking. "S'okay, I suppose." He glanced at Jack. "Your friend has quite the arm." There was a question in that statement, a rise in tone that lingered just after the word 'friend'.

"Strike the set?" I said, "But there's still tonight and tomorrow—"

"No one's coming to see the show anymore," he moaned. "Ma is a wreck, half the cast aren't showing up, and The General says he's never gonna direct again. The whole ruddy thing is cursed." He spat, and it was tinged pink. "So we're closing it up. Mr. Carter told Ma he's selling the building. No more Temple of Thespis."

He looked so dejected, I felt a little sorry for him. "What will you do?"

"I don't know," he stammered.

"And Mrs. Thornton?"

He shrugged.

I decided to press him for an answer. "She'll be out of a job, no place to work, and if Carter sells the building—"

"Ma doesn't really give a darn about the play anymore," he admitted. "I don't know what she's planning to do. She talks about leaving, starting fresh somewhere else. I don't know …" He ran his palm over his sore jaw. "You said you were here to look at my toolbox?"

As I helped him to his feet, I said, "Well, yeah. I don't know many people in Victoria yet, and I figured you might have a great collection of tools. I'm looking for a screwdriver."

Andy, ever helpful, grinned. "Sure, yeah, I've got lots. Back here. Bring the lamp."

I followed him backstage, and limping, he brought me to the same chest. I gathered up the tools I'd arranged on the floor, and with a familiar fondness, he opened the second middle drawer. I replaced them, and he began sorting through the instruments.

"Have a look, see which one will suit your purpose," he offered.

I took one tool and turned it over in my grip. It matched the one in my satchel, only smaller and more finely crafted. The iron knob at the base of the handle was rusted and worn, but it held the same impression of a songbird.

"What is this?"

"The magpie? Oh, that," he said with a thin smile. "They were my great-uncle's tools. He was a carpenter, back in Berkshire, and he had a friend of his—a blacksmith, mind you, a real craftsman—make him a set. He always had a fondness for the magpies that roosted under the eaves of his house." And then, in a childish singsong, he said, "One for sorrow, two for joy, three for a girl, four for a boy." His voice choked. "Aw, shit." He turned away, walked a few feet, and stopped. He hunched his shoulders, hid his face from us in the darkness.

I watched Andy as he tried to compose himself, failing at the task. I marveled at how useless he'd become in the face of his grief.

"Don't stare," Jack said with disgust, "Give the boy a minute of privacy."

"The weapon came from the theatre," I mused, "But it wasn't Andy that killed her. Look at him, Jack. Does that look like a man, capable of stabbing the woman he was about to marry?"

Jack, still rubbing his arm, leaned against the wall and mused over this. "No, I s'pose not." He scowled a little, thinking, and looking at the screwdriver in my hand. "Plus, the kid loves those tools. Can you imagine him ditching it? He woulda cleaned off the blood and put it back in the case, and hid it in plain sight."

Plain sight.

What about the green coat, I thought.

I left the drawers and slipped through the backstage area, and I heard Jack give an exasperated sigh. "Now where the hell you going?" he muttered, but I said nothing. Instead, I led him into the dressing rooms, to the door leading to Mrs. Thornton's shop. I gave a polite knock.

There was no answer.

I glanced at him as I pressed my ear to the door, listening for any sounds coming from within. "Nelly has said she'd given the coat to Mrs. Thornton," I said.

"So?"

"So …" I flipped the latch and pushed open the oak door, and the light spread down the stairs and across the room full of costumes. "This would make a swell place to hide it."

"Ah," said Jack, seeing that my train of thought had followed his own logic, "Plain sight."

The costume closet was a pharaoh's tomb: pitch black, crammed with rich goods, hung to the rafters with colors and delights. I increased the oil to the lamp's wick and the flame leapt higher, casting out a stronger circle of light from which we could more easily identify shades, shapes, and patterns. As I drifted through the rows of dresses, I peered closely for any hint of green, but I found only a few, and all used as trim or decoration: no coat. Shao said it had been known for years that the arsenic in Scheele's green made the wearer ill. I wondered how long it would take for the public to trust the dyers' claims that green cloth was now free of poison.

I passed a lovely cotton shift, barely worn, and a red felted hat trimmed with ostrich plumes. I found a pair of workman's trousers that had been patched with yellow and blue, obviously meant for a clown, next to a thick fur coat of silky mink. It might've been lovely, once, but it was mangy and moth-eaten, and probably only gave the illusion of wealth from a distance.

Then, in a wooden crate by the passage to Mrs. Thornton's shop front, my eye caught a hint of color. It was as bright as the eye of a peacock's feather.

The box was full of fabric scraps: a collection of cutoffs that Mrs. Thornton wished to keep for future projects. There were bits of string and tassels, tangles of soft lamb's wool, and slices of silk. The peacock green winked at me in the low light, and when I fished it from the box, out came a full sleeve.

Jack took it from me and examined it in the light. "That what you're lookin' for?"

I rooted about some more, and found bits that fit together into the shape of a coat. Two sleeves, the back panels, and one collar, along with a pocket and an inner lining. Most of the torso's front panels were missing. The elbow of each sleeve was threadbare, just as Nell had claimed. Portions of the back panel had already been cut and used.

I rocked back on my heels to think.

"It can't have been Andy," I said, more to myself than Jack.

"Why not?"

"Because," I said, laying the sleeves on the ground. "This was not a man's coat."

The sleeves were very small. So small, in fact, they might've belonged to a coat sized to fit me. I thought again of how low the stab wounds to Jess' stomach had been, and how small the murderer must've stood. Not a man, then, but a woman.

But why not destroy the entire coat? Why save the sleeves and the back?

"The killer must've sliced it off the front panels before hiding it here," I said. "They would've been sodden with blood."

Jack studied one sleeve. "Not just the front."

He held it out and ran one thumb over the edge of the wrist. The stitching at the shoulder had been carefully plucked. The threads at the wrist had been scrubbed with something abrasive, and amongst the weave was the barest smattering of dark stains.

"Someone tried to wash off the spatter," he said. "They didn't have much luck."

"Why save it, then?" I asked, puzzling over this fact. "They destroyed the front, but not the sleeves?"

"The front might've been beyond savin'," he reasoned. "But green fabric is rare, and prob'ly worth good money, and not something to part with lightly."

"The sleeves were salvageable."

"Exactly."

A peculiar thought hit me like a slap. "Mrs. Thornton would have known this. She wouldn't want to let go of something so valuable, that she could use in future." I set the fabric down again and pondered this suspicion.

"And Mrs. Thornton," Jack began, "She's a small woman?"

I thought about this, too, but shook my head. "No, the coat won't fit her. She'd be too buxom, too wide for this."

"But she hid it," he prompted.

"And washed out the blood, and plucked out the seams from the part that was most ruined." I ran my hand over the rough weave. "She must know."

Jack walked into the front of the shop with the lamp, and not wishing to be left in the gloom, I followed. His eyes ranged over the room, passed the sewing machines and cutting table, and he moved to the right, towards

Mrs. Thornton's roll-top desk. I was still thinking of the coat, and crouched before the iron stove in the left hand corner. The stove door opened with a squeak. Inside, I found the ashy remains of burned fabric in the grate. It was no longer green in color but its shape still hinted at the cut of a coat's breast.

Jack held the lamp over the desk in the corner. He made a grunt, and when I turned from the stove, I saw him holding two slips of paper, reading them by lamplight.

"If she weren't guilty," he began, "Why is Mrs. Thornton planning on running?"

He held the slips out to me. I took them and read the small, close type: two first-class tickets for the steamer out of Victoria, heading to San Francisco on the fifth of November. Tomorrow night.

"No, these weren't for her," I said, unsurprised, "These were for Andy and Jess."

"You sure about that, kid?"

I looked at them again, then back to him.

"Why?"

"First-class," said Jack, and he cocked one eyebrow. "Ain't no way Jess would've been travelling with the ladies and the gentlemen."

"But …" I looked between the tickets and the remains of the jacket in the grate. "God's teeth," I muttered, "I am an idiot sometimes." I peered once more at the tickets, as if I might see the whole story typed in the little boxes there. "Andy hadn't planned to leave with Jess—these tickets weren't purchased with her in mind."

"So what happened?"

"Mr. Carter happened," I replied, "Plans changed when Andy discovered Jess was going to be a mother. He knew what life would be like for her, he'd seen what Nell had to do to survive as a fallen woman. So, ever charitable and capricious, he chose to elope to California with Jess, save her reputation and make her an honorable woman, and leave behind his original suitor."

Jack looked through the door, towards the passage into the theatre. The acoustics of the theater allowed us to still hear the faint sound of Andy weeping, out on the stage. "Let's ask the boy who he planned on leavin' with."

"I don't think we have to," I said. "Small stature, access to the theatre, and wily enough to take Nell's green coat, just in case she needed someone to frame? I think I know who."

Thirty-Six

November 4, 1898

I went promptly to Constable Grange's office, confident in my findings, and arrived just as the porter opened the front doors of City Hall to the public. I raced up the stairs to the door, but Jack hesitated to enter. He lingered at the side of the street with his hands shoved in his pockets.

"Come on," I urged.

"I'll be staying out here," he replied.

"You're in trouble with the law?"

He gave a cocksure grin.

I took a few steps towards him, away from the door. "Are you going to wait, then follow me back to Mr. Fish's house when I am done?"

He said nothing.

I glowered at him. "You still don't trust me."

"Of course not," he said. "I know what you are, better than anyone."

"But I am reformed," I insisted, "And I do love Shao."

"That I believe," he said. "Everything else might be a lie, but I do believe you when you claim to love him."

"And?" I said, "What can I do to prove that I won't act on any murderous impulse, ever again?" I outstretched one hand in the direction from which we'd come. "I've sought out justice for a woman murdered, I have done everything in my power to make it right. C'mon, Jack—isn't there something in Greek mythology that allows an act of justice to wipe away any blood on my hands?"

Jack faltered. "Now, I don't know about that."

"But?"

He snarled his lip and leaned down to look me straight in the eye. "But if you promise you'll tell Mr. Chen what you've done, then I'll go."

I grumbled at this suggestion.

"Ain't it fair that he knows what he's hitchin' himself to?"

I shook my head. "He won't marry me, if he knows the truth."

"No, yer probably right about that," he said, and hearing him agree raised a sharp spike of anger in my belly. I swallowed it down. Was it anger at Jack, or revulsion at myself?

But I glanced across the busy street, watched the trolley rumble by. The passenger faces in the windows looked bleak, bland, and I forced myself to lock away my anger and replace the expression on my own face with something equally benign. "I solemnly promise, on the souls of all the women that met their end with my father, that I will never kill again," I said.

Jack stared hard at me, weighing the truth of my declaration. People came and went up the steps to City Hall, flowing around us like water, but I hardly noticed any of them. I waited for him to reply, seeing that he was sorting a great number of thoughts in that brain of his.

"You could have a future," I insisted, "A real, honest future, full of happiness. You could have something more than cheap brothels and whiskey and avoiding the police. You could find honest work, marry a woman who loves you, start a family—"

Just a flicker, deep in his slate blue eyes, betrayed his regret at a life lost.

I seized on it with relish. "You've dedicated years to following John Saunders, and now he is dead. You're free," I said, "If you wish to be."

He took a step back, lowered his chin.

"Do you promise?" he said. "Honestly?"

"I do."

Jack lifted his face, straightened his spine. "And Mr. Chen will do his best to keep you outta trouble."

"I know he will," I assured.

He descended a few steps.

"So, that's our good-bye, then?" I asked.

Jack gave a clipped nod. "I suppose it is."

We shook hands, his engulfing my own.

"I wish you well, Ja—" I paused. "Whoever you are. I don't want to know your name. Just, travel safe, and live a happy life."

"Stay outta trouble," he growled to me. Then, without another word, Jack strode quickly away and disappeared down an alleyway on the far side of the street.

For a few moments, I wondered if I had really gotten rid of him. I half-expected to see his face appear in the alley, still watching, still following, unable to release himself from the hunt. He was like a bad dream, skirting the edge of my reality. But five minutes passed, then ten. I saw no hint of him, and I realized he was truly gone. If I hadn't seen that spark of freedom in his eyes, I might not have believed it possible, but he was released from obligation; what man would not seize up the chance to start anew?

'My God, that's the last I'll see of him,' I thought with a start, as if someone had slammed a door, and I breathed a little sigh of relief. Softly, I said to the winds, "Fare well, Jack."

And I meant it.

Inside City Hall, a crush of officers and Chinese men clogged the front entrance, and I heard bellows of anger. Obscenities pelted me from all directions in a range of languages. A raid on an opium den last night, I supposed. No one looked very pleased with the situation.

I found Constable Grange in conversation with a knot of officers. Upon seeing me, he guided me into his broom-closet office and offered me a chair, closing the door behind us to block out the noise. I told him all I knew, every snippet of it, and the constable listened to me patiently, his thin hands folded on his desk.

When I withdrew the murder weapon from my satchel, along with the blood-stained green sleeve, his pale eyebrows nearly disappeared into his hairline.

I finished my story, and he sat for a few moment in quiet contemplation, his brow drawn into a thoughtful scowl and his hands clasped before him on his desk.

"Breaking and entering, theft, disturbing the peace …" he said. "I could arrest you, Miss Saunders."

"You could, I suppose," I replied. "But you'll be giving a murderer a chance to escape. And wouldn't an arrest for murder look better on your record, than picking up a little roustabout like myself for petty theft?" I ran one finger over the sleeve. "Last time I checked, nicking a scrap of fabric is not a hanging offense."

"Very persuasive," he muttered, nodding.

"So you'll arrest her?"

"I shall go and speak with her, but arrest her?" He shook his head. "I can't yet do that."

"Why not?"

"Because I'm not sure if you're correct," he replied. "I need to verify all you've said for myself."

I frowned but could not argue with him. After all, who was I, to him?

"You've been a very clever girl, Miss Saunders," he began, "I dare say, the cleverest I've ever had the pleasure of meeting."

"But?"

He smiled. "But perhaps a little high-strung, and not so mindful of her own safety. I will speak with your suspect, and you ought to go home."

"I never do what I ought." I replied.

He stood and grabbed his helmet from the corner of his desk. "I was afraid you'd say as much, Miss Saunders."

THIRTY-SEVEN

November 4, 1898

Upon opening the door of the tobacco shop, we found Greta's father working behind the counter. At the jingling of bells above the door, he looked up from his task of stocking the front cabinet with clay pipes, and his first reaction upon seeing the constable was to make himself presentable. He smoothed out his moustache and straightened his apron. But, when the constable asked to see Greta, his welcoming demeanor shifted to parental concern.

"Of course, sir," he said, "She's upstairs."

He locked the door to the shop before ushering us up the narrow staircase to their apartment on the second floor, and he welcomed us into a small, crowded home. Everything about the Braun residence was tarnished or chipped. The floral tea cups on the shelf were yellowed and glued together. The rugs were worn so deeply in places that the pile was completely gone. Mr. Braun's eyes flickered to us, showing embarrassment, but he stood as straight and confident as a prince. In a voice that was overly loud, Mr. Braun demanded tea from the portly woman washing dishes in the kitchen, who I assumed to be Mrs. Braun. She was a prideful, peevish woman, who looked quite concerned at the sight of a constable in her hallway, but she kept her lips pinched firmly shut; it was an expression I'd seen on Greta's face when the stagehands teased her, and she was seething angry but not brave enough to speak in her own defense.

"Put out some biscuits and tea for the officer," said Mr. Braun, "Or perhaps some raisin cake. We have some of that left, yes?"

"There's no need for formality," said Grange, "I've come to speak with your daughter."

"Which one?" snapped Mrs. Braun in a German accent, then yelled out, "Girls! You get out here!"

I hadn't come along for tea and biscuits. As the adults talked, I slunk down the hall to the bedrooms, and pushed open the only closed door.

By the amount of beds, this room was shared between four children—perhaps more, if they slept in pairs. A crib behind the door held a small baby, snoring and mouth agape. The floor was strewn with old clothes, papers, bits of string and wood. A horrid smell filled the air; I recognized it as the close, fetid stench of soiled diaper cloths, along with unwashed bodies and filthy blankets. Greta sat on the corner of a bed, closest to the window, where she could mend the ripped knee of a pair of boy's trousers by the morning sunlight.

Her expression soured when she saw me.

"What are you doing here?" she asked me, somewhat tartly.

As the constable stepped behind me, her mouth dropped open.

"You are Miss Greta Braun?" said Grange.

"I—I am," she stammered.

"Greta, at what time did you leave Mr. Carter's home, on the night Jess was killed?" he asked.

"I was second to go," she said to Grange, and then to me, added, "Remember? I told you, Nell and Maude were still there."

"Maude tells me she left immediately after Jess, for she needed to return to her shift at the hotel," I replied. "And you were the one who suggested Nelly had a green coat, correct? But she insists she does not."

"You'd believe Nell over me?" Greta snapped. "She's a woman of loose morals, Miss Saunders. She whores, she lies, she has the coat, she—"

"I found the coat amongst Mrs. Thornton's costumes," I said. Now her face grew thunderous. "How do you think it came to be there, Greta?"

"Are you accusing me?" she demanded.

"There are very few reasons why people kill," I said, "Most of the time, it's for either hatred or love. I wager in your case, it was a little of both."

I turned to Constable Grange. "Greta and Andy planned to elope. When he discovered Jess was pregnant, he decided to rescue his good friend Jess from her predicament, and take her to be his wife." I glanced at Greta. "And your dreams to leave your life in Victoria behind and start afresh in California? They all vanished when he dropped you for her. You knew you had to kill the baby that had thrown a terrible snarl into your plans." I turned back to Grange. "Greta stabbed Jess in the stomach, dumped her body in the ocean, and stashed the coat in the theatre. And when Mrs. Thornton discovered the coat, she dared not entangle her son in a murder investigation, so she covered it up, hoping no one would discover the truth of the matter before the boat departed." I looked at Greta again, and saw that her face was stony and her hands balled into fists. "Safely en route to San Francisco, with Greta and Mrs. Thornton—the only two people who knew the truth of Jess' death—stowed aboard it."

Greta stared hard at the constable, as if she could will him away with the force of her resolve. Her father and mother stood in the hall behind us, and when I glanced back at them, Mr. Braun stared at his daughter, furious, with two bright patches of red on his cheeks. Mrs. Braun had brought her hands to her mouth.

"You have done this sinister thing?" she demanded, "You have done murder?"

Greta shook her head desperately.

"No!"

"But you have shamed us," spat her father. "How could you do this to us?"

"Andy said he loved me!" she wailed, "He promised we'd be happy together! It was all going to be perfect, and then that slut Jess had to get knocked up with Carter's baby, and sweet stupid Andy asked her to go with him—"

"But you would leave?" said her mother, her voice full of disbelief. "You would abandon your family?"

"No!" she stammered, "No! How could I? I could never leave you, Mama! I could never leave, just like I could never kill someone! How could you think it possible that I could do such things?" Greta reeled on me. "I can never leave!"

"No?" I said, glancing at the bed upon which she sat. In a room so small, there were few hiding spots that a girl could call her own. I reached down, hooked the handle, and pulled out a carpetbag. By the way it scraped heavily on the floor, it was clear that Greta had already packed.

Thirty-Eight

November 12th, 1898

Jess was buried the weekend following, and it was great comfort to me that both Greta and Mrs. Thornton had been safely arrested and locked in the city gaol. They had planned to take the ship to California and leave their crimes behind them, but now they would face the judge, and I had every reason to believe that justice would be served. Soon after the arrest, the Temple of Thespis disbanded and William Carter (who had recently suffered a terrible injury to his nose, and now spent most of his time in the privacy of his home, drinking heavily) had sold the building to a dry goods conglomerate, but Andrew Thornton had remained as the building's custodian, for he had good references to support him. Constable Grange took full credit for the arrest, which I truly didn't mind—I had no desire to be embroiled any farther in the affair.

After the small funeral ceremony at the church, we retired to Mr. Fish's house for lunch, and a crowd of people attended, from all stations and occupations. Jess had been well-loved in her neighbourhood, by her co-workers, and by the theater folk, and their affection for her filled the house with warmth.

Shao and I sat beside each other on the sofa in the library. He wore Mr. Fish's old suit, and I wore a black pinafore dress with new stockings, and I didn't give a damn what polite society thought. He studied me with amusement.

"You look satisfied."

"I am," I replied.

"And it doesn't bother you at all that Grange will get the credit? And not a word will be spoken about your hard labor?"

"No," I replied. "I think Constable Grange will do well as an officer of the city. He simply needed a push in the right direction."

Shao chuckled, and lowering his voice, said, "Maybe a push off a pier, if it were my choice."

I smiled and took his hand in mine. "Shao, if I am to marry you, and we are to set up a small business and live the rest of our days in blissful happiness, then I am content to avoid the spotlight. It would do neither of us any favors."

He paused, mid-swallow.

"Is that ..." he whispered, "Is that a yes?"

"Yes," I whispered back, "That is, indeed, a yes."

He held my hand a fraction tighter in his left hand, and bravely, he caressed my face with the right. For a sudden moment I saw how happy we would be, creating a home for ourselves in the seaside city of Victoria. Our future unfurled before us, glorious and full of promise. For the first time in many months, I felt a sense of hope, blossoming like a brilliant rose of sunlight in my heart. My past had been very dark, it's true, but together with Shao, I was determined to make my future very bright.

"I love you, Lizzie," he said.

"And I love you, Shao," I replied.

And I would've kissed him then, in full view of guests and polite society and everyone, but from the front entrance hall I heard Mr. Fish say, "Amaryllis Saunders? Why yes, she is here."

I looked away from Shao as Mr. Fish appeared in the library doorway.

"Lizzie?" he said, and he looked perplexed, "You have a caller."

Behind him stood a face I had not seen in many months. Rufus McGregor had lost weight in that time, but he was still an imposing figure and his face remained the same: misshapen from his days as a boxer, with a large chin and lumpy cheeks, and a pair of kind eyes that glittered under his mop of brown-black hair. He wore a leather coat that was rough from travel, and a bowler hat that cried out for a cleaning, but his boots were polished and his trousers pressed. He did not smile to see me. In fact, his expression was one of sorrow, and it took on a twinge of pity when he saw me. I stood to greet him.

"Miss Saunders," said Rufus McGregor.

"Mr. McGregor! What a surprise to see you here!"

He took off his hat and lowered his voice. "I'm afraid I have bad news, miss."

The conversations around us stilled. Every ear trained itself towards his voice. I, too, leaned forward, and felt the first prickling of perspiration cross my brow.

"A fishing boat discovered the body of a man, not two weeks ago, and by his clothes and his countenance ..." He swallowed, hesitating to say more. "I'm sorry, Miss Saunders, but it's been identified as your father."

Maybe he mistook my stunned expression as grief. I stared at him, mouth agape. My limbs turned cold.

"I'm sorry, Lizzie," he said again, more slowly, "It appears that John Saunders was murdered, and from the state of the body, I believe the act occurred well over a month ago, perhaps at the end of summer."

All the darkness I had cast aside now came crashing back around me. I saw Mr. Fish catch himself against the door frame. I felt Shao's eyes boring into the side of my head. My stomach twisted into knots of lies and deceit, and I whispered, "No, he is gone, he is gone to England …"

"Tea," said Mr. Fish to the women in the hall, "For God's sake, fetch her something to drink! Hurry!"

I felt Shao's hands guide me back to the sofa, and I knew he felt me trembling, and prayed he mistook it for grief.

McGregor continued. "I hate to ask when you've only just heard this dreadful news," he said gently, "But we have a suspect we're seeking and a man that I'm eager to hang when I find." He knelt before me, stared hard at my face, and said, "Have you, by chance, seen Jack Hunter?"

ACKNOWLEDGMENTS

I'd like to express my gratitude to the following people for their help and inspiration through the process of creating this book:

Firstly, a big thank you to my family and friends who continue to support and encourage me. A special thank you to my mom Cindy Bannerman for sharing the family stories about Victoria's early days, and to my grandfather John Bannerman, for his recollections of Vancouver Island's past.

For fielding research questions, many thanks to Miranda Mallison and her lovely friend Shesheshkerbob Yeoman, Danette Boucher, Dawn Williamson, Kate Blood, John Belshaw, Catherine Siba, and Shawn A. Pigott of La Victorian Rose Millinery in Savannah GA.

A big thank you to the beta readers, who provided guidance, asked the hard questions, and rooted out spelling errors with bulldoggish tenacity: Jennye Holm, Jen Thorndale, Kailli Pigott, Tracy Jenneson, Catherine Guiot, and Claire Guiot. A mighty big thank you, too, to Claire for her scrumptious cover and interior design.

Also, a huge thank you to the readers, book clubs, independent book stores, museums, social groups, and history clubs that enjoyed *Bucket of Blood* and who have supported it since its publication in 2011: Laughing Oyster Books, Blue Heron Books, Mulberry Books, Village Muse Books, the Cumberland Museum, the Courtenay Museum, the Goddesses of the Book Club, Rotary, Newcomers Club, Probis, North Island College, ElderCollege, Munro's Books, Tanners Books, and many others. Thank you to the readers who have contacted me, and thank you to those who have shared recommendations in both the real world and the virtual one.

It's been a joy to meet you all, and I truly appreciate the support you've given me. Many thanks to Cara at Bibliobabes and Lee Ann Farruga at Steampunk Canada for your glowing reviews, and thank you to Jo-Ann Roberts at CBC Victoria for boosting the signal.

Lastly, thank you to Shawn, Zoe and Linus. I truly appreciate your guidance, your enthusiasm, and your willingness to join me on wacky adventures in the name of research. I love you all.

Kim